VE[...]
OF
GOD

BY

STEPHANIE HUDSON

MW01068568

Venom of God
The Transfusion Saga #2
Copyright © 2020 Stephanie Hudson
Published by Hudson Indie Ink
www.hudsonindieink.com

This book is licensed for your personal enjoyment only.
This book may not be re-sold or given away to other people. If you would like
to share this book with another person, please purchase an additional copy for
each recipient. If you're reading this book and did not purchase it, or it wasn't
purchased for your use only, then please return to your favourite book retailer
and purchase your own copy. Thank you for respecting the hard work of this
author.
All rights reserved.
This is a work of fiction. Names, characters, places, brands, media, and
incidents are either the product of the authors imagination or are used
fictitiously. The author acknowledges the trademark status and trademark
owners of various products referred to in this work of fiction, which have been
used without permission. The publication/use of these trademarks is not
authorised, associated with, or sponsored by the trademark owners.
Venom of God/Stephanie Hudson – 2nd ed.
ISBN-13 - 978-1-913769-37-6

I would like to dedicate this book to my big/ little sister, Cathy. I would like the world to know that what shapes us in life are the people who surround us and the love we are shown. For me, my sister helped shape me in the best way possible. She was always there for me and even through the rough, together we will always end up finding the smooth.

So, Cathy, to you I say this,

Here is to blue towels and handstands in the water. You are my forever rock in the sea, and I am your forever fish to guide you wherever you want to be.

I wrote this for you.

Big Sister Forever You'll Be

I walked in your shadow When the world was too bright, I slept on your floor, When you were scared of the night.

We laughed on the bed,

When you made puppets of your feet,
You gave them funny names,
Characters I just had to meet,

You were always there for me,
When I was sad or when I cried,
You stood up for me,
When people hurt me or wounded my pride.

You taught me things,
And took me places to see,
We swam together every Saturday,
Just like two best friend fishes in the sea.

We walked hand in hand,
Around our block on a paper round,
You would save your money,
Then buy me treats with every pound.

You did my hair,
And I admit I would wince,
But now I look back on it,
And I would smile with each memory since.

You said to me,
That one day I would go far,
That I would entertain the world,
That I would be a star.

You were my biggest fan,
Went to all of my plays,
Clapped the loudest

Always giving me praise.

You were never mean
Nasty or unkind,
You would wrap up your toys
Every Christmas with me in mind.

You made me into a clown,
Or even a horse,
With paper cups on my feet,
And paper hair of course.

But most of all,
You taught me so many things,
Like how to tie my shoelaces,
And make marble runs with cardboard and strings.

Creating board games
About the scary stuff I adore.
We made a haunted house as the last level,
It took up the whole bedroom floor

We laughed and cried
And yes, I snorted maybe,
But you thought it was cute,
Your little sister, your baby.

And now we are grown
And I couldn't be more proud,
To not only call you big sister,
But to shout best friend out loud

Because you mean the world to me
And gave me the best childhood
And now we are grown and you're still
The best, a sister could...
Ever Be.

All my love,
Your Snessy.

WARNING

This book contains explicit sexual content, some graphic language and a highly additive dominate Vampire King.

This book has been written by an UK Author with a mad sense of humour. Which means the following story contains a mixture of Northern English slang, dialect, regional colloquialisms and other quirky spellings that have been intentionally included to make the story and dialogue more realistic for modern day characters.

Thanks for reading x

PROLOGUE

AMELIA

Foresight is a great thing.

It would have come in handy.

Like when I decided to try and steal from an angry Vampire King. Nope, probably wasn't one of my better ideas. And now he's decided he's done waiting, whatever that means.

He tells me I have pushed the limits of his patience for the last seven years and now it is time to claim what is rightfully his.

Because now it turns out that I am not the only one with an unhealthy obsession. He just hides his better.

Well, he isn't hiding anymore.

And as for me. I am now his prisoner who, unknowingly, just slammed the door to my own cell. And all because I stole from him.

Stole the heart of the notorious,

Vampire King.

CHAPTER ONE

UNLEARNING THE POWER OF LOVE

'The whispers in the morning, of lovers sleeping tight, are rolling by like thunder now, as I look in your eyes...' I started silently mouthing the words, knowing if they'd have been heard it would have come out like a breathy whisper. But pretending to sing any song by the fabulous Celine Dion was as good as it would get as I refused to sully her songs with my appalling singing voice. Another thing I inherited from my mum.

So, as I increased the volume in my headphones on the second verse, I really started to let myself silently sing. I had finally been allowed to work on the box and strangely it felt as though I had come full circle since the day my dad had brought it to me. Only now, unlike that day, Simply Red wasn't singing about holding back the years and instead Celine Dion was currently trying to teach me the power of love.

And just like that day the lyrics started to mean something so much more to how I was feeling. Especially when I started to really give into the impulse of the music, mouthing,

'A love that I could not forsake', knowing exactly who it referred to. I even started to sway my head to the first chorus with the pen in my hand, one I had used to take notes, swirling in the air like I was some kind of conductor. But the lies of the words began, whereas I wasn't *his* lady and *he* most certainly wasn't my man, no matter how much every fiber of my being wanted to make it so!

So, all I had was this song and someone else's words flowing through me and easing my soul, if only until the music stopped. Which was why I couldn't help but sing the next verse whilst looking out the window, asking myself how I would feel if I was ever gifted the moment in his arms.

'Lost is how I'm feeling, lying in your arms, when the world outside's too much to take, that all ends when I'm with you...' I started really feeling myself getting lost now, reaching out my hand, fingers spread wide and shaking my hand, holding it out as if I was mimicking a bloody rainbow across the sky, but I didn't care. It was Celine Dion for God's sake, she deserved the best of me and all I had to give!

So, I started with the air drums the second that louder beat of the chorus hit and a larger sway of my hips and used my pen as a microphone just before the all-important power pull.

'Whenever you reach for me,' I silently sang as I raised my hand into the air and fisted it like I was pulling down a lever of love, one that only existed on the secret stage I was now headlining on. A hand fanned out in front of me as I shook my bum in time with the music before throwing my head back making my hair come loose from its tie and I shook it completely free. Somewhere so lost in my mind I was the one with the amazing voice, up there singing to the world about the love she felt. About the power of it she was ready to learn, despite being frightened. Well, those words certainly hit home.

'The sound of your heart beating, made it clear suddenly,

the feeling that I can't go on, is light years away' I mouthed as I shook my head to the side and suddenly couldn't help myself as I sang for real this time,

"Cause I'm your lady…" Then as I spun around on one foot I saw the flash of someone else in the room with me. I gasped, stuttered and ripped the headphones from my ears, the second I knew my private gig was up. I had been busted and by none other than the very last person I ever wanted to witness my little diva act…

"Lucius!" I screamed the second I saw him standing there casually leaning against the doorframe as if the only thing he was missing right then was a bowl of popcorn and a ridiculously large, bladder busting soda. And of course, he was smirking.

"What the Hell!?" I shouted with a hand to my pounding chest.

"Oh, I wouldn't have said your singing was that bad, I especially enjoyed the ending," he said making my burning cheeks close to crispy they felt that hot. Especially when he winked at me, making me close my eyes and pray to every God out there with the power of mind control to make him to forget the last four minutes. He heard me muttering to myself asking for mercy and chuckled. I opened my eyes just in time to see him push away from the door and start striding over to me.

I had been given this room to work in, amongst other things, like sleeping, eating, and general twiddling my thumbs, all of which came after a full night of biting my fingertips. Oh and let's not forget, listening to hopeless love songs and trying not to cry, along with giving in to the temptation of hunting someone down and begging them to go and get me a tub of ice cream the size of my head.

But I was getting way ahead of myself. Because before this had come the most important moment of my life so far and one that had the power to scar my very soul...*a soul he now knew he owned.*

And it all started with a kiss.

The kiss.

That kiss.

His kiss.

Gods but it was a painful bliss just thinking back to it. But that had been two days ago. Two days since I ripped myself from his arms and tried to leave. Because with only a few words uttered it had plunged me back into the icy river called,

My bitter reality.

TWO DAYS EARLIER

"There is only now...*My Amelia,*" he whispered and before I could put any more words in between us, he kissed me. But it wasn't just a simple kiss, as I knew it never would be with Lucius. No, this felt more like an immortal branding. A way for him to finally mark me as his, declaring me untouchable to the rest of the world. That was what kissing Lucius felt like. As if you were the only being in the world, one that could have been crumbling around us, for he simply wouldn't have cared. He would only have held me tighter to take his prize with him as he stepped into the Underworld.

This was a kiss from a Vampire King, one forged in Hell and given life by the Devil himself. But wait, where on Earth did that thought just come from?

He gripped me tighter, holding me as if telling me without words that I wasn't going anywhere, not until he deemed it acceptable. And really, I didn't have a problem with that, especially not when his touch made me feel treasured and quite honestly, it wasn't a response I'd ever expected Lucius capable of giving until this moment. But then, with his lips on mine, his tongue duelling with my own as he tasted me, fighting me for dominance, there was no other way to describe how he made me feel.

Then suddenly, it all ended, and I was doused once more with Lucius' taste of reality. The moment he growled over my lips and spoke only of pain, not the pleasure we had just shared.

"I wish touching you didn't hurt so fucking much!" he whispered through a hiss of gritted teeth and I swear it felt as though he had just placed both hands on my chest and pushed. Instead I gasped, unable to hold it back before I did to him how it felt he had just done to me. I placed my hands on his hard chest and pushed, making him at least go back a step. I think this was done so more out of shock and really, was he that stupid or just that out of touch with women?

He growled at me the second I staggered backwards desperate to put more space between us.

"Amelia." My name came out as a warning and was snarled as a serious enough threat that it almost had me doing as he silently asked...*almost.* But instead I kept my ground, trembling in my anguish and the second he saw it, he finally relaxed all those tense muscles that had looked ready to make him pounce. Even his hard expression softened and just as he was about to take a step closer my hand shot up and shook as I held it there.

"No Lucius, just...*just no!"* I said tearing my gaze from his, no longer being able to stand staring at him from the other side of the great chasm that was cruelly placed between us. It was one filled with a painful history and hours of tears I just couldn't ignore, even if his kiss still lingered.

"Amelia, let me explain."

"No, no it's too late for that, Lucius. Whatever this is between us, well...let's be honest, it was over before it even began, and I think it's safer it…it stays that way," I told him making him first look shocked before it was replaced with annoyance. I could even hear the sound of leather groaning as he clenched his left hand into a tight fist.

"Now who's the one lying?" he asked folding his arms across his chest.

"As difficult as this may be for you to understand, Lucius, I didn't come here for you!" I snapped back making him raise a brow before granting me a sarcastic,

"No?"

"No, I came here for the box or did the whole breaking into your vault not make that clear enough," I responded making a muscle in his jaw tick and it was the only evidence to how he was actually feeling right then, even if his cool façade spoke otherwise.

"The only thing that is clear right now is that you're running scared." I sucked in a breath of shock and frowned back at him, after first giving him an incredulous, questioning look.

"Seriously?!" I asked making him shrug his shoulders in a nonchalant way that was infuriating.

"You heard me, Princess." I swear I was the one to growl at this.

"For the last time, don't call me that!" I snapped and this time when his jaw muscle twitched, I could see it was because he was trying to fight back a smile.

"Speaking of which, just how did you break in exactly?" he asked making me falter a step in my anger thinking I was now about to tread on very delicate ground. Because if there was one thing I had learned about Lucius as the years went by, was that he had a major problem with all things to do with the Fates. And this included the Oracle whom, according to Pip, he had made no qualms about hating to the point of venomous disdain.

But this was yet just one more thing to add to the list of

hundreds of things I never really knew about Lucius. And really, as someone who had foolishly once believed him to be my Chosen One, then it was somewhat laughable…that was if I wasn't being pathetic and crying over it like a little girl who hadn't been asked to the prom.

Which now put me in a bit of a predicament because really, just how would I have known the things I did enough to break into his vault. In all honestly, I was just surprised this hadn't been the first thing he had asked me. But then again, he had been too preoccupied with taking a mocking trip down memory lane…even if it had ended with a kiss instead of well…the pain of last time.

"I have my ways, Lucius," I told him hoping this was enough. Of course, it wasn't. I knew this when he started walking closer and I in turn started backing up just as if we had been back in his club. But then, knowing how clumsy I was, I fell for his warning the second he nodded behind me. So naturally I turned my head believing that I was heading into something and in fear of falling on my ass and well, making an ass out of myself to boot. But then doing so had been his plan all along as the second I fell for it and saw that there was nothing in my way, by the time I looked back up to question him he had closed the distance between us.

"Ah!" I yelped the moment I saw him staring down at me and the second I took my first step away from him he prevented it by banding an arm around my waist.

"You were saying something about having *your ways*?" he said purring the last two words down at me. I put my hands to his chest and applied a slight amount of pressure prompting him to say,

"That won't work this time, Sweetness."

Unfortunately I visibly gulped, especially when I felt the many impressive muscles in his arms tense as if to prove his point. But then something in my panicked gaze must have made him realise that this was freaking me out, because the moment I started to squirm in his hold he lost his predatory gaze.

"Hey, easy now, I won't hurt you," he said but my look said it all as there was more than one way to hurt a person enough to cut them to the core, with not a blade in sight.

"Lucius, we shouldn't, we can't do…"

"Ssshh, just take a breath and let's focus on what you can do, not what you're scared of doing," he told me and I nearly winced knowing that he knew of my fears and was working around them. I swear but with his eyes gazing down at me like that combined with the back of his fingers caressing down my cheek it had me needing to close my eyes just to escape the intensity of it all.

"I realise that a single moment cannot erase all that has occurred between us, which is why I am willing to give you time to accept that what is happening between us now *will happen*, of that you have my word, Amelia," he told me making my mouth close to dropping in shock.

"Wh…what…are you saying?" I asked stuttering to start, my shock evident.

"Exactly what it sounds like. You are mine." I frowned up at him and his gaze softened to the point where if I could've hazarded a guess at his thoughts, he no doubt believed my reaction to be an endearing one.

"I'm yours?" I almost squeaked this question as utter astonishment and lack of belief that this was actually happening was easy to detect. But he obviously wanted me to take what he said very seriously. So, he lowered his head enough to catch my eyes despite our height difference, then almost growled his reply,

"Most definitely." I started shaking my head as if this wasn't happening.

"You just haven't accepted it yet and that's understandable. So, I will grant you your time, but Amelia be warned…" At this he paused and went to whisper in my ear to grant me the rest,

"My patience to have you is near its end." Then he kissed my cheek and in the time it took me to draw my next breath,

He was gone.

That was two days ago, and in those days, he had done exactly what he had said he would. He had given me time and I hadn't seen him even once. No, instead I had stood frozen to the spot in my utter, complete shocked state before a strikingly beautiful woman had walked in and only stopped when right in front of me.

"Hello human, Lucius sent me, my name is Liessa," she said holding out a hand for me to shake, one that was covered in cute red leather gloves that had three pink bows down the middle finger. She also looked like a supermodel, being slim and at least six foot tall. Although, if she walked down the runway now it would have been for a designer's new line of Stepford wives chic.

She wore a pink sleeveless sheath dress that cut across the collarbone, folded over and was held at the center with a big bow of red. It molded to her slim form, down into a tight skirt to her knees. Added to this was a pair of white pantyhose with a thin red line down the backs of her legs screaming sexy yet classy.

The high stiletto heels matched the outfit, including thick red rimmed sunglasses and of course, her cute gloves. She looked ready for a day at the Grand National as all she missed was a great big hat.

But her outfit, although odd to find in a place like this,

wasn't the strangest thing about her. No, it was her perfectly coiled brown hair that twisted up into different sections and showed flashes of light peach coloured streaks running through it. Added to this were rubber tubes in different thicknesses that entwined in the odd style. Cherry red lips and a pink blush added to her high cheekbones making her look like some living doll. But then she raised her glasses to the top of her head and said,

"Oh, how I do hope you cause this place some trouble like the last human." Then she winked at me and I was shocked to find her eyes were also peach and brown coloured. But then I started to get paranoid, wondering who this other human was that she spoke about. However, she must have read the question in my gaze because she patted my arm and said,

"Oh, don't worry Sweetpea, *it was your mother."*

I gasped.

Because what she didn't realise was that this was the very last thing that eased my mind. In fact, it plagued me for the next two days making it nearly impossible to think of little else. Because the thought of my mother being here with Lucius was like a knife to the gut, one that only managed to sink in deeper every time I closed my eyes and tried to push it from my mind.

But my mind was a traitor and one that seemed to want to continue to inflict pain because I couldn't help but see her being here just as I was now. Yes, I knew that she loved my father more than anything in the world and had chosen him time and time again. But it didn't mean that there hadn't been something between them, Lucius and her. And well, to be jealous of your own mother was nothing short of a 'mind meld' Spock style experience. Or at least one could presume it was.

Which was exactly why when Liessa told me to make myself at home in Lucius' private apartment I had protested...as in profusely. Especially when she informed me his bed was now 'my bed'. Something I outright refused to do and to the point that it was only when she saw me trying to sleep on his ridiculously uncomfortable sofa that she caved in. So, she showed me to a guest room which was more like a hotel suite. I didn't know who it was that used it but after shamefully asking Liessa if it was ever used by anyone I knew, her eyes softened before telling me,

"No Sweetpea, no other human has ever used this room," telling me without saying the actual words we both knew, which was when I decided that I really liked Liessa.

I also found out that when Lucius said he was going to give me time that literally meant he wouldn't even be inside the building. He had left as abruptly as I had ended our first real kiss, informing Liessa that he had business to attend to. Which in Lucius' world, could have meant a number of things, many of which could have been something bloody.

However, one thing at least was Lucius had ordered that the box be kept under my care so I was free to work on trying to discover its secrets. Meaning that the next day Liessa had shown me back into the vault and how to remove the box without setting off the sensors, so I was free to come and get the box any time I desired. I had to say the urge not to touch all the other things I found in there was like a kid locked in a candy store being told there was only one kind of chocolate she could eat.

But working on the box kept my mind from a certain someone…or should I say, mostly. It was just unfortunate that what I was working on included the very grim possibility that whatever was in that box had the power to kill Lucius. And with him being sire to all Vampires, including my mother, well I really hadn't lied to him when I told him he wasn't the reason I had come back to Transfusion. Something he had cryptically asked me what had taken me so long.

Gods but talk about as cryptic as the box I had been working forty-eight hours solid on! Which was something I had yet to discuss with Lucius...the box, not his lack of clear communication.

Which led me to now and the man in question. Someone who I could see was walking his way to me with only one thing written on his face...

His patience was at an end and in turn,

My time was up.

CHAPTER TWO

HELLO MY AMELIA

I watched as he stalked over to me and couldn't help but tense, unsure on how this was going to go. It had been two days, and in that time it had given me a lot to think about. On one hand being with Lucius this way was as if my dream was finally coming true. Finding out that someone you had been in love with all these years was, for the first time, seeing you in a different light was beyond all I had ever hoped for. But then my biggest fear was …*could I really trust him?*

I didn't know whether it was being back here or not but either way it was clouding the happiness my mind wanted to grant me. Like the way I wanted to face him, and the moment he was close enough just throw my arms around him and kiss him. To welcome him home and hope the next step was as simple as him asking me on our first official date.

But that cloud wouldn't let me. Because, what if it was just a kiss to him and I was the only one who felt as though it could be so much more. What if he felt something now but then later on, he decided it wasn't worth the hassle? After all, who was I kidding here, I was human. A mortal who, compared to him, had a pretty shitty lifespan. It was something my parents utterly refused to face. But let's be real, when your own mother looked more like your sister, then there was no getting away from the inevitable. Even if the startling similarities in age were kept from most of the world except their own.

But then there was the worst part. The one that I doubted either of us could ever truly get past…

My mother.

Gods but why couldn't it have even been just another random girl I had to compete with. But oh no, it just had to be a person I loved most in this world, along with the rest of my immediate family. They would never know this, but it was why I was hardly there. Oh, they just believed I wanted my independence, making me wonder if my mum had any clue that this was something my dad had secretly refused to grant me. I knew they must have been going out of their minds with worry seeing as I had just cut and run. But in some way they deserved it…or at the very least, my dad did.

So yeah, these last few days had given me time to think but I doubted it was in Lucius' best interests like he thought it would be. Well, that was if he still truly wanted me. Because my conclusion was simple…*self-preservation.*

That was going to be my main goal from now on. Because I was sick and tired of being lied to. I felt betrayed by everyone around me other than Wendy. My dad had made my independent life in London a lie. My dream job, what were the odds of that being all down to me and my hard work…slim at best, that's what. My apartment that I had saved every penny I earned to afford and made into my little oasis. One of my best friends Ben, who lived across the hall, a person who had been given that apartment as a means to spy on me. And then there was Lucius, another person who'd had me followed.

I felt like something people owned and therefore had the right to decide my fate for me. Hell, but when I think of all I had to do just to get here, when really I was well within my rights to be able to simply get in a cab, drive to the airport and get on any flight I wanted without being chased, stopped, or coerced into doing any different.

And this was all without even dating Lucius.

Meaning I could barely imagine it being worse than what I endured now, but knowing it would be, should I allow him to have me. But deep down I knew that the main reason wasn't just allowing him to have the power over my decision making, but it was more down to when he decided to eventually walk away.

That was power enough to destroy me...*just like that last time.*

So, when Lucius was only a few feet away I turned back to face the breakfast bar I had been working at. Papers covered the surface all with my scruffy notes scrawled across them and even I would admit, I looked like some mad professor minus the white coat and crazy unkempt grey hair. But this was me in my natural element, with what felt like life's greatest puzzle in front of me. My MP3 player now lay discarded, playing the rest of Celine Dion's classics and a cold cup of tea was creating pale brown rings on my craziness.

Oh, and I was also still wearing my pyjamas even though it was six thirty in the evening. So, he was either left to think I'd just got ready for bed really early or that I was just plain lazy. The truth would have been somewhere in between, with an unhealthy dose of obsession thrown in there for good measure.

But then again, I was well and truly done with trying to woo Lucius, so looking sexy was no longer a concern. Which was why I wasn't overly concerned with my baseball style t-shirt that was white with grey sleeves and soft flannel pants in grey and white check. I had now twisted my hair into a messy bun so I could stick spare pencils in it for sketching the different text and symbols. I also wore my thick black rimmed glasses and a pair of slipper booties in fluffy grey with white stars. So yeah, not exactly sexy and added to this was the show I had just shamefully put on by getting too carried away with the music...Yeah, thanks for that Celine!

"So, you're back," I said trying to sound casual and unaffected, which would have been more convincing had it not come out more high pitched than I would have liked. I knew he was getting close but when I heard the two stools beside me being pushed aside, done so to allow him more space, I couldn't help but jump a little. It was like watching a horror movie and every time the music got intense, you knew that something bad was going to happen. And that something bad was always jumping out at you and making you scream. But you still reacted to it anyway, no matter how prepared you were for it.

Well, that was Lucius.

Meaning that when I saw his hands come to rest either side of me on the countertop caging me in, I couldn't help but suck in a shuddered breath. Because despite making the heartbreaking decision not to allow this to go anywhere, it still didn't mean I wasn't weak where he was concerned. A weakness that definitely grew when I felt him lower his lips to my bare shoulder where one side of my top had slipped.

"Any chance of getting a repeat performance?" he asked softly making me roll my lips inwards just to prevent myself from making any further breathy sounds that might give away what his actions did to me. No, instead I swallowed back any witty or even flirtatious response I may have wanted to give, instead deciding it was safer to stick to facts, which included one very big one I was yet to tell him.

Because before that kiss there had only been one thing I

needed to tell him, right before I left for good. But then he had crossed his own line and all rational thinking disappeared...just before he disappeared right along with it.

"We need to talk," I said, trying to sound stern, something he obviously would never have taken seriously enough, as let's face it, this was Lucius we were talking about here.

"We are talking, Sweetness," he hummed against my skin and I was shamelessly starting to get sucked into this new side of Lucius and knew that if I didn't put some distance between us pretty soon, then I was going to find it impossible to do what was needed...like walking away for good.

"Although, before that you were swaying your hips rather hypnotically, so feel free to continue that also, should the mood take you of course." At this I couldn't help it but I laughed, and it sounded how it felt, surprised.

"Ha, you would be so lucky!" I said with a smile I was thankful he couldn't see.

"Indeed." His reply was once again whispered and this time against my neck. Gods but didn't it just feel amazing and dangerously so. Which was precisely why I quickly tried to shift out from between him and the counter. But faster than my eyes could track, his hand went from being casually resting at the bar to snagging my waist. So now I found myself side on with his arm banded across my stomach and a possessive hand gripping my hip, preventing me from leaving his personal space.

"Ah, ah, time's up, beautiful," he told me and as I thought when first seeing him, his patience was at an end. So, I finally braved a look up at him and I swear those grey blue depths nearly had me crumbling in my resolve. Meaning that in order to say what I needed to say next meant digging deep.

"Then the answer is no," I told him and the surprise on his

face was easy to read, and if I had disliked him as I wished I did, then it would have been satisfying.

But unfortunately, it wasn't.

"No?" he questioned, and I took a deep breath and said,

"I get that being told no by anyone is most likely a foreign concept for you, but it doesn't change my decision." At this he frowned and looked as though he was trying to process my response and from the looks of it, well he was still struggling. Even as his hand flexed at my hip and I wished I hadn't felt it down to my toes for how nice it felt.

"I see that two days away did nothing to ease your fears but instead simply reinforced them," he said in a matter of fact way that didn't really give me much insight to his mood. Either he didn't believe I would stick to my word, or they just didn't affect him like I hoped they would.

"Seriously Lucius, what else did you expect...this, us... whatever it is between us..."

"You know precisely what *it is* between us, so don't pretend with me, Princess," he growled down at me and I hated that he used that name when pissed off which he clearly was getting despite trying to keep that famous cool of his. At this I pushed more forcefully out of his hold and this time he allowed it.

"Like I said, I never came here for you, that ship sailed long ago," I told him, looking back towards the door and into a main lobby area that eventually would lead back into his club. Either way he knew what I meant by looking there.

"So, you really did believe you could steal it from me and run?" he asked as if this was a magical feat only achieved by a damn superhero or something.

"I need it," I told him pushing my glasses up my nose and knowing that any minute we were going to have to have the conversation about what I believed the box truly was. But the second he saw the innocent action, one which was typical of someone who wore glasses, he smirked as if he liked the sight. I frowned back at him but he ignored my reaction, instead turning to lean his back against the counter after first grabbing the box. Then he spun it in his hands, and I freaked,

"Bloody Hell, careful!" I shouted suddenly forgetting about space and running up to him to take it from his hands. He frowned down at me in question but didn't say anything as he watched me gently place it back down on the counter as if it was a ticking time bomb. Well, for all I knew it was, only one supernatural in style.

"You're not lying, you really did come back for it," he said as if he only now just got it. I didn't respond because my face said it all.

"So, what was your plan exactly, to change your name, your job, forget all those who mean something to you just so you could run from me?!" he snapped now getting angry. I tore my gaze from his, hating to see that he actually looked hurt by this.

"You have no right, no fucking right, Lucius!" I snapped back and walked away. But he followed me around the corner into the living space.

"I have no right?" he asked incredulously, pointing at himself.

"No! You don't. Not when it was you all these years that made me feel like a damn leper, not when I came here, and you threw me out on the streets to...to..."

"Don't say it, Amelia, because I swear if you do, then nothing will save this room from my wrath," he said interrupting me with a dark gaze and fisted hands.

"And me, what would save me from your wrath?!" I snapped because I wanted to hurt him and I knew it worked the second I saw him flinch and I instantly felt guilty.

"I would never hurt you!" he hissed back and because I felt guilty, I couldn't help myself when I shouted back,

"You already have!"

But then I felt awful as it wasn't Lucius' fault I had been attacked. And he had saved my life. But I also knew that he felt guilty for making me leave his club only for that to happen and what did I do, just made him feel worse about it. But then again, he also knew that what came after my attack had been, well... the most painful moment of my life. And with one look Lucius knew it too. So, before he could utter one word about it, I continued.

"You don't get to play the victim here, Lucius, just as you don't get to just click your fingers and erase the last seven years. It doesn't work like..."

"There's something you're not telling me about the box," he said quickly interrupting me as finally something clicked with him. Because if I hadn't just broken in and tried to steal the box, using this as some kind of ruse to try one last time to convince Lucius that we should be together, then it meant I really was here for the box. And if I really was here for the box then that must mean there was something important. And this knowledge really annoyed him. I guess if I was honest then I couldn't help but be flattered.

"Yes, and I have been trying to tell you since I got here, that is until you left suddenly," I said obviously making his irritation grow in the meantime.

"Well, I am here now, so talk," he snapped back. I took a deep breath and decided it was time we both put whatever was going on between us aside and focus on 'the eradication of a whole race' part of the evening. Oh yeah, this was going to be fun...NOT

"I think you need to sit down," I said and motioned to the sofa, which I was happy to say was a lot more comfortable than the one in Lucius' apartment. Like I said, the whole place looked like something you would have found on the top floor in a five star hotel. It was neither feminine or masculine with its minimalistic décor and practical use of space.

There was a living room that held two oatmeal coloured sofas which faced each other with a stylish glass coffee table in between. This sat on a navy and teal rug that had no pattern just flecks of interwoven colours of the two. The walls were a plain off white with one accent wall of navy blue that matched a strip of colour on the curtains framing a view of the city. There was even a baby grand piano, making me wonder if it was there because it was a beautiful piece and not because anyone in particular played.

Of course, I knew how to play, being taught by my uncle Zagan of all people who was a master at it. Not that many would have known but when I accidently wandered into my aunty Sophia and uncle Zagan's private wing of Afterlife, I had found him sat playing to no one. But instead of shouting at me or telling me off (something he never did) he simply patted the space next to him on the bench and let me sit there and watch as he played. Of course, I was nowhere near as good as he was, but I could at least hold my own. But then, my little flat wasn't exactly big enough for an exquisite instrument like the piano in the apartment. Which made me want to ask if Lucius knew I played, and this was why it was here. Although that felt like a stupid question, because Lucius didn't do things like that...*did he?*

Either way, I hadn't yet had the courage to touch it, just in case it did belong to someone else and they caught me playing it. Meaning that I spent the last two days eyeing up the thing and playing notes in my head from the music I wanted to play on it. Maybe I would ask him... No, what was I saying, I was leaving as soon as I could!

From the living room there were two doors, one that led to the lobby, a space that connected all the private apartments, like Lucius', whose obviously commandeered the biggest space.

The other door led into a comfortable sized bedroom that was probably the size of my whole flat back in Twickenham. A bathroom and walk-in closet led on from there and again, put my little home to shame. But then again, it wasn't my home was it...it was really my father's I thought bitterly.

From this room it ran in a L shape, as up a few steps and around the corner you found yourself in a cute kitchenette fully stocked for comfortable cooking and a dining table opposite, with a kitchen island separating the two spaces.

Liessa hadn't taken long in gathering a list of food I liked an hour after showing me inside, so she could send someone out to stock the cupboards for me. Hence there being no reason why I needed to leave this space in the last two days. Then the next day the clothes arrived and I quickly recognised them to be the ones Lucius had bought for me when my flat had been trashed. After that it strangely felt as if I had been moved in here and the thought had me panicking.

I needed to leave and would as soon as we figured out what we were going to do with this box. After I had said my piece and could then hope this was where the supernatural pros took over. Because I wasn't kidding myself with this one, as I knew this was way out of my league and any help I was going to be didn't realistically need to be done from inside the walls of Transfusion. Which was why I had been working tirelessly on it for these few days.

Gaining all the information I could by making notes and examining every inch of it before I left. That way they could keep me in the loop via email or phone from wherever I decided to go. Because one thing was for sure, I wasn't staying here. At first, I had thought I could handle it all on my own but with so much at stake, then I could never chance it. Besides, if there was one being in the world that would stop at nothing to prevent this, then it was the one who stood to lose the most, like his life and well…that of someone he would no doubt always care for…

My mother.

Gods but would it ever get any easier or any less painful!?

I sat down and was thankful when he did the same, although I would have appreciated more space between us than he chose to give me, seeing as when he turned side on our knees were touching.

"I assume this has something to do with your new obsession?" he stated making me frown when he nodded down at the fact that yes, I hadn't really dressed that day.

"Yes, well I usually save my ballgowns and pantsuits for the really good stuff, like four thousand year old mummies," I said sarcastically making him smirk behind his fingers as he rested his elbow on the back of the sofa.

"But of course, for why should a box that could wipe out an entire race of my people, myself and your mother included, deserve the same glamorous treatment," he said shocking me enough that I blurted out,

"You know!?" He leaned forward at this point and whispered behind a hand in a mocking way,

"Hence the vault."

"But…but…then why, I mean…you never…?" Okay so it wasn't my best come back but surely no one could blame me.

"Amelia, I am a King to millions above and below, do you really believe me ignorant of something as important as this?" I frowned, shocked to hear it was so many but then my father was the same, so why was I surprised. There were millions of demons and angels living on Earth, along with ones ruled under their command down in Hell and above in Heaven. So, like I said, I shouldn't have been surprised to find Lucius' rule to equal my father's.

"But how would you know, as it's not exactly obvious…I mean I only discovered it by accident and even then it was…"

"I am not without my own means," he said interrupting me and I had to admit, the knowledge that he knew someone who also figured it out was, well it was a hit to my ego.

"Right…right." I said looking down in my lap and not knowing what else to say, as now I just felt foolish. I felt his fingers under my chin and he lifted my face back to his.

"Sweetness, don't do that," he said in a tender tone and I swallowed hard before turning my head and getting up from the sofa needing to put some distance between us, especially when he was being like that. I could cope with his sarcasm and his curt and stern demands. But the tender side of Lucius, the one he reserved for who I hoped wasn't just every woman behind closed doors…well, that was the side of Lucius I found most dangerous. Because I knew more than most the power he held over the opposite sex.

"Right, well, okay then it looks like you have this all well in hand. If you could just set up a meeting with this…this person, then I could give him or her, or whoever he or she, doesn't matter which, my notes." Yep, smooth Fae…Gods I felt like smacking my forehead with those bloody notes! And really, did he have to do that infuriating smirk thing behind the crook of his finger like that!

"Amelia, come, sit back down," he said in a way that I was starting to become addicted to the sound of my own name, especially when he hummed it like that. It felt more like a secret promise being whispered in my ear. A name that only belonged to him. And well, as he was the one who predominantly used it, then it felt like it kind of did.

"Why?" I said knowing that doing what he asked was not a good idea.

"Because we still need to talk," he told me.

"No, Lucius…we don't," I said shaking my head enough that I could feel one of my pencils slipping loose.

"No?" he questioned, his tone disbelieving.

"No, in fact, all that is left for me to do is pack a bag, leave you my notes and get a cab to the nearest airport," I said making him raise a brow as if surprised that I could even think about leaving here.

"What, not even a handshake?" he asked this time surprising me, especially when he held out his hand. Gods, but even that turned me on, just seeing the strength in his forearms from the shirt he had rolled at the sleeves. Even the other hand that was covered in leather and was currently drumming fingers along the back of the sofa. It just made me wonder what it would feel like drumming along my naked skin.

I shook my head a little in hopes of dissolving that image from my mind, going back to the rest of what he wore. This time it was a dark grey suit with a black shirt, no tie, no waistcoat, no jacket but still he managed to look the master of his universe, one with so much confidence it was near stifling the room. As if it managed to suck everyone else's confidence from them, only adding to his own. That was what his level of intimidation felt like. Which was why I couldn't help but be drawn into his request, fearful of his next move if I didn't.

So, I placed my hand in his and swallowed hard before saying softly,

"Goodbye, Lucius." He shook it and for those few seconds I held myself so tight, as if any minute I knew the tears of those words would glaze my eyes, telling him all he needed to know. To know what a bullshit liar I was. About how I still loved him and hated that we had to say goodbye. But really, what was the alternative? He held too much power over me, and I couldn't trust him with more.

And in the end, something else I couldn't trust him with was saying goodbye, as the second he gripped my hand tight in his own I realised my mistake too late.

He suddenly yanked me hard to him and twisted my arm over my head at the last moment so when I landed this time I did so in his lap. Then, still holding my hand captive, he wrapped an arm across my torso, trapping my own hand at my shoulder.

Then I felt his lips at my ear as he whispered his own reply at my attempt at saying goodbye...

"Hello, my Amelia."

CHAPTER THREE

DATE WITH A TV

"You do understand this is kind of the opposite to goodbye…right.?" I said after trying in vain to squirm out of his hold. He chuckled behind me and then with his free hand started to pull the pencils out of my hair.

"I do, just as I understand that walking away is the opposite to what I want you to do," he said in reply and I had to mask my breathy inhale. Play it cool Fae, play it cool now. Well, this was easier said than done, especially when even the sound of him dropping the pencils to the floor made me jump. I could even hear them rolling under the furniture. But then the second I felt him removing the hair tie I tensed making him whisper,

"Relax." Seriously, was he joking? How the hell could I relax?! How could I relax when he was currently playing out one of a hundred different fantasies I had of him. Like this one, sat on the sofa snuggled up in his arms whilst he played with my hair…okay so Star Trek Voyager was playing on the TV in front of us and I was very lamely explaining all of Captain Kathryn Janeway's drama as she commanded the Starfleet

starship, the USS Voyager. Oh yeah, I could totally see him being into that…NOT!

I mean really, did we even have anything in common apart from who my parents were?

But my Goddess, I nearly totally forgot what day it was! Okay, so maybe leaving today wasn't such a good plan and speaking of which, why on earth didn't these guys watch TV!

"Now I really want to know where that head of yours is at?" he asked me, as I must have been giving something away.

"Oh, only about 70,000 light years away," I answered before I could stop myself, making him chuckle and really, he had no idea.

"Can I get up now…oooh." I asked but stopped on a moan when his hand started to run through my hair and massage my scalp. Oh dear Gods, why, oh why! This was a major weakness of mine and the bastard just found it, as I freaking loved having my hair played with. Seriously, I would go without basic groceries, like milk and yes, my favourite cereal just so I could go to the salon and get my extras like an Indian head massage.

"Mmm, interesting," he muttered and I chose to ignore him because really, what he was doing now was far too nice to care. But then he let go of my hand and now instead of holding my back to his chest, he used both hands to massage my head, seeing for himself the effect it created. I relaxed even further back into him and couldn't help another moan of pleasure from escaping. Then I felt his lips at my neck and before I could respond he suddenly gripped my hair in a fist and pulled my head to the side making my neck taut and ready for him. Then he growled against my tender flesh making me shudder against him.

"I think I just found your weakness, Beautiful," he whispered by my ear and yes, he was most definitely right, but

he was also most definitely wrong because didn't he realise yet...

My biggest weakness was him.

Which was why all I wanted to do right now was turn around and kiss him. To kiss him and say to hell with the last two days I'd spent convincing myself why that was a bad idea. I just wanted to pick up where we left off and by his actions, then I would say that he wanted the same.

His hands left my hair and I relaxed my head back on his shoulder so he was now free to explore like he wanted to, starting by running one hand down the side of my breast and the other to the front of my neck. I released another breathy moan and it sounded very much like a 'yes' but I couldn't be sure. Not with his hands on me and his lips at my neck. But then with his next words spoken he managed to wake me from the spell he had cast, and it really was the curse of an arrogant king,

"I knew you would easily be mine." At this I froze before suddenly bolting out of his hold before he had chance to stop me. I made it to unsteady feet and pushed all my hair back with one hand and righting my glasses with another in annoyance. Then I whipped round to face him the second I heard him chuckling. The look I gave him should have been powerful enough to cause damage. Damn all the superheroes with all the cool shit like laser eyes!

"Seriously? Does that arrogant shit ever work, or do you just constantly live with blue balls?!" I snapped making him this time throw his head back and laugh, and I swear if the sight hadn't momentarily rendered me breathless, then I would have thrown one of the lamps at his head! Gods, but he was breathtakingly handsome, painfully so, especially given the circumstances.

"My balls survive just fine, but they thank you for your

concern," he replied and I had to turn my face from his just to hide my own grin, as damn it, I still wanted to be mad at him.

"Well, clearly paid services aren't picky," I retorted making him lose his grin and in turn, mine grew. Then he rose from his seat and said,

"Oh Sweetheart, if you think I have to pay a woman to be with me then you are deluded and if you will only let yourself relax long enough in my arms, then you will soon agree that my arrogance is more than justified." At this my mouth dropped before a strangled sounding laugh came out of me.

"Wow, love yourself much!" I commented making him shrug his shoulders as if he was unashamed.

"I will not apologise for speaking a truth, any more than I would for speaking of your obvious beauty," he said making my next witty reply die in my throat at hearing him calling me beautiful.

"I...well, I don't...I mean..." I stuttered for words as yep, that had completely thrown me, and his cocky ass knew it! He started to walk over to me and doing so with purpose.

"Yes Amelia?" The way he said this was again done so in a knowing tone.

"You're arrogant!" I told him and a grin played at his lips before saying,

"Yes, I am."

"And egotistical," I added making him fight that grin again.

"I believe they are the same thing, Sweetheart."

"And condescending," I added this time making him grin outright and again damn him for making it light up his eyes that way!

"Some believe so, mainly those beneath me," he said with a shrug of his shoulders and I gasped thinking he meant me. But then he moved so quickly I swear his body became a blur. Which meant that before I knew it his hand was in my hair, tugging at my weakness along with the strands captured in adept fingers. Doing so now, so he could pull my head back and I had little choice but to do as he silently commanded of me. Meaning I was quickly left looking up at him with wide eyes, to the point that I could feel my glasses slipping down my nose.

"You, however, are the exception," he said taking his time to slowly push my glasses back up my nose as if I was some little doll of his to play with.

"How so?" I asked in a breathy tone, as he knew I would.

"Because I want you beneath me just as badly as I want you by my side." At this my mouth slipped open and I was just about to speak when he growled,

"Enough!"

And then...

He kissed me.

This was also when my world became utterly consumed by everything that was him. His possessive touch, his lips pressed against my own, moving in perfect sync as if we had done this a thousand times before. How it just felt right. That I had been right all this time, how being with him had been declared by the Gods as a perfect match.

Gods, but even the taste of him had me losing myself to a new addiction. I think I could have kissed him for hours if I hadn't feared self-combusting long before I had the chance to do so. And considering his own actions, it seemed I wasn't the only one feeling this way.

One hand remained in my hair, locking my lips to his as if he feared I would pull away before he was ready and from the way his other hand fisted in the material of my top at the base of my spine, then I would have said that he wouldn't ever be ready. And it was a chain reaction because that fist made the once loose and comfortable top as tight as a second skin.

But that fist clenching there also made the tensed muscle of his forearm hard as stone against my side. This was also connected to a bulging bicep I was now gripping onto as if my life depended on it. Well, even if my life wasn't in danger then my legs staying upright most certainly were, which is why they fisted in the material of his shirt.

"Fick mich! Wie müssen die Götter mich hassen!" He suddenly snarled up at the ceiling after first tearing his lips from mine. I tried to make sense of his words but right then I could only translate the first part as being, 'Fuck me', something I will admit to wanting to do very much in that very moment.

But then something started niggling at the back of my mind about the other words that had followed.

"Tonight," he said, gritting it out as though it was being ripped from him when any other words would have been easier to say.

"Tonight?" I questioned in a breathless tone that spoke volumes to what his kiss just did to me. Then he let me go and I wanted to question why, especially when it looked as if he had been forced to do so by his own hand. Had his conscience told him to?

"Be dressed and ready," he told me before walking to the door and I swear I would have accepted his invitation had his sudden and blunt departure not hurt. Which is why I told him,

"But I am busy." He then paused by the door and looked over his shoulder to issue me a single order,

"Yes, by being at my side."

And then he was gone.

After this I sat numbly at the kitchen counter and picked at a sandwich, not even tasting the filling. But when food didn't help, I decided it was time for a bath, in hopes it would be a great place to sort through my confused brain. I just didn't get it, how he was hot and cold, desperate for me in one moment and then near desperate to get away the next. There was no getting away from it,

"It's a mind fuck," I muttered before dunking my whole head under the water and holding it there long enough that bubble islands floated across my face like clouds closing in. I only resurfaced when I was forced to, but to be honest, had I been a supernatural then I would have stayed this way for as long as my body would have let me. But instead, I rose out of the water and pushed my black hair from my eyes. Then I looked to the huge mirror at the vanity opposite and saw more of my father's features looking back at me.

I had his colouring with naturally tanned olive skin and midnight dark hair. But my eyes, well they were all my mother's, big blue ones framed with thick dark lashes and right now, they were framed above by frowning dark brows as I started to question everything about myself. I had spent enough hours to make up years of doubting everything that I could possibly offer a being like Lucius. Because in truth, I may have royal blood in my veins, but I think it was safe to say that it might well have been all of my mother's, because I was all human.

Every last ounce of me.

So, I was a princess of a world I didn't belong in. A princess with nothing to offer a King. It was the reason I had fully embraced the only thing I did have. A stronger connection to humanity. So, after Lucius had cast me aside as nothing more than a hindrance to his world, I had left and never looked back. I had then taken that last step needed to integrate myself fully into the human world. And in all honesty, I had been happy and content. I had made my life work and done the things that made me comfortable.

But now here I was, surrounded by the very life I had run from. Run away from the rule of my father along with the potential rule of another. Because as much as Lucius claimed to want me by his side, how could that be true when it came linked to a demand he had made before leaving. An order he issued like it was just expected of me to obey. Well, my mother had never once obeyed my father's demands. I knew this for a fact.

But then again, my mother had been much more than just my father's Chosen One, she had been declared his world's saviour. So yeah, pretty big shoes to fill with that one I thought with a roll of my eyes.

Because who was I, just some history geek who had told Lucius I was busy because my favourite show was on rerun and finally being shown on Netflix with Season 2.

So okay, after that kiss, if he had then tenderly asked me on a date then yeah, I would have totally chosen him over Star Trek. But as it stood then no, I was not giving in to be demanded to do anything, let alone be some chick on his arm for the night in that damn club of his.

"Screw him!" I said pulling the plug before I gave in and shaved my legs, which really after only a few days since last doing them, then I would have only been doing it for one reason and one reason only. So, I got myself out the tub, spiky legs and all, and wrapped myself up in a towel. Then I walked into the closet and smirked as I totally ignored the line of dresses, instead grabbing a pair of stretchy yoga pants in black that admittedly made my ass look fantastic. Then knowing that he would no doubt see it at some point tonight, when he realised he had been stood up and came looking for me, I picked a top I knew would tease him.

I grabbed a cropped workout top which matched the yoga pants that showed all of my stomach as it basically just covered my breasts. It had a thick white band an inch under my breasts to mirror the thick white band around my hips where the pants rested. The straps, also in white, rested over my shoulders in a halter neck and crossed over at my back, to match the thin white piping along the scalloped V neck. It acted more like a bra as it managed to push my breasts closer together giving me a nice shape.

"Yep, that will serve you right, mister!" I said to the mirror nodding and thinking, that yeah, I didn't look half bad. Hell, I even looked hot! However, I wasn't brave enough to just wear this, as let's face it, I looked more like I was going to the gym than relaxing for a night in front of the TV. So, I grabbed a sweater that was a sheer silver material you could see through and had stretchy bands at the sleeves and waist band. The neck part was wide enough that it fell off one shoulder and hung in a way that it showed just the hint of cleavage.

I was lucky enough not to need foundation or mascara so decided to forget about makeup altogether as that would have been too much. I did, however, rub a fabulous smelling body lotion on to my skin, that had the hint of something shimmery in it so now my skin looked as if it glowed. I decided just to wear my hair up into a high ponytail thinking this too looked casual. Thick white socks added to the look I was trying to achieve.

However, the biggest flaw in my plan came in the form of forgetting there wasn't a damn TV!

"Well, that's annoying," I said out loud and looked to the fancy metal clock that hung at the wall near the kitchen to see that it was 7:45pm. Okay, so I had fifteen minutes to try and find a TV and look relaxed in front of it by the time he came knocking. Oh, who was I kidding, Lucius knocked for no one! More like striding through the door like a damn sultan.

"Damn it, think Fae…umm, could I?" I asked myself when it finally came to me. I had mentioned the lack of TV's to

Liessa when she was showing me around the apartment and she had told me that the only place was in a private room off the club that they hardly used unless Lucius needed a place to conduct business away from prying eyes. I wonder if it was possible to get one from there?

She had even told me it led down from the rooftop garden if I wanted to find it. Well, now I wished I had spent more time exploring instead of brooding inside this apartment for the last two days.

Okay, so it was worth a shot, as I knew there was a staircase that led from the lobby assuming this was in case the elevator didn't work.

I quickly made the decision to do it and left in search of the staircase. But I couldn't help but shudder as I did the first time when seeing the same sculpture sat at the centre of the room just as I had done that night. It was the one similar to the one downstairs that had been facing the back entrance. It sat on a large circular table with its startling centre piece just calling out to be overanalysed by the likes of me.

It was a carved wooden heart that was charred black and opened up as though the two glass hands inside were trying to break free, splitting the heart from within. *A pair of woman's hands*.

I couldn't help wondering once more why this piece? What had drawn Lucius to it? At the time I had convinced myself it was just some rich man's art. But then, as I did that night I broke in, I couldn't help but look off to the large double doors that led to his private space, as if being able to reach inside and ask him through our connected minds.

Then I shook the thought from my head the second I heard voices, knowing that someone was coming, most likely Lucius. So, I ran for the door next to the elevator and quickly ran up the stairs in my socks, trying not to slip by clinging on to the railing. Then I pushed on the roof's metal door I found at the top and stepped into a little slice of contemporary paradise.

The rooftop garden was sweet in its design and looked as though it hadn't long been redesigned as the pale wooden decking looked newly laid and the greenery recently planted. The wall that surrounded it was waist high and at the corners were steel sculptures that acted as unconventional pillars.

They were made up of twisted lengths of corrugated iron rods made to look like barred metal trees void of leaves. In between the two at the end was a quaint seating area under a blanket of ivy that looked as if it had been growing for years and had completely taken over the wooden pergola.

In the centre of it all was a huge water feature that was a hip high glass tube the thickness of a basketball. It was filled with water and in the centre was a mini twister, creating a vortex of water before spilling over the edges. In fact, it looked like a nice space to spend a bit of time in, seeing as it offered a stunning panoramic view of the city all lit up at night. But then I thought back to my main goal here and scanned the rest of the rooftop until spotting a spiralling metal staircase that Liessa must have been talking about.

So, I quickly made my way down it and pushed on the frosted glass door at the end, finding myself next to a small bar. The long open room was definitely a private space and looked like one with the sole purpose of spying on the main VIP room. This was thanks to the wall that was seventy percent made up of a two-way mirror, acting like a window to the other side. One that I noted was in full swing…literally as it looked more like a demonic sex club. Well, I was just glad to find this particular room empty and not currently accommodating an orgy.

A row of stylish black leather sofas faced it, with a throne style at the centre showcased by winged sides and an arched high back. Dark wooden flooring matched the drinks' tables dotted around and also the dark wood panelled wall that was adorned with bleeding glass tears the size of dinner platters.

So, this was the VIP to his VIP, I thought with a wrinkle of my nose, hating the idea of what he did in here or more to the point, of who he invited in it. I suddenly looked down at myself and then back up at the large room full of tempting beauties beyond the glass, knowing that he could sit upon his throne and simply take his time in choosing one. And me, well I was here trying to steal a TV off the wall, dressed like a yoga instructor, when in reality, I had tried it once and after farting in front of the whole class decided I was safer at home. You know, so I could break wind in private and giggle about it like a five-year-old, would.

In the end I shrugged my shoulders and focused on why I had snuck in here to begin with. Most of the screens were raised high above the frame of glass, attached on TV brackets. Meaning that to get to one I would need two things, a screwdriver and a high-top table. I scanned the room again and thought my best bet was the bar area as surely there would be something there, I could use.

So, I checked all the cupboards and under the sink shouting in excitement when I found one in a tool kit.

"Bingo!" Then I pushed one of the tables closest to the bar over to the window just under a 22inch TV screen.

"Whoa!" I said as the round table wobbled a little as I climbed from the chair, on to it. Then with bent knees I steadied myself before I got my balance enough to straighten my legs. Then I yanked the cord out of the plug socket hidden behind it and twisted the TV on its stand, thankfully it was one that was on a moveable arm.

"Four screws," I said to myself as I pulled my screwdriver out of my waistband ready to try my luck and take this puppy down. I had managed three screws just fine, knowing now the thing was only held there by one. So, I loosened it a bit and put the screwdriver in my mouth as I held on with one hand and with the other at a difficult angle tried to take out the last one by hand.

"Cumon," I said with my mouth full. Then I heard a tutting sound and looked up to see once again a masterful figure stood leaning against the doorframe watching me.

"Trying to steal from me again, I see," he said with a devilish glint in his eyes. And I swear if I had been able in that moment I would have thrown up a hand, looked up the Gods and shouted, 'Oh come on!' But this didn't happen.

No instead I went with mumbled and clumsy,

"Ucius!" I said in shock. A startled cry that was unfortunately followed by an even more unfortunate reaction.

Letting go of the screen and in true Amelia Faith fashion…

I fell.

CHAPTER FOUR

OH, HOW THE WICKED FALL

I say I fell but by the time it took me to cry out I was caught by Lucius.

"Gottcha," he said and my mouth dropped open, something that evidently happened a lot around Lucius. He smirked down at me as the screwdriver rolled from my mouth in what could have possibly been the most unsexiest sight in his entire history with women. It landed in between us and rested against my heaving cleavage thanks to this wonder workout type bra.

Then he lowered my legs to the floor, and I was just about to speak ready to explain when something stopped me. Movement above my head made me look up just as the screen was about to crash down on us. I winced, waiting for the impact but when it never came, I opened an eye peeking at the sight of Lucius' arm held above us as he had caught it one handed.

And what stupid shit did my brain conjure up to say,

"Looks like you got yourself a bogof." He placed the screen

down on the high table I had been using and then with questioning eyes my way, said a clipped,

"Excuse me?"

"Buy one get one free, bogof…erm, you know, because you caught me and the screen," I said trying to explain my very lame and weird statement. He grinned at this and said,

"You can't buy what you already own." I frowned up at him and snapped,

"You don't own me." At this he scoffed and replied with a cocky,

"Don't I?"

"No, you…" I started to say but was stopped the second he plucked the screwdriver from my chest with a knowing smirk and quickly interrupted me,

"So, are you going to explain to me why you were trying to steal a security monitor instead of meeting me like I requested?"

"You mean ordered," I said folding my arms over my chest in annoyance.

"I'm waiting, Amelia," he said sternly making me roll my eyes at him. But then I heard a growl and my eyes snapped back to his serious steel blue gaze.

"Did you just roll your eyes at me?" he asked in a dangerous tone that had my heart rate kicking up a notch.

"Erm…" I didn't really know what to say, other than give in to the temptation to turn around and bolt for the nearest door as he started to stalk towards me. Instead I kept my eyes on him and started slowly backing up and he, in turn, continued to slowly close the distance between us. His predatory gaze scanned the length of my body and suddenly my choice of outfit didn't seem that lame as his eyes grew heated and hungry.

"Oh, screw it!" I shouted before turning and running for the frosted door I had entered through. I made it about three steps, and this was because I think he must have wanted a moment to enjoy the sight of me running from him before capturing me… he was sadistic like that.

I felt his arms wrap around me before they twisted me around so I was facing him and before I could speak, he had my face framed in his large hands and was tilting my head back so he could growl down at me,

"Next time you will be over my fucking knee, girl!" Then before I could lash back at him, he was slanting his lips over mine and shutting me up with a feverous kiss. I gripped onto him just as I always did, fearing the way my body would probably crumble if he were to let go suddenly. Gods, but why did he have to kiss me as though I was the only girl in the world. Like he worshiped every inch of me… *like he had been made to wait a hundred lifetimes to have me?*

In fact, I was just about to lose myself completely into all that was Lucius when he tore his lips from mine and denied me my pleasure.

"Now you can explain to me why you are in here and not where you were supposed to be, or more to the point, why I very nearly ripped off the head of one of my subjects when he came to tell me that you weren't there to be escorted to my side like I asked of him?" I gulped at the question that came the second he had finished kissing me. So, in my ultimate wisdom and one I could only blame on the kiss, I blurted out,

"They are playing a re-run of Star Treks Discovery season two on Netflix tonight." He jerked his head back a little as if he were questioning if he had heard me right, something that was quickly followed by an almost comical,

"Come again?"

"It's a TV show," I informed him, noting that I was still locked in his embrace, as his hands had left my face at some point during the kiss to wrap around my waist. Then he cleared his throat and concluded,

"So, let me get this straight, not only am I being stood up by the prospect of some out of space nonsense on a screen..."

"Oi, that's..." He gave me a pointed look that told me to be quiet, which I wisely did so he could finish,

"...and without so much as a word of apology on your part, but instead, in my furious and panicked search to find you, I do so only to find you nearly falling on your fine ass before the screen you are about to steal crashes onto your pretty head, and one I would very much like to keep looking the way it is now and for the foreseeable future...*am I correct?*" Oh Gods, but there was just too much in all of that for me to overanalyse. However, with that one eyebrow raised I knew I didn't have the gift of time to do so. Which meant I homed in on the few bits I did focus on.

"You like my ass and think I'm pretty?" At this his lips twitched before trying to slip back into being stern.

"Out of all that, this is what you chose to focus on?" Now it was my lips that were twitching as I tried to contain my grin, something he didn't miss.

"Okay, so first off, there is no such thing to a girl like me as 'out of space nonsense' and secondly, I didn't stand you up as I told you that I was busy, and thirdly, you shouldn't get angry at one of your men for simply telling you the facts, as it wasn't his fault I wasn't there to be 'escorted'..." I said pausing so I could pull my hands up between us and create quotation marks with my fingers at this last part, making him fight a grin.

"...fourthly you should have come to my door yourself like a gentleman, not got one of your lackies to do it for you and fifth and six...erm, ly...I only fell because you scared me, hence me having to let go of the screen that never would have crashed on my head because I did have it all under control

before you swooped on in like Master of the Universe and...
well you know, acted like you do." I told him making him
display an array of facial expressions as my list was reeled off,
nearly bursting out laughing when I tried to say fifthly and sixly
which just didn't sound right.

But then he decided to also focus on the parts he wanted to
and proving a point when he did it. Because suddenly he
gripped my ass in one hand, and his other fisted in my hair as he
growled down at me,

"Do I seem like a fucking gentleman to you, Sweetheart?!" I
visibly gulped and let out a whoosh of breath before telling him,

"Well...erm...not right now you don't but I know you can
be," I bravely reminded him and also, near breathlessly thanks
to how much his rough and sexually dominant treatment of me
was doing to my woman bits.

"Umm, well in that case, it must be your pretty face that
brings it out of me....but this ass, oh now that only brings out
the demon in me because what I want to do to it is about as far
from *gentlemanly* behaviour as one could get," he said growling
the word gentlemanly, as if mocking the first part of the word as
the way he still gripped my ass was far from gentle. Possessive,
animalistic, rough and forceful, yes...gentle, no. I also think it
was safe to say that the yoga pants were a big hit and a useful
piece of information I definitely filed away under a plaque
called 'big guns'.

But right now, with the way I was looking up at him it must
have switched something inside of him. Because he raised a
hand up to my face and cupped my cheek.

"But these eyes, these beseeching eyes of yours that could
pierce the heart and soul of any man... now those are the eyes
of a woman with the power to bring the Gods to their fucking
knees!" he said fiercely before once again yanking me hard to
him and kissing me. But this time when my legs near failed me,

it didn't matter as he was pushing me against a wall, holding me there with his weight just shy of crushing me. Gods, but it felt as if he was trying to brand the memory of what I tasted like to his soul and after his words, then Hell, I was doing the same.

I jumped when a hand suddenly slapped to the wall above me and I heard it crack from the force. That was when I realised what this was…he was trying to hold himself back because I was human. The thought was like dousing my libido in a bucket of ice. Because I knew then I could never fully be what he needed me to be.

I wasn't my mother.

This was when he must have realised something in me had switched because he loosened his hold on me, placed his forehead to mine and released a sigh before whispering,

"And she's gone again." I didn't know what to say to this so said nothing as he let me go. Then he held a hand out to me and said the very last thing I ever expected him to say,

"Come on, let's get you your Star Trek fix." And strangely, it was one of the sweetest things he had said to me so far.

"Can you believe it's got Captain Pike in this season!" I shrieked over the phone when Lucius finally gave in and let me call Wendy so we could watch it together like we always did. This was of course after I first had to play catch up, and in a way where unfortunately it meant lying about pretty much everything. Because really, what could I say…I managed to make it to the airport without getting caught then decided to go break into a vault in Germany because the fate of an entire supernatural race, aka Vampires, rested on my shoulders. Oh, and in this it included saving who I one day hoped to be my soulmate and also my mother, who just so happened to be the one he still had the hots for...yeah, no I didn't think so. Gods, but not even Jerry Springer would know what to do with that shit!

So, I had kept it simple, saying Lucius found me, said he needed my help and convinced me to go to Germany to work on a project of his. It was lame I know, but it was at least something she kind of believed. Of course, this was after she explained what had happened once Dante had discovered the switch, seeing as he first scared the shit out of her. But this was because he had ended up saving her from being mugged. I had freaked when hearing this but discovered pretty quickly that she must have been fine, because she focused nearly every second of this story on the part Dante played in it, being that he was now her hot, southern gentleman, American hero.

I had even asked her if anything had happened, as in an X rated something but she had simply said,

"You first." To which I declined like she knew I would. This was what tipped me off that she really liked him. I had to say that I suddenly felt bad for her and also guilty that I had encouraged it. Because really, where could it ever hope to go... considering what he was. Meaning that in the end, the only bit of advice I was able to give her was a lame,

"Just be careful okay, after all, we don't really know this guy." Meaning that, *she* didn't know him at all and the things I knew weren't exactly what I would have called 'boyfriend material'. Not after experiencing it first-hand after the 'Ben incident' something that clearly Lucius hadn't been informed about. And thankfully, because I dread to think what his reaction would have been seeing as just being told I wasn't in my room was enough to near render some poor sod headless!

However, my advice was swiftly followed by one look at my own brooding male in the room and then really, I decided who was I to judge?

After Lucius' last kiss where he felt me mentally retreating from him, he had taken my hand in his and led me back into the lobby area. But then when he had been about to walk me into his apartment was when I had pulled back.

"I...I mean, can't I just go back to my own room?" I asked making him question my reason but doing so silently as I could see it there, the questions working their way into his mind until finally something in my gaze must have clicked.

He nodded after his gaze softened and he then escorted me inside, telling me he would be back shortly. I didn't know what to expect but it wasn't that ten minutes later two guys would walk inside carrying a huge flat screen TV, followed by two other guys carrying a stand to put it on. Then four more guys walked in and started to rearrange furniture so it made viewing the TV a more comfortable angle, meaning that now the sofa wasn't just for awkward conversations reserved for Lucius and me about boxes of death.

But what was even weirder was that not one of Lucius' men looked at me, let alone even spoke to me. I only knew why when Liessa showed up, issuing orders and before she left, she looked side on at me and said,

"Don't take it personal, they aren't permitted to look at you...*you're for their King's eyes only, doll face,*" she added with a wink and a naughty whisper like this was the best thing to happen since the cold war. Something a day ago she remarked as 'oh those were the fun days'.

Something I really didn't get, as in... Not. At. All.

Then five minutes after that, Lucius strode in to find me getting comfortable on the sofa with the remote in hand logging into my Netflix account. He was on the phone issuing orders at someone, so I got an acknowledging head nod before he went out of sight to where the kitchen was. To say that this wasn't distracting would have been a lie because I wasn't used to having him in my space and well, after two days I had claimed it as such. Well, at least until I made plans to leave which I was hoping to do the next day.

"You are so crushing right now, aren't you?" I asked Wendy as Captain Pike was issuing orders.

"But of course, aren't you?" she asked and just in that moment I leant back ever so slightly over the armrest and saw Lucius taking off his jacket, throwing it to one side in what looked like frustration. Oh, and he was still on the phone but this time he was talking German and doing so far too quickly for me to fully catch more than a word here and there. But there had been a distinct part where he had looked at me and said 'No, she is going nowhere' doing so slow enough for me to translate in my head.

I turned my head just in time so it wasn't obvious that I was eavesdropping, even though I *obviously* was.

"On Captain Pike...? No, not right now," I confessed making her laugh at me down the phone.

"I take it there is far better eye candy for you to be crushing on at the moment." I scoffed and said,

"Oh yeah, the butler is hot." At this she giggled and said,

"Yeah whatever, Smock." But I wasn't listening as Lucius walked from round the corner now minus a suit jacket and with two beers in one hand. Then he said,

"Get it done and don't fucking bother me again tonight." Then he cancelled the call and threw his phone down on the coffee table before starting to loosen his tie one handed in a way that made my mouth dry. Holy mother of God, could he be any sexier?!

Then he twisted the bottle cap off one beer and handed it to me before doing the same to his own.

"That Sci-fi crap still on?" he asked making Wendy shriek in outrage on the other end.

"Oh my God, please do not tell me you are going to let whoever that jackass is, say that and live!?" Lucius raised a brow at her response, and I tried not to laugh when all I said was,

"I have to go and give 'em Hell, laters, Kirky," I then hung up. I turned back to Lucius and the first thing I noticed was him now looking down at me as if…well, as if the Devil had flipped a switch and now…

A Vampire King looked hungry.

I cleared my throat but this only enticed a primal grin from him as he scanned my body and oh mother of every Goddess out there, but that one look alone made me feel as though I was lying here naked like Kate Winslet in the movie Titanic. Gods, what was next, was he going to fish around the floor for one of the pencils he had plucked out of my hair earlier and start sketching me?

Because now I felt as though I was being stalked by some predator that was eyeing up his next meal. Of course, he knew what he was doing as his knowing grin grew the second I started to squirm uncomfortably under his lustful gaze. Now I was really rethinking my outfit choice wondering if it was too late to rush into my closet and grab my unsexy PJ's.

But then there was the other part of me that really liked that I had this effect on him and it made me wonder what his response would be if I ever got the opportunity to wear something really sexy for him.

No! Jeez, Fae, get a grip…not going to happen!

But then one look back up at him and I had to say, it looked like we both had two different ideas of the future. For me, I was intent on leaving but for him, it was clear…

He was intent on keeping me.

CHAPTER FIVE

WORDS

"U mm…going to give me Hell, yeah?" he mocked, and after I had marginally gotten over the smouldering look of lust coming from him, I shrugged my shoulders and said,

"I'm pretty sure it's hard to do when someone already has their own holiday home there." This made him scoff,

"Yeah." And then he raised his beer bottle and took a long swig, also making this another sexy sight to add to the long list that was named 'Hot Lucius moments'…yes, I was just that sad of a human being. But then I wondered if my reply had hit a nerve as it wasn't the response I had been expecting. Smart ass and arrogant yes, but a broody 'yeah' was not.

"Well, either way there should be a punishment for making such a comment," I said once he'd finished drinking.

"Trust me, Sweetheart, being made to sit and watch it will be punishment enough," he told me, shocking me so that my only response was an,

"Err…" Then I watched as he nodded for me to give him

room so he could slip in behind me and put his back to the armrest as I had been doing. I was so dumbfounded that I did as he asked by shifting my body forward but then I felt his hands at my shoulders so he could pull me back and his chest became my backrest instead.

"Relax, Sweetness, isn't this what most humans do?" he asked as he casually lounged back and faced the TV, now watching it with me. I swear it was probably the most surreal moment of my entire life so far and if anyone had told me that I would have been in Transfusion, drinking beer and watching Star Trek snuggled up to Lucius on a sofa like a real couple, then I would have called more than bullshit. I would have screamed it from the bloody rooftops and thrown it on people passing by like a damn monkey at a zoo! Okay, so no I wouldn't have and *eww*, but you get the point.

"So, explain to me what this is about," he said after a few minutes of watching Captain Pike explaining the next mission they faced. But his question made me frown wondering really, who was this man at my back and where did he put Lucius?

"Well, they are all on a spaceship named the Discovery, that Captain Pike just took command of," I said making him chuckle, before leaning closer to my ear and saying,

"Yeah, I gathered as much." This time I pulled back so I could turn to look at him and said,

"You did?"

"I may not be as smart as you, Sweetheart, but I do like to consider my skills in basic observation adequate enough to deduce as much."

"Whoa there, slow down Lucius, or pretty soon I will be calling you a Trekkie geek with the best of them."

"A what now?"

"Never mind," I commented drily with a roll of my eyes, this time one he couldn't see as I turned back to face the screen.

To be honest, I was just surprised he was interested but then as he continued to watch, something that I had no doubt he had assumed would be total nonsense, he started to get into it.

I could tell this as he started to ask me questions about, I quote, 'the hot black chick' also better known as Michael Burnham. He wanted to know her back story, which I started to tell him because, hey, I was always excited to talk about Star Trek. I think what helped was watching the asteroid scene, where it was pretty much on the edge of your seat type of stuff. But then most men were suckers for action packed entertainment…even two-thousand-year-old Vampire Kings that were probably bored there hadn't been a war to fight in for a while… *apparently.*

But then it finished and just because I didn't want this evening to end, I asked him if he wanted to watch the first season. I even found myself tense as I waited for his reply, hoping he would say yes. Which meant that when he did, I found myself smiling. It just felt so comfortable being like this with him to the point where I could even convince myself that this might be what it would be like if we were ever a couple. Of course, all I had to do was look to the door that would lead us back into his club and that thought was quickly squashed under a giant boot called reality.

Because no matter how much we could hide our massive differences inside this private space, unfortunately we couldn't stay in here forever. Which meant at some point I had to face facts and doing that meant leaving, despite what he thought and had told whoever it had been on the phone at the time. Because I couldn't stay here, not like this, not spending my time with him in such an intimate way. It was already messing with my head as it was, making me argue with myself that this was what it could be like, if only I trusted him enough when he said he cared.

But then the rational side of my brain was screaming at me not to trust this. It was screaming out questions like why now? Why was he suddenly paying me all this attention, or acting as if something had held him back all these years and now he'd hit some kind of limit?

I guess my biggest fear was the only logical answer I could come up with and it was the one I was most afraid of discovering. Which was if this was all just a ruse to keep me here and out of danger. Doing it for someone he felt loyal to, say, someone like…*my mother.*

Had he promised her at some point during my mortal life that he would do anything in his power to protect me and keep me safe? It was an awful thought, that this was just all an act to keep me here, playing on my obvious feelings for him and using it as a tool to manipulate the situation. Of course, I hated this idea and really tried to convince myself this wasn't the reason. But then that little voice at the back of your mind, the one that tries to steer you away from danger and hurt, the one whose nickname is doubt, couldn't keep quiet, no matter how much I tried to just enjoy this. Because this had been something I had been secretly dreaming of since I was a teenager.

It sounded pathetic, but it was my reality and something I had been trying to ignore since the day I ran from this place. But then instead of answering me, he took the remote off me and clicked for the first episode to play from season one. Then he wrapped an arm back around me so it rested across my torso as if silently telling me that I was going nowhere.

I think it was easy to see that I was nervous because I had been picking at the beer bottle's label in my hand by folding back the edges. It gave me something to do with my hands instead of giving in to the urge to bite my fingertips as was my bad habit when nervous. It had been empty a while now which was why it was soon plucked from my hands and placed on the coffee table by Lucius.

"Relax," he hummed behind me, making me blush, one I was thankful he couldn't see.

"I am," I muttered back, making him chuckle.

"Is that so?" he asked in a knowing tone.

"Lucius, I am lying back against your chest with my feet up, if I got any more relaxed, I would be dead," I lied.

"Yes, and such a position means I can feel enough tensed muscles to know when someone is ready to bolt from my arms the first chance they get...now fucking relax will you," he told me, issuing this order at the end. But when I didn't do as he asked, he decided to take matters into his own hands...literally. He shifted behind me and I moved forward a little to allow him to move, but what he had planned was placing both hands on my shoulders and working my tense muscles with adept fingers. I swear I nearly muttered a curse with how good it felt and had no choice but to lean back into the motion of him massaging my back and shoulders. Gods, but where had this man come from with his hands from Heaven? First my hair and now my back, what was he trying to do, kill me with tenderness and cursed words!

"Holy..." I whispered on a moan that couldn't be helped as I let my head roll back, trying not to wonder how he acquired such skill, not wanting to find the answer in the most obvious place. Because if there was one thing that no girl wanted to think about, it was the person she was secretly obsessed with in the arms of another woman...or should I say that woman in his very capable hands. And seriously, did his hands have to be so big and manly, couldn't there be just one thing on him that wasn't bloody perfect! I even found myself wishing that maybe his feet resembled those of a hobbit or even an orc...bloody

hell, but at this rate I would even take ingrown toenails and sweaty.

In fact, I was just getting into it, relaxing back and getting lost in the bliss he created when he suddenly framed my neck each side and held me in a hold that anyone would class as threatening being only a slight squeeze away from taking my breath. Then whilst trapped in his hold he leaned down to whisper in my ear,

"Right, now that I have your attention, I am going to issue you a warning and only do so once…" I swallowed hard, an action he no doubt felt due to his hold on me.

"You never fucking joke about your death again…do you understand me!?" he snarled in annoyance and it confused me enough to take pause, despite where his hands were. Because his words contradicted his aggressive actions, meaning that he would never hurt me. Hell, if he got like this over some silly comment about me being comfortable enough to be dead, then hurting me would be last on his list. Which was why the second he released me I bolted up out of his arms now standing before I whipped around to face him.

"Just what the hell do you think you are doing!?" I yelled down at him.

"It's simple, I am teaching you the rules," he replied casually and I picked up the remote and muted it so I could argue what I thought was a very important point. Like the fact he was obviously a psycho!

"What, by putting your hands around my neck!?" I shrieked.

"Word to the wise, Sweetheart, if I want you to take something seriously, then I take serious action."

"Serious action! Gods give me strength!" I said adding this last part to myself as I turned my back on him and rubbed a hand down my face.

"Did I hurt you?" he asked in a knowing tone.

"Well no, but that's not exactly the point here," I argued, even though it kind of was.

"Isn't it?" he questioned, damn him!

"What exactly are you saying, that because you didn't hurt me you think it's acceptable to…" Suddenly I was cut off the second he reached up and snagged my hand before yanking me down hard enough that I fell on top of him on the sofa. Then he ran a hand up the side of my head, embedding his fingers in my hair before growling,

"Yes, I fucking do…" then he kissed me, holding me to him in case I thought about pulling back. But come on, with Lucius kissing me like he was addicted to me, then what were the chances of ever pulling away from him. Especially when his arm banded around the base of my back like steel anchoring me to him. My hands also found his sandy coloured hair as I too held him to me, losing myself in the burning heat of our kiss.

I swear but I could barely think of anything else when he had me like this. And just when I thought it couldn't get any more intense, he grabbed the waistband on my yoga pants and tugged hard enough that when he shifted to one side, I easily slid underneath him. Then he pulled back from the kiss and his eyes burned amber when he claimed in a dangerous tone,

"…You're mine, Amelia…*mine!*" Then before I could respond he was back to kissing me again, this time with both hands finding my own so he could entwine his fingers with mine and pin them over my head. I felt myself rising up, my back bowing and pressing my breasts up like peaks I near begged him to feast on. Gods, but this was the most delicious torture!

My wanton behaviour only seemed to push him further or at least, push at his limited restraint because he growled down at me the second he felt me hook a leg over the back of his thigh. I was even about to remove it, thinking I had done wrong but then just before I could retreat he snarled,

"Don't you fucking dare put space between us!" Then he kissed me before I could react, leaving me to secure it back to ensure we were as connected as we could be...*well, not entirely.* But then again, he didn't know what I knew. He didn't yet know how I had pathetically waited for this moment with him for what seemed like forever. He didn't know that I had saved myself for him, in some hopeless attempt at it meaning something to him when, or more like *if,* the time ever came. But now I wasn't so sure. Because this was not a man who would gently take my virginity like some gentleman lover who offered roses and making love by candlelight after sweet words of adoring sentiment.

As Lucius wasn't a man who made love...*he fucked.* Plain and simple. He was the type of man to get what he wanted, when he wanted it. And me, well I hadn't wanted my first-time making love to a man, my once in a lifetime moment, sullied by some quick fuck that would become meaningless by the morning to one of us and it didn't take a genius to know who would wake feeling that way. No, I couldn't give him that power, not until I trusted him to take care of something like that. Not until he knew the value of what it meant to me...or in my dreams, *what I wanted it to mean to him.*

So, even though I was near desperate to discover exactly what that hard steely length pressing against my stomach felt like in my hand, I knew I had to stop this before I ended up losing my virginity on some sofa like some teenager whose parents were out of town. Meaning that despite his warning, I let my leg fall and turned my face away breaking his kiss.

"Amelia." The way that he whispered my name was like a plea from a man only used to giving orders. He had whispered this against my cheek and the second I opened my mouth to

speak he buried his head in my neck and spoke just below my ear after first kissing his way there.

"No, don't do that...don't pull away again."

"I...I can't do this, I just..." My own plea was cut off the second he took a bite full of my tender flesh in between his teeth in warning and even though it made me lose my restraints, it did so in the most erotic way for I couldn't help but moan in pleasure. I didn't know why feeling myself at his mercy this way clicked something inside of me, but it just seemed that if he actually took that step, then it would mean that he would own me completely...well, almost.

But then I knew what kind of commitment that would mean as once we exchanged blood then he would be binding himself to me and me to him in return.

And this was when I made the final decision. I would only become his, giving that last part of me, when he gave me it back. When he bound himself to me, then and only then would I give him the whole of me. Because he already had my heart, he just didn't know it. And as for my soul, well the Gods had already deemed it destined to be his for the taking. But my body, well that was my own to gift and one that had to be earned in exchange for the everlasting eternal commitment his people could make.

One, deep down, *I knew he would never give me.*

And how did I know this, because it suddenly came to me what he had said earlier, when he had torn his lips from mine before issuing my order to join him that evening. And it was out of my lips in a muttered whisper of pain as his words finally hit me,

"Wie müssen die Götter mich hassen." This was when he paused letting my skin free from his hold before he slowly came to look down at me. He then took in the blatant tears welling in my eyes and whispered my name one more time,

"Amelia..." But it was too late, he didn't need to explain because I already knew what it meant. And well, there was no other way to take his words,

Words that cursed the very Gods that had bound my soul to his.

Words I could never forget.

Words, *I could never forgive...*

"How the Gods must hate me."

CHAPTER SIX

PERFECT PUNISHMENTS AND CRIMSON KISSES

That night I dreamed like never before.

It was a haunting dream that felt more like a memory, only it wasn't one of mine. I was running, the earth was dry, and nothing grew. It was as if it had been baked beyond death, like the only place on Earth that resembled Hell or at least that was what it was soon to become. But then as I looked down I saw my footsteps sink into the ground like wet sand, only instead of water seeping up from beneath, it was crimson. As if I was walking on the shore of an ocean of blood.

I frowned asking the question in my mind,

'Why am I here?' Only this question seemed to echo all around me, but it wasn't in my own voice…

It belonged to Lucius.

'Why?' I questioned again and once more it was Lucius asking it. I spun in all directions and only saw a vast desert staring back at me. Only then in the distance I could see blurred figures walking towards me, distorted in the haze of heat coming from the sun scorched earth.

'I am no traitor.' This time I felt my lips moving but my voice never followed. No other voice did but his.

Then there was an eerie moment of silence and I opened my mouth to scream before I saw it coming. However, this time the second the blade sliced through my gut, the only sound to be heard was my own and there was only one name I cried out for in the middle of my nightmare…

"LUCIUS!" I bolted upright and the second I opened my eyes I realised where I was. I was gripping the sheets as if they had the power to ground me to the real world and not back to the death that awaited my dreams. I was also panting, trying in vain to drag in air but feeling it burn like poison.

Then suddenly the bedroom door burst open and I screamed before realising it was Lucius, now stood in my doorway looking both ready to commit murder and worried that he had been too late to save me from my own. It was also clear he had been resting or Gods forbid something else, as now all he wore was a pair of black drawstring pants that looked as if they could have been worn to work out in as well as sleep in. So who knew exactly what they were, other than what Lucius deemed as casual.

But this was a minuscule detail in the background of what my mind was really focused on which was his bare chest. And holy shit, if I hadn't just had an horrific nightmare then I think my instinct to whistle would have come out no matter what. Thankfully though, this didn't happen, as I was still in the throes of my nightmare and unable to breathe at a calm pace.

But then I also wasn't sure this wasn't down to the abundance of tight abs that looked completely void of all fat, leaving nothing but solid muscle. This was followed swiftly by those delicious lines at the side of the abs that I was sure were called obliques. They reminded me of metal grills, as they looked just as hard!

But mainly it was his broad chest, something much more than just a pair of chiselled, toned pecs, but full on muscle that was what obviously separated the men from the boys. And then there was the main attraction, his arms…Gods but those shoulders looked big enough to throw me over with room to spare!

Something he would have no problem with when picking me up, not with the size of those mountain biceps and rippling triceps. To be honest, it was every inch of him that had my mouth going dry and I wondered if tasting every bit of him would help in bringing back moisture in my mouth, for surely getting close enough would make me want to drool.

Gods Fae, get a bloody grip! So, he's hot, okay maybe hotter than hot, but big deal! Just get over it, he's an ass remember. And so, what if biceps have been the symbol of strength and machismo for centuries, he could just go right ahead and use that exquisite body on some other poor sap!

But then he was now bringing that body over to me so he could comfort me, and I swear my reserve crumbled the second he took me in his arms and held me to him.

"You had a nightmare," he stated without question. I could only nod as he held the side of my face to his chest, hopelessly trying not to let my emotions get the better of me, but even I felt the few tears slip free.

"Sshh now, just try and concentrate on taking deep breaths for me." He spoke in a tone so tender that it alone was almost heart-breaking. Which was why I didn't trust myself to speak, not after earlier. Because the moment I had remembered what he had said and translated the German for cursing the Gods, saying they must hate him for giving him me, well then there had only been one thing left for me to do…*run.*

I had thrashed in his hold until he decided the best course of action was to let me go. The second I stood I had said only one thing,

'Get out!' To which he had released a sigh before standing to face me, then he said,

'I can already see that there is no point in discussing this whilst your mind is in a venomous place, but make no mistake Princess, *we will* be talking about this!' After this he left and I shamefully sank to the floor and cried, hating how weak I felt. I also hated that he had gone back to calling me 'princess' knowing now that he only reserved it for times he obviously wanted to piss me off.

But now here he was being sweet and caring, holding me close like I was something precious to him. Like I mattered. Like I wasn't something to damn the Gods for and fool that I was, I hung onto him as though I had forgotten. As if this knowledge had been drowned out and carried off by an ocean named doubt, not to return until the tide.

"Do you want to talk about it?" he asked after a few minutes of me trying to calm myself. But I couldn't speak, not yet. Because when I finally did, then that would only make this a reality I didn't want to face. And going back to the way we were wasn't something I was ready for.

But now this Lucius, the man with his arms around me, holding me close as if scared of me breaking without him…now that was the Lucius I wasn't yet ready to let go of. So, I said nothing but shook my head. However, this obviously wasn't good enough for him as I felt him hook a crooked finger under my chin. Then he lifted up my face so he could look down at me.

"It frightened you?" he asked softly, and I swallowed down a lump mainly named lust and just as I started to nod, he raised a brow telling me silently he wanted my words.

"Yes, it frightened me," I whispered with my voice hoarse

due to what I gathered was the time screaming before I eventually woke.

"Then I will stay," he said before pulling me down with him on the bed making me try to splutter out,

"That's…but, it's…no it's…" But then I soon found myself being manoeuvred to where he wanted me and evidently where he wanted me was resting in the crook of his shoulder and chest. And with the weight of his arm holding me there, I had no choice but to relax into him, something I found far easier than I should have, especially when I should have still been angry at him.

I also didn't know where to put my arm and it was only when I started making it obvious where I didn't want it to go, was when he once again took matters into his own hands. He did this by reaching across his torso with his left hand and grabbing my own with the leather from his glove groaning as it held on tight.

Then he rested it across the tight abs on his stomach making me roll my lips back inside my mouth as I felt myself getting hot. I just kept saying to myself not to move my fingers as all I wanted to do was trace the dips and lines between his six pack. But it was when I felt him vibrating beneath my hand with the muscles tightening that I knew he was silently laughing. This was confirmed when I looked up at him and saw that he had been looking at me the whole time and obviously my expressions were giving me away.

This was confirmed when he tipped my chin up again and whispered down at me,

"You can touch me, Sweetheart." Well, at least I was back to the sweet endearments now and not 'princess'. But then he brushed the back of two fingers down my cheek, no doubt trying to see for himself if the skin was as hot as it looked. Well, I could confirm that like this, with him lying half naked in my

bed, then yes of course it bloody was! Now did he have to look so satisfied about it, no he didn't! But then again this was Lucius we were talking about so could I really be surprised?

"Amelia…"

"Yeah?"

"Are you going to touch me?" he boldly asked making me swallow hard before shaking my head, something that again made him chuckle softly. I waited for the vibrations to end before looking up at him knowing what I would find with him already looking down at me.

"Then go to sleep," he ordered gently making me want to argue but then again, he was surprisingly comfortable to lie against despite how hard the abundance of muscle was. So, in the end I just whispered a small,

"Kay." And then did as I was told. But this time when I slept, I dreamt of my current reality…

Being safe in Lucius' arms.

The next time I woke it was because I felt myself being shifted and an arm slipping from where my head had been resting. I didn't know what was happening on account of still being stuck somewhere between a conscious state and dreaming of him still holding me. However, when I started to feel the loss of his heat and soft skin I knew he was leaving me.

"Lucius?" I spoke his name before I could stop myself and found a hand reaching out to him, too weak to prevent the want in both the needy reaction and breathy sigh after it. At first, I thought I had been too late but then I felt the bed dip to my side and a gloved hand came and cradled my cheek.

"Ssshh, go back to sleep, my Šemšā," he whispered before leaning down to place a kiss on my forehead and then, just

before I could say another word, he must have decided it wasn't enough for the next second I felt that same tender kiss on my lips. But just as I was about to open up for him, he took away his kiss and left. I know this because I finally sat up and saw the empty room with not a Vampire King in sight.

That's when I noticed that my hand was still held out reaching for him, one that quickly turned into a fist and landed on the bed next to me. A clear sign of my frustration. I looked back down at the bed and swear I could see the memory of what we must have looked like together, entwined like lovers after the act. The way he had held me had been as perfect for my obsession, as it had been damaging. Okay, so it was time to face facts, definitely more damaging!

"I'm so screwed," I said aloud running a hand through my hair before falling back onto the bed with an umf sound, now knowing that there was only one thing for it, I needed to get the Hell out of Dodge.

I had to leave before I did something stupid, like giving Lucius all he wanted from me before I was then left wide open and exposed for him to use when and how he wanted before he simply left. Because what else could I expect from Lucius? If he believed me to be his Chosen One as I knew him to be mine, then he would have acted on it long ago. He wouldn't have pushed me away. Which again made me have to ask myself what had changed for him to be acting this way now? A question that now seemed to constantly plague me.

I had tried to run away from my life, that's what, something he clearly didn't like. Something he had tried to prevent, like my father had. That was why I didn't trust this. Didn't trust him. How did I know he wasn't just using my weakness against me? Because, it was as clear as day what my weakness was after the night I had turned up at his club, *dressed for him.* Something he had cruelly mocked.

And now here he was, being everything I had ever dreamed he could be. No…of course, I couldn't trust it. Or myself.

Which was why I had to leave.

Like right now!

So, with this in mind I got up and washed, whizzing through my bathroom routine and putting in my contacts this time, forgoing my glasses. I also told myself that this wasn't because it was easier for him to kiss me without them. Absolutely not.

Then I dressed in a pair of jeans the colour of indigo and matched it with a soft grey T shirt and a plaid shirt that I tied into a knot at my belly. After dragging my hair up into a high ponytail, I found the stuff I had arrived with, which thankfully included my wallet, money and passport. Of course, trying to take the box would be a mistake, as I knew there was nowhere safer than in his vault but then again, *I* had been able to break in.

But then what if I was to just hide it? Of course, I would eventually let Lucius know where it was but after first using it as leverage for him to leave me alone. Because I knew that once I left, then I would only end up with him trying to find me again. Whether this was for my mother or my father I didn't know but right now I just needed to be alone. I needed to be able to think and I definitely couldn't do that here or anywhere that Lucius was.

He was too much of a weakness for me.

So, I made the decision to hide it, now knowing what to do to disable the alarm after watching Liessa. Clearly, she wasn't too concerned with me or considered me a threat, that was for sure. And I think it was obvious that even Lucius didn't think me crazy enough to try and steal it from him again. Ha, well little did he know just how crazy this human could be!

I saw that it was still dark out but without a phone I couldn't say what time it was without being bothered to check the clock on the wall in the kitchen.

Which reminded me Lucius must have taken back the phone he had given me to call Wendy last night, but I had long ago memorised her number so I knew I could still contact her once I was settled somewhere. Something she had been convinced of me already being after speaking with her last night.

Well, she may end up being worried for a few days, a week at most but I was sure she would understand once I could explain. Now I just needed to google how long I could be on a call before it could be traced because if Dante was still working for Lucius, then I could pretty much guarantee that he would have her calls monitored.

Gods, but I think downloading the Borne Identity was top on my 'To get the hell outta Dodge' list just for some tips on how to do this. So, with that in mind I decided it was probably safer to leave my bag hidden until I'd had chance to get the box. But first I had to hope that Lucius hadn't just gone back to his own bed and was going to catch me sneaking in.

I was just glad that Lucius wasn't paranoid as there were no guards or security back in the private space Lucius obviously called his home. So, this meant that sneaking in was the easy part, although I already had my excuse ready, saying that I woke up and couldn't get back to sleep without examining it, as I had some kind of cryptic epiphany. Although he had also once said that my lying skills were as shit as my mother's, so I didn't hold out much hope for this to work.

But in the end, this wasn't needed as it soon became clear he wasn't here and what's worse, neither was the box! I frowned before true panic started to set in wondering exactly what it was he had planned to do with it? I mean this wasn't just his life we were talking about but my mother's!

I backed out of there, relocking everything and as I turned around, I did so only to walk straight into someone.

"Shit!" I screamed jumping out of my skin.

"Something I can help you with?" Lucius asked raising his brows in question and I looked down to see the box in his hand. I swear but the relief whooshed out of me and before I could stop myself, I put a hand to my chest and said,

"Thank the Gods."

"I think we can leave the Gods out of this for the moment, don't you...? Now answer the question, what are you doing in here...*again?*" He added this last word in what can only be described as exasperation. I didn't answer straight away but instead took note that he was now dressed, and I wasn't the only one looking casual.

He wore stone washed grey jeans that looked well-worn enough to be soft and a long-sleeved charcoal black T shirt that was pulled up at the forearms, showing off his usual black leather glove. To this he also had on thick heavy-duty biker style boots that told me relaxing in his home was not on his agenda.

"I came to get the box." At this he folded his arms across that solid chest of his, (one I now had burnt to my memory in a folder unfortunately labelled 'utter perfection')

"Believe it or not but the power of deduction told me as much," he replied sarcastically, all trace of the sweet and tender Lucius gone, making me frown and snap back before I put much thought into what I was saying or more like giving away,

"Well, I could have been coming to see you, you know after you left me in bed and erm..." At this he smirked down at me before his obvious bullshit detector kicked in and I knew this when he nodded over my head to the massive vault at my back.

"And hoping to find me locked in there, were you?" I

couldn't help but roll my eyes at him, totally forgetting his earlier warning about doing so.

"No, of course not!" I said but then the second I took note of his eyes darkening was when I realised my mistake.

"Did you just roll your eyes at me...*again?"* I visibly gulped the second he started to walk me backwards until my back was up against the door. I had to arch my neck just so I could keep eye contact, feeling that doing so was like taunting a wild beast. But then again, what was it he was going to do to me if I did...kiss me again?

"Maybe... oh come on, Lucius, what are you going to do about it...I mean you are not really going to...AHH!" I suddenly shouted the second he dropped the box, obviously not taking its threat seriously enough not to punish me, because the next thing I knew I was being pushed up against the wall. Then even more shocking, before I could fully react to what was happening my jeans were unbuttoned and yanked down my legs.

"Lucius!" I screamed his name but before I could grab the waistband to yank them back up, I was hauled up over his shoulder. Then with my ass up near his face and feeling close to naked in just my plain white boy shorts, he swiftly raised a hand and smacked my backside.

"AHHH!" I screamed more in shock than in pain as it wasn't too bad but Holy Hell, what in the Gods did he think he was doing.

"PUT ME DOW...AHHHH!" I was cut off in my demands to be put down when he smacked me three more times in quick succession, making the skin burn and also shamefully, my panties damp. Because souls alive it was the hottest thing that had ever been done to me! However, shamefully Lucius' super Vamp scent detection became my mortification when he then placed his face against my bare thigh and inhaled deeply. And this time when he growled, he did so low and guttural, like the beast he was currently acting. I even started to feel his fangs lengthen and this was when I became worried, so stammered out his name in question,

"Lu...Lucius?"

"You smell so fucking good! The Gods don't hate me Amelia, they just want to fucking torture me by giving this beast a fucking Goddess to feast on!" He snarled against my skin before kissing and nipping at it as though he wanted to do so much more but was holding himself back...*barely.*

But then this was when his words confused me, if I smelled so good to him and he wanted me so badly then why think the Gods were torturing him? I just didn't get it. Did he mean it to protect me against himself? Was there more to what he had said in German, but I had taken it wrong? I seriously think I was missing something big here.

"Lucius, I don't understand," I said in a small voice making him lean his forehead to my thigh and release a deep frustrated sigh. Then he slowly pulled me back from over his shoulder and before he spoke, he pulled my jeans back up over my now heated flesh. Then he looked down at me, zipped me up and redid my button silently.

"I know you don't, *my Khuba.*" I frowned and asked,

"What does that even mean or the other thing you call me, Semsa or something?" He gave me a grin and said,

"Maybe I will tell you one day." I actually pouted at this but he didn't care or the fact combined with me crossing my arms over my chest it must have looked a sight, one that I could see made a grin play at the edges of his perfect lips.

"Is this before or after all the other stuff you have yet to tell me!?" I snapped.

"You're not ready," he stated as he picked up the box and turned to the control panel so he could punch in my birthday.

"I think that's my call."

"Fine, *then I am not ready,*" he said rewording his earlier statement, but I wasn't going to leave it alone.

"Ever heard of the term, knowledge is power?" I threw at him and just as the door opened, he looked back over his shoulder at me and said,

"Not in this case it isn't...it's a curse." Then he walked inside and went straight over to the wall where there was an empty spot waiting for him to place the box. The damn box that had started all of this.

"Bullshit! I think you are just afraid!" I barked back at him, with fists balled by my sides in anger. But he granted me a look of surprise at my outburst.

"It is not my fear I am acting on *but yours,*" he said emphasising this last part as nothing short of a warning, one that had me backing up a step and shaking my head.

"So, this is what you call protecting me!? Fucking with my head is what, some kind of noble version of getting your cake and eating it too, but just not too much, is that it?" I snapped out the question like a verbal slap, hoping that it felt like that. His scowl told me I'd hit a nerve at least.

"I am going to ignore that last comment and put it down to the rants of a young girl who doesn't know what she is talking about!" he growled back and this was when I officially lost my shit!

"A young girl?! I am twenty-seven years old for the Devil's sake! I am not a fucking child!"

"Then maybe it is time to stop acting like one, Princess!" he snarled back after grabbing my hand and pulling me from the vault so he could lock it.

"DON'T FUCKING CALL ME THAT!" I screamed at him yanking my hand from his and gaining an incredulous look in return. I then stormed back into his personal area knowing he would follow. Because I'd decided enough was enough. It was time to get this done and over with. It was time he knew exactly how he made me feel. So, I took a deep breath and said,

"Really! Is that how you see me Lucius, as some childish little spoilt princess that doesn't know her own feelings...?"

"I never said..." he tried but I just kept going.

"...That what I feel for you is just some passing fancy or attraction I feel like indulging in?"

"No, I didn't ever..."

"You think this is easy for me, being back here after all these years knowing that the last thing you said to me in this room was something I could never possibly hope to get over!" I shouted knowing that I was going too far with letting him know these things, but I just found I couldn't stop now, not even when he told me to.

"Amelia, just stop."

"NO! Lucius, you want to know what I know, something you obviously think is very little, well here it is...You ever wonder why I left Afterlife, moved to a different fucking country and left my home for good?!" At this he actually did look as if I had slapped him, as he tore his gaze from mine and nodded,

"I can guess."

"You can guess...you can guess! Well, here Lucius, let me finalise that guess for you should I...? I left because I could no longer stand looking at my own fucking mother! I left because I loved her and hated myself for feeling nothing but jealously around her! That was what you did to me, you didn't just break my heart, you tore it to fucking pieces and then left me with nothing but scraps left for those who I loved around me," I yelled making him flinch as if I had truly struck him this time.

"Amelia, I didn't..."

"Yeah, well you may not have intended that Lucius, but it

doesn't change the past and it doesn't change that was what you gave me! So, don't give me that princess, I don't know anything crap, because news flash here, I am not the one that is fucking clueless and running scared!" I shouted back at him making him grimace, even though he looked as tightly wound as a predator waiting to strike.

"But hey, I was foolish enough to believe that something had changed. That maybe…"

"What?" he asked suddenly as if needing to know. So, I took a deep breath and gave it to him, knowing it was too late to take it all back now.

"That…that you finally looked at me like a woman you wanted and not just some naïve princess that foolishly thought she had a chance at being with someone like you," I told him before deciding I couldn't do it anymore, I had to get out of there before he saw me cry, something I'd vowed not to let him do again. However, even the best laid plans fail and in my case it was always one named Lucius. This meant that I didn't get far in my dramatic departure as I was soon grabbed roughly and spun around to face him,

"Where the fuck do you think you're going!?" he shouted back at me making me shout back at him,

"As far away from you as I can get!" Then I yanked myself out of his hold and unless he wanted to hurt me, he had no choice but to let me go. But this was only so he could try again and this time, I was ready for it,

"Oh no, you don't princess!" And just as he yanked me back, I brought my hand around and slapped him right across the face, and this time, it was one he didn't have a chance at stopping as he never saw it coming.

"I said don't call me fucking PRINCESS!" I screamed up in his face, one that had cracked to one side and was still held there in his utter shock. Then he slowly brought it back round to face me, with eyes burning like the Persian sun and I knew I might have just gone too far.

But it was too late to take it back now and anyway, I wasn't sure I even wanted to, even with how truly terrifying he looked right now. Despite this, he was still the most beautiful strikingly handsome man I had ever seen in my life and as I stood there panting through my rage something else started to seep on in there and before I could stop myself I snarled at him,

"Gods, but I hate you, Lucius!" Then I grabbed him by the neck and shirt, tugged him to me and kissed him like my damned cursed life depended on it!

Now, if I thought he had been shocked by the slap then this clearly had him dumbfounded, if only for a few seconds before he started to kiss me back in earnest. Then he tore his lips from mine, growled down at me, as his fangs grew in length past his lips.

I shivered in response, but this wasn't in fear, it was in hope. One that seemed to be held precariously in the balance. It was like being suspended on a tightrope, with one end the safety of the door, my chance to escape, my exit. My last opportunity to leave this all behind me. but on the other was Lucius, whose next action managed to tip the scales. Because he knew what he wanted and the second he grasped my ass with both hands to lift me up, he made his dominating move. Doing so by positioning my spread legs around his waist, something I automatically responded to by tightening my thighs. And that was when I knew there was no running from this now.

Especially not when in three long and determined strides later I found my back pressed against a wall. Then with my legs gripping onto his waist he shackled my wrists and held them suspended above my head, trapped there just like my pounding heart. After this he took complete control of the kiss, devouring my taste like a man starved of it for far too long. Gods, but he made me feel so wanted it was like being drugged. A heady weight fogged my mind of what was right, of what it wanted, what it needed all merging together and giving me only one answer...

Lucius.

But then his fangs stung as they pricked the skin, making me yelp and he pulled back with a mouth full of my blood with a devilish grin on his crimson lips. Then, whilst looking down at me, his eyes burning like the sun, he licked them slowly as if savouring the taste. My own widened in response as I licked the pooling blood on my lips as he had done, making his eyes seep into a deeper flame, as if I was now staring straight into the pits of Hell.

Gods, but it looked like the making of a beast I had unknowingly just released and the thought both frightened me and exhilarated me. To know what I was capable of doing to him, with just my blood alone. Well, then being his Chosen One actually felt possible. Especially with the way he looked to be trying to savour even that small taste of me.

This caused his head to fall back, so he looked up at the Heavens and this time, I could barely breathe, because instead of cursing them, he whispered his thanks...

"Gifted with fucking perfection!"

CHAPTER SEVEN

HIS PRISONER

"*Lucius…?*" The moment I spoke his name it seemed to jerk him from wherever it was he had been lost to, because his gaze snapped back to mine and his grip on me tightened.

"No Amelia, no fucking way!" he snarled making me frown up at him in question,

"If you think for one minute that I am going to let you walk out of here, especially after all you just said to me then you aren't in your right mind," he threatened on a growl.

"Well, I did just slap a Vampire King, so I think it's safe to say my state of mind is questionable at this point." After this and my attempt at using humour to calm the situation down, he released a ragged breath before his lips twitched in amusement. But then just as quickly he turned serious again.

"You're not running from me, *not again.*" This time it didn't just sound like an order, it sounded more like a vow.

"But don't you see, this, whatever this is…it's not going to work, Lucius," I said trying for reason, because what we were doing now, well it didn't seem like we would ever get past it...*That I would ever get past it.*

"You know exactly what this is, so don't you dare choose now to ignore it, not after all these years of holding on," he said moving his hands from my suspended wrists and down my arms to come to rest at my neck. I lowered my arms, frowning at his words and hating how pathetic they made me seem. Because the arrogant bastard knew it all. But right now his words, as little sense as they made, weren't coming from arrogance.

So I shook my head,

"I don't understand, what is it you want from me here, Lucius?"

"I want the freedom to do as I please without fear of guilt or repercussions against us," he said cryptically and I swear I felt like gritting my teeth and cursing the Devil.

"Guilt or repercussions? Lucius what are you talking about?" At this he wrapped his arms around me and buried his head in my neck to breathe me in before whispering,

"I wish you knew it all, as much as I hope you never discover the truth." Then he pulled back from me when he heard me suck in a startled breath, because really, what could be worse than him loving my mother?

"The truth? The truth about what?" I asked pulling back and letting my legs fall from being wrapped around him. I slid down, now nowhere near his height but still trapped between his large frame and the wall. He didn't answer me straight away but raised a hand to my bleeding lip and ran the pad of his thumb down the centre. Then he nearly crippled me with his next admission,

"About what I did to you." This was when his thumb found his own mouth so he could have one last taste. It was as if he knew his phone was about to ring and I found it odd that during such an intense conversation he would answer it.

"They have come for you," a voice told him on the other end as for once I was close enough that I didn't need supernatural hearing to listen.

"I know. Three minutes," Lucius replied calmly without taking his eyes from me.

"Yes, my Lord." A deep and burly sounding voice replied.

"And Clay..." Lucius said his name, taking pause to make sure he was being heard.

"Sire?"

"No one follows me." At this I narrowed my eyes in question, wanting to know where Lucius intended to go to and why no one should follow.

"But that isn't..." It was obvious that this Clay person didn't agree.

"This is an order, not a request...understood?" Was Lucius' stern reply.

"Fine...and if something goes wrong, what then?" Clay snapped back telling me that whoever was on the phone was someone extremely close to Lucius and most likely on his council as I couldn't imagine many being able to get away with speaking so bluntly to him.

"Then naturally you call in the big guns and the one who is best known how to use him," Lucius replied, now back to being calm, making me wonder where exactly it was he was going, or who it was that had come for him?

"Great, that's all we fucking need," the one named Clay grumbled making Lucius smirk instead of getting angry. And through this last part Lucius had been looking off to one side with an arm rested above my head telling me that I was going nowhere as he'd promised. But for this next part he once more turned his attention back to the body he had trapped in his frame by looking directly down at me. Then he said,

"And one other thing."

"Yeah?" Clay waited but sounded very much as though he knew what was coming.

"The girl doesn't leave, *at all."* I swallowed hard at the sound of the strength in that order and even the guy on the other end said,

"Yeah, last I checked, I'm not suicidal Luc, of course I won't let her fucking leave!" Lucius smirked at this and said,

"Now that's two minutes." Then he hung up the call.

"So, I'm some kind of prisoner now?" I snapped, making his smirk turn into a knowing grin. Then he snaked an arm around my back and yanked me hard to him before telling me on a growl,

"No, you're not just *some kind* of prisoner...*you're my fucking prisoner!"* Then he kissed me as I gasped in outrage, one that was swallowed up by his consuming kiss and one that spoke only of possession.

And one that took up the last of his spare minutes.

"I shouldn't be long and then when I get back, we are going to talk about all the things you said to me and all the things you *think you know,"* he said this framing my face with both his large hands before kissing my forehead and then walking away, but when he got to the door I couldn't help but ask,

"And what about all the things that I don't?" He paused with his hand on the handle and lowered his head in what looked like some kind of personal defeat, before granting me one last look over his shoulder before saying,

"Those too... even if I have to chain you to my bed first so you can't run from me, *then I will."*

Then he left and in doing so missing the stunned look on my face. Because now all I had left to question was what was so bad he thought I would first need 'chaining' to his bed before he risked telling me!?

What exactly had he done to me?

But more importantly…*would I still love him after it?*

———

I don't know how long it was before I shook myself from staring at the closed door, bombarding my own mind with two thousand questions, one for every year he was older than me and a couple of extra for good measure! Then, thinking back to his phone call, I wanted to know where he was going and who it was that was there for him? Because of all of the times to leave, now wasn't exactly what I would have called convenient and if there was one thing I knew about Lucius, it was that he didn't do anything he didn't want to. Which was why I doubted he would have wanted to leave unless…well, unless he was forced to?

I thought back to him leaving me in bed, only to find him a little time later putting the box back in his safe…did that mean it had something to do with it? Well, I was damned if I was just going to sit here as his 'little prisoner' and wait for my answers to probably never come. So, with this in mind, I ran over to the window in his apartment that I knew faced the front of the club, meaning that I had a 50% chance of catching him leave, as I decided the front was most likely my best bet. And I was right. Because I caught him just in time to see him walking towards a blacked out SUV with the door open waiting.

But it was the two huge bulky guards who were escorting him that worried me the most.

"What are you doing, don't get in the car!?" I asked no-one in particular, with my hand gripping onto the frame hard enough my knuckles turned white. Only it was in this moment that Lucius looked up at me, as if he had heard my panic, and knew I would be standing here watching. He gave me a head nod, and I wondered if this was supposed to give me comfort or Hell, the broody demanding bugger might have just been telling me to get back to being a good little prisoner. Who the Hell knew with Lucius but getting in that car, then even I knew that was a bad idea.

But then my fears were ignored as I watched his large muscular frame disappear inside the car and I swear my heart was in my throat. Especially when I was forced to watch the door close and the car pull away, taking him away from the club and his men. Why wouldn't he want people to follow? Did he know how important his life was!

"Damn it, Lucius!" I snapped hitting out at the frame and ignoring the pain from doing so. Then I just slumped down where I stood and put my back to the full-length window where I let my head hang in my hands. I just needed to think. But then that was easier said than done when there was just too much to think about.

What I needed was answers but other than Liessa, then who could I ask? More like, who would even tell me, but then there was one person who I had heard that would definitely know what was going on and that was this Clay person. Now of course all I had to do was find him...*or did I?*

An idea started to form because really, what Lucius had said to him, warning him that I wasn't to leave, well surely to get him to appear then all I would have to do is try. Umm, well there was only one way to find out.

I left Lucius' apartment and looked to the private elevator, knowing that if I went that way then I might be giving away my last option when it came to actually leaving here. Although Lucius hadn't asked me how I had snuck into the building or how I even knew the combination to his safe? And why not, surely these would be the first things he would have asked. And really, what would I have said if he did, that some crazy chick with mad driving skills told me how to get in, oh and she just so happened to be the next oracle.

Okay, well I liked to consider myself to be an intelligent sort of girl but right now I felt as dumb as a post for only asking myself these things now. Alright, so admittedly I turned into a mushy bumbling idiot around Lucius, but then that's what decade old obsessions would do to you. And now I had seen him without his shirt on, then I feared it would only get worse. Oh, that and I now knew what it felt like to be kissed by him. But then that wasn't a strong enough word for it.

Being kissed by Lucius felt more like willingly stepping into a trap that you knew had the power to cage you, to consume you, to imprison you for however long he wanted you locked there. It was like signing up for the type of pleasure you knew also came with the power to torture you afterwards. This being the part when he would inevitably walk away, taking those consuming kisses with him.

Because no matter how much Lucius made you feel as though you were the only being on Earth he wanted and with an intensity to fool you into believing he needed it as much as he did his next breath...Lucius was owned by no one. Meaning that I knew the commitment would only ever be one sided...it had been for over ten years. A gift I stupidly had been keeping for him in some kind of twisted fairy tale notion he would one day realise I was the only girl for him. That I was...

His Chosen One.

Damn my parents and their ridiculous love for one another. Honestly, what did I expect? Growing up and having to witness that type of commitment, that depth of love and adoring, Gods but it was no wonder I was so messed up. I know what you're thinking, what's wrong with that, isn't it what every child wants and yes, deep down I wouldn't have it any other way. My parents were and always would be an absolute in my world. But the downside to this was it created impossible expectations of the future. It made me ache to have what my mother had in a husband, partner, soulmate or more like, Chosen One.

All around me, the Kings of my father's world would meet their Chosen souls, bring them to events, balls or even council meetings and the look of utter adoring love in their eyes was sickening to someone who had been dreaming of finding it for herself most of her life. Foolishly convinced it had been there for the taking in Lucius. Sometimes I liked to convince myself another was out there just waiting for me and Lucius had just been the first one I latched onto with the silly and naive notion.

But then just being in the same room with him and I knew my mind and body hadn't just manifested these thoughts because it was convenient...hell, it was anything but convenient, seeing as the guy didn't want me.

Well, until now it seemed.

But it wasn't just a passing fancy. No, my body literally ached to be near him. My heart felt like it started to beat in tandem with his own whenever he was near. My mind and body were both drawn to him as if he were the eternal flame and I was but a moth desperate for just one touch, even though I knew the dangers of getting burnt. That pull, the incessant tugging at my heart, wanting nothing more than to offer itself up for his mercy.

I knew he was the one and because of it…

I was cursed.

CHAPTER EIGHT

MISFITS AND MASTERS

So, this was my curse. This was my secret. The power he held over me, as if at some point in my life he had stolen a part of me, and I wasn't just talking about my heart.

I shook these thoughts from my mind and got on with my task because I couldn't help but have a bad feeling about where Lucius had been taken to. I also had a feeling it had something to do with that damn box. Had he discovered who was behind the attacks and the people who were hexed to silence?

Leaving the elevator out of this, well then my options were pretty limited. I knew the floors below held other apartments, like Liessa's who I discovered was married to a man named Caspian. Someone who apparently was a brute, her words not mine and ones she seemed quite proud of. There were also other rooms for Lucius' council members on the floor below but the only ones on Lucius' floor was what now seemed to be my temporary apartment, Lucius' private space and a locked apartment that I knew belonged to my aunty Pip and Uncle Adam.

Okay, so they weren't related by blood but Pip was my mum's best friend and pretty much lived in Afterlife. Meaning that I grew up with her around and like a quirky second parent at that. She was also one of the most bonkers, fun and funniest people on the planet and I loved her dearly. She was another reason leaving my home was one of the hardest moments of my life. Just like leaving the rest of my family was.

But I hadn't lied to Lucius when I said I'd had no choice. Because I loved my mum and wanted it to remain that way, so to save our relationship, I left. And thankfully for everyone involved, no one had any clue why...well, other than my aunty Pip who had been here that day I found out. But she had made me a vow she wouldn't say a word and I had to trust that, as I knew she would never lie to me.

Hell, she had been the only one I had ever cried to about any of this. I shook off the memory of being on the private plane with her as we travelled back to Portland, Maine. The image of me sobbing in her colourful arms as she softly brushed back my hair and handed me tissues. She hadn't tried to brush off my tears, or talk reason into how I was feeling, telling me bullshit like it would pass and I would feel better once home. No, she simply listened, silently letting me get it all out. She was the one and only person who knew how I felt about Lucius and after that moment, how I also felt about my mother. Which was why I hadn't been the only one crying by the end of the flight.

After that, I didn't think I could love my aunty Pip any more than what I thought I already did. So, although I was curious as to what was behind this door, as knowing Pip, it no doubt would have been like walking into a sex-crazed wonderful land adventure novel, it was locked.

Oh, Gods but it was times like this I missed my crazy aunty, along with my actual aunty Sophia, who was just as mischievous. Actually, it was times like this that I missed everyone in my family, but then I thought about my dad and my heart ached with the lies he had told me.

I adored him, I really did. Growing up I was definitely what you would have called a daddy's girl but because of that, he'd clearly had the hardest time in letting me go and watching me grow up. He was also what you would call a slight control freak and to be honest, I kind of understood why. Being King wasn't exactly an easy job. He most definitely wasn't as easy going as his brother, my Uncle Vincent, that was for damn sure.

Stood now in the lobby I circled the large sculpture that still seemed to tell a story I wasn't yet getting. Then I eyed my limited choices knowing there was really only one door that was an option, it just so happened it was the last one without an apartment behind it. It was the doorway into his club. I knew what I would find in there, a lot of bad memories and ridicule. So, before I did anything stupid, I needed some fresh air first. Which was why I retraced my steps from earlier and decided to go back up to the rooftop garden.

Once up there, I took in a deep breath wishing I had grabbed a jacket or something as the cool air nipped at my skin. Which was why I ended up holding my arms around myself as I gazed out at the city, knowing how most of it still slept at this early hour. My guess was it was about three in the morning, which made me question even more what Lucius could have been thinking going with those men?

It made me wonder if something like him leaving would have gone any differently had we been a couple. Would he have told me where and why, or still kept me out of the loop, doing as he wanted without feeling the need to put my fears at ease?

"What's the point," I muttered aloud, knowing it would

never happen. What Lucius and I had was far from what convention would ever dictate as being a couple or class as normal, which included things like being informed what he was doing and why. And why should it? He had no one to answer to. Never had anyone's feelings to consider. That much was obvious.

These thoughts also made me question if even my own father had struggled when he first met my mother? He shared everything with her but then again, I doubted my mum knew the depths of crazy my dad had gone to when it came to controlling my life. If anything, my mum was my biggest advocate for trying to live a normal life, saying I needed to experience my humanity before it might suddenly change. Hell, but it was almost as if my mum knew something that I didn't when she said these types of things.

I walked over to the small seating area under a blanket of ivy, hugged my legs to my chest and let a stray tear roll down my cheek as I thought about my mother. God's what I wouldn't have given in that moment to be able to talk to her. To have her here with me, just so I could lean my head against her shoulder and hug her. But in reality, it had felt like a small forever since we had been like that. Since I had allowed myself to be that daughter again. The guilt I felt was just as heart-breaking as the reasons I had stayed away.

But what other options did I have. It wasn't as though I could talk to her about any of this, even though I knew that she was far from stupid. Of course, she knew something major was wrong. She had since the day I arrived back home. But then again, staying in your room for a whole week without wanting to talk to anyone was obvious enough. I remembered the way my dad had stormed through the doors all pent up and angry, ready to demand an explanation from me. But the first sight of my blubbering tears and he had lost his anger with me pretty damn quickly.

But that was my dad. All hard and a mighty warrior ruler on the outside but utter mush inside when it came to those he loved. Gods, but once he wanted to buy me a pony just because I fell off my bike and cried after grazing my knee. It had been my mum who had told him not to be ridiculous. That I was a Draven and therefore she picked me up, dusted me off and put me back on the bike. Then telling me that I was doing great and to keep showing my bike who was boss, much to my dad's horror in thinking now that all bikes were evil contraptions that needed to be wiped from his kingdom like spinning wheels from Sleeping Beauty. It was sweet and endearing but totally impractical.

Which was why in the end, and thanks to my mum, it was the only emotional time my parents ever let me have to myself without pushing for answers. Oh, but I knew my dad had been forced to do so by my mum. But it did also made me wonder if this was why he had taken it upon himself to take control without my mum's knowledge, once I made the decision to leave. Did he not trust me to be capable of living my life solely after this moment? Well, knowing my dad it certainly sounded like something he would do.

I didn't know how long I ended up being up there but it was still dark and I was also too cold to stand it for much longer. Besides, I was getting nothing done. My plan had been to just try and escape and see who came running first to ask for answers. But after my time up there I decided to just pull up my big girl pants and walk straight into his club and start demanding them from people. After all, it wasn't like they could hurt me, as I was pretty sure Lucius would have killed anyone who tried. He had certainly made those sentiments clear enough, especially if he hadn't even let some of his men look at me without a threat if doing so.

Which was why I walked back into the stairway and jogged down one floor back to the lobby area. Then I came face to face with the one door I didn't really want to walk through but knew that at some point, it was inevitable.

If I were honest with myself it was also the reason I didn't want to meet Lucius last night, telling myself Star Trek had been more important. But in reality, cutting my damn toenails would have been more important than being made to walk back into that place.

Truth was that I *hated* Transfusion, as in utterly loathed it! The club had haunted my dreams ever since the first time stepping foot inside, as the very memory of the place was like a rot to my soul. Now, would I have felt differently walking back in there as Lucius' girlfriend? Who the Hell knew...not me for damn sure because even the thought of becoming something like that to him felt more like some cosmic joke! Something that these days felt as if even the very Gods themselves were laughing at.

Then again, if I walked in there now then what was the worst that could happen. For starters the biggest threat wasn't even in the building, so the rejection I was most scared of wasn't an issue. It wasn't as though I could get thrown out this time, if anything it was the complete opposite. As according to Lucius, I was now his prisoner, meaning my prison was this bloodthirsty place.

Oh, the name fit alright, but a pint of blood felt like only half the sacrifice. To be fair, I didn't really know what went on in there as over the years it was quite possible that my imagination had warped my traumatized memories of the place.

Well, there was only one way to find out, so I opened the door and walked inside and the first words out of my mouth were...

"Oh shit."

This was muttered in a barely heard whisper but for the people all now congregated around a large table, it could have been said in a damn megaphone for the reaction I received. The whole club was obviously shut for the night and even the VIP was almost empty. Or at least it would have been if not for every council member that was now sat around a large oval table where the huge gothic sectional sofa had once been. Oh, and at the sound of my entrance all eyes turned to face me.

"Erm..." This was the only lame sound that escaped me, and I wished I could have just given in to the urge to turn around and bolt through the door. However, my parents didn't raise a coward and it was time to put all that 'Princess' usefulness to well, to good use. It was time to act like a Draven and get my ass back on the damn bike Fae.

See, my mum once told me that she often felt the same way, totally intimidated by so many supernatural beings and often those who were the strongest of their kind. It was daunting and it was overwhelming, especially for a human, which pretty much meant bottom of the food chain in this gig. But that was when she first met my dad who, as she described it, had been the most intimidating of them all. And no wonder really considering he was the King of Kings and pretty much ruled everyone but Lucius.

But then this had also been because, well, in her words, when they first met he had been a bit of an asshole, to which he would roll his eyes and mutter something about mortal sensitivity and leave the room after growling at my mother. But I could tell with the twinkle in her eye it was something playful between the two of them, as the adoring exchange couldn't be ignored.

So, due to this sound advice, being that all of these supernatural macho men basically had a bark much worse than their bite, her words had been that if you gave them a fearful inch, they would then take the intimidating mile.

Of course, trying to put this advice into practice, especially around someone like Lucius, was most definitely easier said than done. But around these guys, who I knew could bark at me all they wanted and get away with it, I also knew that was all they could do. Because anything more and Lucius would roar bloody murder back. Of this I had no doubt. Because in his mind, I belonged to him, even if that meant something unquestionably different to me than it ever would to him.

Which was why I metaphorically pulled up my big girl pants like I said I would and strode into the room as if I owned the joint, saying,

"Right, well now the big bad royal ass has gone, where can a girl get a real drink around here?" Everyone was silent, all but Liessa who threw her head back and let out a long breathy laugh and smacked her hand on the table in her hilarity. Of course, this made everyone have to throw up their arms to protect themselves as ink burst out from beneath her palm the second it made contact with the table. They all moaned in annoyance, as I could see some of the black substance sizzling skin and burning like acid, now telling me why most of the time she wore gloves.

However, the man next to her, aka 'The Brute' and who I assumed was her husband, growled at everyone before taking her hand in his and started licking at her palm like a dog. Then when he was finished with that, he placed her hand on his lap before bending his colossal looking frame over the table and then licked that clean too. More astonishing was that not a single person said a word against this. But then again, just looking at the sheer size of him and it was of little wonder, seeing as he would have made a good contender for my once personal guard Ragnar, yet another person I classed as family.

Ragnar was over six foot seven inches tall and was built like the term, 'a brick shithouse!' He had muscle where you didn't think there should even be muscle. He was also very mean and scary looking, with scarred skin and a short shaved mohawk. Of course, to me, he was like a giant teddy bear and used to let me ride on his back as a kid as I pretended I was riding a giant wolf named Fenrir. Fenrir, also called Fenrisúlfr, who was a monstrous wolf of Norse mythology. He was also the son of the demoniac god Loki and a giantess, Angerboda.

I knew this from listening to stories sat on Ragnar's lap as a child as he told me all about the Norse Gods. I should probably mention that Ragnar had also once been a Scandinavian king before of course he had been thrown into a pit of snakes and poisoned to death. After that was when my father saved his soul and contracted with his Gods to have him serve him on Earth as his head of security. He was then resurrected as one of the Devourers, meaning he had literally been gifted with the blood of a Norse God.

But now, whatever this Caspian was, beyond being obviously terrifying and extremely different looking, I didn't know. He was incredibly wide and even though he was sitting I just knew that if he rose from his seat, he would mostly likely have been as tall as Ragnar.

However, that's where the similarities ended. His hair reminded me of what you would find on a fine silver wire brush and it framed most of his face, from his pierced lips, where it came down into a long and shapely point, and the top of his head where the unusual style was pulled back from his forehead and shaved at the sides. It was held atop of his head in a 'man bun' in a metal spike sticking from the top with three prongs like Poseidon's trident.

He wore what looked like well-worn biker gear, with a tight faded Rolling Stones Tee under a leather cut. And from the looks of things everything that could be pierced was. Three bars on the bridge of his nose, multiple ones through his lips, silver balls at his chin as well as either side of his lips. Tattoos painted his pale skin but I was too far away to make them out. But from what I could see they looked old school in their design, like the type you would have expected to see on sailors or tattooed people headlined as freaks at the circus a hundred years ago.

He also currently wore shades like Arnold Schwarzenegger had done in Terminator 2, something I knew because I had the figure sitting on my shelf at home in my newly decorated flat. Thanks for that one, Lucius, I thought with a grin.

Next on the table was who looked like a punk rock teenager, who obviously liked all things black, including the colour of his nails and eyeliner. He also liked Fall Out Boy, according to the T shirt he wore over a long sleeved dark grey one. Of course, he also had a thing for belts and blades as they were everywhere you could naturally fit them on your person. He was tall, slim and had a baby, but handsome face, despite it holding what looked like a permanent scowl. Fingerless gloves, leather straps and chains were what completed the outfit. Oh, and not forgetting what looked like untied skull covered Doc Martins boots that were actually up on the table as he leant back in his seat.

Next to him was a small man who wore a dark hooded jacket, covering most of his face and skinny tight jeans with the same style boots as the teenager next to him, only his had flowers and a paisley pattern all over them which I could just see from this angle.

But then moving along and I really didn't think you could

get much stranger than the misfit bunch I had already noted in detail. However, I was wrong, because I came to the strangest of all.

This man, like the other adult males around the table was as muscular as the rest but sat with his arms crossed and unmoving in an unnerving way. He was clearly of native American Indian descent and boy was he beautiful to look at. Even with his harsh unwavering stare. What with his toffee coloured skin, almond shaped eyes and long silky midnight black hair that hung straight and split in two halves reaching his naked and rippled abs.

Now if this had been it, I would have said other than sitting there half naked in only a wrap-around skirt, one that was belted with thick, coarse leather, I would have said there was nothing unusual about him. And this would have been the case had he not had his torso wrapped in some weird thick metal wire. One that looked spiked in sections, like some hellish barbed wire.

It wrapped around him in no particular way, just crossed over and over again in different directions, but was thicker at the arms and neck, where it made a collar and cuffs. Stranger still, it didn't look as though it confined him in anyway. But hey, what did I know, seeing as the guy barely moved an inch. I mean Hell, he could have danced the bloody macarena with the best of them for all I knew.

Although I didn't exactly see him as the dancing type, now serious and pissed off, then yeah. But maybe that was just down to the intimidating black ink he had painted across his eyes. A strip just over an inch thick that was a straight band spanning from one side to the other. But like I said, there was something beautiful and totally alluring about him. Almost like you just knew if you ever had the chance to witness him smile, you knew it would have been breath-taking.

The last figure at the table was another huge man, one that wasn't as tall as Caspian but one definitely as wide. But he would have definitely been the yin to Caspian's yang, although that sounded kind of wrong and rude at the same time. But I suppressed a childish giggle at the thought, and it was a good job too as neither of them looked like the teasing type. Caspian was as white as snow and this guy had skin like melted chocolate, and yes, it looked just as lickable!

He was the most jaw dropping gorgeous black man I had ever seen and with eyes that looked as though they could be as tender as they could frightening. An unusual navy blue colour, they added a depth and dimension to his personality that made a woman just want to dive right in and start peeling back the layers.

Short black hair just a few grades away from being shaved completely, and dark stubble that dusted a strong square jaw and chiselled features. And that body, then Gods, but this guy looked like he was getting ready to join some strong man competition or something equally as manly.

Jeez, I mean what was it with these guys, did they all eat other people's muscles for breakfast or something. Did their protein shakes have the powdered bones of virgin angels and demon tears as a secret concoction that made them all look like fallen Gods!

"Is this her, my Wench?" Liessa's husband asked with an accent I couldn't place and a deep grating timbre to his voice that made me want to shiver. Of course, I also couldn't help but frown at hearing what his nickname for her was. But then she certainly didn't seem to mind as she draped herself across his shoulder, walked two fingers provocatively across his massive muscle and said,

"That's her, told you she was cute." Then she granted me a little wave and a wink, especially when her husband growled low as if jealous. I tried not to frown in reaction to it and was about to take my first steps up to the table when I felt a presence step up behind me. Then, before I could turn around to discover who it was, I felt an arm band possessively across my chest and pull me back against the solid presence.

"She is indeed." A masterful voice spoke behind me, making me shiver and whisper a single breathy name...

"Lucius."

CHAPTER NINE

LUCIUS' COUNCIL

Well, so much for well laid plans. Like discovering which one Clay was and then asking him where Lucius had gone.

"You're back?" I whispered, feeling suddenly shy being like this with him in front of his people. Clearly however, he didn't feel the same way, as he tightened his hold on me and whispered down at me,

"And you're cold." He said this as though it annoyed him without questioning why I was. As if he already knew. Something that was confirmed when he released me so he could drape a large leather jacket over my shoulders. The warmth seeped into my cold frame and I had to hold back the urge to moan and snuggle deeper into the warmth of the material inside. It was clear that he must have been wearing it recently as it was warm and it smelled amazing, and exactly like him. Sandalwood, a hint of citrus all wrapped up in leather turned out to be the scent and heady mix of raw sexual masculinity. Meaning it was enough to mess with my head as all that was

Lucius surrounded me completely, with his body at my back and his scent caressing my senses like a lover's touch.

But this was when I noticed that Lucius was not only wearing different clothes than he had been wearing before he left, but his hair was now slightly damp. Which confused me because if he had just got out of the shower, then why the jacket?

In the end I didn't have long to think about it as he issued his next command,

"A jacket next time Amelia, that is not a request." His tone was stern and absolute, telling me that he somehow knew exactly where I had been. In fact, I would have said something sarcastic or thrown back some sass about how I was a grown woman and could do as I damn well pleased, but admittedly I was still stuck on the fact he was clearly concerned about my health and wellbeing. And not only that but he had no problem with letting his council know it either.

"So, did you miss me, my cold little beauty?" Then, before I could answer him, he spun me so fast I had no other choice but to reach out and grab onto his shoulders so I wouldn't keep spinning like some sort of cartoon character and go flying right out the window.

Then with barely a gasp being my only startled response, I was being lifted clean off the ground with one arm snaked under the jacket and banded around my waist, so I was at the right height for his lips. Lips that suddenly kissed me, and when I say kissed, I mean the kind that was long, and deep and what felt very, very close to being X-rated.

But stranger still, there wasn't a single sound to be heard from one member of his council as their boss and King basically just entered a room and started ravishing a random girl they'd only just this second met.

Which was when the painful thought hit me, maybe it was

because it was a sight they were used to seeing. This made me instantly tense in his hold and he groaned over my lips the moment he felt it. Which was why he pulled back a little and after making sure he had my eyes, he muttered,

"There she goes again." Then he set me back on my feet and I started to make my excuses to leave. Especially now that he was back and because seriously, it was still dark outside and quickly becoming the night that just would never end.

"I will just…"

"Oh no you don't," he said grabbing my wrist and pulling me back to his side. Then he settled me in front of him, with his hands at the tops of my arms, so I had nowhere to go but to be back facing his council.

"It's time to introduce you," he told me and I turned my head to the side and whispered,

"Please." But it was a plea he ignored as there was no chance with one as powerful as he, that he wouldn't have heard it. But at the very least, he must have been contemplating what to do next as he remained unmoving. Then I felt him lower his lips to my ear so he could whisper,

"Be brave, little one…" After this he ran his hand from the top of my arm over the leather until it came to my hand, which he first had to fish for inside the sleeve before taking it firmly in his own. Then he spun me again, tapped me under the chin and said,

"…And show me that fire in your eyes that I fucking adore." I swallowed hard as I played back his words and found myself having to hide the biggest grin from how that compliment made me feel. Of course, this also meant that I gave no resistance when he walked me over to the table, because right now, all I wanted to do was make him proud.

Gods, what was wrong with me and where on earth did that thought come from!?

There were two chairs free around the table and both were opposite each other. But it was obvious which one belonged to Lucius as it seemed the similarities between Kings were obvious to someone who had grown up around them. For starters it had a higher back than the rest of them, which were quite contemporary in their design. The only 'gothic' element was the black leather material buttoned in a diamond shape like you would find on an old chesterfield. However, these chairs looked as though that leather section had been melted over a carved wooden frame that was the colour of a stormy sky. The feet part were giant demonic claws that dug into the dark flooring, but it must have been a trick of the eye as otherwise how could they be moved?

But Lucius' was the same in design only instead of the wilted style sides, the back part went up in a high arch attached to a carved twisted frame. So, seeing as this was clearly his seat, I continued to walk past the others to get to my own, when I was quickly tugged back.

"You sit with me," he stated firmly, making me frown first at him and then down at the single seat. I knew that my father often sat with my mum in his lap, even during serious meetings.

I asked her once if she ever got embarrassed about it, but she just shrugged her shoulders and said that she used to a long time ago. But now, well she would start to worry and dread the day that my dad didn't want her in his lap anymore. However, that was my parents. That was love. And this...well, to a man like Lucius it meant only one thing...

Ownership.

"No," I said just as firmly, and I knew without looking that every one of his council members were now staring at my back as they witnessed me denying their king. But instead of looking perplexed he smirked down at me before cryptically saying,

"Ah, but there she is." Then he held a hand out to his side

and pushed it back as if something was there for him to physically touch. This slight action made his throne suddenly go crashing backwards, only stopping when it smashed into the wall behind. I yelped and couldn't help but flinch, something he blatantly ignored.

Then without comment, he looked over his shoulder at some of the other bits of furniture that framed the room as if making his choice. Oh, and boy didn't I just know it when he found the one he wanted, as he first granted me a knowing look and a wink before making it slide towards us as if being pulled by an invisible cord.

Damn him but did he have to look so freakin' sexy as he played the badass king thing off to a damn tee!

The seat he chose was a quirky take on an old-fashioned wingback chesterfield, like the others were. Which must have been the theme in the VIP, but instead of having a wilted flower head look, this was more traditional in style. It was also upholstered in black velvet and was two chairs of the same style fashioned together. A style that made it kind of look like conjoined twins, as a thicker sectional piece in the centre was what connected them both.

But each seat had their own elaborately carved back and each side a padded arm rest. Meaning that I had no choice but to share the one seat, especially when he snagged the waistband of my jeans and pulled me roughly to him. Then, before I could protest further, he stepped me backwards until the back of my legs hit the cushioned rim. So, with nowhere else to go I sat down before he leant over my space, trapping me in with one hand to the armrest and a gloved hand gripping the chair's carved back, and issued his condescending praise,

"Good little princess," something that instantly pissed me off and made me growl back at him, cursing myself for not being more threatening, or someone who could ever hope to match him. And he knew this because he tapped my nose and chuckled once before he turned back to face his council who now all stood in his presence.

"Fuck all that royal bullshit and sit your asses down, as now is not the time for it!" he snapped, making me frown in question, asking myself why was I the only one he was not in a foul mood with? Not that I could really complain about it and a pissed off Lucius wasn't exactly a treat to deal with.

"I take it the meeting went well," the teenager remarked without looking at Lucius and with a snigger as he was now chipping away at his black nail polish with the tip of one of his blades.

"Yes, and was about as useful as a fucking hole in the head, which reminds me, where is that little prick you hired recently?" Lucius barked at Liessa, who had been too preoccupied with running the tips of her fingers around her husband's ear and poking her finger through the large hole in his lobe thanks to the sizeable ear gauge. The other one had a large black horn through it that curled through his ear and all the way round to where it started.

"You mean Puck the Fuck?" Caspian answered for her and it made the hooded one giggle.

"Damn it, I knew I should have attached a little bell to the guy," Liessa said with a smirk.

"I don't give a shit whether you attach a leash to the kobold, as long as he does his fucking job and gets me a damn drink!" Lucius snapped in complaint before finally sitting down next to me. I then turned to him after first giving him as much space as the double chair would allow and said in hushed tones whilst looking down to the side,

"You swear an awful lot, you know that?" Lucius then looked at me and smirked before saying,

"Yes Pet, I know I fucking do," then he winked and tapped

me under the chin before turning towards the small hooded man and said,

"Percy, if you please." And I had to say, I was utterly dumbfounded and for more than one reason. First, this was the most polite I had ever heard Lucius speak to anyone other than me and secondly…was this '*the* Percy?' as in, my mother's Percy?

The small hooded man nodded and said,

"Bbbuth of courseth, my ssssire," he hissed with a heavy lisp and then he slipped away towards the back of the club where I could see a long bar set back within the wall, making it look as though there was no way inside.

"Is that my mum's Percy?" I asked before I could stop myself from mentioning her in front of him, but he didn't seem to care as his reply was flippant,

"No, that is *my Percy.*"

"You know what I mean, the one who helped save her?" I pressed further.

"I do and yes, he is the one who saved your mother, along with many others and multiple times no doubt considering your mother's past record," he said in a tone that spoke of contempt and I would have questioned why if we hadn't been surrounded by his council members.

I was surprised to be honest that he spoke of her in such a blatant way and looking at his face now, I was expecting to see some kind of deeper feeling there, but there was none. If anything, it had been as if he had been talking about someone he was merely acquainted with, not someone he had deep feelings for. But then, as he must have felt my gaze on him, he looked down at me making me quickly look away before I could be caught with the obvious question in my eyes.

"So, I take it by the blood still stained under your fingernails that the meeting ended the way you thought it would?" Liessa remarked making me suck in a sharp breath and instantly my eyes fell on his hands, seeing that she was right, the tips were stained red. My eyes shot to Lucius expecting him to explain or at the very least look somewhat remorseful but instead he smirked and then looked to his own hands.

"Mmm, it's no Krombacher dark, but it will do," he said before sucking on his own fingertips making me flinch back in my seat, not really enjoying seeing this darker more sinister side to him.

"Problem?" he enquired when he realised I wasn't exactly clinging on to his every word, as he started to explain things I just couldn't follow seeing as, well my mind was most definitely preoccupied.

"You killed someone?" At this it was the punk who chuckled darkly and said,

"Yeah, better get used to that as our Lord doesn't usually issue revenge with words... or did you think he would just swear at them?" The sideways look of disdain added to this attitude making me instantly dislike him.

"Ruto, that's enough," Lucius replied on a stern growl, obviously not liking his particular tone being directed at me. And I wasn't surprised that it worked, as I didn't think there were many who would have disobeyed him, well apart from me obviously, Miss Slap Happy here.

I wanted to ask what he meant by revenge, but this was when Percy came back and did so with two bottles in hand.

"I thound the Kobolthddd," he stammered, although clearly perfectly at ease.

"Yeah, did he have his head in between a pair of tits again?" The big black guy said in a gruff voice that matched the one I had heard on the phone to Lucius, telling me that this was 'Clay'. Percy chuckled but didn't comment, instead he handed Lucius the beer and said,

"I broughth thissh ssso you didthn't haveth to wait and one for tthhe pretthhy lady," he added giving me a nod and this made his hood fall back a little showing me a glimpse of scarred burnt flesh that was puckered and twisted around his features.

But he was smiling, and his stunning green eyes sparkled as if nothing in the world could ever bother him now. In fact, he looked like one of the happiest people I had ever met, and I couldn't help but smile back at him as it was infectious.

Besides, I owed him my thanks for he once saved my mother's life and for that I was eternally grateful to him, even if he didn't know it yet. So, the second he put down the bottle in front of us I first tugged up the long sleeve and reached across Lucius so I could grab his scarred hand. I ignored what I knew was Lucius' intense gaze on me and gave Percy's hand a squeeze before telling him,

"Thank you, Percy," knowing that my expression spoke of so much more than just for the drink and kind compliment he gave me. He looked shocked for a moment and I wondered if it was maybe from the contact with his burnt flesh or my blatant show of thanks. I didn't know which but by the time his eyes came back to mine, he actually looked bashful before he nodded and said without a single lisp,

"You're welcome." Without the stammer his voice sounded completely different as if there were two sides to him, making me question if this was the one he wished took more centre stage.

I didn't know where that thought came from but as he retook his seat, I watched him just as Lucius continued to watch me. But I continued to ignore the intense look I could feel Percy's master giving me. Instead I took the bottle, reading the label as the beer that Lucius had mentioned before cleaning the bloody evidence off his fingers. Then I pulled up my sleeve yet again and took a swig of the beer, realising it was the same brand from last night only a different kind. This had less of a honey aftertaste and more chocolate hints with caramel and that tang of bitterness. It was nice but a little heavy for me.

But then, as Lucius had obviously made watching me his new hobby, he plucked the bottle out of my hands. But before I could ask why or protest, he took my hand in his so he could start folding back the far too long, sleeves of his jacket. He didn't say a word during this but instead spoke to Clay about increasing security during the club's open hours. I could feel a blush blooming over my cheeks and even creeping down my neck at the attention he blatantly showed me in front of his people, and it weirdly felt as if I belonged to him. As if I was his to care for and do as he wished, whether his people were there to witness it or not.

This gave me mixed feelings, as on one hand it made me feel kind of treasured. But on the other, I wasn't sure being 'owned' by Lucius was ever a good thing. Just look at how he acted when finding out I had been sat out too long in the cold. Yes, it had been nice to see his concern but demanding I have a jacket next time, as though he had somehow become my boss. Was that how a relationship with Lucius would go, that he would simply bully me with his intimidating ways into doing as he wanted? Well, if that was the case then this King was about to get a shock and a cold hard dash of reality, because I had run from the control of my father for a reason. Which meant I wasn't about to jump out of the fire and into the sizzling and yes, arguably unbelievable sexy hot, frying pan.

All in all, as sweet as these little gestures were, they were also confusing the hell out of me and only seemed to be adding to the very long list of reasons why I should still be trying to leave. Something I had so far only being saying I would do without the actual…you know, doing part.

Once Lucius had finished re-dressing his little 'doll', he reached for my bottle and handed it back to me before retaking his own. I was then forced to watch the sexy image of Lucius with his lips around the bottle, shamefully wishing they were latched elsewhere, like sucking on my neck. He really was a stunning sight, with his chiselled jaw line, that perfect nose, corded neck that I wanted to lick up the length and see if he moaned like I knew I would.

Gods, I needed to get a grip, I scolded myself and quickly turned away the second I caught him turning his attention back to me. So instead I turned my own attention back to the table, realising that out of everyone there was only one who I didn't yet know. Which wasn't really surprising seeing as it was also the one who never seemed to speak...the beautiful Indigenous American man. Which was why I couldn't help but lean into Lucius just enough to turn my head and whisper the question,

"Who is the quiet one?" Not knowing what to call him but knowing that the 'strange one who looked like a bandit caught in some wired trap' sounded lame. Lucius looked down at me as if surprised I had asked the question and when his eyes widened, he must have realised something. So, he slammed down his beer making me jump and flinch back. It was an action he didn't seem to care for, as he hooked me behind my neck and pulled me closer to him. I was just about to protest when he tipped my face up and growled down at me,

"I like keeping you close." Then before I could respond, with something along the lines of, 'get off me, you big lug' he turned back to his council and started to introduce them to me one by one. Starting with his left,

"This is Clay, my head of security, next to him is Percy, who you know." Percy gave me a little cute and endearing wave I couldn't help but smile at.

"Next to him is my current right hand, Ruto." At this the

teenager decided to mimic Percy but instead waved a blade at me with a knowing grin. But I ignored the rude response, too shocked to care. My wide eyes must have given away my thoughts at hearing that Ruto was who Lucius considered as his right-hand man.

"Yeah I know that look...don't let my youthful good looks fool you, Princess." Ruto commented dryly but this made Lucius snarl at him after a fist pounded the frosted glass table,

"It's Fae to you and you will not forget it. The same goes for the rest of you, am I understood?!" They all nodded, including a now sullen teenager who looked pissed off as if he had just been told to tidy his room or not play with knives, like he was currently doing. But I was just shocked that he had ordered them to call me something even he didn't ever call me...was that why he chose it? Was Amelia his, along with Princess when it was clear he wanted to piss me off? It certainly seemed that way.

I felt him squeeze my neck where his hand still lingered, doing so now to gain my attention back.

"You know Liessa of course and this is her husband Caspian, my head enforcer." Caspian barely even acknowledged me, but he did home on to his title.

"And speaking of enforcing, when exactly can I get back to doing that, starting with the human dicks that think they can mess with us?!" he snapped cracking his own empty beer bottle, one that must have been consumed before I got there. I felt Lucius, who again still wouldn't let go of the back of my neck, start to draw circles at the top of my spine in a soothing way.

"Be patient, as after tonight, they will most certainly need to recoup after their losses," Lucius replied, still without moving his eyes from me. I felt like some damn pet of his and Gods, if he wasn't turning me on so much, I would have slapped his hand away when he ran the back of two fingers down my cheek.

Of course, I also didn't think it wise to disrespect him in front of his council, especially since over half of them were scary as Hell. I mean yeah, I could be fiery when I wanted to be, but I wasn't 'let's just crash the Enterprise into a random planet just for the sheer fun of it', crazy suicidal!

"And no, I didn't kill anyone...*this time,*" he commented as if it was important that I knew this.

"But I...well, the blood and..." I started to try and find the right way to ask about it, when he cut me off with an answer,

"And, I didn't say that they weren't beaten to a bloody pulp, I just said I didn't finish the job," he said making me close my eyes against the image. But it was no good as I shuddered anyway just thinking of Lucius going on some interrogating rampage having witnessed just a small slice of what that rage of his could do and to a mortal no less. I swallowed hard, something naturally he didn't miss and asked,

"Then what did?"

"The Hexes did," he replied coolly before turning his gaze from mine and taking another long swig of his beer.

"Wait, you mean the same hex that killed the other guy back at the museum?" I asked thinking back to what was definitely the most disgusting thing I had ever seen to date. However, the thought of what could have happened to me had Lucius not made it in time, might have been the reason why Lucius was now scowling and clenching a leather fist around his beer bottle, making the material groan under the strain. It was also probably the reason why his other hand at my neck tensed, hardening his grip but thankfully stopping just before the point of pain.

"Yeah, the same," he grumbled irritably, without looking at me. Okay, so note to self, me nearly getting shot was obviously a sore spot for him and it was probably a smart thing to avoid in the near future.

"So, this meeting, other than ending in a pool of mortal waste, did it serve a purpose?" Clay asked leaning back and folding his massive arms over his chest. Lucius smiled and it was one that spoke only of violence.

"It did."

"And…are you going to share with the rest of the class?" Liessa asked with a knowing smirk and winked at me, closing one stunning eye that was light brown with flecks of peach running through them.

They were certainly unusual and always seemed to hold a mischievous glint in their depths, like everything she did had a playful purpose. This was despite usually looking like she had just stepped out of the pages of some 1950's Good Life magazine or something.

However, tonight's choice was a little more provocative than usual. She wore a figure hugging, tight blouse that was in a sheer cream material so you could clearly make out she wasn't wearing a bra. The shirt was tied at her neck in a big floppy bow, meaning that even though she was covered up to the neck, she might as well have been naked, as you could easily make out the rosy tips of her nipples poking through the transparent material. To this she had what I could see were wide legged trousers that had a split up the centre of her leg which only stopped at the tops of her thighs.

If there had been a contest for sexiest school teacher, she would have won it hands down. And boy didn't her husband know it!

In fact, she seemed to be the only one he didn't constantly scowl at, only doing so on occasion whenever he deemed her sexually teasing him, which was something she obviously took great pleasure in doing. Like the way she would touch herself in a suggestive way whenever she caught him looking. Or the way she would lick the rim of her bottle after taking a swig, no doubt mimicking the oral act he seemed to ache for. Well, if the shift in his seat or adjusting of his trousers was anything to go by.

I mean, I might have never personally taken part in the sexual act, like most woman my age had, but I wasn't a bloody nun! I watched porn and I masturbated, so I wasn't that naïve as to what went on behind closed doors, or where Lucius' club was concerned, *in plain sight.* Something I was just grateful I wasn't witnessing tonight, seeing as it was closed due to the late hour and a time I was reminded of when I couldn't help the yawn that escaped.

"Are we boring you, human?" Ruto asked with an obvious distaste for me. I was about to open my mouth to respond, making sure to add the word asshole, when I was cut to the chase by Lucius,

"My human is tired and will be in *my bed* before long…you would do well in remembering that, Ruto." His words were like ice as he pronounced me being 'his' with a barely contained snarl of displeasure.

Ruto jerked as he made a scoffing sound but other than that, he wisely remained silent and I was thankful for it. But this was for him as well as me, as I didn't think Lucius would have held back in drawing blood…something I didn't really want to witness. And well, no matter how rude Ruto was to me, I didn't exactly want to see Lucius tearing into a teenage boy, no matter how old he actually was.

Besides, my mind still lingered on his words, being declared as his (which I wasn't) and finding myself in his bed soon (which I also wasn't) wondering at what point his feelings about me switched so firmly? Ever since I had arrived here it had been as if someone had flipped something within him and no matter how much I wanted to, I didn't and wouldn't allow myself to trust it.

"In answer to your question Liessa, its purpose was simple, they wanted to know if the box was now in my possession. I wanted to lead their interest away from Amelia, so I confirmed as much. Which was why two lambs walked away from the slaughter with their lives. But it seems it was also a test," Lucius said making me shiver at the easy way he spoke of death and Clay frowned but not for the same reason,

"A test? Of what, our security or just how easy it was to get you in a car?" Clay asked clearly displeased, as it was obvious he hadn't wanted Lucius to go at all.

"If you believe a handful of humans to be a threat to my being then I fear my rule must be lacking and my reputation slipping," Lucius said in a dangerous tone turning his serious face in challenge to his head of security. But I found it was me that couldn't help but speak up.

"Yeah, well, immortal badass Vamp King or not, you wouldn't put up much of a fight to a bomb strapped under your seat or a bazooka aimed at your head! After all, us lowly humans don't exactly fight fair, but we do fight with what we've got, something you had no idea of when getting in that car!" I snapped before I could stop myself, knowing that the idea of Lucius putting himself in danger like that annoyed me and I wanted to put it down to all the lives he had risked with it. But really, it was his own life I cared for just as much as I cared for my mother's.

I knew I had spoken out without thinking, even if I gained a nod of respect from Clay and more surprisingly, even Ruto, who granted me a brief look of surprise. But it was Lucius' reaction that I was most concerned with. Because he turned to me with eyes hard as the steel colour that circled the pupil, one that was growing smaller with the intensity of his predatory gaze. He looked like an exotic beast about to strike and suddenly my heartrate matched the panic, something I knew was ultimately a smart person's natural response.

Of course, a smart person wouldn't have spoken at all. Because now here I was, caught in his world and unable to escape.

Escape a Vampire King that I had unknowingly just made...

Furious.

CHAPTER TEN

PERFECT LITTLE SUN

His hand tightened at my neck so he could exert his will over me by pulling me towards him. This meant that I had no other option but to move into the position he obviously wanted me, which soon put me having to twist my body and shamefully crawl across his lap. I tried to wriggle free, only his hold on me was unyielding, putting me now face to face with him as I was forced to straddle his lap. I tried to put what space I was allowed between us but the second my back bowed, he wrapped his free arm around my back and pulled me hard against him.

"Lucius, what are you…!"

"Silence!" he snarled and a yelp of mine was soon cut off when his hand inched up my neck and fisted my hair so he could yank my head back. The sting shocked me enough not to fight him. Especially when he placed his lips at my shoulder and kissed his way up my neck. The gentle sensation became a contradiction to the tug of pain on my scalp as his hold on me

was brutal and unyielding. Oh yeah, he was pissed alright and this was nothing short of a warning never to speak to him like that again in front of his people. Because it was one thing to show my sass in private, but this was nothing short of a message, or more like a lesson to be learned.

"Do you think my senses any less than your father's?" he asked, his tone dangerous and calculated. I swallowed hard and purposely held my tongue, not knowing if it was safe to speak.

"Do you not believe me capable of scenting deception or the stench of your kind's cowardly weapons, the scent of explosives or the weakening resolve of humans, knowing they could only accomplish their devious task by forfeiting their lives for nothing but a hope and a pointless prayer?" he questioned making me realise my mistake. A mistake for making my lack of confidence in him only come across as a weakness he thought I believed of him. Not the truth. Not that I was simply worried. He was taking my concern as an insult and nothing more and I had to say, that it hurt.

However, utterly oblivious to this, he continued in a venomous tone that had me wincing, along with the gentle assault he continued up my neck, caressing my tender skin with his lips.

"Did you know what I did with your *vile race* the moment I stepped into their domain...*I made every one of them kneel to me,*" he snarled against my cheek making me close my eyes against his verbal attack.

"With each step I took each mortal fell to their knees like the bringer of death was upon them and it was, for I made them suffer...every single one suffered at my hands...these hands that touch you now, that hold such sweet innocence in my grasp," he said letting go of my hair so he could soothe a hand down before fisting both hands at the opening of his jacket when speaking of what he held. I shuddered beneath such strength when hearing the leather groan, knowing that this was him battling with himself and there was nothing I could do or say to stop him...*or was there?*

"And do you know why they suffered, my sweetness?" he asked me softly, a tenderness I knew not to trust. So, I turned my head away and he used this opportunity to speak directly in my ear,

"Because they tried to make me suffer by taking *you from me*... because their plans involved *you*. To use you, to cause you pain and force you into helping them. To torture your mortal and breakable body until you gave them everything. So, the Hex might have been what killed them, but all before it... well, that my Amelia, *that is why they suffered,*" he said in a dangerously dark voice that spoke only of the death he had enjoyed being a part of. I swallowed hard and then looked at him, before asking quietly,

"Why are you doing this to me?" His eyes sparked like the grey had been set alight for a moment before he replied,

"Because it is what I am, what you have chosen to sit beside," he said in nothing short of a warning for the future, one I shook my head at, because I knew then that this was his way of pushing me away. I winced, hating this side of him and knowing it was time for me to get away from him. I needed to think! But he also needed to know the truth before I did.

"I only said those things because I was worried about you," I told him in a small voice that spoke of my reluctance in admitting it. At this I saw him close his eyes for a moment as he took a shuddered breath, doing so as if he was savouring those words of care and feeling before, well before what he did next which was shatter them,

"Worried for me, *or for your mother?"* At this I gasped and pulled back, something he allowed before I shook my head, telling him silently I couldn't believe he had said that. Yes, of course my mother played a factor here but to use what was nothing short of an admission of how I felt about him and throw it back in my face like that! Well, what came next couldn't have been helped, even if I was in front of his damn council!

I turned away from him and the second he took it for something else, my anger couldn't be contained,

"I thought as much!" He threw at me and I in turn pulled my hand back and went to slap him, only unlike the last time, he caught my hand. Then he growled before yanking me back to him with the hand in his grasp,

"I warned you once before, and now it's time to see where it got you, my little Šemšā," he snarled referring to when I tried to slap him back at the museum after my tour. But unlike then, now he was in his own domain, in front of his own people, and now I was the example to be made of. And the way to do this without actually causing me physical harm was to put me in my place with his greatest weapon against me…*humiliation.*

So, before it had chance to come to fruition, I took control and this time fisted a hand in his hair and slammed my lips over his, lifting myself up over him to do so. Then, just as his hands fisted the material of his own leather jacket, I lowered myself down on him, grinning over what I could feel straining for freedom behind the zipper. He growled in my open mouth before he took control of the kiss just like last time and the second he started to get lost in it, I pulled back enough to whisper over his lips,

"You don't get to humiliate me sexually ever again, you heartless bastard!" Then I tore myself out of his arms before he had chance to react, only to do this I ended up having to scrabble back over the tabletop to get away. Everyone was

clearly shocked by my reaction, but I didn't care, nor did I care when bottles spilled, and glasses smashed to the floor.

I held his stunned gaze long enough to feel liquid soak through my jeans as I crawled backwards through the pool of alcohol on the frosted glass top, but I didn't care. I just continued going until I reached the far end. But the second he made a grab for me, I yanked my ankle just out of reach before I jumped off the other end of the table. Then I ran from the room, already feeling the bitter sting of tears rolling down my cheeks, wincing when I heard the roar of anger coming from both his snarling lips and the sound of the chair being smashed into glass.

But I didn't stop. I simply ripped off his jacket and threw it off in the lobby, not caring where it landed. Then I just ran back to my room, wishing I could have gotten away with just grabbing the bag I had already packed and making a run for it. I needed to be gone from this place. I needed space between us. But even I wasn't stupid enough to believe it would happen this way. Because I knew he wouldn't just let me leave like that. So, I grabbed my bag and threw it angrily inside the closet before I started tearing off my wet, sticky clothes. Then, as I was down to my underwear I walked into the bathroom, slamming the door behind me in my own rage. Angry hot tears still falling in my frustration at both Lucius and myself.

I turned and locked the door to the lavish bathroom that was all white marble walls and grey slate floor. Twin sinks were carved out of a long solid length of marble that rested on top of darker carved stone that matched the slate of the floor. An elegant roll top bath that was black claw footed and big enough to fit four of me inside it. Or just me and one large alpha male who was currently brooding as though his favourite toy had been taken from him.

I shook my head and got that ridiculous thought of the both

of us in there from my wishful mind. Instead, I looked to the large shower that was like a room itself. It was glass fronted with two marble walls that faced each other. But the back wall was faced with a puzzle of uneven slate pieces that framed a jagged glass mirror at the centre. Meaning that you couldn't escape your own image whilst in there, or in my case, my very hopeless and sad image.

It had a concealed panel on the outside that controlled the water, along with other things like temperature, pressure, direction of the water, and even things you didn't need, like change of lights, music or even the choice of a cooling mist. I swear I just wanted a shower not a damn disco!

So, I pressed what had taken me the longest time to figure out as I just wanted water and I wanted it hot enough to steam. Then the second it started to rain down from the ceiling in a large square pattern I unclipped my bra and pushed down my panties, kicking them off to the side. I then yanked the hair tie from a now messy style thanks to being manhandled by Lucius, letting my hair rain down my back. I decided to leave my contacts in, as in my haste and annoyance, didn't think it wise to start clawing at my eyeballs in frustration.

I opened the double doors, (that's how big the shower was) and stepped inside, instantly taking a deep breath the moment the water caressed my skin, heating it instantly.

My mother always used to say that there wasn't anything that couldn't be solved by a good soak in the bath or a relaxing shower. But then again, she was usually joined by my father, so she would say this.

I, on the other hand, was well and truly alone, so I could only think a shower would serve two purposes right now, one was getting me clean and the second was washing away my tears and making them disappear the moment they re-emerged one after the other. Something I could see thanks to the mirror that now showcased a heartbroken girl who felt as if she were simply put there to continually make mistakes. That stupid fancy mirror that wouldn't fog up with the steam, just like the glass doors, so everything remained clear around me. Everything remaining the same, reflecting back the only mess in the room and one trying her best to remain upright and strong. After all, I was a Draven. Dravens didn't just give up and crumble under pressure. No, we stood tall and faced the enemy head on. But then what if you were the enemy...what then?

Because as much as I fought with Lucius, I knew I was fighting with myself just as much. Like now, instead of just grabbing my bag and taking my chances on the run, I had trapped myself in here by my own doing. Believing what, myself safe behind a locked door? Just how stupid was I?! Because a locked door couldn't save me. Not from him. Not from myself. Not from that passionate anger that obviously wasn't done with me from both sides.

This became obvious the second I suddenly heard a door being ripped from its hinges and my teary eyes rose to stare at him through the mirror, now stood panting in the doorway.

His own eyes looked startled at first but quickly darkened as they scanned the length of me. I didn't know what he had expected when barging in but finding me now wet and naked in the shower obviously hadn't been it. But those eyes were drinking me in, from the tips of my toes all the way to my hair that was now plastered back like a dark glossy length of ebony between my shoulder blades.

My wide eyes, a startling blue and ones made glassy through my unshed tears locked onto his that were glowing silver, like molten steel this time, all traces of warm amber lost to something deeper and far more sinister...his lust. Like mine they were framed by a blanket of thick lashes, only unlike his mine were adorned with tiny droplets of water clinging to them like morning mountain dew. I knew from my reflection right then, that I didn't look of this world. I looked as though I belonged to another and all that separated us...separated our worlds was a single pane of clear glass.

But for how long it would, I didn't know, for his gaze was as it had been in the club, that of a predator stalking his victim. His once steely grey eyes now ablaze with the sight of me naked before him and the second he took a step forward I placed my hand on the mirror and shook my head, a silent 'no' from my lips. A desperate plea for him not to do this. Not to give me anything more. Not to add to the mountain of reasons why this was already too difficult to walk away from. Not when all I needed was one good reason for me to leave. Something he had just given me. But by him being here now, well he was either going to add to that reason or he was going to take it away with his touch, destroying my resolve to leave.

But then he made his decision as he ignored my plea and took another step forward, making the sight too much to bear watching. So, I closed my eyes, flinching when I heard the door to the shower open. I kept them closed as I felt the large presence invade my space, seeing his image in my mind's eye, thinking that was enough.

However, *it wasn't enough for him.*

I knew this when I felt his thumb and finger capture my chin, forcing my head back first through the spray of water before my body was pushed back against the cool wall away from the jagged slate.

"Open your eyes and look at me...Look before you, look at what you believe is your fate, my virginal little Princess," he told me making me wince even with my eyes closed as he delivered what sounded like sweet endearments that I knew were nothing more than an insult. One masked and hiding in the shadows of a tender voice and gentle wet leather hand, that he held at my naked hip. But his words felt like a lash against my skin and because of it I tore my face from his hold. Then I opened my eyes and let him see for himself the level of my weakness in my tears but the strength in my determination. Then, even as I felt my tears fall, I looked him up and down and said with my voice unwavering,

"I'm looking." And I was. I took all of him in, now every inch of him with his black t-shirt soaked and clinging to every muscle like a hidden promise of the perfection that lay beneath. A pair of jeans that once dark grey turned to ominous black just like his shirt, making him look even more menacing. And the threat of him was real. The threat of a temptation so great it felt as if it was blazing within me, until with only a single touch and he would know, as my skin burned for him.

At this his eyes scorched with such intensity, I was surprised I even survived it. Then he brushed away my tears tenderly before his hold on me started to change. His hand left my hip and wrapped around my lower back just as his hand left my cheek to push all my wet hair back from my forehead.

He was looking down at me, his hair now the colour of wet Persian sand that was hanging forward with droplets slowly running down the strands. The harsh and handsome lines of his features looked formidable under the spray of the shower, and I found the sight a breathtaking one. Gods, but with just that one look alone it felt as if he had striped me bare, where I was already naked in his arms. And with his next words, it seemed as if I wasn't the only one.

"Curse the Gods, but your beauty has the power to bring a man to his fucking knees!" he told me in a harsh tone as if the sight of me was his weakness. And the moment he started to lower himself to his knees, now that was when I took his words seriously. I sucked in a sharp breath at the sight, asking myself if this was even real!? Surely a man such as Lucius, a King of such power would kneel to no one?!

"No one but you," he told me as if he could hear my thoughts and I would have asked if he could but then his eyes fixated on my bare breasts like a starved man stumbling upon a feast. I gasped the second his hands ran up my sides from where they had framed my waist, their destination clear the moment they each cupped a weighty breast. One of bare skin and the other of wet leather, a combination that made me question my damn sanity because it didn't feel real. Then he ran both thumbs over my hard and waiting nipples, making my head fall back slightly as a moan slipped free.

"I knew your clothes hid even further perfection..." he told me and I opened my mouth to speak yet nothing came out. Just the sight of him soaking wet and on his knees before me was enough to render words useless, for nothing could be said to explain how I was feeling. Especially when his fingers plucked at my nipples and palmed my breasts before they left me simply wanting more. But he had other plans and for those plans he would need his hands. I knew this when he lowered his gaze down to my naked and bare sex, one I'd shamelessly shaved bare ready for him and had continued to do so for years in hopes that one day he would see it. The secret knowledge only managed to heat my skin further.

Until he finally touched me.

Then I really burned.

He ran the backs of two fingers over the soft mound of my sex and I shuddered, my embarrassment was like torture and I wanted so badly to shy away from him. My reaction must have pleased him before he granted me a satisfied look, then he told me,

"You are bare for me... *I am pleased...*" he said making me blush scarlet and hold back the urge to throw an arm over my eyes. Something I was soon to do for other reasons,

"...Now it is time to taste my sweet perfection," he said before dragging his wet t-shirt from over his head making my mouth go dry at the sight of those wet, massive shoulders come into view. I even found myself flinching at the sound of wet material as it slapped the tiled floor.

"Easy, my little Šemšā," he cooed as he ran a gentle hand up the inside of my calf, past my knee and then I sucked in a breath as he caressed my thigh, getting higher and higher. But then before he could reach what I was getting desperate for him to touch he travelled back down again. I shamefully meowed in protest unable to stop the sound which along with my bare sex pleased him also. I could tell this as he looked up at me, a knowing grin playing at the corners of his perfect lips.

Then, without warning, he grabbed my calf in a strong hold and started to lift my leg. This soon became obvious why he did this, as he started to position it over his shoulder, giving me no choice but to go on my tiptoes and flatten my back to the wall just for added support. But the second my legs parted I felt far too vulnerable and open, so started to squirm in his hold. I also placed a hand to his head in panic, telling him,

"I...I...well...I have never..." thus making his eyes turn soft and tender before he told me,

"Good, then death falls upon no man in the name of my jealously, for you are mine...and with it your sweetness." I swallowed hard digesting his words of possessiveness and shook my head trying to make sense of them. But then the second I felt his fingers trail a path down my mound to the centre where I knew I would feel it the most, I jolted causing him to say,

"Don't worry, *my Khuba*, I will take care of you, *just as you will take care of my thirst.*" He whispered this last part as he parted my folds and dove right in, drinking in my lust and tasting the depth of it for himself. And the second his tongue ran up the length of my core and circled that tight bud of nerves, my head fell back as though it was no longer attached.

"Oh Gods!" I shouted on a loud and breathy moan, thinking that such pleasure wasn't really possible! That all these years it had simply been a myth suddenly come to light, doing so in such a way that it nearly blinded me! As if I had unknowingly died at some point and this was not only my Heaven, but a gift I had somehow deserved from the Gods. Of course I had touched myself over the years but this…this was something else entirely. The way he sucked me in and let me go so his tongue could go right back to teasing me again was near torturous and sending me out of my mind. I even found myself clawing at the back of the wall just for something to hold onto but there was nothing there.

"Fucking Heaven! You taste like the Gods be damned elixir of life!" he growled before he was once more moaning against my sensitive flesh in between lapping me up as though he was quickly getting addicted to my taste. Gods, but the thought of him loving the flavour of my sex was just as intoxicating as the feeling of him devouring it. But then he shifted his hand, no longer holding me still to the wall in favour of drawing two fingers up through my dripping core. I jolted in his hold and he growled over my abused clit when I backed away from his onslaught of sensation.

Needless to say, he didn't like this much.

"Be still, now!" he ordered roughly, a command that was near impossible as I couldn't help but quake. Not as I felt my release building like a storm and one gaining strength as if it ripped its way through the earth. But he allowed me these little movements which told me his earlier complaint was in fear of me taking his meal away from him for good. Not something he would allow.

However, the second he gathered up my dripping arousal, coating his bare fingers in it, I knew what was coming before it happened. But even so, a gasp of pleasure tore through me the moment he pushed his fingers inside me that had me coming in seconds. I cried out, screaming my release as he both fingered me and bit down on my clit at the same time.

"Lucius, Lucius, Lucius!" I cried out his name over and over asking, no begging him for something I couldn't understand. Maybe it was for him to take me, to exchange his fingers for something else?! Or was it to stop him, as his continued assault on my nerves was getting far too intense the longer he carried on. But it was as though he didn't want to stop and because of this, the second he flicked his tongue over my clit again I was now grabbing a fist full of his hair to hold him to me as I rode out another orgasm, trying to slam my hips down on his fingers.

"Ahh...Fuck yes! Yes, yes, Gods yes!" I screamed as my hips bucked against his face and my insides milked his fingers, keeping them captive and drawing them further inside my core. However, I knew that he was holding himself back, not giving me their full length for a reason.

"Take care, sweetheart, for when I finally break you, I do so with your virginal blood coating my cock..." I sucked in a startled breath at both his filthy hot words and the way a leather hand now gripped my ass, yanking me forward and closer to his face so he could growl at me,

"...and I can't fucking wait!" Then suddenly, as if hitting his own limit, I felt his fangs lengthening dangerously but before I could do a thing to stop him, he suddenly decided to turn this meal of his as bloody as his thoughts were.

"AAAHHH!" I screamed as this time the last orgasm that

ripped through me felt as though it had the power to destroy me! It was unlike the other two but double, even triple the intensity! It had my knees buckling and suddenly his hands came up to hold my waist, keeping me upright until he had finished his feast.

I felt him sucking in my blood around my painful clit, but with each tug, I felt my body spasm as another zap of pleasure fired my nerves like a live wire of electricity. It was only when he felt me going limp in his arms that I felt his fangs retract with a pop. After that he licked at me, no doubt trying to heal the tear in my flesh and lapping up the last of his meal.

Then he laid a soft and tender kiss over the abused flesh before gently placing my limp leg from over his shoulder back to the wet shower floor. After this he rose back to his full height in a graceful way yet still continued to hold onto me so I wouldn't fall. I felt and looked like a limp wet flower battered from the storm that was Lucius.

Once he was looking down at me from his usual height he took more of my weight in only one arm as it snaked around me. This allowed him a free hand to brush back my hair so he could kiss my forehead, tasting the beads of salty sweat for himself.

"You were utter perfection, sweetness," he whispered, gently praising me as he rested my head against his shoulder, knowing that my body was utterly spent of energy and no wonder, from the three most intense orgasms of my life and added blood loss.

"Now let me care for you, my little Šemšā," he said picking me up and turning us both so the water now showered down my back and all around us. Then I felt a soapy hand start to wash me, but I could feel myself falling down the rabbit hole that Lucius had purposely pushed me down. Quickly getting lost in his tender touch and losing all sense of reality to it. However, there was one thing I wanted to know before I gave in to unconsciousness.

"What is a Šemšā?" I asked in a voice that spoke of how close I was to sleep. He murmured softly in a different language into my hair as if speaking to himself first,

Before he then told me...

"It is you, *my little sun."*

CHAPTER ELEVEN

LUCIUS KNOWS

I *was his sun.*

This was all my mind seemed to fixate on. Which meant that those memories took me back to two very different points in my life. Both of which were two firsts for me. But thinking back to all those years ago came at a price. Because it was when I first came here and he cruelly turned me away, only to end the night by saving my life. I had been in his arms after the brutal attack, barely conscious. He had been speaking to someone else, a voice I now knew belonged to Ruto at the time. I had been safely tucked away in his hold and the moment I started to stir he cooed down at me,

'Ssshh now and sleep, my girl.' Then just as Ruto had started to speak Lucius interrupted quickly,

'We will speak of what is to be done later for she is restless and listening...isn't that right, my little royal Šemšā?' Lucius had whispered down at me, humming the foreign word and one that at the time I didn't understand. Then I had fallen back to sleep to the feel of Lucius' gentle hand stroking my hair and him

holding my hand as if I was something precious to him. Something the next time I woke I had convinced myself had all been a dream, for it wouldn't have made sense to me considering the agony I then had no choice but to endure at his words.

But now I knew the truth.

Just as I did when thinking back to the other first, when seeing him again all those years later. It had been the night of the gala, after concluding my private tour and this time when he had called me it, it felt more done so in mockery. Because it was when I tried to slap him after he had warned me,

'Nasty? Oh, sweetheart, you have no fucking idea.' But like tonight, he had caught it before contact was made and snarled the same warning at me,

'Try that again and see where it gets you, my little Šemšā.' Well now I knew where it got me and that was quaking and shuddering in the shower before passing out after the greatest orgasms of my life. A time that stole my breath along with the ability to remain standing.

But if this had been his secret name for me, then did that mean that I had always meant something to him? And if so, then did it just mean he had spent nearly half my lifetime denying it? Hiding from it or simply just ashamed? And if he did, then the most burning question now on my mind was the one that felt like acid on my tongue…

What of my mother?

Was this the reason he was torn, denying me all these years because he sickeningly loved us both? Gods, but the thought was a torturous one! Which made me now question the other name he had called me, what did Khuba mean? A name he had only said twice and both times since I had been here. Did it mean something more?

"That no longer looks like a peaceful sleep, sweetness." The moment I heard his voice I opened my eyes to find myself lying on my side facing him. He had one arm under my head and the other lay casually over me with his fingers creating lazy circles on the small of my back. Oh, and I was still naked. My eyes widened the second I realised this, and I quickly grabbed the sheet that I felt gathered at my thighs, yanking it up to my neck, covering us both.

At this he threw his head back and let out a throaty laugh, one that had me near hypnotized it was that rare a sight. By the Gods but it was beautiful, so much so it blinded me to the rest of the world around us.

There was only Lucius.

Only this man of my dreams.

"I think it's a little late for modesty, Amelia," he said, the humour still coating his words along with giving his usual broody features a light and easiness to them. Adorable little creases by his eyes and a boyish smile that for once didn't speak of violence or death. Gods, but like this he looked years younger and more human. Especially seeing as he too was gloriously naked and in my bed.

"I must be dreaming," I whispered before I had chance to stop it, because this couldn't possibly be real. Lucius wouldn't have allowed such a reality...*would he?* No, he was probably still brooding and destroying furniture in some kind of Supernatural overlord man paddy!

"Then I am blessed, for we dream the same dream," he told me softly before he left my back and instead took one of my hands in his so he could bring it up to his lips to kiss. My eyes widened at both his gentle touch and his tender words, the type of words I had yearned to hear most of my life from him. Oh yes, it was a dream indeed.

"So that really happened?" I asked feeling myself getting

hot as flashes of what we did came back to me...or should I say, *what he did.*

"Gods, but I hope so or that damned box has claimed my life sooner than I would like and Heaven must certainly be a forgiving place," he said winking at me, and I pulled from his hold, rolling to my back and throwing an arm over my eyes. Then I groaned as my embarrassment soared to new heights making him chuckle.

"I don't...I mean I have never...you know," I said stumbling on my words and still hiding myself from him, something he didn't allow for long as I felt my arm being forcefully removed from my eyes. Then he turned my face to look back at him by cupping my cheek.

"Yes, I got that, sweetheart." At this my cheeks burned even more, and I wanted to bite my fingertips so badly.

"So, now you know," I said, the shame written all over my face as up until now I had assumed he had just always called me a virgin to be cruel or mean. His features softened and he caressed down my cheek to my neck, running his fingertips tantalisingly over my collarbone.

"I have always known, Amelia," he confessed in a gentle yet knowing way. But despite how tender it sounded, I couldn't help but frown in question, one I didn't need to ask because there was only one question to a statement like that...*how?*

He released a sigh and ran a hand through his now dry hair. Then he admitted,

"Having you watched isn't just a recent order I issued," he said surprising me. At this I grabbed hold of the sheets, shifting to give myself space from him so I could sit up. Then I shook my head trying in vain to find the answers myself but coming up empty.

"But why? Why would you even bother...you don't even like me?!" I said, even realising myself how stupid this last sentence sounded. But even more so when he laughed once without humour before nodding down to himself and saying,

"Does this look as though I don't like you, sweetheart?" I allowed my eyes to trail the length of him only to find the proof he was indicating, which was the impressive sized tent his obvious manhood was making under the sheet. This time when I blushed it no doubt looked like someone had smushed strawberries into my cheeks!

"But...but..."

"There is still a lot you don't yet know, Amelia, and for the moment it will remain so." I frowned at this and jerked back a little as if he'd struck me.

"Are you joking?!" I snapped making him frown back at me but remain quiet.

"Even after what we did in there, you still think what exactly, that I am not ready?!" I shrieked in annoyance and disbelief.

"You're not," he stated bluntly.

"Bullshit!" I shouted back wondering why it was that we always ended up back in this place. The wrong way around, the storm after the calm.

I shifted off the bed dragging the sheet with me but in doing so it left Lucius as naked as...well, as the day he was born...*twice over.* But of course, my eyes homed straight on in there, unable to help myself. My eyes went impossibly wide and shot to his, noting that self-assured bad boy grin along with a cocky raise of a single brow. But I was unable to stop the first thing from blurting out of my stupid, stupid mouth!

"Holy shit, you're huge!" Then I slapped both hands over my mouth forgetting about my sheet which fell to the floor. Gods, but could this moment get any worse! I screeched and quickly bent to pick it up but ended up tripping over it instead and sacked it to the floor with an ungraceful 'Umpf' sound.

Meaning that I ended half wrapped up at the end of the bed with an arm thrown over my eyes wishing, no *praying,* to every damn God out there for some emergency to make him suddenly bolt from the room. That or the earth would swallow me whole and I found myself quickly visiting my grandad in Hell. Oh, and I should probably mention at this point that doing so naked wouldn't have exactly been weird or out of place in my Grandad's realm. Not seeing as he was the President of Lust in Hell. He was also like a dirty, but admittedly, handsome older man, who kind of looked strangely like my father but in his fifties. But then he told me once that he did this just because he liked pissing off my dad, making me laugh.

Needless to say, my parents preferred I didn't see him too much.

But even that awkwardness would have been a picnic compared to right now. Especially when I peeked a look and saw that Lucius had shifted on the bed. He was now lying on his front, and had his face rested in his palm with his elbow to the bed, looking down at me over the edge. Then with his other hand he started plucking playfully at the sheet that covered my breasts.

"Now I have to say, that was quite a show," he said in a teasing tone and I lifted my arm to shoot him a deadly look and tried to ignore how handsome he looked when trying not to smile.

"Shut it, Vampy," I said making him chuckle.

"I do feel inclined to ask what my punishment would be should I choose not to give in to your demands," he asked, and again in a teasing and even playful tone.

"By asking that question is you *not* giving in to my demands," I reminded him without looking but snatching the sheet from his fingers as I felt it starting to be pulled slowly from my breasts. He chuckled again.

"Then by all means, dear girl, punish away," he said in a cocky tone.

"I could slap you again and see where it gets me... as at least I know one in every five make it through," I commented sarcastically.

"Oh, I agree. In fact, I am starting to like where it gets *me,*" he said and I glanced a look at him to see he was now looking hungrily at where he had not long ago been feasting on. I felt myself getting hot and bothered just thinking back to it.

"Don't count on it, buddy!" I commented even though I was pretty sure at this point my libido wanted to bitch slap me for even speaking such blasphemy. At this he laughed in a knowing way that called my bullshit without needing to say the words.

"So, are you planning on staying down there much longer?" he asked coolly and I felt him once again start playing with the sheet, this time at my belly.

"For the foreseeable future, yes," I answered unable to keep my lips from twitching as I forced down the grin.

"Very well, I see I will have to take matters into my own hands."

"Wait what!? Ahhh!" I shouted the second the sheet was fisted in his hand and then pulled from me, leaving me naked on the floor. So, I quickly jumped up and lunged for him on the bed, trying to wrestle the damn sheet from his hands, even though my wobbly bits (mainly my breasts and ass cheeks) were dancing everywhere and most definitely on show.

We ended up in some kind of tug of war which he most definitely could have won but obviously playing this game was far more entertaining for him than claiming victory. Or who knows, maybe this was *his* idea of a victory, as we were no longer arguing about the mountain of answers he refused to give me.

But by the end, none of it mattered to me, not in this

moment. One so perfect I felt as if I were soon to burst with happiness. A smile big enough it ached and my chest heaved from laughing so hard. His hands snaked out and tickled my naked skin, gently pinching at me whenever he saw an opportunity to try and make me drop my side of the sheet. I would slap his hand away trying to be stern, but my scowl was tainted by joy and he knew it as his eyes heated to honey amber.

But then there was a knock on the door and the second my eyes shot there he took his opportunity whilst I wasn't looking. He grabbed my ankle and yanked me hard so I fell backwards from my crouch position before he dragged me towards him. Then he landed on top of me, holding his weight so as not to crush me but covering me all the same. And before he even acknowledged the door, he kissed my nose and told me,

"You lose." Then he shifted his gaze to the door and as if someone had flipped that switch again, he snarled,

"And if anyone walks through that fucking door right now, I will redecorate this room with their blood!" And yep, there it was, my crazy bloodthirsty Vamp king was back, and I shuddered beneath him. Something he felt for he lowered himself enough to coo in my ear,

"Ssshh, be still."

"I will wait." The sound of Clay's voice said through the door with a slight knowing chuckle.

"Let me guess, duty calls?" I said in a breathless tone and not solely down to our tussle.

"That depends, are you going to slap me if I say yes?" he said in a hopeful tone making me giggle before asking,

"Do you want me to slap you?" His answer came after he first placed his forehead to mine,

"Most definitely," he said on a growl that turned me on to the point close to panting, as it was quickly becoming our thing. As it was clear that it was starting to mean something lustful

was sure to follow and let's face it, just how hard could a slap from me to Lucius be? However, I couldn't resist teasing him just a little as I snaked a hand up between us and tapped him on his cheek in a playful way, making him smirk. Then I asked in a cheeky tone,

"What's that one worth?" I could see the grin on his lips grow as he held back a laugh. Then he shook his head a little as if asking himself if I were even real or not. Doing so before he lowered himself close enough so he could kiss me and when he did, it was slow and soft and above all, gentle. More like the morning kiss granted from a lover and one that said goodbye for the day.

But because I didn't want it to end, I reached up and gripped on to the back of his neck, one hand entwining my fingers in his hair as I held him to me so I could deepen it. I was overjoyed when he let me and basked in my victory for a delicious minute before he pulled back and growled out a soft warning,

"Behave, my beauty." Then he snapped his teeth at me playfully. After this he got out of bed and I was happy to see that I wasn't the only one who looked reluctant to let the other go. I released a sigh as he disappeared inside my closet, obviously having clothes in there himself for this very purpose…wow, cocky much? Wasn't that like making sure that you had a condom in your wallet before leaving for a first date?

Oh, who was I kidding, for a man like Lucius, of course at some point I would have become a sure thing. Either way the thought irked me. But then he walked out of the closet wearing a fresh pair of dark jeans and a long-sleeved T in a dark maroon colour, a sexy sight that had me taking a breath.

I got up onto my knees, still holding the sheet to my breasts and couldn't help but tease him one last time just as he reached for the door.

"Wow I must say, I can't wait to see what will happen when

I go all the way and punch you," I quipped making him pause just as he had opened the door a crack, before he lowered his head and shook it slightly.

"Ah fuck it!" he barked, hitting the door closed with the side of his fist before he turned on a heel. He was by the side of the bed in a second, hooking me behind my head, fist in my hair and pulling me the short distance to his lips as he lowered his head to mine.

This time when he kissed me, by the Gods it was all consuming! It wasn't soft, it wasn't gentle and there wasn't an ounce of tenderness or playfulness to be found. It was rough, it was hard and holy shit did it turn me on, especially when he tore his lips from mine and ripped the sheet from in between us. Then he pulled my head back so I was looking directly up at the ceiling as he started to bite, suck and lick down my taut neck before he then used a free hand to lift up a breast to his ravenous mouth.

Once there he sucked in my nipple deep and held it between his teeth. I released a guttural moan as if it was being torn out of me by the Devil himself. Then I felt his teeth grind down and the pain bloomed like the Devil's flower into a sizzling pleasure that nearly had me coming undone in his arms. He rolled the abused little bud in between his teeth and I cried out just on the verge of both stopping him and begging him for more. Just as he then soothed away the hurt with his tongue, circling it and sucking hard.

But it was when he felt his own fangs started to extend that he knew if he continued, he would only end up feeding from me again, and who knows, maybe more. Something he was obviously not ready for yet as he pulled back, letting me go with an audible pop.

Then with one last lick, he let go of my hair and he looked up at me, his lips still close enough to my breast I thought he would go back for more. And as I looked down at him, I don't think there was a sexier sight in all my life, other than the one of him on his knees making a meal of me in the shower.

But it lasted only seconds as he rose back up to full height and licked his lips slowly, leaving me with the need to rub my thighs together in frustration. Especially as now I was so turned on it was hard to even concentrate on his face any longer. And the bastard knew it as his grin said it all. Then, before I could even open my mouth to complain at him leaving me all hot and bothered without release, he suddenly gripped my throat.

I gasped in his hold, but he wasn't hurting me, no it was done in a possessive and commanding way that told me he demanded my attention. Then he got close to my face, captured my eyes and told me sternly,

"You are not permitted to touch yourself, do you understand?" My mouth dropped open in horror and shock...*was he serious?!*

"I..."

"You. Will. Not." he said cutting me off before he pulled me forward with his hold still on my throat and this time the kiss he gave me was most definitely one of goodbye. Then he let go and I was left kneeling on the bed, the sheet pooled around my legs, top half of me naked and I was panting with a stunned look on my face.

"And Amelia..." He said my name and I numbly turned to look at him waiting by the door. I didn't reply just waited for my shocked state to be complete as he gave me a word of warning,

"If you do..." he paused, his eyes flashing amber before he said,

"...I will know."

CHAPTER TWELVE

ESCAPE PLAN

It was little wonder that after this demand of his I tossed and turned, kept just on the cusp of sleep. But it wasn't only because I was turned on and too afraid to take the chance and disobey Lucius by doing the finger flicking deed. Even if admittedly my hand snaked down the sheet quite a few times during my time trying to sleep. No, but it was also as I replayed the night's events back in my head. Lucius was quite possibly the most changeable person I had ever known and he just so happened to be the one person I was intent on being obsessed with…damn him!

When back in his club, I had started to ask myself where I had gone wrong. Okay, so I knew when, it was doubting his abilities to survive. Something he quickly proved to be a simple situation for a powerful being like him. But looking back now and it seemed as if it was more than just a simple wounding to his pride or ego. And I was determined to find out what.

Which was why I got up and dressed, forgoing the shower, especially seeing that it became clear Lucius had actually taken the time to wash my body and also my hair. Oh, after I had passed out on him first of course. I could only imagine that this had been a feat in itself and I blushed just thinking about it.

I looked at myself in the mirror and for once I looked a little pale and wondered if being with Lucius, I would need to invest in a bulk order of iron tablets or something. I brushed the many knots from my hair because let's face it, washing my hair was about as far as it was going to go with Lucius, as I couldn't see him then plugging in a hairdryer and going the full hog in styling it too.

Meaning that now my hair had some wicked kinks in it, and I am not talking the naughty kind. So, I tried to tame it back the best I could into a hair tie, putting it into a messy knot. Now dressed in a pair of soft chocolate brown cords, I added a big roll neck knitted sweater with cute bell sleeves. The look was a bit seventies meets winter chic, but I thought it went well with my dark hair and olive skin. I then made sure to wear a little navy blue cami-vest underneath just in case I got too hot, as I hated that.

Once I was ready, I went in search of Lucius, stopping short the second I saw my kitchen counter had been laid with a small buffet of food. The second I saw it, my stomach rumbled and I thought back asking myself when was the last time I had eaten anything? Well, if you couldn't remember then the answer was too damn long ago.

I also found a note by the jug of orange juice that made me grin and feel strangely giddy, like one of those ridiculously happy 'in love saps' you wanted to slap silly telling them to get a grip.

It read,

I would like you to eat,
your belly rumbling sounded

like an angry bear...
A cute one.
See you later beautiful x

P.S... Good Girl ;)

I think my mouth dropped at just the thought of Lucius drawing a little wink face in such elegant script, but his words made me feel all warm inside. So, I sat and ate and as I did, I thought about all that was Lucius. I thought about the change in him, a new side I never expected to see in Lucius, he could be tender, soft and gentle along with carefree and playful. Gods, but I didn't know which side I was attracted to more, the masterful ruler who seemed utterly cutthroat and merciless or the one he seemed to reserve just for me. Making me question if he had ever been with a woman like me before. One he could just sit and watched TV with, or play fight on the bed over the covers? Something told me no and I had to admit I freaking loved the idea that I could be a first for him, as much as he was for me.

But then I thought about his gloved hand and what had happened for him to feel the need to keep it covered. I also asked myself why he had spent so many years pushing me away when it was now becoming clear he did so against his heart. But then the biggest question of all, did I really think that in that heart he held love for me?

Well, that was as they say, the million-dollar question.

Did Lucius love me?

In all honesty, I didn't know but I think it was clear that he certainly cared for me, enough to feel possessive over me that was for sure. But was it enough for me to chance staying? He had admitted to having me followed in the past and really, I wanted to know the extent of that. Especially seeing as right now, my naïve view of what I thought was an independent life was a bit of a sore spot for me. What with my father's interference in that and basically discovering everything I thought about my life was a lie.

So yeah, the idea of Lucius having me followed close enough to know that I was still a virgin was a big no, no for me. Talk about hard limits, I mean what did he do, put an ad out for stalkers for hire? I shook my head after ripping off a piece of freshly baked bread and dipping it into some kind of stew that was delicious.

But then I asked myself what would have happened had I met someone, and I mean someone more serious than Peter. Would he have intervened? Would he have stepped in and stopped it before it had chance to fully begin? I started to think back to the few dates I'd had wondering why none of them had ever called back for a second. Hell, but some had even cancelled before we had even managed to go out, never to call again. Not that I had been too bothered at the time, as apart from Peter, I hadn't really been with anyone long enough to even claim to have a boyfriend and even then, the title sounded too committal to say aloud.

But it did at least get me thinking whether or not Lucius had something to do with it. I had to admit, that as annoyed as I was at the idea, I was also secretly a little excited by the idea. Excited by the thought that his jealousness and possessiveness towards me had in fact started years ago, as confusing as that thought was to fathom.

Gods, but men thought women were complicated and sometimes came with emotional baggage! Well, Lucius had nothing on those types of women! But thinking all of this just made me stuff the last of the bread in my mouth before getting up and finishing the rest of my juice. I looked outside to see that it was getting late, as by the time I had gotten ready, most of the day had already come and gone. Wow, a few more long nights like that last one and I would soon be on Lucius' time, even though the light didn't affect him, something not all Vampires could claim.

But like most supernaturals, I had learned pretty quickly that growing up surrounded by them if you wanted to join in, it was a nocturnal kind of gig. Hence being left out a lot as a child. I remember how many times I would end up sneaking into the club after my bedtime and if my mum wasn't around then my dad would always give in and let me sit on his lap until I fell asleep. Oh, he knew he would get in trouble with my mum, but he didn't seem to mind that either. Well, now I was older I knew why this was, as what did they say…there was nothing like makeup sex. Not that this thought wasn't a 'eww' one for me as let's face it, as great as it was my parents loving each other and all, but no daughter wanted to think of her parents doing it…as in, EVER.

So, sneaking into things like parties and such was something I did often, unable to wait until the day I could dress up as pretty as my mum. My mum who I'd always known as being a queen, meaning I knew I had also been a princess and well, all I wanted growing up was the chance to finally dance with a handsome prince.

But it never happened like that.

Not once.

Oh, as I got older I was allowed to join in but by that time came, it was too late, I had already felt as though I didn't belong. No, instead I craved a different type of social life and it was the one with my own kind. But then I wasn't allowed to go to these either, because it just wasn't safe. Needless to say, I led a very sheltered life and felt as though I was living in a gilded cage, one that the second I was old enough I thought I had broken free from. Which was why finding out that I was still caged, just by the invisible bars my father had built around me, was a huge sore spot for me.

But even when I thought I was free, I still craved the night. With true bred Vampires, the light wasn't an option but with the powerful hybrids that Lucius changed, then it just depended on what they had started out as.

At one time I was told that Lucius didn't like the daylight but why this changed I was unsure…like most things to do with Lucius, I was now the one in the dark. And to be honest, I wasn't sure just how long I could cope with being forced to stay there.

Which was why I started to make my way to Lucius' apartment, hoping that he was there and I didn't have to go looking for him inside his club. I couldn't lie to myself, I just wanted to see him again. But when I knocked there was no answer, so I tried the handle finding it unlocked, telling me that he might have been inside in the shower, or something.

So, I walked inside thinking that after what we had done not long ago, then would he really mind me invading his personal space? I hated that I was unsure, when really after the bathroom then I shouldn't have been. But the truth was that when it came to Lucius, I never seemed to have a clue on what to do or how to act, not knowing what reaction I would get in return. And besides, I knew that we should have been working on the box trying to find a solution to the 'supernatural vampire race' sized problem we had on our hands. And when I say solve a problem, I meant it in a way that was more than just getting into some random car and bringing mortals to their knees with just a thought…oh yeah, before they all melted from the inside out before becoming a puddle of human goo.

Eww and Eww again.

But it was a problem that seemed to have somehow taken a backburner and remained in the background as our strained and strange relation took centre stage. But it was a problem that didn't seem to concern him as much as I thought it should. And I had to ask myself was it simply due to being overconfident, or did he know something I didn't? Well, being in his room now was a sure way to find out wasn't it?

But then I thought back to when he had caught me yesterday when I had been about to take the box to hide it. I'd had the right idea then, well maybe now it was another option. Because I couldn't help but feel as if something bigger was going on right now and sacrificing humans was just the beginning. After all, the plot made for the best movies and was simply named misdirection by causing a big hoo-ha over in one corner, whilst the real crime was happening where you least expected it.

Was that what the bad guys were doing now?

I checked that the apartment was empty and walked into Lucius' closet hoping this time I would have more success. So, now knowing how, I opened up his vault room and stepped inside, walking straight over to where the box was situated. Of course, I also now knew the right protocols and waved a hand over the hidden sensor before attempting to remove anything, which was where I had failed the first time. But really, no amount of Bond movie binge watching was going to prepare me for shit like this.

However, I still kind of wished I had a bag of sand to exchange for it just like I did the first time. Only now it was more in a 'so as I could badass Indy style just for once in my life' type of way, even if Mission Impossible would have been a better fit in a room like this. Because, really, all glass and chrome was about as far away from the 'Peruvian jungle' as you could get. Yes, I knew which jungle it was because well, I kind of based my whole future career on those three movies...not the fourth though, because well, that was pants.

"Gods Fae, get a grip, girl," I said to myself before picking up the box and taking all of about two seconds to discover the problem, meaning that by the time I walked out with it, I was swearing,

"Lucius, you son of a…ah!" My curse ended with me tripping over the slight step by the vault door and catapulting myself into the railing opposite. I ended up landing inside a mountain of suits but I did however manage to hold back the box like a rugby ball and put a hand out to brace myself.

"What the…?" I left the question hanging there in the air like a broken speech bubble, when I felt a section of the wall give way in my hand, knowing that I had stumbled across something. So, I shuffled the material out of the way, seeing now a secret panel had popped open, revealing a more traditional looking safe in the wall. I looked behind me to check I wasn't being watched and went back to the safe, thinking it couldn't hurt. So, I turned the dials to my birthday, expecting to hear the click.

Turned out that this time,

It wasn't my birthday.

———————

Twenty frustrating minutes later and everything was back to where it should be, and I was once again moving through his apartment intent on finding him and giving up on him coming back here. But then I heard the loud beeping of a horn outside and got curious. So, just like last night, I walked over to his window and saw for myself Lucius was once again being escorted into yet another car. However, this time it was one that was blacked out and a lot more expensive. I knew this because I had been brought up a rich kid and had been driven around in enough luxury vehicles to know every make and model.

But then again, my dad was a car buff, so it was a given. Of course, he also collected weapons, so sadly I also knew the difference between a claymore and a bastard sword, and a mace and a flail. Oh, and I also had a replica bat'leth hanging on my old childhood bedroom wall at home. But then the Klingon weapon hung between two Star Wars' lightsabres, which I am pretty sure could get me a whole number of death threats in the geek community. I didn't care though, as I thought it looked cool when lying on my bed looking up at the way the red and blue lights reflected off the polished metal in between.

Of course, my dad had also made sure the thing had been practically welded to my wall so there was no chance of it accidently falling during the night and chopping my head off. His paranoid words not mine.

But then again, it wasn't surprising really, as he was known to be a bit overprotective, my dad. The thought sent an ache in my chest as I thought about how he must be feeling right now and half of me wanted to just put him out of his misery. I mean, my mum must have given him hell over it by now, as I very much doubted she knew the level of intrusion my dad had gone to and all in the name of my safety.

I could hear his argument at me now, 'just you wait until you have kids, then you will understand our worry'. I scoffed aloud just thinking about it. Well, if that conversation ever did happen, then my reply would be the conversation killer of all conversation killers,

'Right, so I am free to just go and have sex with someone and make babies, yeah dad?'.

Oh yeah, 'cause I was sure that would have gone down well, because I was sure that to my dad I was still five years old asking for a Star Wars' band aid every time I got a 'bang bang' as I used to call it. Of course, this was because my aunty Pip always used to let me watch all the action movies I wanted. Meaning every time someone looked hurt and in need of a bloody big band aid, then it usually happened after the 'bang bang' of bullets ripping through them. Did I happen to mention that my childhood was an unusual one.

But enough of that, the main question now was what the hell was Lucius doing by getting into another car, and this time a Maybach? I saw him nod at his men telling them to stay back and this time even though something told me he knew I was up here watching him like the first time, he purposely didn't look. I had to say it hurt, but then I quickly tried to convince myself it was to protect me in some way.

"What are you playing at, Lucius?" I asked aloud as the door shut behind him and the car pulled away. I didn't know what it was, but this time, I had a really bad feeling that he was walking into a trap. What if the first time he went willingly was just to lead him into a false sense of security? What if this time when he got to his destination it was to a room full of powerful supernaturals that all wanted to bring him down?

After all, Lucius wasn't as invincible as he liked to believe, the ancient text on the side of that box told me that. And even though I still didn't know exactly what was inside it, I knew that it held the key to his destruction in one way or another. I just hadn't figured out all the details yet.

No, something bad was going down, I just felt it. But I also knew that none of his people would act against his orders and it was clear what they had been ordered to do. Diddly shit that's what! Well, that left only one person crazy enough to go against him and I wasn't about to just let him walk into a trap. At least if I got my proof somehow then I could call in the cavalry. Now I just needed to write down that licence plate quickly and then ring a friend who had the right connections for tracing the address the vehicle was registered to. Thank you very much, Wendy.

I also had to hope that it was going to the address or I was hitting my first hurdle after a simple taxi ride. So, I raced back into my apartment to grab my phone, coming up short the second I saw the massive bunch of flowers now sat in the centre of the coffee table. When did they get there? Was it when I was in the vault? Were they from Lucius?

But then if they were, it was the colour that struck me to a dead stop...*light pink*.

I frowned, wondering if I was thinking too much into it and walked dumbly towards the large bouquet sat in a vase of black glass. Then finding the note I plucked it from the holder and read it.

'Beauty in exchange for beauty and I thought the colour of innocence wouldn't be lost on you.
Now don't disappoint me and let them die,
Luc x'

I realised my frown had deepened significantly because everything about this message was wrong. For starters I never called Lucius 'Luc' nor had he ever indicated that I should, even though I knew some of his people did, like Pip always referred to him as such. But the most obvious part was the colour of the rose, as he stated it was to represent innocence, but I knew it didn't. Was he making a point, like a hidden message? Because a white rose meant innocence and pale pink, well that only meant one thing...

Sympathy.

"Oh Gods," I uttered, covering my mouth with a hand knowing that my feeling had been right, something was very wrong here. But then I read the last line, telling me not to let them die...did he mean not to let him die? Did he mean for me to do something?

"Damn it, think Fae!" I scolded myself with a childish stamp of my foot, done out of frustration.

"Come on, I am supposed to be the smart...wait!" I suddenly grabbed the vase and ran towards the kitchen, having a thought. He told me not to let them die, well that meant adding water, which strangely the vase was lacking. Obviously, whoever brought it up here didn't think too much about it and neither would the person who delivered it. But then again, if you read the card, even that wouldn't tip you off unless you were already suspicious, which I was. So, I quickly turned on the tap and filled the vase waiting for something to happen. However, it was when the water started to hit the bottom that I could see it wasn't black glass there, it was just black paint and the water was now washing it off.

So, I dumped all the flowers into the sink and swirled around the water so it took away more of the paint, revealing words beneath etched in the glass.

'Staircase.
Backdoor 18.06pm
Alleyway'

"Oh shit!" I shouted quickly looking to the clock to see it was nearing four minutes past six! I then quickly dropped the vase in the sink and ran out the apartment with little thought of anything else but that secret message. So, I quickly scanned the lobby seeing it was empty and ran for the staircase taking it down to the bottom getting there just in time. I knew this was my signal to run as an alarm started blaring throughout the whole building before I had even touched the back door, the same one I had used when I first arrived.

This told me that someone had tripped the alarm somewhere else, meaning they wouldn't suspect anything until it was too late. They had obviously missed me on the security cameras too, making me wonder exactly what it was they had their hands full of.

Well, either way it meant I opened the door without it alerting people and ran around the building, back to the cut in the fence leading to the alleyway and basically retracing my steps that brought me here less than a week ago. I squeezed myself through the fence, cursing the sweater I wore the second the wool snagged on the wire, needing first to unhook it before I could go any further. Then I saw a car pull up just outside the entrance to the alleyway and I held back at first hoping this wasn't a trap. But then I saw the window go down and my mouth dropped open when I saw the Oracle waving frantically at me to hurry up.

So, I took a chance and ran for it.

"You know we really need to stop meeting this way, now get in Bitch, we gotta go!" she said, looking like her usually sexy badass self.

"Bess! What are you…"

"You remember last time we did this?" she asked cutting me off as she ground the car into gear.

"Erm yeah, why… whoa!" I ended shouting as she skidded the car around the tight space before speeding the little car out of there.

"Then hold on!" she said changing gear and not needing to remind me that she was crazy behind a wheel. We went speeding quickly past the front of the club and I now saw what it was that had caused the security to concentrate all their attention on the front of the club. As now there was a car on fire smashed into the wall, with a crumbled front end and pieces of the stone building in rubble around it. Oh shit, Lucius was going to be pissed and I didn't just mean about the mess to his building.

"Did you do that?" I asked grabbing hold of the handle above the door as she took a corner using her handbrake. Gods, but where did this chick learn to drive!?

"Yeah, I did that," she said with a smirk as if destruction was her middle name. Well, she was most certainly different from the first Oracle my mum had talked about, that was for damn sure!

"And you sent the flowers?" I asked the obvious, which was exactly what her raised brow told me but still she said,

"I had them delivered and knew Liessa would take them to your room thinking they were from your favourite Vamp, she's a sucker for romance that one," she said making me feel bad for her, as I just hoped she wouldn't end up getting into trouble for it.

"You two do it yet?" she asked suddenly, making me screech a,

"No! Jeez, what are you…"

"Never mind, forget I said anything," she said quickly interrupting me and I didn't know why but she looked tense, as if she knew something I didn't. It put me on edge.

"Anyway, I knew you were a smart girl, besides, Luc isn't really a flowers type of guy, wouldn't you say?" she said, letting on that she obviously knew Lucius and most likely a lot more than I did, being an Oracle and all. Well then, she knew a lot of things about a lot of people. And well, if I hadn't currently been clinging on for dear life then I would have asked her a few things. But currently we were still in the throw of making our getaway. And speaking of getaways, I looked behind me to see that no one was following us this time, which made me say,

"You know I think we are good, you can slow down now." Something she ignored for the minute as she expertly manoeuvred us through the busy streets of Munich's end of the day rush hour traffic. It certainly was a beautiful city and one I might have enjoyed taking in if it hadn't all just been a dramatic blur due to our speed.

"I can't," she finally responded coolly as if death defying speeds were as dangerous as picking daisies with bees buzzing overhead.

"Why not?" I asked but then this was when it got complicated as she turned to me and said the only thing that was needed,

"Because Luc's about to walk into a trap and he doesn't know it yet, but they have the means to force him to give them the box and we can't let that happen," she told me and after my gasp of horror, my only other response was a panicked,

"Does this car go any faster?"

CHAPTER THIRTEEN

DEMONS, ANGELS AND THE ORACLES IN BETWEEN

"So, what do we do now?" I asked feeling like some kind of spy or newest member of mission totally fucking impossible! We had driven out of the city and I soon found myself staring bugged eyed at what looked like an unbelievable task.

"What do you think we do, we break in and save the King," she said as though we were talking about something as simple as picking out a damn china pattern for our wedding!

"Oh right, duh me…so don't suppose you packed your A team and Tom Cruise in the back pocket of those leather pants of yours, did you?" I asked sarcastically because basically it helped my panic.

"My what?" she asked with a frown that arched a perfectly shaped and heavily pencilled brow.

"Seriously, don't any of you guys ever watch TV?"

"I'm sorry, is my lack of pop fucking culture going to be a

problem for you?" she snapped making me realise I was being a bitch.

"Sorry, I am just freaking out okay, I find sarcasm helps...so what is the plan here, and I mean, not in what we hope to achieve but more, how we have a hope in hell of achieving it?" She flashed me a knowing grin this time at my mention of Hell. Wow, definitely not what I expected from a new Oracle. As in... At. All.

"You'll see, come on," she said before shifting from behind the wall we were currently spying from. We had driven to a massive mansion that was most likely only a turret away from being classed as a bloody castle! It was pale stone that had too many architectural details to mention and even if you did, unless you were an architect yourself, then all the different terms and names for things would have been lost on you, just as they would be for me.

But simply put, large pale yellowish stone blocks made up most of the front, with smooth rendered towers that were topped with dark tiled pointed rooftops that reminded me of gnomes' hats. Windows of every shape and size were dotted at the multiple levels and each was framed by an elaborately carved stone arch.

The building itself, despite all the sectional rooms that jutted out from the main building, was primarily a large square building. The grand entrance was a semicircle of arches and pillars with a fan of steps leading up from the gravel driveway, one that was attached to a turning circle that surrounded a huge water fountain in the middle. The building was also lit up as if they were throwing a damn Christmas party in there! Floodlights were aimed up at the stone walls, creating an ominous feeling as if the building itself was actually glowing.

Shadows were cast from the gargoyle figures that seemed to stand guard, perched there at the ready and looking down at us like winged demons. Each sat from angular plinths about to swoop on down and snatch unwelcomed guests before even making it to the front door. I shuddered.

I followed Bess, keeping to the shadows best I could and wondering if now was a good time to mention that stealth wasn't exactly my middle name. In fact, it was kind of the opposite seeing as I had been known to fall over when trying to achieve the most simple of tasks...like dressing. So, sneaking wasn't exactly my forte, especially when I looked down and saw that even my laces were loose. Damn it, I knew I should have double knotted the bloody things.

"What are you doing!?" Bess hissed when she saw I wasn't following.

"I'm just tying my..."

"Get your ass over here!" she snapped and I scowled at her knee-high spiked boots, wondering how the hell she walked in them, much less ninja style crept around in them. I rolled my eyes with a pull of my laces as I redid them and then hurried along to catch up. The look she gave me said it all.

"What, I am kind of a health hazard with my clumsiness, and that's without adding spy shit to it," I said nodding down at my high-top sneakers, ones that didn't match my brown cords in any way. But then I was in a rush so what was a girl to do. Now, if I had known what evening exploits I would have been up to, then I also wouldn't have worn a cream coloured, knitted sweater that was pretty much like waving a great big white flag in their faces. And when I say faces, I meant all the guards that patrolled the grounds.

Oh yeah, we were so screwed.

"So, what's our next move, Nancy Drew?" I asked her once we had reached a walled garden around the side of the mansion. She raised an unimpressed brow at me yet again and I shrugged my shoulders, telling her,

"Sorry, nervous sarcasm, remember?"

"They are holding one of their rituals tonight," she told me without taking her eyes off the building as if waiting for something. But my hands flew to my mouth as I gasped.

"Oh Gods, but they aren't going to sacrifice Lucius are they?!" She frowned only this time flattened her lips and said,

"No of course not, you do remember who he is right?" she said now being the one to use a sarcastic tone.

"Okay wait, I am confused...I thought you said he's in danger."

"No, what I said was, that they have found a way to make him give them the box, not that he was in danger...jeez, dramatic much," she grumbled this last part as I released a whoosh of relief.

"So, let me get this straight, we get this leverage back and..."

"Bam, threat over," she finished for me and just as I was about to ask what it was they were hoping to use, a car started to pull up, its tires crunching on the gravel of the turning circle. It pulled to a stop and we both watched as a door was opened by the driver before a man got out dressed entirely in black. His face was covered in a matt black Devil's mask that matched his suit.

Even from here I could see that it covered most of his face other than his lips and chin. It also had high brows that made it look angry, with a flat triangular piece at the forehead which a pair of horns were attached to. A long pointed nose and pointed ears finished the look, making me want to roll my eyes. Gods, but if these stupid mortals actually saw what a real demon looked like, then they would think twice on trying to replicate it for some Devil worshipping masked ball.

I scoffed at the sight and I could feel Bess' eyes on me, but for once she didn't comment. Then shortly after that another car turned up and she nudged me saying,

"This is our way in." I grimaced the second I saw two barely dressed girls get out, both wearing short white dresses and had white masks on. Because now I was pretty sure what her plan was and the thought of it kind of also made me want to vomit with nerves.

"Please don't tell me what you're thinking is what I think you're thinking...as in, pretty please," I said making her smirk at me, her pretty features twisting into something cunning and kind of badass.

"That depends, I think a lot of great things...come on, they will be heading this way," she said walking low and remaining out of sight. Thankfully, the main entrance was framed either side by landscaped gardens that each mirrored the other. High neatly trimmed hedge walls in interlocking patterns made for a great place to hide and this was where we waited as like Bess had said, the girls were being directed to one of the side entrances.

We stalked them and I had a bad feeling about what was going to happen next like a chill that slithered down my spine. I mean I wasn't stupid here. I knew we weren't just going to ask them politely to give us their clothes and then kindly miss the party. But I also wasn't expecting Bess to hand me a cloth soaked in chloroform out of her back pocket and telling me to take the one on the left.

"Bess, I don't think..."

"Do you want to save Luc?" she snapped and I nodded, knowing that I was being backed into a corner. Finally, her harsh gaze softened and she said,

"Look, we have about thirty seconds here, so make your decision, because if you want to do this, then this is our only way."

"I know," I sighed and finally I took the cloth from her, nearly gagging at the scent of ether as it wafted up my nose, with that strange sweetness to it that just seemed wrong.

"Good, now come on…besides, it's not like we are going to hurt them," she said, obviously being totally fine with this, making me wonder if she had seen this all play out. Did she know this was our only way in because she saw it that way? Isn't that the way it worked with Oracles?

She made a signal like she was a navy seal or something, letting me know to make my move. And the second she grabbed the back of the girl, I did the same. However, she was like a bloody kidnapping expert because the girl was dropping to the floor in no time at all. Mine on the other hand, well what I got here was a fighter and what we ended up playing was more like buckaroo!

Besides, I hadn't really taken into account her damn stripper heels, and that put my short ass at a bit of a disadvantage. Meaning that I was being swung around like a damn cat trying to cling on to her head with the cloth only just covering her mouth.

I looked to Bess who was just rolling her eyes at me as she lowered her own burden to the floor, dragging her body behind the bushes.

"What the fuck do you…!" The poor girl never finished as I had enough of this shit, so jumped up and literally wrapped myself around her like a damn monkey on her back. Then I covered her mouth and nose this time, putting my arm around her neck to keep her head still.

"Gods woman, just breathe in this shit, would you?" I hissed in her ear as she started walking us both backwards and I instantly had a bad feeling about this. I knew it was true when I felt her starting to pass out and I gave Bess a premature 'Look I

finally made mine pass out' face when I felt myself going backwards.

"Oh shit," was the last thing out of my mouth as we both tumbled backwards over a hedge and I landed with first a painful thud to my back and then one to my front when the woman fell on top of me.

"Fae?" Bess called and I groaned letting her know I was still breathing and hadn't cracked my skull open like it felt I had done. But in case she hadn't heard me I lifted a hand over the hedge and gave her the thumbs up, telling her the deed was done.

I was, in that moment, officially the un-coolest spy in the goddamn world!

Five minutes later and we were both now looking the part. Although Bess certainly worked it far better than I ever could.

"You ready?" she asked as she pulled down her skimpy white dress that was almost completely backless if not for the thin spaghetti straps that crisscrossed her shoulder blades. However, none of the shoes fit her so she just went with her knee-high boots, that I was sorry to say now made her look more stripper than badass.

I was fortunate in this department as one of the girls had what must have been only half a shoes size too big for me. But thankfully they had straps around the ankles so stayed on when I walked. The dress however, I had needed Bess to help tighten up as it had a corseted back with thick white ribbon. The front was a plunging neckline and because of the back, it smushed my breasts together in a way that made me want to keep pushing them down, just so they looked somewhat decent. But other than that, the dress was kind of cute and definitely the less 'trashy' out of the two. Even though I kept my thoughts to myself on that one.

The white dress had thick straps over my shoulders and a deep sweetheart neckline. It was tight to my waist, clinching me in and giving me a wicked curve as the full and double layered skirt flared out as if I was some kind of ballerina, stopping about six inches above the knee.

"Here, we will need these," Bess said, handing me one of the masks we had knocked off during our struggle. Oh, what was I saying, she seemed like a damn pro, me on the other end was a laughable criminal now with bruised ribs.

"Wings," I uttered in response to the style of the masks which looked like angel wings that would fan out across our eyes.

"Yep, time to be an angel," Bess said before walking straight up to the side door and knocking three times. I was just thankful that no one had caught us taking down the two woman or was likely to find them anytime soon in the bushes where we had hidden them. Bess assured me that they wouldn't wake for a few hours, and after convincing her that there was no way I was leaving them out there naked, with a sigh she finally gave in. She then helped me redress them both in what we had been wearing.

And I had to conclude that if I had a 'hardest shit ever list', then trying to redress an unconscious woman was definitely up there at the top, right along with trying to get comfortable after breaking my coccyx when painting your bloody toenails...damn that gorgeous Hawaiian Fuchsia!

The door opened and we didn't even need to say anything to be let inside.

"Wow, that was easy," I murmured to one side so only she could hear.

After this I kind of expected to be walking in on a scene

from Stanley Kubrick's Eyes Wide Shut, not the normal looking masked ball party we did. There were no creepy masked kisses or from what I had gathered in five minutes, rooms filled with very elegant looking orgies. Of course, there was definitely a theme, as all the women looked the same, white dresses in different styles and the same angel wing masks hiding half their features. It was only their hair that gave them any semblance of who they were and the same was with the men.

Each was wearing a Devil's mask like the man who I saw getting out of the car. And each was wearing an all-black suit of some kind but still, it didn't look any more than a party. Most of the girls were stood together on one side of the large room, as if waiting to be picked by one of the men, which made sense seeing as they entered through a side door. Making me wonder if all these girls were actually paid to be here. Well, if that was the case, then maybe all the sex was still to come, and this was just the selection stage of the night.

"Hey, does this seem right to you?" I asked pulling Bess to one side and nodding to the room. She scanned the room and shook her head.

"I think this is a façade for the humans," she said making me think the same thing, which meant we still had to find where the real stuff was going on.

"Come on, let's keep going," she said gesturing over to what looked like a hallway. The manor, mansion or even castle, whichever it was known by, was typically opulent and exactly what you would have expected in a home as grand as this on the outside. All lush fabrics, gold threaded wallpaper and every type of grand moulding you could imagine existing, adorned each right angle or corner a room had. Chandeliers hung down from carved roses on the ceilings and the floors shone with wood polished to such a high sheen it almost looked like liquid.

The hallway was no different other than the age-old

masterpieces that decorated the walls. And it may have sounded conceited but places like this didn't impress me. Not when you have grown up in every type of luxury there was to experience. The world's best hotels, my father's centuries old homes, from grand Scottish castles to Italian lake house villas, even a palace in Venice. He had every type of home around the world and I had seen them all.

Now, what did impress me was natural beauty created by nothing more than nature itself. That, and ancient beauty found in far gone civilizations and the history they left behind. The puzzles and mysteries they had hidden for us to find and study in their long-passed footsteps. Those were the things that impressed me.

So, a room full of the rich, celebrating their personal victories wasn't my bag and never really had been, including my mother, who refused to let anyone clean her toilet no matter how rich she was. Well, that mentality had kind of rubbed off on me, hence wanting to make it on my own in London. And also, the reason why I never felt as if I ever belonged in places like this.

"I'm thinking the doors at the end," Bess said when we came to two large carved doors that were guarded.

"Password?" One guy said and I couldn't help but roll my eyes and mutter,

"Seriously?" so only Bess would hear.

"Ssshh...Succubus," she said after first hushing me and again I wanted to roll my eyes. The guard nodded and opened the door for us to walk through and I had to bite my lip to stop myself from saying something sarcastic.

"Really, a sex demon?" I questioned making Bess wink side on at me. I would have questioned further when suddenly Bess spotted a staircase and grabbed my arm to pull me that way just before another set of double doors opened. I hurried along with her and we snuck up the stairs without a sound thanks to the thick red carpet that was kept on each step thanks to the gold rods keeping it in place.

"Come on, we should have a better view from up here," she told me as we rounded a corner and soon found ourselves on a surrounding balcony. It framed three sides of a large white ballroom below that was covered in red veined marble.

Gods, but it was creepy, and made it look like the whole room was bleeding beneath non-existent cracks. It actually made me shudder but what was worse was the man that I noticed now stood at its centre looking just as masterful as he always did.

"There he is!" I whispered feeling a huge weight off my chest at just the sight of him and thankfully seeing him unhurt, as had been my biggest fear.

"Ssshh, or they will hear us," she said pulling me back into the shadows of the arched surround. The whole room reminded me of some kind of modern church. It was longer than it was wide and surrounded by an open balcony. At the opposite end to the large double doors was a huge stained glass window and below it was a raised dais where an altar stood as if just waiting for an unwilling sacrifice. I don't know why, but in that moment I got a sickening feeling in my stomach as a flash of my mother on one just like it felt like a knife to my gut.

I shook my head, trying to rid myself of the horrific image. In front of the altar were three men and even I could tell that only one of them was human and that was from all the way up here. It was just something in their stance. Like years upon this Earth had bored them of humanity instead of teaching them something more about it. They stood as though life was eternal and nothing was ever going to change that. It was more than just arrogance or knowledge, it was an absolute power.

Yet still, as powerful as they were, even I knew the man

they now faced was more powerful still. Which made me whisper,

"What is it they have to make him give up the box?" because from up here it seemed like nothing could defeat him.

Nothing could ever own him.

Hence Lucius' own arrogance.

And why not, after all, what could beat him but the possible threat of what was in this box. He was a man without weakness, without anything to...*lose.* And this was when I finally got that 'oh shit' feeling in the pit of my stomach that told me I had just made a huge mistake. I knew this when I started to back up and suddenly turned around the second the hairs on the back of my neck started to stand on end.

But I was too late.

"You!" was my answer.

The arm with a gun was already coming crashing down over my head. I didn't even have time to scream as the butt of the gun collided with the back of my head and suddenly pain exploded as I went down. Then in blurry sight, I looked up at my attacker with only one question on my lips,

"Bess...why?" She looked down at me, now with cold dark eyes that spoke only of hatred and a dark black soul that consumed her.

"Bitch, my name isn't Bess..." then she laughed and bent down on a knee to get closer as she lifted me up by the hair and just before she smashed my head down on the floor,

She snarled...

"It's Layla."

CHAPTER FOURTEEN

OWNED

"Sire, they are here as expected and requesting…" I waved off one of my guards, a demon named Henry of all fucking names. But he was as loyal as his name sounded and had been working for me for at least the last hundred years or so. To be honest, it could have been two hundred for my head was, as it usually was these days, *elsewhere.*

In fact, fuck trying to kid myself as I knew exactly where my head was, and it simply wished I would get my ass back there to join it…*or more like her.* Gods, but having her wake in my arms was a vow I made to myself in making it happen from here on out. I knew she didn't want to give in and sleep in my bed, but it was going to happen at some point, one way or another.

But now I understood her reasons why a little better. At first just knowing that she hated being in my private space, well it angered me enough that I lost my shit and punched a hole in the concrete wall of whichever space I was occupying at the time.

Despite this frustration, I also knew that I needed to give her space and now that she was safely contained in my own domain, I hated to admit it, but I loathed doing so. At first the reason why I had refused, thinking forcing her to live in my home would be enough to help her settle to the idea of staying there permanently.

But then Liessa had informed me she refused to sleep in my bed so I gave her the order to situate her in the apartment next to mine. I even ground my teeth in memory of her telling me she found her asleep on my couch. But after anticipating long ago that this may happen, I'd had the space refurbished next to mine with Amelia in mind. Although admittedly, if I had known the true depth of her character more, then I would have covered the place in vintage movie posters and had Pip do most of the decorating.

Besides, doing so served its purpose, as I managed to keep her close and still grant her a space of her own, something I knew she needed. After all, I wasn't a fool and I knew when to push her and when to back off, and this had been one of those times.

Because I tried to see it from her point of view. Remembering back to when she had first been in my bed, finding out about the past between her mother and I. Undeniably, she had been horrified and it had only succeeded in pushing her away at the time that I needed her to be at a distance. But what she had heard hadn't been the truth. A mistake so to speak and a spoken exaggeration of what many people had been led to think. However, the real truth would all come out in time. But as for right now, well I knew there was still too much between us to explain that side of my past to her.

It was too dangerous for her to run from me and I didn't have the time to hunt her down as I would be forced to do. So, I told myself soon. Soon there would be nothing between us, no matter how much I wanted to protect her from the truth of my crimes against her. Then I would claim her fully. I would make it happen. After all, where Amelia was concerned, I was a fucking master at patience and waiting for what I wanted to possess.

Just as I was in revenge.

But then in reality, when thinking back not only over the last few days but weeks since I first invaded her world, that famous patience of mine was wearing far beyond thin, it was near fucking see-through!

I had been nearing my end as it was, for seven long years I had waited to make my move. Gods, but just thinking back to when she had first arrived in my club all that time ago. Of course, I had known the second she had landed. Just as I had known her every move the moment she left the safety of Afterlife. As her father wasn't the only overprotective bastard having her followed. But she had no clue and nor would she, not if I had anything to do with it...*which I did.*

I walked over to my window and looked down, seeing for myself the car that was waiting there. Umm

who I had to kill this time, I thought with a grin. I located my phone from the counter and rang Liessa, who I had put in charge of Amelia's care since she arrived.

"Yes, Mr Big Bad Royal Ass?" she answered with a chuckle making me raise a brow in question.

"Care to explain?"

"It's what your little bird called you before you arrived last night," she said calling her what all my council had been instructed to do, as this had been her codename for all these years. For keeping the knowledge of what she was to me had been vital for her safety. But her hearing what she had named me brazenly in front of my own people, now this did make me grin.

"Oh, did she now?" I asked with a voice that promised punishment, the fun variety of course. Mmm, just thinking about it took me back to throwing that sassy ass over my shoulder and spanking her beautiful behind like I promised. Well, I was a man of my word after all. Besides, from the mind-fucking scent of her, then I was beyond fucking delighted to find that she obviously got off on it. And well, it only spoke of good things to come as that was merely a taste of the deliciously sinful things I wanted to do to her. Our time in the shower had just been merely plucking my fingers at an hors d'oeuvres, for just a taste of her and I now wanted to gorge myself for hours. And I knew exactly what my main course would be. But I would need new restraints for that, for that silky soft skin of hers only deserved the best. And well, the more comfortable the restraints, the more her will to fight against them, a sight I couldn't fucking wait to see.

"She was adorable," Liessa said, who I could tell already had a soft spot for the girl.

"I have no doubt. And speaking of such, I want you to arrange food be brought to her apartment, her stomach was growling at me," I said making her chuckle,

"Aww now I bet that was cute," she commented sweetly making me wonder at the polar opposites of her and her husband, for he was one hard bastard. But then again, so was I and we clearly all had our weaknesses.

"Indeed. Now go make it happen before she wakes," I said before ending the call. Then I walked to my desk sitting down with a grin, knowing I was letting the bastards downstairs wait, making a point of doing so. It was a power play, letting them know that I do what I please, when it pleases me and that I was only choosing to go with them out of nothing more than curiosity. Of course, there was a little more to it than that, but the human lackies they sent this time didn't need to know that.

So, I took my time in writing her a little note asking her to eat, taking the opportunity to tease her, knowing that she would not defy me by touching herself. Hell's Gods but I had a feeling that teasing her would quickly become my favourite pastime. It certainly had been during my short time with her in London.

But then I leaned back in my chair and thought back to the past when she first entered my domain. I had admired her obvious courage, although it had been easy to see that she had grown up in her father's world. For she most certainly acted like the princess I mocked her for being. The way she had waltzed in here as if she knew nothing could hurt her because of who she was. Of course, she had been right but also very wrong, as she believed herself untouchable because she was a Draven, her father's daughter.

But in truth, none of that mattered the moment she crossed over into my world. No, the reason she was untouchable was because I made it so. Because she was mine, plain and simple. But she was as clueless now as she was that day. Something I had spent all this time trying to accomplish. But that time was now at an end, and all those years I now had to make up for in convincing her of the opposite.

It was a battle and one I couldn't fucking wait to win.

The war on claiming her heart was mine for the taking, with only one thing in my way…

The Truth.

A truth that would have to wait for now, as I knew I had to tread carefully. Especially with this new and very real threat. A thought that made me look to the window once more and see the enemy at my door.

Of course, the box was indeed a threat and one I knew about even before Dom had rung me, asking me to intervene and help his daughter in discovering more about the box he'd found. At first I had been silently furious with him for involving her in this but then secretly rejoicing for it gave me the excuse to intervene in her life like I fucking craved to do!

But the moment he had mentioned where he had acquired it, I wasn't the only one who saw red flags. The Skull and Bones, The Order of 322 or also known as The Brotherhood of Death was an undergraduate senior secret student society at Yale University in New Haven, Connecticut. It was also seemingly harmless to the rest of the world. Nothing more than a group of wealthy young socialites wanting to feel a part of something elite. Dabbling in the mortal fascination with the darker side of my world, one they had no real clue about. It would have even been laughable, though undeniably it wasn't without its power as some of the world's most influential mortals had been members, including US Presidents.

However, it was unclear if they really knew what the society held at its core, for its heart certainly wasn't beating to a mortal tune. It had always been on the radar with rumours among my people as being something more than what it innocently portrayed, ever since it was founded back in 1832.

I wasn't yet entirely sure on all the details surrounding how Dom had acquired it, but I was sure of one thing, it had been something the Order hadn't even realised they had until it had been too late and had been stolen from them...or so my sources told me.

Well, it was said they had stolen a number of skulls, including the likes of Martin Van Buren, the eighth president of the United States between 1837 to 1841. Also, Geronimo, the prominent leader and medicine man from the Apache tribe and Pancho Villa, who was a Mexican revolutionary general and one of the most prominent figures of the Mexican Revolution. But why, I had no fucking clue as it all seemed pretty pointless to me.

But either way, needless to say, it was about time they too had something stolen in return. Of course, for me its importance quickly became apparent after Amelia's attack, as I knew the moment those stuttered, fear laced numbers had been spoken from a dead man's lips that the mortal society had been the ones involved. Now the biggest question of all was who was it from my world that was truly behind the Skull and Bones pulling mortal strings?

Gods, but just thinking back to it had my blood on fire in a blinding fury, that threatened nothing more than bloodshed should I only allow myself the violent impulse. But then, once the threat to her had been eliminated, I then remembered my utter astonishment at seeing the evidence to her own version of bloody violence that she had inflicted.

Even now I found myself shaking my head at the memory. I would have thought it best to hide her from the brutality of my attack when I was left with at least one to deal with. I was even close to telling her to close her eyes, especially when she shouted out 'No' in panic.

I had even found myself in my rage snarling at her like a wild beast with someone trying to take away my promised kill. But then those big blue eyes of hers rendered me unable not to grant her whatever the Hell it was she wished of me in that moment. After all, I could have just killed the guy later. But then she had nodded fearfully to the back of the room and asked me with beseeching eyes,

'Don't damage the artifacts,'

Gods, but in that moment I found myself in two minds and

neither of them included the mortal death I craved. I didn't know whether to throw my head back and laugh or to reach for her in the three strides it would take me and kiss her fucking senseless!

Instead, of course, I granted her wish and protected what she deemed most important, shaking my head in surprise when she gave me two thumbs up for doing as she had asked. Hellfire, but had she always been that funny had been the question I had been asking myself at that point.

But then, after comically saving another damn artifact, as I asphyxiated the guy up against a wall, something she seemed utterly unaffected by, she then thought it best we try and interrogate the guy. I had to say that in that moment I hadn't remembered the last time I'd had so much fun, and the guy bleeding in my hand for once hadn't had a damn thing to do with it.

No, it had all been her and Gods, but the times I just wanted to kiss that sweet smart-witted mouth of hers had been ridiculous! Even when I felt her nudge me and tell me to show the bastard my fangs. Well, little did she know that in that moment I had wanted nothing more than to just crush the guy's skull with my boot. This before snagging her around the waist, hauling her to my chest and showing *her* my fangs, right before I sank them into her sweet-smelling flesh.

But I hadn't yet been free to do so, making me crave the days that I was, knowing now of her exquisite taste and the addiction just waiting for me to indulge in. However, knowing that she would taste so addictive hadn't been surprising. Not when I knew, just like everything else about her, that she would be fucking perfect for me.

What had surprised me though, had been her ability to defend herself. Even though her explanation of being taught how to fight by her father most definitely made sense. Like I had said, I remembered being utterly astonished to find two of them on the floor unconscious and clearly beaten. I believed my first assumption had been to question if they had turned on each other. Her response I would never forget as long as I lived. The way, when my disbelief in her ability to render two unconscious and the other bleeding, was replied with her crossing her arms over her chest, cocking out her hip and said,

'Yeah, Lucius, I did this.'

I swear in that moment I nearly had to bite my own lip just to stop myself from grinning. Especially when I scanned the men again and made a mental note of their injuries. But that hadn't been enough as I had asked Ruto to get a more accurate account during their interrogation of what had happened. One had been punched in the face twice, breaking the bridge of his nose from a downward punch which knocked him out. But before that a punch to the throat and a knee to his testicles and one hard enough that Ruto had informed me he was still cupping his balls when he died.

Naturally this thought made me happy.

The other man had a busted lip from receiving an elbow to the face, before her knee also got a little more action by making him even more bloody. Oh, and then there was breaking his arm, to rid him of the knife being wielded at her. Something she had been successful in, along with embedding it in the last man's shoulder when she threw it at him. Of course, if she had known that the guy had a gun, then that knife would have ended up in his heart, of this I was certain.

Meaning, I think it was safe to say the girl could handle herself and by the Gods, I couldn't wait to see her abilities for myself, wondering now how long it would be until I could get her in my gym and on the mats. The thoughts of taking her down for myself before fucking her there had my cock hard in seconds.

I rose from my seat and walked back into her apartment, knowing that she was now in the bathroom, for I could hear her there no doubt getting ready. I was in two minds whether or not to go in there but knew that if I did, then I would never fucking leave. So instead, I walked to the kitchen counter, where food had been placed there ready for her. I poured her a glass of juice, drinking some myself and licking the edge with a sick satisfied knowledge that her wet lips would soon be around the rim. After that I placed the note next to the glass and left.

But once more as I made my way down to speak to the head of my security, I couldn't stop myself from thinking back to that day at the museum. It was after showing me the box when she made contact with my skin and by the way she reacted, I would have said I hadn't been the only one affected. Which was why I quickly slipped my fingers from beneath her own. Knowing that if I hadn't, then I would have ended up pressing her against the nearest wall and forcing her to feel a lot more than just my fingers. Not that I thought this would have been much of a problem for her, as it wasn't solely my arrogance that told me she wanted me.

No, it was the way her heart would beat faster, her pulse rate spiking whenever we did touch. Or the way her breathing hitched when she watched me remove my jacket, drinking in my form with her eyes, a knowing blush creeping down her cheeks to her neck. Gods, but it made me feel like a fucking lion playing with a mouse, and therefore I couldn't help but use this to my advantage.

I was starting to crave those little subtle reactions from her and found myself continually trying to entice them from her at every opportunity I got. Like seconds later when I caged her body to the desk, leaning in close, trying to prove some point I cared not to remember. No, I had far better things to focus on, like the way she held her breath and started to squirm under what I knew was an intimidating gaze.

But I also knew that I was a cruel bastard as she stood there caged exactly where I wanted her and all the time asking herself if I was going to kiss her. Gods, how I would have liked to, but in that moment, I knew that it was too soon.

I first needed her right where I wanted her...*At Transfusion.*

However, I still couldn't help but tease her, calling her this time *my little puppet.* Oh, it made her angry alright, but I quickly found myself fucking loving it when she showed me that spark of fire I knew only I could ignite from her. In that moment though I was once again stunned by her, acting no doubt as if she had just slapped me. Something since that day, she had tried to do, many times in fact.

Now why that thought had me grinning was still a mystery to me. Usually I liked my women obedient and submissive but with her, it was different. I actually found myself enjoying it when she challenged me. It made my time with her unpredictable and when you were as old as I was then this was, more often than not, a welcomed distraction. Besides, it only made the times that she did submit to me all the sweeter, as there was a reason she had earned those particular endearments from me.

But even so, she had changed so much in the time I had last been so close to her, back before the night of the gala and seven years ago when she boldly presented herself to me. She had changed from a shy, trembling and unsure little beauty, into someone who was confident in the world that they'd built up around themselves.

In some ways she suited living in the mortal world, as it was clear it was where she felt most comfortable in being herself. But even knowing this, it wouldn't ever stop me from forcing her to live in my own, ensnaring her in it until I was sure she was solely rooted there and unable to escape me. I had just been biding my time. Now did that make me a selfish bastard, yes of course it did.

But did I care, *fuck no!*

The girl was mine.

And spending those few days in her presence only confirmed that waiting was no longer an option, not for her and most definitely not for me. Because up until that time spent with her, I hadn't believed she could have been any more perfect for me than I already knew she was. But Hellfire, I'd had no fucking clue. Because all those years watching from afar had taught me most things about her, yes, but not the most important. Like how funny she was or how stubborn she could really be when I was demanding things of her. But there were other things too, like how brave and strong she could be. Oh, I knew of her intelligence but knowing of it and experiencing it first-hand had been completely different. Just hearing the way she spoke about her work with such passion, as she had done at the gala, well then I found myself utterly captivated. A knowing grin playing on my lips nearly the whole time watching her. Just knowing how difficult she was finding my presence was fucking intoxicating!

Gods, but I was sick!

A sickness for her that I knew would never leave me, unable to burn itself out and instead, it continued to reach for my core, intent on scorching my very soul.

But despite these intense feelings that raged within me, I also knew that I had to take my time with her. Because I knew with me leaving for Germany, that if the threat continued on her life, like I had selfishly and secretly hoped it would at the time, then it gave me all the reasons in the world I had been waiting for to finally take her. But if it hadn't, then I knew it would only have ended up fucking with her head even more if I had shown her my true feelings, especially if I only intended to walk away again.

So, I waited and in doing so started putting plans in place to situate her in Transfusion under the guise of her own protection. I had even been on the cusp of ringing Dom and convincing him that his daughter needed my protection. Telling him that if she wished to continue working on the box, as I needed her to, then she would have to do so at my club.

But in the end, my plan hadn't been needed. Because from what my spies had told me, she had found out about her father's interference in her life and now refused to speak with him. I confess that her reaction to her father's meddling in her life didn't hold much hope for me. Because if she thought his interference bad enough, then he would look like a fucking saint compared to my intense control of her life.

Wisely though this was something I'd decided was better left being drip fed to her little by little. For right now, what she didn't know wouldn't hurt her and even better, it wouldn't fucking hurt me or my chances at claiming her either. Because once I had her, finally breaking through the last barrier between us and exchanging our blood, then there was no escaping me.

She would be mine forever, whether she wanted to fight it or not. Because I wasn't like her father was when meeting his Chosen One, I wasn't the self-sacrificing type, walking away from her because I believed she deserved better. I already knew she deserved better than the Devil she would have in me. But did that mean I was going to let her go, fuck no!

Yes, I may have kept her at arm's length all this time, patiently waiting for my moment as was fated but I always knew that one day this would happen. Which only strengthened my decision when my little bird had flown right into my cage, foolishly doing so of her own accord.

I couldn't help but think back to the moment that Dante told me that he had lost her…

ONE WEEK AGO

"Come again?" I said in a deadly calm that I knew wouldn't last long if Dante repeated the word's he just said to me.

"I lost her," and there went my calm.

"You lost my Chosen one!" I roared, my voice no longer one that solely belonged to me but more to the Devil's son. If you could describe the sound of a flinch, then that was what I heard on the other side of the phone. But I was too far gone in my rage to pay attention to such. A rage that exploded into something even noted as deadly to my own kind, as my entire VIP stopped. Now frozen in life and at the sight of their master's wrath, hitting heights they had rarely seen before. The only sound was the echoing of glass cracking all around the large space. Every single window, tv screen, the near entirety of the bar, even panels shook in their frames… the Gods be damned beer bottles even cracked.

"Lucius I'm…"

"*You* fucked up! Now it's time to explain how!" I snarled and I heard the heavy swallow down the other end before he started to explain it to me. He told me how she had swapped clothes with her friend and after putting on a show, she left pretending to be this person named Wendy. This was obviously after discovering that her friend's apartment had been bugged. At the very least Dante had been following her friend, and I could think of no other reason for this than his own personal interest in her. But I didn't give a shit, I was only thankful for it, as it meant that they were also following my own personal interest.

But their double cross was also discovered quicker than she would have anticipated, and this was thanks to the Manushya-Rakshasi demon I had placed in the flat opposite her own, charged with befriending her. Of course, had he not preferred the opposite sex and had no interest in females at all, then I would have picked another. But the demon was sired by me and therefore had no choice but to do my bidding. And well, there was nothing quite like someone who could come and go in her personal space than a friend she entrusted with a key.

This had been my answer to spying on her without giving in to the temptation of bugging her apartment or installing a camera. Because I may have been a bastard, but even I knew that was crossing a big fucking line. However, I had still found myself annoyed at her at the time when hearing how her 'friend Ben' had a key to her place. Even if I already knew and had issued for this to be one of his objectives. But my annoyance came when I found her too trusting and this was proven, for she had no clue who Ben really was.

It was a double-edged blade I had used to carve out the path of her adult life. Because having him there and integrating himself in her life had been his job. It had been how I knew exactly where she was at all times, that and the fucking team I had watching her twenty-four seven.

But then after the threat, I had called in the best and the Drude might not have been one of my own but he owed me, and I was fucking collecting. Something I was starting to regret.

Thankfully though it had been Ben who had rung Dante and explained how she was upset after she had found out about who he was, now believing his friendship with her was nothing more than a masquerade. But his loyalty to me remained worthy, for he had led her to believe that it was her father's doing.

In fact, she believed everything had been down to her father, including the whole building being filled with men loyal to him. Something that was somewhat true, as there were those that lived there under her father's orders after first having them installed there. But that's the thing about loyalty...*it can often be bought.*

Just like the building she lived in.

The one her father never owned.

But the one that I did.

CHAPTER FIFTEEN

BIRD IN MY CAGE

I owned her building and I didn't know what type of bastard it made me to let her believe it had been her father. I knew I should have felt guilty, any decent person would, but I was as far from a decent person as you could get. And if she blamed him over blaming me, then I was more than fucking happy to let her. I mean it wasn't as if daddy dearest was squeaky clean in all of this, he just wasn't quite as bad as I was.

But then we were two kings who ran this world, and to him she was his dear mortal daughter. However, to me, she was my Chosen One, and in my book that meant more than the first. Being mine, belonging to me, took precedence over ties with her family, even if she wouldn't ever agree that it did.

Gods, but it felt like I was soon to be at war with Dominic Draven all over again, or at least I soon would be once he discovered how I owned his daughter and didn't intend on giving her back or ever letting her go.

But as I sat here now, on the fucking edge of losing control just knowing the shit she had just pulled and I had to say, if I hadn't been beyond fucking furious that she had gone on the run, then I would have taken the time to be impressed by her cunning nature. Even if I knew she wasn't necessarily running from me this time. That knowledge managed to calm me enough not to destroy any more of my club...*at least for now.*

But either way, she had managed to fool us both and I had to give her credit for that at the very least.

My clever little princess.

"We underestimated her," Dante commented, making me growl back,

"Yes, and I overestimated you! Now the next call you make better be the one with you telling me exactly where she is, and I warn you Dante, it had better be in five fucking minutes...now piss off and make that shit happen!" I said cutting the call and having to consciously take care not to damage my phone any more than the cracked screen my rage had created. Now, once I got that call back telling me exactly where she was, then I wouldn't give a fuck what happened to my damn phone!

"Problem boss?" Clay asked the moment he entered the space and took in the damage, his sizable black muscles tensing in preparation for what he no doubt hoped was a fight. Thankfully the club below hadn't yet opened to the public, otherwise they might have believed a fucking earthquake was making the glass close to shattering.

"I want one of my planes fuelled and ready to go the second I have a destination...and I want it done fucking yesterday, understood?" I snapped feeling myself on the edge of tearing this place apart as I felt the minutes passing. In seven fucking years there hadn't been one fucking second of it that I didn't know where she was at all times! And now, well I could feel that sinking feeling crawling up my damn spine, just as it had done that night. That fucking night I had let her walk out of here, letting her think me a heartless bastard and my personal punishment for that had been what happened next.

I knew that I could scent something different on her, not realising until it was too late that she had been drugged. But then when I found her in the back of that van, I swear the demon in me, the one only Lucifer himself ever saw fully, being the one who created me, came full force to my old mortal vessel. It was one that I showed the first mortal of what Hell actually looked like…or should I say the wrath of the beast that ruled it.

I had just been thankful at the time that Amelia had been mostly unconscious, for I doubted she would have ever looked at me the same way ever again. Now that would have given her a real reason to run from me.

Speaking of which, thankfully my phone rang. I looked down at the time first. Four minutes the lucky bastard.

"This better be good news, for your sake, Drude," I threatened.

"My men found her." I released a sigh of relief not giving a fuck who heard it, ignoring the shocked glances my council members exchanged with one another.

"Where is she!?" This question came out as a rumble of sound, grated and rough, as if torn from some dark depth of me. Gods, but I hoped that she never heard me like this, she would have been fucking terrified.

"She's at the airport. She switched clothes with her friend, so once we got a description from…"

"I don't give a fuck! Just tell me where she is heading, and I will handle it from here!" I snapped this time making him sigh.

"She bought a ticket to Dublin." I frowned, feeling every Gods be damned muscle in my body tense, to the point that I swear if I had flinched right then I could have fucking snapped my own bones.

195

"I'm not sure why as my men found no connections she has there, so I don't know why she…"

"She has none, that is why," I interrupted and then hung up without giving him anything more. Besides, her options were no doubt limited as she would have had to have picked a flight leaving before my chance at finding her. Also, one with a destination close by, as she would be using her cash knowing we could trace her card. Because if she was clever enough to even get to the airport without detection, then she was clever enough to know the easy ways in which she could be tracked down.

I swear my palms were itching just at the thought of now being the one to hunt her down and when I finally caught her, oh what fun I would have in punishing her. I had to wonder how she would take me bending her over my knee and palming her ass, till red and burning.

Would she whimper for me?

"Call the pilot, tell him we are flying to Dublin." I barked out my order and Clay had his phone by his ear before I had even finished. Fuck, but I knew I should have entrusted her detail to my own men, they wouldn't have been fooled so easily.

Just in that moment my phone rang again and I snatched it up like a live cobra ready to strike, doing so with the mentality, 'what fucking now.'

"Don't bother with that flight, she's no longer going to Dublin," Dante said making me frown.

"Where?" I asked through gritted teeth as they ground together in frustration. But then his answer came and finally I could breathe without wanting to break someone's face, mainly Dante's.

"Munich…looks like she's coming to you."

Good, my sweet bird was finally flying home.

The moment I knew she was on her way here, I knew tracking her was pointless as there was only one reason for her to come to Munich…*she wanted the box.* I was sure of it. The question now was why now? Had she discovered what I already had my own people discover? That the box held some kind of weapon against me…did she know and had come all the way here to warn me? It stood to reason as no matter how strained her relationship with her mother was because of me, she still cared deeply for her. I knew this thanks to her friend Ben, my spy. And this wasn't discovered through what she did say but more what she didn't, for she never really spoke of her family and for Amelia, that spoke volumes in itself.

Meaning any threat against those she cared for and Amelia would have been there. Now I had to wonder if I too was included in that list. Well, I was soon to find out as the second she was spotted outside my club I knew it was show time. I nodded for Clay to pass me the expensive tablet that now held six images from different security angles.

"Did you disable the alarms?" I asked him, because I wanted to watch this little break in of hers for as long as possible and doing so by leading her into a false sense of security and right into my trap.

"I did, as you instructed."

"Good, then it's time for me to enjoy the show," I said with a knowing grin and looking down just as she entered the alleyway that led to the back of the club and secure parking lot we had there. Again, I felt my pulse quicken at just the sight of her, knowing I would only relax my muscles the second I knew she was inside, once all chances of escape were eliminated. Because she had no idea by coming here what she had done. It was like sneaking into Hell's prison and handing herself over to a demon warden.

I tapped on one of the images by the fence so it enlarged giving me a better view of her taking off her full jacket. At first, I wondered what she was doing, as I half expected her to start trying to climb it. But then I saw her begin to roll it up into a ball to protect it. Then she passed it through a hole in the fence as if she knew it would be there. That's when something about all of this felt off.

How would she have known?

"Did the girl arrive alone?" I asked the question to Clay, who should know being that he knew everything that happened within Transfusion and just beyond its walls.

I was currently sat in the centre of the large sectional sofa that faced the rest of the club, instead of the VIP area, which I knew was in full swing behind me. It no doubt had looked more like a demonic sex club to the naïve eyes of a twenty-year-old Amelia when she first saw it.

Gods, but that blush upon her skin and the way she was near desperate to give in to the impulse to bite her fingertips, an endearing habit of hers, was nearly enough to break my restraint on tasting her.

Clay placed his finger to his earpiece that let him communicate to his team, which included the humans downstairs. I heard him ask the question.

"They said she was alone," he told me, which meant one of two things, either she did come alone like I hoped, or whoever had been guiding her had the ability to mask their presence.

I watched as after placing everything carefully through the gap, she then started to crawl through. I swear the sight of her on all fours had my cock twitching along with the corners of my mouth as I fought my grin. I even felt my anger dissolving with every second I watched this little break in attempt of hers unfold. It had almost been worth the worry experienced.

I watched as she must have been talking to herself, no doubt congratulating herself that she had got this far. She put her heavy jacket back on as she looked up trying to locate the dummy cameras we had and then move around the building trying to keep in what she thought were their blind spots.

She also continued to look around her as if any minute she was ready to bolt at the first sign of her getting caught. She reminded me of a jittery cat that knew it was where it shouldn't be.

"Oh sweetheart, you have no idea just how close you are to being trapped in my web," I said aloud, not giving a fuck who heard me as I swigged back my beer. Now her next test came and the answer to my question would be revealed, the code for the back door. I had Clay ready to unlock it remotely either way, but first I wanted to know if she got it right, because if she did, then I would know she had been helped.

I nodded to him and he slipped his phone from his pocket at the ready to do what was needed. Now she was going to either think herself the luckiest human alive in guessing what the code could be, or she already knew it. I tapped on the live feed, enlarging each camera image as she went and the second she slipped through the door, I leaned forward and looked to Clay.

"Well?"

"She knew the code," he informed me, making me sit back, place the tablet on my lap and steeple my fingers in thought.

"What do you want me to do?" Clay asked knowing I was thinking something. I was starting to regret my choice to allow her to come here without being followed from the airport.

"Get me the security footage from the airport and any on route of her getting here from the streets."

"That will take time," he informed me and I nodded

accepting that and no longer feeling the burning need to know right in this moment. Not now I had her right where I wanted her...or at least soon would do.

"She had a card," Clay commented in annoyance and as head of my security, then I could understand that watching someone gain access to Transfusion was not easy for him to accept.

"Now that is interesting," I hummed, still feeling the grin there just below the surface. Of course, if it had been anyone else breaking in then I would have wanted to peel back the flesh from their bones. But her, instead I just wanted to tie her up and leisurely lick every inch of her skin.

"It's an old card, not one that's been in use for a while," he told me and Ruto, who had been taking all this in silently swore in Gaelic. I turned to him and nodded, knowing he would now make it his mission to know who that card had once belonged to, as it wasn't as though we handed them out like fucking loyalty cards.

"I will find the fucker!" he snapped, sliding the blade he had been playing with back into the sheath strapped to his thigh. I don't think I recalled a time he didn't have a blade in his hand as simple obsession wasn't enough to describe his habit.

"She's in the lobby...what now, should I have her brought to you," he asked and I held a hand up to stop him and shook my head.

"Not yet, for I am curious," I told him and I was. I wanted to see for myself if she was really bold enough to try and steal from me. So, I watched as she first took a breath, staring at the doors into my apartment before her resolve won. She slapped both hands to the doors and opened them up, storming inside as though she owned the moment. Gods, but she was magnificent when confident like that, just as she was adorable in her insecurity. Both were just as captivating as the other and I was torn as to which made my cock harder. Her brazen replies or her breathy little murmurs. I fucking loved them all.

"You think she will find it?" Clay asked me, speaking about my vault, and one only my council knew about. There was naturally no security inside my private space but there was inside my vault so all there was left to do now was wait.

"I think if she made it this far, then it is more than likely," I told him.

"Do you want me to apprehend her as soon as she does?" he asked and this time, I welcomed what I knew was a sadistic grin to develop with ease.

"No, I have a better idea for our little thief," I said smirking down at the screen the second I saw her appear, stepping inside. But of course, she knew the code to this one, as it was her birthday. Something I knew she had seen when I had paid for her meagre groceries, wanting to laugh aloud just thinking back on her cereal addiction.

Gods in Hell, but she was fucking adorable, the way her eyes widened as she took in the room, a small collection of all the things I had acquired over the many years upon the Earth. The most important of which was still embedded beneath my flesh, now very much a part of me since that day I helped her father save her mother...his price had been the blood of Christ, hers the blood of a Vampire King.

Ironic then now, as I had Christ's blood to compete with the blood of the Venom of God. Well, that will serve him right I thought with a barely contained snarl.

I quickly lost those dangerous thoughts and watched as she marvelled at all before her. Then the shock at seeing my most prized possession and one Dom had also managed to steal from me at one point during our feud, *my Caliburnus*. Many knew the sword as its more common name, Excalibur. The sword had long ago been gifted to me by the lady of the lake, fated that I would one day need it in my rule. But see, the thing with the Fates was how little they could be trusted, something Dom had learned the hard way, despite the outcome all those years ago.

Me, on the other hand, well I didn't hold much faith in the Fates, nor did I listen to a fucking thing they had to say! I had been charged for too long with keeping track of the damned Oracle, for Lucifer's obsession. But now Pythia was no longer my concern and in the only place she should be, his prisoner in Hell. Although, I doubted she was complaining as torturing her would have been the last thing on his mind. But then again, he wasn't the only one obsessed with a mortal girl, I thought as I ran a fingertip down the length of her frame on the screen.

I watched as the longer she was inside there her unease grew, with the way she looked over her shoulder at the door as if contemplating whether or not she should run.

"Be brave little bird, just a little longer so I can have my fun," I said urging her on for my own amusement, even though she couldn't hear me. I just couldn't wait to watch her reaction when she tripped the alarm and found herself locked inside knowing that she had been caught. Fuck, but I felt my fangs growing in anticipation, not giving a shit who saw and questioned my reaction. Because really, this had been the most fun I'd had in years. It felt like having a plaything to amuse myself with. An unsuspecting little mouse as she made her way through my maze and well now my sweet little Šemšā had just found its centre.

I watched as trepidation made her hand shake as she reached out for the box, knowing deep down that something bad was about to happen. But she couldn't stop herself as she had come this far. I even found myself holding my breath and leaning forward as she did as the second she touched it, she triggered the hidden sensor she wouldn't have known about and the whole place came alive around her.

Heavy metal doors started to slam down all around the room and her head snapped to the sound, her sweet mouth opening in shock, her lips making a perfect O shape. Again, the sight made my cock hard like the sick bastard I was.

Then her mind finally kicked into gear and her panicked gaze shot to the door that was closing. She ran to it far too late to stop it and ended up pounding her fists on the heavy metal, silently I could see her scream the word 'No' before she cursed over and over again. I found myself wishing it had audio just so I could have heard it for myself instead of being left to imagine what it was like. That intoxicating breathy panic coming from her would have been like fucking music to my ears. I was even tempted to rise and go to her in that moment just in hopes to have caught the end of it.

But this wasn't part of my plan.

"What now?" Clay asked and I grinned without taking my eyes from her and said,

"Now it's time for a drink." I said clicking my fingers and the second a waitress appeared, I relaxed back and said,

"And time for her punishment."

CHAPTER SIXTEEN

PRESENT DAY

MY KIND OF KINDNESS

I grinned as I walked through my club thinking back to that day. The day she walked right into my trap a week ago. But then I also thought over the days and in them how far we had both come since that night. The night I finally let myself kiss her fully for the first time.

The night this Demon found Heaven.

The thought had me looking up from the bottom floor as if I would find her there, on the top floor looking down from the VIP. The club was empty at this time, so being free of humans I was free to speak as I wished.

"The girl…"

"Yeah, I know, she doesn't leave no matter what. I told you, I ain't suicidal," Clay told me in that gruff tone of his. I nodded to him before doing the same to Ruto, my right hand who looked yet again beyond pissed off that he was missing all the fun.

"You will have your time, I am sure," I told him, making him scoff at me with a nod and that was all. I turned to leave, and this time resisted the urge to look, just as I did when I exited my building and folded myself into the car they had waiting for me. Because I knew if I had looked up and seen her staring down at me like last time, then I never would have left.

But even when in the car, this time being ignored by the mortals that had drawn the short straw being picked to escort me, I found my mind elsewhere. Because despite the seriousness of the situation and current threat, I still found my thoughts more in the past than the present.

Just the idea of her trying to leave had me playing back my fears all over again. The Gods knew the anger I had felt just knowing that she had planned to steal from me before sneaking out and to what, to run forever. Did she really think she could hide from me? Oh, she could change her life all she wanted, her home, her job, even her damn name, disguising herself as much as she thought she would have to, but all of it meant nothing. Because I would have hunted her to the ends of the Earth and beyond if I had to. Just the thought of her believing she could escape me made me near boiling over furious and the men in the car could pick up on it. Their fear was a stench, unlike Amelia's where it simply made my mouth water. A delectable scent I craved like all the rest of them, one in particular being my favourite…

Her arousal.

A thought I quickly tamped down before I ended up sat here with a damn hard on and these assholes added sexual deviant to the MO of being the cold-blooded killer I was.

So, I allowed my mind to seep right back into my earlier thoughts. My sweet bird flying into my cage the way she had still made me grin, something else the mortals in the car could add to their fears, I was clearly fucking crazy.

But despite her being a clever little thing, my girl, she was also an idiot if she believed herself more capable than me. And the second I saw her slump down to the floor of my vault, that was the moment I knew she had finally started to get it. She was obviously a quick learner. Learning that she couldn't beat me.

However, she still showed me that fire in her when after about twenty minutes of letting her ask questions of what would happen next, as was her punishment, she then raised her hand to the camera and gave me the middle finger. I remembered shocking the entirety of my VIP the second they witnessed their King's hilarity as I threw back my head and laughed, doing so harder than ever before.

'I think she has hit her limit,' I had said before nodding to the doors that led into the lobby, telling Clay to get his men to fetch her. But then she had appeared and as much as I relished watching her struggle with her fears, being that I could taste her fear from here and it was fucking delicious, I also didn't have it in me to make her suffer.

Gods, but she had been a treat and a fucking feast for the eyes too. As the second she had been escorted inside my club, I swear the urge to snatch her up, throw her over my shoulder and kick open the doors to my apartment had me near snapping the back of my chair where my arm lay looking far more casual than I felt inside. But I was the master at hiding my emotions, or the beast inside me was, one that admittedly these days was far too close to the surface, especially when our Chosen One was around.

But even after I had beckoned her forward and offered her to take a seat, I could see the defiance in her eyes as she refused me. But there was something else there hiding in the shadows of her eyes. And it was when her breath caught the second I stood to go to her that I knew what it was. It wasn't just her fear of me, but of me as I was in the past.

I had known then in that moment she believed that by being here, in front of me now, just as she had been seven years ago that she was about to relive that night. That's when I knew it was time to rewrite the past and in doing so, righting a wrong. Starting with the dress I knew she wore underneath the heavy material of her jacket. However, the second she had admitted that this time she hadn't worn it for me, I found myself forcing myself to relax enough that I wouldn't simply rip the offending item from her. I needed to go slow, I needed to gently erase her fears of an impending rejection that would never come...

Not this time.

No, this time, I had been determined to get what I wanted, no matter the consequences. So, I had begun by luring her in, tempting her, teasing her with this new side to me, one she had yet to discover. But then she had thought it done only to humiliate her and that was when I knew the true depth of the hurt and pain I had inflicted that day. Years had not weakened its memory as I had hoped it would have but instead, only managed to preserve it for me as punishment until she was here once again.

After that I knew there was no more slowly bringing her around, but only immediate action would have any chance at convincing her. Which was why I had simply picked her up and carried her into my private living space, intent on having my way with her. Yet another time my hopes had been drowned out by her doubts.

I swear I had nearly choked when she told me how she didn't believe I even liked her. Gods, but she really didn't have a fucking clue and I wanted to shake my head at myself, questioning had my act of disdain and indifference towards her really been that convincing? Well, my obvious answer had been staring at me all wide eyed, with the disbelief written in the depth of her eyes. The feeling powerful enough to fucking drown me in an ocean of guilt along with that fucking hope!

It had been in that moment that I realised I had gone too far in pushing her away and my only wish was that the damage made wasn't irreparable. My first step in doing so being the one I had wanted to take since first learning of who she was to me. But restraint had become my middle name and I had quickly become a fucking master at it!

Well, no more. So, I took her lips like I craved and the second I had first kissed her I knew that for as long as I took breath, that I would never stop owning them. That I would kiss her at every given opportunity, and in these last few days I had made good on my promise. My only limitation had been going at her pace, for if it had been left up to my desires, then I would have never let her go that night. And the space I forced myself to give her would have been no more than ten minutes not the two days I had.

But then again, I knew I had something to keep me busy.

The hunt.

Which brought me back to this next meeting and what it may hold. I was naturally hoping for more bloodshed, being this time the ones making demands and issuing the orders. Because the quicker I got this shit done and eliminated the threat, the more I could concentrate on her. Although, admittedly if I had to continue the ruse of a threat just to keep her under my roof without a fight, then I was a big enough asshole to do so.

So, getting in this car alone was my plan, despite how my council disagreed, Ruto and Clay especially. But this was done as a show of strength because if I had walked in there surrounded by my people, then I was giving them power in the misplaced knowledge that they were needed. But by showing up alone, then I took that power from them with my obvious lack of concern. After all, the sight of one man who believed he could take on an army made each man question why. And if a man questioned why, then fear of what the answer may be was sure to follow.

But naturally my people were protective over me, just as much as they were over their own lives. It was also why, being the one who sired them, it was incredibly difficult for one of them to ever betray me. Unless of course, they found the extremely rare means.

Besides, I now had an advantage after the night before, where twenty or so mortals forfeited their lives. Their show of numbers supposed to impress me. As I hadn't lied when I said that had been a test. One that had ended in bloodshed the second I found out that they had been a taskforce hired with only one purpose. To get the box back at all cost. Which meant they would have had to kidnap my girl and torture her until I agreed to give it to them. This had been their plan. I knew that the moment I walked inside. How, after the deaths of their comrades, they would enjoy sending me the fucking pictures and pieces of Amelia in boxes, doing so until I complied!

Admittedly the second I had read the thoughts of one in particular, a twisted mortal's mind on all the ways he wanted to fuck Amelia, well then I had lost my shit pretty quickly. But no one in that room had to be blind to my secret, which meant I had no beast to contain. Besides, it had felt good to get my hands dirty and release him of the Devil's chains…if only for a minute or two.

But then, as the car continued through the streets of my home the city of Munich at the end of its working day, I thought back to when I had left Transfusion the first time. Getting into a different car than I had done this time. The jolt to my heart was one I couldn't ignore, when I saw her looking down at me as I got inside. The worry for my safety plain to see.

I couldn't tell you what such a sight meant to me. I had nodded to her, a subtle way of telling her it would all be fine. But then, after I got in the car, I looked behind me as the car pulled away to find her hitting out at the frame before admitting defeat and sliding down its length, clearly upset at the sight of my departure. There I watched as she hunched over with her head in her hands and I didn't know in that moment whether I cursed my supernatural sight or not.

Fucking Hell, but I had been in a mind to bring this car to a stop just so I could go back to her. But then I had taken one look at the mortal cretins that had thrown every threat my way. Threats to get me to go with them, something they were clueless to know was actually no threat at all as I chose to go with them, nothing more. Because no one on this Earth made me do a damn thing that I didn't want to do.

I had almost given into the urge to smirk as they had assumed by me looking back at my club that I was concerned about leaving its safety. I knew this by the cocky stench of self-assurance that filled the car, that and their obvious grins. I would have rolled my eyes had I not yet wanted to give away my intentions of not letting a single fucker live.

Well blood was blood, and I was...well always up for a good meal and there was nothing sweeter than tasting the blood of your enemies. Well, nothing until last night. Because I swear that the second, I had finally given into the roaring impulse I always had around her, by piercing her soft skin and tasting her blood, well then, my entire fucking world had stopped. There had been nothing before that moment in time.

Thousands of tastes had coated my tongue before, victims of circumstance, enemies of wars...even the exotic tastes centuries of this world had to offer, Gods, but even my favourite dessert SholehZard, and not one fucking thing compared! Although I had smiled at the time, thinking back to her reaction to trying the Persian dessert. One traditionally served on the occasion of festivals such as Tirgan, as well as Ramazan, and at the memory, had I been alone I would have laughed aloud. Her reaction and face alone, now forever changed the experience of the dessert forever more.

But like I said, now nothing compared to the taste of her. Her blood was like drinking in life itself. It was like my very own elixir created by the Gods and offered to me in the vessel of a fucking Goddess! It was most certainly the closest thing to Heaven that I would ever experience that was for damn sure. Lucifer's blood, but even thinking back to it now as I licked at a fang, wishing that I hadn't already savoured every last drop, was temptation enough to have this car turn around, just like the one the night before.

But then I caught sight of the mortals eyeing what I knew was a demonic grin and licking at my fangs that I hadn't realised until now had grown just thinking about her. Well, now they actually started to allow their fear of me to morph into doubt, unlike the fools the first time. Good, it was about time they started to take who they had in the car with them seriously.

That was why I didn't have this car turned around. Because pretty soon I would know who was behind all this and then, like last night…

I would have my bloody fun.

After my bloody fun I found myself desperate to get back to Transfusion, only because being apart from her even for this short time wasn't something I liked. Gods in Hell, but it was like some fucking cosmic joke. I had put space between us for so long and learned to live with my obsession from afar. But now that she was actually in my home, constantly within reach,

I found myself unable to think of little else. But well, being this far apart now felt like a blade embedded in my chest that would only be removed once I could touch her again.

Because I couldn't fucking relax knowing that she was where I wasn't. Yes, I knew my men competent enough to do their jobs, as Clay hadn't been kidding when saying he wasn't suicidal by letting her leave. Because if I didn't get things my own way, I could be a mean, moody motherfucker, who relished in making those around me suffer.

Like I said, I was a true bastard.

I was what the Devil had made me.

But in regards to my men, it was why now I only turned those I considered the best, surrounding myself with an army of warriors of the highest power. Oh, there were those who wanted me to grant them the gift of becoming one of my creatures but not many passed my test. And once they discovered the level of control I had on my turned, well then let's just say that binding their lives to me wasn't for everyone.

But right now there was only one being that I wanted to be bound to me and she was the one I was fucking growling like one of Cerberus' Hellhounds to get back to.

And just like those beasts, I fed and I fed well.

Which was why a little time after first arriving I was left to simply pluck the now bloody keys out of the jacket of one of only two survivors. One of which was currently on the floor bloody and beaten and the other was huddled in the corner rocking and praying to Christ to survive this, clutching his broken arm to his chest. Yeah, good luck with that one mate, I thought with disgust, as me and Christ had fucking history, and not one I spoke of...*ever.*

Of course, the broken mortal had pissed himself, along with other things and was one of the reasons I decided not to dirty myself with his stench of vomit, piss and shit. Instead I would use him to deliver my message, knowing he would. Especially after the threat to find him, rip out his tongue before making him choke on it, should it slip his mind to do so.

Then I stepped from the room of death, now flooded with the mortal waste that a death hex left a body after they had melted from the inside out. I looked up to the ceiling of the warehouse they had brought me to and closed my eyes, breathing deep and scaring birds with the satisfied growl that rumbled from my chest. Then to the sound of panicked wings, I sucked the dripping blood from my fingers as I made my way down to the parked cars out the front of the abandoned space. I pressed the fob for the SUV we had travelled here in and used it to get back to the club.

Back to my girl.

Thankfully, the place they had taken me to was no more than fifteen minutes from the city and combined with the twenty minutes of torturous fun and bloody feeding I'd enjoyed, I would be back sooner than I thought. The moment I parked the car in my own underground parking, one with a hidden entrance, I used the private elevator to the top floor. Then I made a call.

"Where is the girl?"

"She's sat in the garden, looking fucking depressed if you ask me," Clay commented dryly making me snarl,

"I didn't ask...Now how long has she been there?" I asked, only because I was curious, especially now I knew she looked forlorn. I also found myself caring enough to question why, something that in itself shocked me. Was it because I had left? I shook my head at myself, scratching my head, as I wondered if this what was it would be like, guilt and irrational thoughts plaguing me from here on out?

"About forty minutes." I frowned knowing that there was a chill in the air and that humans were susceptible to catching all types of shit. Which was why the question was out of my mouth before I could stop it.

"Does the girl have a jacket?"

"Seriously?" Clay asked his shock understandable, as apart from her mother, Keira, I hadn't shown care for anyone's health before other than those few brief occasions.

"Just answer the fucking question," I growled making him release a sigh before telling me,

"No, and seeing as this time you are asking me, she looks fucking cold." My only response back was an annoyed rumble in my chest.

"If she isn't back inside in five minutes, let me know and I will go and get her ass back down here. Raise the table and inform the council, I will be there shortly," I told him and hung up, knowing I was free to enter my apartment without her seeing me soaked in the blood of others. Not exactly an enticing sight a potential lover would wish to see no doubt...well, a mortal one, I thought with a knowing grin.

I showered quickly, changed my clothes, setting everything alight other than my boots, which weren't beyond a simple clean. So, I threw them in the shower after me, letting the water run long enough to do the job. Because despite what people would think of me, in my mind being rich didn't give you the right to get people to clean your shit, and that included the blood of your victims. I had been in enough damn wars to know that a true warrior cleaned the kill off their own weapons after battle.

By the time I got out and was rubbing a towel over my damp hair, I saw a message on my phone that said one thing,

'Your bird just flew down from her nest and found your vipers.' Umm, now that was interesting, seeing as I had been hard pressed to get her back inside my club after that first night, when in that instance she'd had no choice. But now she had just walked straight in there knowing I was gone. Now the biggest question was, why? Was it the memory of me in there that kept her away or the desire to know where I was and the only answers to find were with...what did Clay call it, *my vipers?*

There was only one way to find out. But first, I made sure to grab a jacket, putting it on so when I forced it upon her, she would have no choice but to wear the scent of me surrounding her. The thought made my cock hard, just like most other possessive thoughts of her.

But then, as I walked into my club and saw her standing there, I knew nothing would stop me from putting my arms around her stating my claim, even in front of my own council, one that already knew of my obsession. After all, it wasn't as though I could hide it and nor did I care to, for they would soon get used to the sight of seeing her by my side.

So, after scolding her gently for not wearing a jacket and hiding the depth of my annoyance at finding her cold, I led her to my table, telling her to be brave when I saw the reluctance in her gaze.

I had to say, after a night of death, then having her sat next to me at my council table felt strangely right...*peaceful even.* Not something I expected to feel after losing myself to bloodlust.

I even found myself unable to hold back touching her, getting protective when my unruly second would snipe out at her, just as he did with most new people. In fact, the only person I had ever known him to take to instantly had been Percy.

A being who had become like his shadow over the years and the only person he still tolerated without his usual look of disdain. Of course, there was also myself, his master and sire, someone he pushed on occasion like tonight but ultimately, he obeyed me without question.

But then as the night progressed and talk grew to earlier events, I found myself furious as Amelia questioned my ability to handle myself. Did she really think me so weak that I was unable to handle a room full of mortals on my own?! Did she not know of my power? She surely wouldn't have questioned her own father's ability! Gods, but I found myself furious at her!

I found myself needing to test her. To show who it was she questioned. Who she was fucking with! I was near blind with rage, insulted that she didn't think me capable of protecting her. So, I told her why those men suffered, tempted even to go into detail. To explain what it felt like in my hands to snap bones as easily as breaking twigs. How stepping on their bodies was like stepping on glass. How I wanted to howl in victory like a fucking animal the second I heard the sweet music of their agony, or their begging cries for mercy. But I wasn't a merciful being, far fucking from it. Not when I was coating my tongue with their blood and gorging myself on their life like a man determined to get drunk from their favourite beverage.

But I didn't say these things. Because I didn't want her to know just what a savage beast I was. No, she would discover that out for herself soon enough. But for now, I wanted her how I wanted her, and the look of disdain and disgust was most certainly not the thought I had in mind.

So, I warned her in the calmest way I knew how, with her ass sat in my lap and her warmth surrounding me. It centred me, stilled my anger down to a simmer and enough that I could be soft with her. I could be gentle despite the angry bite of my words.

But then the moment she admitted why she had said those things had been because she had been worried about me, an emotion I wasn't used to feeling took hold of me and morphed into something dark and cruel. And like a bastard I had lashed out at her intending to hurt her the only way I could, *with my fucking words*.

Because the truth was, I might be rough with her, if only to give her a glimpse into what her future with me would be like, but actually hurt her physically, well the idea made me feel sick and a stomach of blood threatened to reappear at the thought.

So, I had hurt her with what I knew would work,

'Worried for me, or for your mother?' the second I had said it I had to mask my regret, for I wanted to kick my own ass. I wanted to fucking cut out my own tongue and offer it to her as payment for my foolishness. The way she had recoiled back from me, I had no choice but to let her. Because the very mention of her mother was like her own brand of venom, a bitterness she couldn't get past, not until she first knew the truth…but right now that wasn't something I would permit. Not when the only outcome would be her running from me. No, first I had to bind her to me so running wasn't an option.

Only then when I was assured of being able to hunt her with ease, would I chance easing her pain with her mother.

But with that ease came a whole different kind of hurt…

My kind of kindness.

CHAPTER SEVENTEEN

MY THREATENED HEART

Punishments.

Was it hers or mine?

Because of my need to punish her that night, in return she went to slap me yet a fucking again! But then something in her switched and my punishment wasn't the sting she tried to inflict but her actions after. It started when she took me completely off guard, doing so by taking control when she practically threw herself back in my arms and kissed me as though I was her own fucking God to worship.

The way she had ground herself down on my straining cock had me close to banding her to me and walking from the room with only one intention. Finally making her mine and breaking through the last barrier between us...*literally.*

But then, just as quickly as she gave herself to me, she was tearing herself away, giving back as good as I fucking gave her with the cruelness of my previous words. The second she snarled,

'You don't get to humiliate me sexually ever again, you

heartless bastard!' After this she ran from me, and I was in too much shock to react quick enough. Hell, even my council were as fucking dumbfounded as I was! I even remember reaching out for her and her getting away, something I allowed her to do just so I could react the way I wanted to without her witnessing it. The fear in her eyes would have been my own brand of venom hissed back at me and I didn't feel like getting stung anytime soon. So, I let her go, knowing that I could have been at her before she even made it three steps from my table if I'd wanted.

But instead I waited until I heard the door slam behind her before I erupted out of my chair and threw the fucking thing through the glass barriers that separated the VIP from the rest of the club. The sound of glass exploding before the echoing of the chair smashing into large splinters two floors below, did little to ease my burning rage.

"FUCK!" I roared, throwing my arms behind me, so far lost in wrath I felt as if my skin was going to split wide fucking open and allow the Devil's beast to take control completely. I even ignored the shocked looks of my people as they had rarely ever witnessed such uncontrollable rage in me before. Calm, collected, brutal rage yes, but one that burned like the pits of hot Hell, ready to destroy a fucking city rage...then no.

And I knew why it was, because I had yet to claim her. I had yet to break through the barrier that was my right to do so and claim her the way no man had ever done before or would ever get the chance to after me. The girl was mine and the thought of anyone taking that from me, let alone her doing so herself, well it had me blind fucking murderous!

My need to take her was growing with an intensity that pushed at every part of my dominant personality. It made me think of nothing else and I knew it would only get worse. Putting space between us all these years had been the smartest fucking thing I had ever done, as now, being this close to her, well this was nothing but self-inflicted torture!

But I knew now that there was no going back. I couldn't walk away now or put space between us once more. It was too late for that. I was too far gone. Even now my body itched to take her, or at the very least taste her again. Which was why I was doing yet another stupid thing and that was demanding that she not play with fire ever again. She needed to learn her damn lesson one way or another, whether I had to pin her to the fucking wall and keep her there until she understood who the fuck she was messing with!

I managed to calm enough to speak, first taking large rumbling breaths before doing so.

"The two I left alive, I collared them, track them and find out who else has a fucking death wish!" I snarled out the order before going in search of my next prey, one considerably more delicious than anything I had ever tasted before.

I had barged through the doors, hearing the crack as they hit back against the walls, wood splitting the moment they did. Then the second I found my leather jacket discarded on the floor in the lobby I picked it up and twisted the leather around in my hands as my undiluted rage continued to get the better of me. I knew I was free to leave my men in charge of finding out who was at the top of the mortal food chain, one that would now be easier since I had marked each with a unique marker that Hakan would be able to track, as was one of his gifts. After all we called it being collared for a reason.

And more importantly, this allowed me the time to show Amelia exactly who she was fucking with or more like what happens when she taunted the beast...*she would get my fangs.*

I had then stormed into what I had declared as her personal space, dominating the air around me with the power of my rage and frustration. Something that the second I found her, escaped me in a single heartbeat, and as quickly as if some unnatural force was sucking me dry of it only to replace the intensity of my emotions with a blinding lust. I had heard the shower but didn't think to stop, knowing the possibility that she could have been in there. Of course, the second I broke open the door, angered that there had been any barrier between us, I had ended up rooted to the spot at just the sight of her.

She was fucking exquisite!

I didn't know who it was that invented the shower glass doors that wouldn't steam up but I was ready to write them a check for millions in thanks. For now it offered me the clear view of what I could easily declare as the most beautiful sight in the world.

My Chosen One naked.

But not just naked, *wet and naked.* Gods have mercy on my damaged soul, for what I wanted to do to this woman was nothing short of Hellish and sinful! All that naturally golden tanned skin. That midnight waterfall of glossy black hair cascading down her back, as dark as the fringe of thick lashes that framed the most beautiful eyes in the world. Gods in Heaven, below she was fucking perfection. She actually stole my breath away from me and as much as I wanted to pounce on her, I was also actually afraid that when I did, I would simply pass right through her.

Because in that moment I felt too blessed to even believe she was real. Like it was a trap and she was in fact some kind of siren luring me to my death, a life I would have signed over to her in my last heartbeat. But she had no clue as to the immense power she held over me. To the point that even when she shook her head, telling me not to come closer, I knew no force alive would have stopped me in that moment. *Not even her.*

I just had to taste her and fully this time. Not just the bare sample I'd been tortured with on her lips. No, this time I wanted it all, starting with the cream of her sex, produced only by her lustful want of me. So, I hadn't stopped. I hadn't given into her silent demand. Instead I had taken what was mine and it had been nothing short of a feast fit for the Gods.

Fucking divine.

I had feared that once I started, I wouldn't ever have let her go and to be truthful, I could have done so for hours. Hell, I wanted to get drunk from her flavour and drown in her soft moans as she came with my fingers inside her and my teeth firmly embedded at her clit. I had remembered to take care at least, making sure not to break the barrier of her innocence with my fingers, knowing that honour was for my cock alone. Something when finding her bare, wet and ready for me had nearly been done in the fucking shower. But in the end, I knew that I wanted her first time with me to be what she deserved. Time would be taken, care shown and not the result of my mindless lust at seeing her naked for the first time like a rutting teenager!

No, for now I knew that the three orgasms I had given her and the blood I had taken was enough, especially when her body could no longer support itself, weak from her sudden blood loss. I knew then that I would have to take care, learning restraint around her for I didn't want to accidently harm her in anyway.

After all, being with a mortal was new to me. Oh, who was I lying to, for it was all fucking new to me! Every Gods be damned feeling I now had was all new, and in honesty I didn't know how Dom had fucking survived it when meeting his own Chosen One. I felt as though I was willingly signing myself up for insanity!

Just like the second I felt her go limp in my arms feeling that moment of panic. Just like I had that night when finding her taken from my club.

Panic.

Fucking panic!

I didn't panic, ever! I was a fucking King and son of Lucifer for fuck sake! But if that was the case, the second she lost consciousness, this little mortal beauty in my arms, why did I have the urge to protect her, to care for her, why was it taking over me?!

The reason why I gave into it and when I was assured she was safe and her breaths deep and even, I took care of my girl. I held her in my arms, lowered us both to the shower floor and then took my time washing her. It felt in that moment as if caring for a fallen angel, one that simply had found the world too much to bear and decided to sleep through life. She looked so peaceful, as I wrapped her body in a towel and carried her to her bed, before laying her down facing me, so I could simply watch her.

And never, in all my years on this Earth, had I ever taken so much time and care when being with a woman. In fact, I barely even remembered my time before I had turned, which included all the women I had bedded. One face in particular I should have remembered better than all the rest, but after over two thousand years, I was sad to say that her image had long ago blurred from my memory. But I wasn't that man anymore, nor had I been for a very long time.

Christ had seen to that.

I had been thankful to see her sleep and to do so peacefully in my arms felt like another gift. Another gift after the one she let me abuse with my mouth and hands in the shower. But when she did finally wake, she had gotten all shy after what I had done to her and I had confessed to knowing that she had never been with a man before. And, well, if it made me a bastard preventing such from happening then so be it, I would claim the title gladly. For she had been destined for me by the Gods themselves and really, it was about fucking time I was entitled to my due.

But then I had been surprised, for after a brief moment of annoyance on her part and confessing only a few of my sins against her, on the whole she had woken up playful. A side to her I had only seen brief glimpses of before. Starting with when she had tried to hide her modesty. Something that had been utterly pointless at this juncture, considering I had just spent a good few hours not only staring at her naked form, when making sure the sheets didn't cover her entirely, but also after I had washed every inch of her body.

But she had pulled up the sheet, her embarrassment being nothing short of adorable. But then in doing so, had exposed myself and when her eyes homed right in on my very obvious and hard arousal, her reaction had been priceless. Shouting out loud about how large I was, I am not going to lie, was a compliment I was claiming whether it was said more in panic on her part or not. However, her reaction after blurting this out was to cover her mouth, dropping the sheet in the process.

By the Gods, but I would never forget the sight of her reaching for it, only to end up in a pile on the floor tangled among the covers. It had been the cutest sight I had ever witnessed, still amazed that I could find the sentiment both amusing and a great fucking turn on! For all I wanted to do was scoop her up and kiss every inch of blush on her body, one I could see growing when I shifted to look down at her over the end of the bed.

Shortly after this and a little teasing later we ended up playfully fighting over the sheet, and I found myself feeling something I never had before. A lightness in my heart as if someone had replaced it with one no longer cold and hard like stone but one that actually beat.

A heartbeat only for one woman.

But then when that knock on the door came, I had wanted to cover her body with my own and snarl at the door *mine*. I had wanted to hide her away and force my will upon Clay to piss off and leave me to my Heaven found. Gods, but I fucking deserved it after all this time.

But then my rational mind had kicked in as I knew why he had arrived. I still had a fucking job to do. Like the whole race of people to protect, including her mother. But mainly, I had a Chosen One to keep safe and that included removing this thorn in my side...*permanently.*

In the end I had given in to the impulse but doing so by finishing our game and winning my victory after sliding her slight body beneath my own, making sure I didn't crush her with my weight. It wasn't lost on me our considerable size difference, and if anything, simply made me even more protective of her fragile and mortal frame. I knew that when I took her for the first time, then I would have to take care, and not lose myself to my other side. The side that craved her beyond all rational thought.

But then she started to continue her playful ways adding that wicked and easy humor to it, and I couldn't help but shake my head, asking myself if it was even possible for someone to be so perfect. She was unlike any other I had ever met before and the knowledge that she was mine, *made for me...* well, it was like a fucking gift I would have stolen had it not been given to me freely!

But then she went once again throwing sass and fire my way and I found myself unable to just leave without one last taste, something she craved just as much as I did. Especially when I tore the sheet from her and feasted on her beautiful breasts the way I had always wanted to. Gods, but even her breasts were utter perfection and her skin tasted better than I ever imagined it would.

But then getting her all hot and bothered I knew what would happen the second I closed that door and the thought made me want to growl, because I was a fucking madman if I could get jealous of her own damn hand touching what was mine!

I honestly didn't know if by the time I had her it would end up calming my obsession and possessiveness or actually just make it worse? Either way, it was happening even if I knew which was the most practical of the two to hope for. Because I couldn't imagine it much worse than it was now, short of locking her in a damn comfortable prison cell and tying her to my bed each night! That or I was close to losing my fucking mind! The only time I felt at ease was when I was with her, surrounded by everything that was my personal little sun.

Because long ago Keira may have had the ability to blind me with the sun on the few occasions we kissed, but with Amelia, she didn't just show me the sun.

She became it.

She was the heat that warmed my heart and didn't blind me but instead bound me to it, wrapping me up like a heated cocoon and holding my newly beating heart safely inside it, never again letting it turn to ice. That was when I knew that Keira had only led me to my destiny, she had never been the true source of it.

But I knew the issues Amelia would face with our history, her mother's and mine. Especially once all truth came to light. And to be honest I couldn't blame her, for to a lot of people it would have sounded wrong. But the difference between being mortal and immortal was time.

Time was a very different concept for us, and for me I had quickly come to learn that my fascination with Keira had solely been based on an unknown future. I knew that now. For I had never felt the way I felt for Amelia about anyone, Keira included. And even though small elements of her mother shone through in her daughter, her distinctive humor and clumsiness being two of them, she didn't remind me of her in the slightest, for she was totally unique and utterly made to be mine.

Now all I needed to do was convince her of that fact. But all in good time.

And speaking of time, fate had just brought me to my enemies door.

Brought me to my second night of death.

The car pulled up to a large mansion which was one of the few in the neighborhood of Schwabing, just north of the center of Munich. And seeing as Munich was Germany's most expensive city, then Schwabing was one of its richest neighborhoods. In fact, I myself had a few large apartments in the area for investment purposes and not as ones I ever lived in. There was little point seeing as I spent most of my time between Transfusion and my hidden castle at lake Königssee. But Schwabing was no more than twenty minutes' drive from The Neue Rathaus, the new town hall and one that held a particular memory for me.

It was a magnificent neo-gothic building from the turn of the century which architecturally dominated the north side of Munich's Marienplatz. But it also happened to be one of the few places I liked to go and contemplate, something I had done many times after that night. It hadn't been long after saving Keira from the auction house, and at the time, finding her dressed as a damn bird hanging trapped in a gilded cage. It was at a time I thought my love for her was without compare and well, it foolishly had been. I had known what Dom had done and shamelessly used it as an excuse to have her for myself, knowing that she was hurt and vulnerable at the time.

I had come so close to owning her, but then fate had intervened, and it was one of the only things I ever thanked the Gods for doing. Because in that moment, naked together on that clock tower and under a blanket of stars had been when the Gods had spoken, giving me a glimpse of what awaited in my future.

Giving me my first glimpse of my Amelia.

I swear I had torn myself from Keira so quickly, I felt fucking whiplash. And since then, I thought to how many times I had been back there just staring at the fucking moon like some hopeless romantic and nearly giving in to the impulse to fucking pray just for one more flicker of her image, as I had seen it that night. Asking myself how long I would have to wait until I could finally have her, until she was to arrive in the world. Something at the time I had no idea would actually come as a result from the immense love between Keira and Dom. I had no idea at all and wouldn't have believed it even if someone had told me. Not until I saw for myself.

Not until I saved her life for the first time. The first time our paths crossed and not yet classed as the woman she was today. Just sixteen years old and already getting herself into trouble by sneaking into the Devil's Ring, a fight club owned by the King of the Hellbeasts, Jared Cerberus.

But that night changed everything.

Because I knew the draw, the connection, the once foolish belief of love I had for Keira was all because of what she would give me. The life she would create, at the time it also felt like some fucking cosmic joke the Gods had played on us both all the time. Of course, Keira knew who her daughter was to me, for she was no fool. She had even once pleaded with me to make my move. But at the time I had believed this a desperate attempt at keeping her daughter an immortal, knowing a lifetime of my blood would change her as it had started to do with Keira back when she too was mortal and first met Dom. But there was something she didn't yet know.

That no one knew.

And if they did, then I doubted even she would have believed me worthy enough for her little girl. But I was done waiting and done with my loyalty to Keira, for what I owed her had come to an end. Because I had paid my dues. The Gods knew how much I had fucking paid them, I thought feeling my gloved hand clench at the memory.

The reason for seven years fucking waiting!

It was of little wonder why by the time I entered the opulent residence I was seething. For starters they were the reason I was here now and not back with the girl I had waited twenty seven lifetimes for! Yet another offense I would have them pay for along with the mountain of others building. Meaning as I was escorted into the building, I found my strides self-assured and with deadly purpose.

I glanced off to the side and scoffed at the masked ball that seemed in full swing. One filled with members of the Skull and Bone, mortals each of them playing at being a demon for the night, an angel on their arm and every single heartbeat totally unaware as to what was really going on beneath their very noses.

They believed it just to be another event held by a senior member of the society. Some eccentric rich businessman inviting everyone to Germany for its annual ball, this year finding it being hosted in Munich. I'd had my people do enough research into the society to know enough that most mortals had no clue to the true nature it hid behind. Liessa had done well, but then again, with the age of social media, there was always someone who couldn't help themselves in thinking the world cared enough to know what they were doing on the weekend.

I had once feared that Amelia would have willingly put

herself at risk in following the decades old trend, but thankfully she was smart enough to refrain from joining any online social sites.

Besides, I already knew of her addiction to donuts without needing the pictures to prove it every time she bought one. Mmm, maybe that was why she was so sweet and gifted me with enough curves it made my mouth water. Hell, just thinking about the little bite marks I would soon leave on them had me fighting myself before I simply became a walking hard on.

But just the idea of seeing her body marked by my touch had me forcing down the image before I walked into this meeting with a fucking hard on that could have hammered nails into a block of Quebracho. Also known as quebrar hacha, which literally means axe breaker in Spanish, for it was known to be one of heaviest and hardest woods on Earth. Yeah, think of wood Luc, that will fucking help, I thought rolling my eyes at myself this time.

Although having a piece of that wood in my hands right now would have helped in focusing my mind more on violence than lust. I even found myself cracking my neck to one side just as my body hummed at the thought of the carnage that I knew would shortly ensue from behind the double doors I was being led towards. Finally, I was about to come face to face with the fuckers who thought they could hurt my woman and steal from me!

The door opened either side by two servants dressed in white suits and masked with the faces of what I could only think were supposed to depict that of a tortured soul. I shook my head thinking that they had no fucking clue on what a tortured soul looked like, but then again, what type of guest would I be if I didn't correct them.

Time for a little show and tell, I think. My grin was pure evil the moment I stepped inside the large ballroom that was floor to ceiling marble with a startling blood red vein running through it. The only difference was the introduction of black marble in the checkered design on the floor, making the blood vein stand out even more against the gloss of darkness.

Three figures stood by an altar at the end of the room and as I approached, I scanned my surroundings, sending out a wave of power to find any hidden minds tucked away in the balcony that surrounded three sides of the room. The large glass window in front of me was an exact replica of one of the stained glass windows in the Duomo di Milano, the cathedral in the center of Milan. It was one that depicted a war between Heaven and Hell. Armed angels from above striking down at the demons below.

Well, if they wanted a war, then it would be short lived for this demon didn't need an army at my back and walking in here alone proved that. But my wave of power detected that although no life was hidden in the shadows above, like a sniper with the sight of my head in his scope, it did detect some power. One human and two of my own kind...

"Rogues." I hissed the moment I felt them like a stain on my soul. A mistake I wished I had the ability to claw back, taking from them what I had once given far too freely.

Rogues were hunted down and destroyed, killed for abusing the power I had once granted them. I thought I had caught them all and they were the reason I now only selected the most powerful demons for the change. Because once I did then that power would become my own, adding to my strength and making it even harder for them to become rogue.

But this decision had only been in the last few hundred years or so, as before then I simply built my army based on numbers, foolishly believing that was where my strength lay. As those that were weaker easily passed through my radar and were easier to succumb to the likes of a powerful casting of a witch. But even then, to twist my ties to those I sired was not an easy feat and often ended up killing the demon, hence why there weren't many rogues for me to contend with once that tie between us was severed, of which only two ways were possible, one by a witch and the other by my own doing.

Although the second often meant a death sentence, as without me they wouldn't often survive unless finding themselves a very powerful witch or warlock, and there weren't many. One was my own, a witch I turned named Nesteemia, and the other with that level of power was named Rue, who was loyal to Dom. That left only two others to name and one from all accounts of my people had died by my hand long ago.

I watched as they lifted their blood red cloaks with a roll of my eyes at the theatrics. For surely my kind should have known better than to give in to the fanatical whims of what humans believed my kind to be. I even suppressed a chuckle when Amelia had threatened to call me Dracula back at the museum. I would have thought the mortals' notion of my kind far surpassed the likes of Bram Stoker by now.

But saying that, I believed Dom still carried out the traditions when a new soul was to pass to a new vessel when the moon was right and shining down in his temple. But then again, he was as old as dirt, so it was of little surprise. I, however, thought the sight was a ridiculous one and unless I was dressing as something I wasn't for one of Pip's outlandish parties, then I would wear what I damn well pleased and this would be without a fucking cape or hooded cloak!

We were well past those times, thank the Gods!

"Ah the King grants us with his presence at last," the mortal in the center said and I frowned asking myself where I had seen his face before. It wasn't often I would ever forget...

"You," I snarled the moment it came back to me making him grin, one that slipped slightly when I took a threatening

step forward. The mortal cretin before me was the same one who had dared touch what was only mine to touch.

It had been the night of the gala when coming to the end of Amelia's charming little tour. I had decided to sink back into the shadows to observe her in private, for I knew my presence was throwing her off her game. But then I had watched as the man placed a hand on her shoulder, squeezing it slightly as if to gain more of her attention before saying some extraneous nonsense about stepping back in time.

Well, I could see now that my punishment for that was still in the form of a cast on his hand, for I had broken his fingers with a thought before sending him on his way.

"Ah yes, I have you to thank for this I suppose," he said with a misplaced air of authority.

"And the promise of more to come, I can assure you," I replied looking down at my ungloved hand and allowing my talons to grow, smirking back at him when he paled significantly. Then I turned my attention to the other two which were of my kind and soon I was recognizing them as well, snarling the moment I did. The hatred in their burning crimson eyes was easy to see.

"So, this is your next plan is it, swapping the use of mindless mortal cattle in a penniless colony, to a cult better dressed...ones just as foolish through the guise of their rich society, I see," I said nodding to the human in the middle who glared at me. But as calm as I seemed I was seething inside. Because now I was thinking back to the scum of the 'fathers' who had kidnapped Keira and made her believe she was someone else for almost a year, poisoning her mind and forcing her to live within the colony they created.

These two were the only ones who managed to escape, running from the fight at the first chance they got, it would seem.

"You won't be saying that soon, not when you will find yourself repeating history before too long." I frowned in question, as there was all manner in which those words could be taken. However, they weren't wrong for the doors opened behind me and the second they did Lucifer's blood froze in my cold black heart.

A heart Amelia had brought back to life.

The heart of a masked angel and...

My heart now threatened by a blade held at her own.

CHAPTER EIGHTEEN

WEB OF LIES WE WEAVE

The moment I watched as Amelia was dragged into the ballroom by her hair, I felt the cracks branch out around where I stood as my rage built to new heights. Instantly I sent out a wave of power, expecting my will to be obeyed and my enemies to all drop to their knees. But when this didn't happen, once more a frozen chill crept its way up my spine, like the Devil himself had dipped his talons in ice and was now using them to drag his body up my fucking back.

They were immune.

I knew then that they hadn't simply become rogue but in fact had a new master, one that held their will for his own and therefore they were impervious to mine. Something that had never happened before. Meaning only one thing, this new master of theirs held a power of will that matched even the strength of my own.

Something that should have been fucking impossible!

I sucked in a deep breath, now knowing that I had to play this situation very fucking carefully, because this had most certainly changed things. Which now meant I had no other choice but to exercise my other gifts, one of which was a seemingly ice cold reserve that was infallible.

Of course, this would be easier said than done, especially when seeing the way my girl was being dragged forward with a blade to her chest and I had to witness my Angel wincing in pain. Because that was exactly what she looked like right then, dressed all in white, with feathers framing her wide eyes full of panic. But there was also a hint of something else...*relief.* She was glad to see me, and I wished in that moment that I could have gained access to her mind. To infiltrate her thoughts so I could have told her all the things I needed to. The main one being for her to trust me.

I knew she thought I was about to make my move, and I would have liked to but then I was also very aware of the blade that quickly shifted from her chest to her neck as soon as she was forced to stop a few feet from the door. This was done on purpose so I had no hope in getting to her before that knife slit her throat. Now, if it had been a mortal hand holding that blade, then it would have been different, but it wasn't.

Because the rogue had been right, this was history repeating itself. I knew that when her name was hissed from between my fangs,

"Layla." She smirked when I said her name and I swear if it was the last thing I ever did, I would cut it from her face, preventing the sight ever to be seen again.

"Mast...oops, I almost forgot, I don't have to call you that anymore, not since you cast me out and left me to die without you," she said, her face twisting at the end as the memory resurfaced. Oh, but she had waited a long time for her revenge and with that fucking blade against my Chosen One's neck, then I would now say it was fucking complete. Which was why I knew I had to play this one carefully, seeing first what they knew and playing one of my biggest strengths, the ability to keep my shit together and my emotions so close to my fucking chest, no fucker would have a clue at what I was thinking.

"You survived well enough I see," I answered in a flippant way that had her frowning in question. She had expected more of a reaction and the brief look of surprise to the rogues at the altar confirmed my suspicions. I knew then that she had convinced them that Amelia meant something to me and was worth using as a bargaining chip.

Fuck! But what I had to do next would feel as if I was being forced to eat the burning hot sands of Persia. But then again, it wasn't as if I hadn't had to lie before. And looking at that blade by her throat, I knew her safety came first. Speaking of safety, how the fuck had they even managed to kidnap her in the first place?

"You were saying something about swapping mindless mortal cattle?" One of the rogues said in a tone that was laced with confidence. I had to hold back a growl and instead replace it with a feigned act of indifference.

"Ah yes, you're right, I see now that I can add a disgruntled ex-lover to the list and one who foolishly believes she holds something of value to me beneath that blade," I said with a nonchalant and unimpressed tone. I heard Amelia suck in a sharp breath in between her teeth and I held back my body's natural instinct to flinch, unsure if her reaction was to my words or to Layla's rough treatment of her. I tried not to eye that blade, knowing this too would give away my concern for her.

But I knew it had worked as each of the three in front of me shot annoyed looks to Layla, telling me this had been her plan in the making. She glared back at them before turning her cruel eyes back to me. Then she tore off Amelia's mask and sneered,

"Cut this shit Lucius, I know you care for her!" I scoffed at this and replied,

"If you are referring to any attention shown towards her, I can assure you it is nothing more than a tactic to keep the girl in her place until I can palm off the burden to her family. But then again, if you have been keeping watch on Afterlife, as you obviously have on Transfusion, then you will know for yourself that they were on their way to Munich for that very reason," I said calling their bluff, something that was starting to work on the three who seemed to be calling the shots, for they each looked to the other in question. Amelia this time sucked in a startled breath before hissing her curse at me,

"You bastard!" The urge to close my eyes and grimace was one I fought, replacing it with a knowing smirk sent her way in confidence adding,

"Sorry Princess, but fun's over, time for mummy and daddy to take you home and finally off my hands."

"Why you, you! Gods damn you Lucius, it was all a fucking lie!" she screamed at me but when she started struggling against Layla, I nearly fucking cursed her for real, hissing for her not to be stupid and stay fucking still!

"Of course, it was a fucking lie, you really believe I would give a shit about a spoilt, little mortal brat who is pathetic enough to believe herself in love with me and more foolish yet, that my love could be returned!" I snarled this time acting out my annoyance and I swear the second tears welled up in her stunning blue eyes, I felt myself close to fucking breaking right alongside of her!

But I knew it was working as the human in the middle snapped,

"Layla, you were wrong."

"What!? He's fucking lying, it's what he does!" At this point Amelia finally let loose her tears and whispered,

"Hhhow could... you...how..." A sob tearing from her

throat cut the heartbreak off and I forced my breathing to stay steady, along with keeping my body relaxed.

"Quite fucking easily, I assure you…but I will tell you princess, the blood certainly helped," I said with a fake grin, granting her a wink and a lick of my lips, acting exactly as the bastard she had claimed me to be.

"I fucking hate you!" she screamed and would have turned her head away had the blade not still been there as a threat, but in Layla's frustration she had at least let it slip slightly. I blew Amelia a mocking kiss and laughed before facing the three, demanding,

"Now can we move this shit along, as I take it the real reason I am here is you want to bargain for the box," I said making the mortal cross his arms as if this would aid the older man in being more intimidating. Well, I wondered how intimidating he would find himself to be without the two rogues at his sides.

"It belongs to the Skull and Bones, you stole it," he snapped making me want to roll my fucking eyes.

"Ah, ah, ah, get it right asshole, her father was the one who stole it, not me. I was simply charged with taking possession of it," I told him nodding back over my shoulder to who no one in this room knew was my fucking soulmate at the mercy of the whims of a crazy bitch. How the fucking God's name I was keeping my shit together I had no fucking clue!

"Yes, and if you remember, he did so by killing how many mortals, all in the name of protecting this, what did he call her, a spoilt, little mortal brat…seems to me to be a big fucking hole in your story there Luc!" Layla spat out making me snarl back at her in response.

"You want to fucking challenge me, Lahash, then kick the girl aside and come and get it!" I said making her grin.

"Ah, so you do want me to let the girl go?" she said as if she had just proved a point.

"You see, I was right!" I made a show of rolling my eyes for real this time and said,

"I was unaware that you had the ability to beat me with a mortal hostage in tow...I have to say that's impressive. Well, come now, let's see it..." When she didn't take a step towards me I growled at her,

"No, I didn't fucking think so!" I then turned my attention back to the men and knew it was time to drive my point home and in the worst fucking way possible.

Words that were unforgettable the first time.

But the second, *they would be unforgivable.*

"Not that it is anyone's fucking business but I made a promise to her mother to protect her daughter but that promise only goes so fucking far. The bitch means nothing to me, I assure you... now her mother on the other hand...well, I think Layla remembers all too well the level of love I hold for the King's Electus, seeing as she tried to kill her for it...quite a few attempts if memory serves me right...oh but wait, did she fail to mention this?" I said grinning the second I drove those doubts in Layla home and fucking buried her under them. Amelia on the opposite end of this looked as if I had just fucking broken her in two. She kept whispering a hopeless,

"No, no, no it's not...it...can't be true."

"Now, if you want to continue to discuss this, then two things happen, first get that psychotic ex of mine out of my sight, for I think I have already established that she is fucking useless to you and clearly knows nothing!" I snapped snarling back at her over my shoulder and trying to ignore the way her hand that held the blade shook. By the Gods, I would fucking rip her apart should she hurt my girl! This thought at least eased my rage enough to continue my act.

"And the other?"

"What! How dare you, you would…"

"Shut up, Lahash!" One of the rogues growled and with the way he did, I would say that they had some power over her at least. Good, because I would need that to be the case, for she was about to get ordered to let my girl go.

"Release the girl, let her walk out of here untouched and I will consider your terms of a possible exchange."

"YOU SEE! He wants you to let her go! I told you he cares for her!" Layla shouted quickly and I growled low before saying,

"You want a fucking war with the King of Kings, then go right fucking ahead, but I am warning you now, hurt his precious daughter and the wrath of Gods will be nothing in comparison. And as for her mother, if you know our history, then you will know who it is I am talking about…you know, the one with enough power she fought the fucking Titans *and* won…what do you think will fucking happen, uh?" At this the mortal who obviously had no clue looked to the other two each side of him and they each nodded at the silent question, now looking more fearfully at Amelia.

I couldn't help but feel my gloved hand tense, clenching at my side as I knew I was mere moments from them letting her go. And it couldn't have come soon enough either for I could feel my rage about to snap and my beast about to erupt. Too fucking close.

"Let the girl go, Layla!" One of the rogues ordered and I had to force myself not to take a deep breath in relief.

"WHAT! I can't believe this, don't you see, you are falling for his bullshit, just like he wants you to!" she shouted back and I swear it was only the image of crushing her skull beneath my boot that was holding me back from ruining all of this.

"I gave you an order!" he roared making her flinch. I could

almost feel my victory, for what they didn't know was that the second Amelia was out of the line of threat, then I would be free to set my plan into motion. Oh and there would be blood and it would look fucking beautiful decorating this room adding to the vein of crimson with something real. But with her in here I couldn't risk her getting caught in the crossfire. She was my main priority and I needed to get rid of the risk first.

But Layla wasn't yet ready to give up her prize. And like a dog with a bone she now felt backed into a corner enough to have a point to prove.

"No!"

"What did you say to me?!" the rogue demanded taking a threatening step forward.

"I promise you, that if you let her go now then he has no reason to give you the fucking box! You will be giving away the only thing you have to bargain with and the only thing that is keeping him from ripping you all apart, besides it is not your call to make!"

"He put me in charge, Lahash, remember that!" the rogue said, giving away the fact that, just as I thought, there was someone else at the top giving the commands and these three were just a level up from a lacky, that most likely meant that I had to at the very least leave one of them alive. Although I wasn't sure that the mortal would survive as he would no doubt have a damn heart attack when he saw what I had planned for the rogues.

"Yes, and just think about what he has the power to do to you should you fuck up his one opportunity to get the box and he knows it was you that ordered the girl released!" she argued but the rogue feared my words more than hers, so told her,

"I will take that chance, because a war with the Dravens isn't what he would want either. Now, let the damn girl go!" he ordered this time showing his fangs…ah yes, I would rip those out first I think, maybe make him choke on them.

"Fine, I will fucking prove it!"

"NO!" I roared but it was too late as it was being drowned out by Amelia's cry.

"AHHH!" The sound of Amelia's scream of pain was the limit that cut my cord of restraint because Layla's way to prove her point was to suddenly yank her head back and start cutting her throat, doing so slowly enough that it just broke the skin. But it was enough that blood poured down the front of her chest and white dress, soaking half of her crimson.

"STOP!" I roared making her still her actions.

"If you don't fucking let her go, I swear to you Lahash, I won't just rip out your heart, I will take fucking days torturing you before I fucking devoured it! NOW LET THE GIRL GO!" I bellowed this last part with enough power that marble split all around me, until it even travelled up the fucking walls. But it was a threat she didn't take seriously as she proved a point,

"I know you're fast Luc, but even you won't be able to stop me before I gut this bitch and slice her open. Bet you wished you had that power of will over us now don't you?" I snarled at her and fucking hated that she was right.

"LET. HER. GO." This time my demon spoke, and it shocked her to hear it, along with Amelia, who was now sagging slightly in her hold, despite the pain to her neck.

"And there is your proof…I told you, he cares for the bitch," she stated proudly, looking to the three and making the urge to do something potentially stupid growing by the fucking minute. Because even though I knew Amelia wasn't in danger of bleeding to death, it was clear that she was in pain and the sight was fucking with my head!

"Fine! We will seek our master's council and await his

word, but for now, have our men escort him to the prison you have ready." At this Layla grinned happily, before saying,

"Oh, it will be my pleasure. Now Luc, remember to behave now, as just think, I have this bitch at my mercy," she said removing the now stained blade and tapping Amelia on the side of the head with it, making me growl. Then she whistled, her grin slipping long enough to do so before it was back in place.

The doors opened and the lackies who had escorted me here, came back inside ready to take me to my cell. Layla had already started to walk both herself and Amelia back off to the sides, keeping out of range enough to know I wouldn't reach them in time before she had chance to kill my girl.

Meaning that I had no choice but to walk out the door, noting how the guards all kept their distance. The urge to tear into them was nearly too much to contain, but then I knew that they had me on a fucking leash. Because they could hurt her at any point should I start killing their men. The look I gave Amelia was one I hoped told her to hold on, to be brave a little longer. That I would save her, if it was the last thing I ever fucking did on this Earth!

"Oh, don't worry, if you're good she will join you shortly," Layla called back to me and the look I gave her over my shoulder promised nothing but pain, doing so until she was out of sight when the doors closed behind me.

I was then escorted down into the lower levels and inside what I assumed used to be a wine cellar that had been converted into a makeshift cell. I knew this as the scent of cork and wine still lingered as if it had seeped into the stone walls. The hallway was slightly damp and branched off into arched alcoves on each side.

The space at the very end was where I was intended for, as this was where the obvious money had been spent. Reinforced steel doors, similar in thickness to that of my own vault door faced me now and I wanted to laugh if they thought it enough to keep me caged. Because they could have been made from paper and it would have still done its job simply because they had Amelia at knife point. Had she not been a threat, then I simply could have killed the guards with a mere thought and walked right out of here.

But with her life threatened, I had to continue to 'be good' as Layla had put it. But the second I was inside and the door locked behind me, I found myself pacing the floor like a caged beast, concerned only for my girl. I worried about the cut to her throat, replaying it over and over in my mind, still trying to convince myself it wasn't deep enough to be a threat to her life...but what if I had been wrong?

I took in my surroundings again, just for something to focus my mind on and a distraction to alleviate my growing tension and worry. The room also had once been used for storing wine, but it would have been where the barrels had been kept.

Although the building didn't look that old my guess was that whoever commissioned this house, wanted it to have a 'grand English mansion' feel to it. That then included a more authentic looking wine cellar. And if you would go to the expense of making it look this way, then barrels were also part of the design. So, three large arches were against the back wall, each with a stepped inlay on the floor with wooden runs where the barrels would have sat.

A long padded bench covered in old red leather was also built into the walls, and obviously an addition added for the owner to sit amongst the rustic setting and enjoy a glass or two. At that moment I could have drunk fucking methane and breathed fire for my rage was building to near uncontrollable, as taking in the minute details of the room no longer helped.

Of course, I spotted the camera as soon as I stepped foot inside, knowing that they would be watching me. I wasn't sure if it was the kind to pick up audio but there was a speaker incorporated into the wall.

I decided to test the theory and roared loud enough that stone dust from the ceiling rained down around me,

"BRING ME THE GIRL!" Then I hit out at the door hard enough to cause it to buckle around my fist but not too hard to destroy it completely. After all, this was a test and I couldn't risk them hurting her.

"Bring me the girl and I will calm, or I will assume the worst and will break down this door, kill every last one of you and burn this house to the fucking ground!" I threatened making sure it was wordy enough. As expected, Layla's voice came through the speakers giving me exactly what I wanted.

"Wow, that looks like a full on man paddy in there. However, your roaring rants and threats are useless, Luc, no one can hear you. Besides, I'm being kind and giving you a roommate as Samson thought it best you heal your girlfriend just in case our master wants her in one piece. Who knows, he may want her for himself." I bellowed in anger at the thought, hitting out at the door again and this time actually cracking the hardened steel.

"Now, now, enough of that. Here she comes but I must warn you, if you try anything, escaping and such, once you have her then I will flood that room full of gas and set the whole fucking place alight before you have chance to stop me. So, if I were you, I would play nice…remember, I will be watching." I bared my fangs up at the camera knowing now that she couldn't hear me. That was one thing at least as when Amelia was finally brought to me, at least we had some shred of privacy.

Gods, but what was I to say to her after everything I had already said in the ballroom? The thought of her reaction was clawing at my insides. I had never been so unsure of anything in my whole life as I was in this moment. All I could hope for was the chance to explain and for her to be made to fucking listen long enough to accept my words as the truth.

Well, now was the time as I could hear footsteps approaching from behind the door. The second I heard the large locking mechanism shifting, I braced myself for what I may find. I swear if they had hurt her any more than what Layla already had, then I wasn't sure I wouldn't simply lose myself to the Hellish spawn I was reborn as.

Thankfully though, other than her injury, she seemed unharmed any further. However, the second she was pushed inside hard enough to go stumbling to the floor, I lost my shit. I managed to grab her before she landed, spun her to the side and grab the fucker's arm all before he had chance to close the door. Then with one quick movement I bent his arm back against the steel edge of the door and snapped the bone in one strike. Then I let him go and with him still howling in pain the door slammed shut.

"Tut, tut, Luc, that wasn't very nice," Layla's voice said over the speaker with a chuckle and I just gave the camera the finger, reminding me of what Amelia did back in my vault. Then I turned to face Amelia, putting my back to the camera. The first question came out quickly and in an unintentional bark of impatience.

"Are you alright?" She nodded slowly so as not to aggravate her wound, one she had been given a cloth to hold over to try and stop the bleeding. Then her sad, tear filled eyes looked up to the camera in question.

"They can't hear us." I told her and I saw her take a deep breath in relief.

"Good, that's good because I..." she said and was about to open her mouth to say more but with that one look, I knew it wouldn't be good, so I got in there first.

"Wait, just listen first and then you can hate me all you want but not before I have had chance to explain."

"Don't Lucius, there is…" she started but I cut her off.

"Yes, there is a lot to fucking say and you are going to listen, whether you damn well like it or not!" I demanded in a stern voice that brooked no argument, so she wisely shut up.

"I had no choice but to say those things, but you need to know that I didn't mean one fucking word I said. You are too important to me, my only Gods be damned weakness and if they knew just how much, then fuck knows what they would have done, what that psychotic bitch would have enjoyed fucking doing!" I took a breath and dragged a hand through my hair in my frustration before going right back for more,

"Hell, but she could have done so much worse than she already did, so you need to understand that my words meant nothing, but your safety does. I made a decision and for that part I won't apologize!" I snapped and the second her eyes became damp with emotion I caved,

"I am, however, sorry that you got hurt in the process, both physically and emotionally. You have to believe me." It was the most I had ever come fucking close to begging, but Gods she certainly deserved it after what I had put her through and not just in the last thirty minutes *but the last seven years*.

It was everything I should have said to her long ago but I had never had the desperation to push me into doing so before. Never felt the fear that I had up there in that ballroom. The way I saw the heartbreak in her eyes.

But then it was clear that once again I had underestimated my girl, just like I had done before. Because she simply said,

"I do."

"Come again?" I asked after jerking in some sort of double take asking myself if I had heard her correctly.

"I believe you." I frowned as if she was the one I didn't

believe in that moment. But then she stepped forward and fucking shocked me to my core when she said,

"You're not the only one who can act, Handsome." Then she winked at me before she pulled back her arm and let it go in a whoosh, cracking my cheek with her palm, sending my face to the side on impact.

As she once again,

Slapped me.

CHAPTER NINETEEN

HEALING HEARTS

I watched the way his face turned back so slowly, and my heart hammered in my chest in anticipation of his reaction. Needless to say, he didn't disappoint.

"You knew?" he asked on a rumble that sounded as if he was holding himself back. I rolled my lips inwards and nodded but then the second I hissed in pain forgetting my injury for a moment, his eyes lost their playful menacing side and grew intense. Then he took hold of the hand I was using to hold the cloth to my throat and after exerting a bit of pressure, he slowly pulled my hand away so he could assess the damage for himself.

"The bleeding has stopped at least," he said taking care not to hurt me further when examining it. But then when he wanted to see how deep it was I sucked in a breath through my teeth and he gave me an apologetic look in return.

"I will fucking kill her for hurting you...I will kill them all," he said with pure hatred coating his vow.

"Not a fan of your ex then?" I asked making him grant me an unamused look.

"She tried to kill your mother...many times," he stated in a furious tone.

"Yeah, I got that part."

"And then she slit your throat, so what do you fucking think?" he snapped, so I tried for humour again as he continued to examine the wound.

"Honestly?" I questioned before going on to joke,

"That she is just a crazy bitch and in fact you don't just want to kill all your exes... because no offence, you're hot and everything, but not sure I want to chance dating you if that's the case...so just friends, yeah?" At this I finally saw his lips twitch as he tried not to grin but instead hold on to his anger.

"*Absolutely not*...now stay still," he replied making me want to smile this time, knowing that he didn't want to be my friend. Because I had to confess, as much as I knew he was only saying all those things in the ballroom to save me, it still managed to hit a few too many nerves. Nerves that were already near shot to pieces. Which was why I couldn't help but say in what I knew was a small voice,

"You were very convincing up there."

I wasn't sure it was supposed to come out quite as vulnerable as it sounded, but it did. He lifted his eyes to mine and held my gaze for a few seconds longer than what was comfortable before replying with,

"I wasn't the only one."

I knew he was referring to my performance, one I knew I had no choice but to play along with. And in truth, it had been nice to know he had been worried that I hadn't believed him, blurting his reasons for lying as soon as I was thrown in here. Well, after he broke that guy's arm first.

I shrugged my shoulders, wincing again as I kept forgetting the pain it would cause.

"I told you to hold still!" This time he did growl at me and I knew it was because he was concerned, as it was obvious that seeing me hurt was pushing at his control to keep his temper. And boy did it hurt, I felt like my skin on was fire!

"Alright, Mr Bossy Pants, jeez anyone would think you were the one in pain," I snapped back because, well, because I obviously couldn't help myself and it was in fact helping in ignoring the pain. But then again I think the adrenaline was still keeping me going.

"And if I was, then I would know when to...Hold. Fucking. Still!" he shouted down at me. In fact, I was surprised during this whole thing that he was still being as gentle as he was, despite our little argument. But he did have a point so I let him have that one, with nothing more than a roll of my eyes.

"Seriously, did you just roll your eyes at me?" He snapped out the question and I would have gulped if I wouldn't just get told off for it and besides, my throat really did hurt like a mother fudger!

"I might have, but then again I might have had something in my eye... or *both of them,*" I added this last part slowly, when he raised a stern brow at me clearly silently calling me on my bullshit.

"Oh, come on, what are you going to do, spank my ass in here and give them a show whilst I bleed on the floor?" I asked making a growl rumble from his chest and I had to then question why I was pushing him.

"Let's call it an IOU should we, now take off your dress," he demanded making me frown and then shoot a look to the camera.

"Erm, why?" I asked, thinking the time to get naked wasn't really now. This was when he started walking me backwards and up against the wall, doing so under the camera and in what must have been a blind spot. I felt his leather hand come to my hip to steer me, and then before my back could hit the stone, he placed a hand there to stop me. Then he got closer to my face and said,

"Because the scent of your blood is driving me near fucking wild, and I don't know how much more I can take before my restraint snaps completely that, my Amelia, *is why.*" I suddenly looked down at myself and for the first time realised he was right, as I must have looked like a giant, walking, talking candy bar to a sugar addict!

My white dress I had stolen was soaked with my blood all the way down to my waist after that bitch had slit my throat. And that was when it hit me,

The shock part of being hurt.

"Oh Gods...Lucius I...I..." I started to shake as the adrenaline had chosen that moment to run dry and one look from Lucius and he knew it too.

I was crashing.

So, he took my face in his hands, making sure I stopped moving it as the pain of doing so was just making my panic worse.

"Ssshh, calm for me now, I will take care of you...Amelia, give me your eyes..." he asked and only when I did as he asked, did he repeat his promise,

"I will take care of you, okay?" His voice was gentle and soothing making me about to nod but he held me still.

"It's okay sweetheart, you are okay now, just be brave for me, just a little while longer, yeah?" I swallowed hard and my eyes watered as the pain was worse now that my adrenaline had up and left me.

"Okay," I said in a small voice that didn't sound like I had much more fight in me, but then again, I was here in his arms, so I knew I didn't need to fight yet, not with Lucius protecting me.

"I am going to take this dress off you now," he told me, taking over and I had to say I was glad to let him as I was shaking so much that I didn't think I would have been able to get the zip down. But Lucius had no problem. At first, he looked as if he was simply going to rip the thing off me but then must have thought better of it. Maybe he was scared that the quick action would jar my neck or maybe he just knew in that moment I needed a gentle hand. Whatever the reason, he reached behind me, stepping closer as if hugging me, which made me realise we had never hugged before.

But right then, in that moment, being in his arms with him unzipping my dress, it didn't feel like a hug type of moment. No, it felt like an 'I am undressing you before laying you on the bed to make love to you' type of moment. This was because he did it so slowly it felt more tender than the previous times we had been together. Because all those other times, it had been like a frenzied need to kiss each other but like this...well, in this moment between us, it felt too raw, too intense and too connected to be anything other than profound.

And from the looks of things I wasn't the only one feeling this way. His heavy breathing, tense muscles and intense gaze down at me told me so. Especially when he took half a step back and with both hands drew the straps of the dress down my shoulders. He did this so softly, I sucked in a breath as he skimmed both his bare fingers and leather clad ones down my arms until my bloody dress was falling from my body.

Then, unbelievably, I watched as this time he was the one swallowing hard as his eyes scanned the length of me in nothing but a blood soaked bra and white panties. And I had to wonder at the moment, knowing it was only with a Vampire that being soaked in blood could still be a turn on. But then, what did that make me, being the one soaked in blood and still turned on?

"Move away from the fucking wall and show yourselves!" The second his ex's voice filled the space, crackling over the speaker, I wanted to curse her for ruining the moment between us. But then again, Lucius got in there first, when he took a step back and made his thoughts clear when he looked up at the camera and said,

"Fuck off!" Then he reached up over his head and pulled off his T shirt before stepping back into me, despite her warning. I then watched as he looked to my neck and then back to the shirt in his hands. He must have been questioning the best way to do this, before he fisted the neck band and tore it a couple of inches.

I couldn't hold back my grateful smile as he dressed me, taking care of my injury. But he was soon looking sorry when I couldn't help but suck in a harsh breath when it hurt going past my neck even with the slightest touch. But then again, I would say that the sight of him now bare chested certainly helped. Because holy hell, but the sight of Lucius in nothing but a pair of jeans was droolworthy and most definitely managed to take away some of the pain.

Once I was wearing his T shirt that fit me like a short dress, he held out his hand for me to take so I could step out of the bloody dress that was now pooled at my feet as I was still wearing the heels. This at least put me a little closer to his face but then again, I doubted that we would be kissing in here with what we knew was at the very least an audience of one.

"Now let's see what we can do about that cut, shall we?" he said, leading me over to a bench on the opposite side to where the camera was, meaning we would be in view once more. But I think this was done so that whatever threat she could throw at us wouldn't end up hurting me further.

He lowered me down to the seat then knelt in front of me, putting us even closer in height.

"They can't hear us, and with me blocking you this way, they won't be able to read our lips. Tell me everything, how did they manage to kidnap you and were there any losses to my men?" I frowned at the question and then realised the level of shit I was about to be in.

"Your men are fine, no losses," I said after first swallowing hard, wincing in pain and thinking this the safer of the two parts to that question, even if I had hurt myself.

But he frowned, no doubt wondering how, without a full blown war against his men, I had managed to get kidnapped. Yep, I was in big shit. Which was why I said,

"If I tell you, can you promise you won't get angry?" It was lame I know, but right in that moment I didn't think a full blown argument was the way to go and besides, I liked this tender side of Lucius too much to want to lose it right now.

"Amelia." The moment he said my name in warning I had my answer.

"Then perhaps we should wait until you have healed me first," I said thinking this would give me more time. But then he decided to be blunt.

"Alright, but I should warn you, to do so will make you cum." I would have spluttered out some intangible sound if it wouldn't have hurt my neck, so instead opted for my mouth dropping, before then going with,

"Err…come again?" Two words we both used when being astounded by the other's unexpected answer.

"Depending on the severity of the injury, when one of my kind heals a mortal, it can be very intense and the only way for your mind to make sense of the intrusion…"

"Intrusion!?" He ignored this high pitched word and carried on,

"...is to do as it would with any other..."

"Intrusion?" I said, this time making use of the same word to finish off his answer making his lips twitch again as he fought a grin. Gods, but I loved it when he found me funny.

"So, let me get this straight, you're going to touch my neck and I am going to have an orgasm...is that correct?" I asked and he grinned before saying,

"Yes...didn't you ever learn this?"

"Off who, my parents because eww, that's gross?" This time he laughed.

"Point taken. Now try to relax."

"Yeah, well according to you in five minutes, that won't be a problem." Again, he grinned and then shook his head a little as if his inner thoughts of me amused him.

"Yes well, it will sting at first." Okay so that part didn't fill me with joy, not like the first. Although if I could choose, then having an orgasm in a cell whilst being watched by his crazy ex, didn't really do it for this naïve little virgin.

But then, instead of waiting for me to let him know I was ready, he simply bit into his hand and placed it over my neck before my gasp of shock was even finished. And he was right, at first it stung like he had just set it alight, but then as I started to fight to get away from the pain, he wrapped an arm around me and held me to him, whilst he continued to do his thing.

"Easy, it will pass, just hold on...*hold on for me, sweetheart*" He whispered this last part in my ear, after his arm had shifted at my back. His hand started caressing its way up my back before cupping the back of my head so as to keep me locked to his hand at my neck. But then I started to feel it, and it was like he said, the pain was only seconds before a warmth started to seep into my body and started blooming at what felt like the core of me. I must have tensed in his hold as I felt the intense feeling coming over me.

"Easy my Šemšā, easy now. Don't fight it...just let it happen," he said just as I felt my fingers grip onto his bare shoulders, before digging my nails into his back unable to help myself. It was the strangest sensation, feeling the rise of pleasure without actually being touched anywhere other than on my neck. But I was torn, feeling shame at what I knew was coming and my reaction to it, as though it felt wrong somehow. But even so I would have begged for it not to stop. I felt the tingling at the base of my spine, and I squeezed my legs together as a whimper escaped despite my closed lips.

Then I felt him softly chuckle before telling me,

"My stubborn little bird obviously needs my touch," he told me and then he started kissing and sucking at my shoulder, one that was easy to get to as his t shirt was too big for me and also torn at the neck. This time I opened my mouth and let out a breathy moan, allowing the feeling to flow instead of fighting it.

"Open up for me, girl," he said and I don't know why but I loved it when he called me that, doing so in that demanding tone of his. But I was also questioning his words of what he wanted from me, because my mind was fogged due to the pleasure.

"Spread your legs, princess," he demanded and I found my legs opening of their own accord not even caring that he had called me that. Not this time, because the way he hummed it, almost purring it against my cheek in a deep silky voice, then I loved the sound of it too much to be annoyed.

His hand left the back of my head and instead rested at the base of my spine at the same time his denim clad knee settled between my legs. Then without warning he pushed against my back, making my backside shoot forward on the bench and with my legs open and exposed, his knee ended up parting the lips of my sex. The second contact was made, I sucked in a startled breath.

Then he started rocking me forward on his knee, with his hand at my lower back doing so in a maddening rhythm. Oh Gods, but it felt so good, so dirty riding against his leg this way. The way the denim rubbed against my clit, well it was no wonder that in less than a minute doing this, I ended up coming against his knee, soaking the denim. I also let my head fall backwards pulling away from his hand and realising now that I was healed. Hell, but I could have been cured even before he put his knee to my core for all I knew. But I didn't care as I opened up my mouth to cry out my pleasure as the orgasm ripped through me. He grabbed the back of my head and this time pulled me forward so that my cry ended against his bare chest where I stayed until I finished shuddering against him.

Then, once it was done, I looked up at him through my lashes and found him looking down at me. I swallowed hard, no longer feeling pain and decided because I was embarrassed and needed to speak, I went with a very lame,

"Was it good for you?" At this he threw his head back and roared with laughter, before pulling up my face with both hands and just before he was about to kiss me, I pulled back and said,

"But what about the…" I never got to finish as he growled low,

"I don't give a fuck!" Then he kissed me, no longer caring about the show of indifference. One I think we could have still continued because healing me was always expected to end in a sexual release. But then kissing me afterwards, well that only showed them one thing, that *he cared*. But then, it was most likely one ship that sailed when she had slit my throat and the bitch ex of his knew it!

I would have said I cared but right then with Lucius kissing me and the euphoria still clinging on to my mind, then his lips on mine was all I could concentrate on. It was all I cared about. It was like a damn addiction as the second he kissed me...Hell, but the moment he even touched me, the entire world seemed to evaporate around us. Nothing else mattered, not even this place, being captured and our unsure future.

There was only him.

Only us.

Of course, this intensified the second he tore his lips from mine and said,

"I need to taste you and...and...*I. Am. Not. Fucking. Sorry,*" he said emphasizing each word in between each kiss down my neck to where my blood still remained. But then the second he made it to the first of my crimson stained skin, his hand fisted in my hair and yanked my head back suddenly. I yelped in shock, but it died the second he kissed, licked and sucked my skin clean, and his rumbling in pleasure was fucking just as addictive as him kissing me. Gods, but just knowing what I could do to him was like a drug, and I moaned at both the pleasure gained and the pleasure my blood gave back in return.

But then the sound of the door opening, cut our time short and Lucius suddenly banded both arms around me, holding me so close I could only just breathe. Then he turned his head to the door and snarled like some wild beast over his shoulder, my blood still coating his lips and tongue, whilst his fangs were without the stain. This was because they were used in warning and hadn't been used to feed from me, something I could imagine he wanted to do right now.

"Time's up for the lovers!" Layla said striding in, still dressed like a hooker only playing at the virgin by wearing white. But then the second she clocked back the hammer on the gun she now pointed my way, I wouldn't have exactly been in my right mind to say,

'Hello slut bag, how you doing?' Because well, I didn't fancy a bullet in the brain as I didn't think any amount of knee rubs or magic touches would fix that shit. And I kind of liked my brain where it was and not decorating the walls with its gooey pink matter.

"I have this aimed at her head, Luc, so don't try anything, as I doubt she could come back from something like that," she said taking my fears right out of my mouth.

"Now back the fuck up off the bitch and let's go...it's time to bargain." Lucius tensed, tightening his hold on me and I didn't think he would do as she asked at first. So, I raised my hand to cup his cheek and said to him,

"It's okay, trust me this time, yeah." His eyes burned down into mine, seeping from blue grey into amber in a way that was beautiful to witness.

"Oh, how very touching...now fucking move before I vomit!" she snarled and even I knew it was an act, as the jealousy of this woman was still easy to see. Lucius looked as though he wanted to rip her head off and go bowling with it, after stuffing it full of explosives that was...or wait, was that just me?

"Put the gun down, Lahash, as you know well enough that I could simply catch that bullet the second it fires," Lucius said now moving from where he had still been kneeling on the floor in front of me and standing to his full height, looking beyond impressive and intimidating with it. All that glorious muscle on view, Gods, but he was terrifyingly magnificent.

"That maybe so but are you so sure you could catch them all...Thanks, but I think I will take my chances with the gun. Now move," she said motioning us to go ahead of her with a wave of her gun. But then she backed up out of the cell making sure she didn't get too close to Lucius, no doubt scared that he would make his move.

Lucius took my hand in his and refused to let go, even when Layla made her threats.

"Not fucking happening," was his only reply to that and she obviously knew with his tone that this was one demand of hers she wouldn't win. And it was obvious she was under orders as I wasn't sure I would have survived if not, because it was clear she hated me almost as much as she hated my mother.

Something she had taken pleasure in taunting me about when I was alone with her in the ballroom. Threats like, 'I should give you the full mother daughter experience and stab you and push you into an icy lake'. But then I turned around to face her the second she had to let me go and snarled back,

'Yeah, and how did that turn out for you?!' In that moment she would have followed through with her threats if it hadn't been for the three at the end that were calling the shots so far.

After this I had been escorted down to the cell and the rest was a kneeing humping history.

Which lead me to question, what would happen next?

Lucius' hand in mine at least gave me the strength I needed to walk back up into the ballroom where the three 'hopefully soon to be dead' amigos were waiting for us. I couldn't help but grip his hand a little tighter the second those large double doors came into view. I would have also shot him a panicked looked if I wasn't too determined not to give bitch face the satisfaction.

He squeezed me back, telling me silently to be strong and for him, I would be. So, we walked back in there hand in hand with what felt like the full force of our enemies all around us.

And I knew that this time,

For me...

It was showtime. .

CHAPTER TWENTY

A KINGS DISAPPOINTMENT

The moment we stepped inside it became obvious that this time, they were definitely more ready for us. Now situated all around the balcony was what looked like a team of mercenaries all dressed in black fatigues with large assault rifles in hand. And every single one was currently aimed down at us. Okay, so my panic most definitely spiked at the sight and I found my other hand going to Lucius' arm as I pressed myself closer to him.

So, he let go of my hand and instead wrapped an arm around me, drawing me as close as I could get to his side. I looked up at him to see him too looking at the men that surrounded the room and concentrating hard as if trying to achieve something I couldn't see. But it obviously wasn't working like he hoped, as he shot those he had named the 'rogues' a threatening look and snarled at them.

"Ah, I see now that our witch was worth every penny, well done gentleman," the man in the middle said, who I remembered from the gala and thinking at the time he looked like Pierce Brosnan in his sixties. He had said something to me back then that felt slightly creepy, combined with his hand on me. But then his fingers had sort of snapped back suddenly and he had left. Well, it was easy to understand now why that had happened, knowing how possessive Lucius was. Well, that and the black cast that was on his hand.

But then I processed what he had just said and suddenly it clicked what was happening. Lucius had been trying to force the 'wannabe swat team' above us under the power of his will, but it wasn't working. This now meant that, as capable as Lucius was at stopping bullets, there was no way for him to stop that type of fire power raining down from above...*or was there?*

"Looks like King Vamp is without any power here," the Pierce look alike added making the other one next to him snarl,

"Shut the fuck up, DeMars!" But it was too late, as the second I glanced back up at Lucius, I saw that his eyes now looked like molten steel, glowing with rage. Suddenly I felt the floor beneath me start to shift, rumbling as if an earthquake was building. Then, just as his arm around me tightened his hold, an almighty thundering sound erupted as the marble floor started to crack, doing so with enough force that it shot out from around us. It branched out long enough that it travelled up the walls, making the small army shake, each of them now quickly grabbing onto the walls and balustrades for support.

But then I screamed as one person's gun went off and it was one aimed at Lucius' head. But acting like a Gods be damned superhero, Lucius snapped up a hand and caught the bullet like Superman! Then he snarled at the person who had tried to shoot him and as he dropped the bullet, Lucius flung a hand outwards, making the man fly through the air, hitting one of the marble pillars. His body then made a sickening snapping sound on impact, as if too many bones all broke at the same time, before he then slumped to the floor.

"Anyone else want to fucking try that?!" Lucius snarled to all those who still surrounded him and the intense fear in their eyes was understandable. Hell, even I could smell it and I wasn't a supernatural.

"I will!" Layla said, after grabbing an automatic weapon off one of the guards and pointing it, not at him but at me. Lucius growled low and menacing at her.

"Now lose the bitch." This time he bared his fangs at her, snarling like a Hellish beast and it was a sound I hadn't heard coming from him before. It was frightening as Hell and if I hadn't been plastered to his side in his tense hold, then I would have probably moved back a step in fear. It was for me an irrational response, seeing as I knew he would never hurt me, and his reaction was one because they threatened to take me from him. Even so, it was still 'wet your pants' level of scary.

"NO!" he roared back and even she flinched at the sound.

"You want to bargain for the box, then fine, give me your fucking terms but you will do so with her by my side or not at all!" Lucius demanded now turning his attention back to the three. The two rogues at least looked like they gave this some thought and it gave me time to take in the two cloaked figures in greater detail.

The one who did most of the talking had very prominent facial features, starting with a long pointed nose that was beak shaped. This, combined with his high forehead and hollowed cheeks, gave a distinct creepiness to him, especially with his tall, slender frame.

The other one, a far less creepy looking Vamp, spent most of his time actually looking bored, as if running cults, kidnapping and murdering was all just a sideline hobby for him. Making me wonder if there was some far less creepy Mrs Vamp at home waiting for him right now with dinner on the stove. Of course, I wasn't sure what poor soul would be on the menu but still, the guy looked about as harmless as a bible salesman going door to door. Shortish build, a face you would forget. A voice barely heard and hair the colour of soot…and about as far away from the handsomely pale and mysterious race portrayed in romance Vampire novels as you could get!

Nope, these guys wouldn't sparkle, they would just bore you to death and make you pray for anything more exciting, like doing your tax returns!

"Very well, my people are stationed outside your club. Give your men the order to let them enter and take the box, once they have it in their possession and are safely out of the building, then we will let you both leave unharmed," Rogue 'bore you to death' on the right said who, as I mentioned, had hardly spoken up until this point.

"The fuck we will!" Layla shouted making the one on the left snarl at her,

"Silence! If it is what the Master wills it to be, then you will comply!" I had to say, I kind of liked watching her getting a verbal lashing. But then I saw Lucius weighing up his options and I started to see it all playing out before he even spoke. I even looked back at Layla wondering if in this moment she was going to act the way I thought she would. Well, I was about to find out.

"Fine, you want the fucking box, then you can have it, it's fucking useless to me anyway!" Lucius snapped, making the guy in the middle snigger,

"Let us worry about that," Mr bored rogue on his right glowered down at him but didn't speak…*big shocker there.*

"Then I suggest that someone give me a fucking phone!" Lucius demanded and all the while I could see Layla frowning, as if her cogs were turning and I could see that they were ones powering her suspicion.

Creepy nodded down at the human, silently giving him an order to do as Lucius said,

"I'm not fucking going near him!" he shouted in panic making Lucius grin before saying in a sinister tone,

"What's the matter human, afraid I will make them both match?" nodding to his other arm, although knowing Lucius it would have ended in nothing short of a body cast.

"Just put your fucking phone on the floor and he will do the rest," Creepy snapped and the human did as he was told, getting it out of his suit jacket and placing it on the floor. He never once took his eyes off Lucius as if he feared that when he did, he would only find the Devil looking back at him in his place.

Lucius made a slight gesture with his hand and the phone slid along the floor towards him. Then without needing to bend to pick it up, it flew up to his hand with all the back section scratched up. Hurray for small victories was all I thought with a childish grin.

Lucius then rang who I assumed was one of his men and started making orders. But I didn't miss the information he was being given first, as Lucius looked down at me and said in a severe tone,

"Yes, I have her."

After this he engaged his Master of the Universe mode and started telling his people what he wanted them to do. Then, after he had finished, he said,

"Call me on this number when it is done...oh and Clay, tell Ruto to put away the blade in his hand...*at least for now.*" Then he cut the call and looked back to the men in front.

"It is done."

"And now we wait," the human said folding his arms and looking as though he had any bloody control here, which was laughable really. But then, it did make me question why they needed him in the first place? Was he just to keep the other humans in line? To keep up pretense that the two sides were working together. I mean, just looking around the room now and I knew that someone must have been paying these guys.

"You made the right choice, Lucius," the one on the left said making me scoff and Lucius' arm tensed around me as if in warning not to speak.

"Yeah, a little too easily if you ask me!" Layla piped up as she started slowly circling us, coming closer to the three at the end of the room. I watched her now as she looked side on, telling them quietly,

"Something is wrong, he wouldn't give it up this easily."

"Ha, we have forty guns pointed at his fucking head, and you call that easy," the human said first, scoffing at her words.

"For him it is," she replied looking wary. The sound of the phone ringing in his hand cut through her doubt and Lucius answered it and I was just surprised that it wasn't crushed in his hand.

"Understood... Your men have been shown to my vault," he said after cutting the call.

"And have they been shown inside?" the usually silent rogue asked.

"Not yet, first let the girl go and I will give you the code," Lucius said, still trying to bargain, making both rogues glare back before creepy said on a snarl,

"That wasn't our deal, Lucius." But he shrugged his shoulders before telling them,

"Things change." I also frowned wondering what he was up to now.

"Not this time," the same rogue replied and nodded to the balcony who all aimed their guns back at me this time and Lucius quickly dragged the rest of my body to his front, covering as much of me as he could before snarling at them,

Then after taking a few harsh breaths, he conceded to their demands,

"Fine! Tell them the code is 1705," he said telling them my birthday but giving it to them the way it was said in Europe, not in the States, where they put the month before the day. Which meant it also could have meant a historical year for him, making me briefly wonder where in the world he was during this time. Probably wearing powdered wigs and walking down the halls of some manor home with his heels clicking on expensive marble. Oh, but thank the Gods jeans were invented, that's all I could say.

"Check it," Creepo said, who was now on his own phone and had already given his men the code, repeating the number Lucius had given them.

"Something doesn't feel right," Layla whispered frowning.

"It opened, now is there anything else he needs to know?" the rogue asked after ignoring Layla's mistrust again.

"There is a hidden sensor, tell him to scan his hand under the box first before removing it," Lucius told him, but only after first seeming hesitant.

"I am telling you, he is giving in too easily!" Layla said, now a little more forceful this time making Lucius tense at my side.

"He has the box...well done Luci..."

"No! He is lying, he is double crossing you, can't you see!" Finally, they decided to listen to her, and this was when Lucius turned to stone next to me.

"What makes you think so?" Mr bored asked, obviously feeling as though it was time to show a little more interest.

"Because I fucking know him that's why! Unlike you two, I was sired by him long ago and have been with him since the beginning," she said not taking her eyes off Lucius as she said this.

"Meaning?" Creepy asked,

"Meaning, that I know how the bastard thinks!" she said making me now the one to tense by his side as her words hit home. She had been with him for thousands of years?! Surely not? But then as if Lucius knew exactly what her words would do to me, he looked down at me and whispered so only I could hear,

"Whatever you're thinking, unfucking think it." Well, alrighty then. I guess I was unthinking what I was thinking then.

But what she had said hadn't only had an effect on me, as now the rogues were mulling over her words and taking a moment to actually listen.

"He has the box in his hand, Lahash, I don't think…" Boring said before she snapped back,

"No, you don't, that's the fucking problem! And I don't think our Master will be best pleased to know we didn't do everything we could, when we had the opportunity to do it!" Both rogues growled in unison this time but weirdly refrained from arguing back, instead snapping,

"Then what would you have us do!?" She looked thoughtful a moment and then her eyes widened, and a grin replaced the once unsure gaze.

"Tell him there is a safe hidden behind a row of suits and use the same combination." Once again, I could feel Lucius was killing mad next to me, as his whole frame nearly shook from the intensity of his wrath. Meanwhile I remained silent, wondering how this was all going to play out. I didn't have to wait long.

"He found it, but the combination isn't the same," Creepy said, now looking to Lucius who was obviously livid.

"You have the fucking box, now tell your men to leave and we will be on our way!"

"If that is the case, then you won't mind proving it. Give us the combination and let my men check it's not there, proving that you are a man of your word," he replied, making Layla grin as though she wasn't just the cat that got the cream, she was the bitch currently fucking bathing in it! She would have crossed her arms had she not already had her arms full of weaponry. But she started circling us and Lucius snarled at her, telling her,

"Don't you fucking dare come any closer to her!"

"You see, I told you so...you underestimate me Luc, I fucking know you, remember that!"

"You never fucking knew me bitch, as if you did, you would have known I couldn't fucking stand you, hadn't done for over a millennia..."

"You tell yourself that!" she snarled back in anger at what sounded like very honest words to me. But then again, I had known the real her for only a few hours and even I wanted her to go skinny dipping in shark infested waters!

"No, I am telling you that! Fucking blind, Lahash, you always were..."

"Shut the fuck up!" she said, this time hating the truth she heard because deep down she knew he meant his words. But Lucius, being Lucius carried on regardless,

"...you were either too crazy to see it or just not fucking smart enough to ask yourself why...why I was always sending you on assignments that took you as far away from me as I could get you!?" he told her making her scream in anger and he was waiting for it. But unfortunately, his move backfired. As the second he made a piece of the balcony she was stood under crumble on top of her, she shifted quickly, using the distraction to grab one of the guards to send him hurtling our way. Lucius let me go, so I wouldn't get struck, pushing me out of the way. But Layla was ready for me, as with impressive speed, she grabbed me, and spun out of reach before he could react.

He had the guard in a head lock using just one arm, making the guy desperately trying to free himself, as he clawed at Lucius' arm with little to no effect.

"LET. HER. GO!" Lucius's demon was the only one speaking in that moment as his eyes were now burning crimson as if being infected with blood on fire. Then, to put power behind the demand, he suddenly snapped the guy's neck with both hands before letting the dead man fall to the floor. And holy Hell, if I thought Lucius terrifying before then this was something else. But Layla wasn't affected. She simply angled the large gun at my head and said,

"Come and fucking make me!" Then she dug the end of the gun into the side of my temple making me whimper as well as forcing my head to the side and it fucking hurt!

"Yeah, that's exactly what I thought, now give them the combination and I will let her go!" Layla said now digging her nails into my skin where she held a hand at my bicep, with her arm banded across my chest.

"Please don't, you're hurting me!" I said as she dug them in further making them bleed and me wince in return.

"I promise you, I will fucking kill every last one of you for this!" Lucius snarled now he had calmed his beast slightly, doing so in that moment so as not to do anything rash that might, well basically *get me killed*. But then Layla kicked out my legs and I went down on my knees hard. Then I felt the gun's end forced against the back of my head and her free hand gripped onto the back of my neck!

"FUCKING STOP! I warn you, if you harm her then I give the order for my people to slaughter your men and burn the box to fucking ash...now, I will not tell you again, LET HER GO!" Lucius said still trying to get them to let me go.

But I'd had enough of this shit show and decided now was about time to take things into my own hands.

Enough was enough.

"Please stop! Fucking stop okay, I know the combination!" I shouted making Lucius flinch the second I said it.

"Amelia, don't." he said, the threat clear.

"No Lucius! It's not your fucking head with a gun to it!" I snapped back. I felt Layla chuckle behind me, and her hand moved from my neck and she lowered herself enough to cup my cheek, before kissing it and patting me there, telling me,

"There's a good little girl, just the fucking coward I knew was in you." I swear I wished I could have stopped playing victim for just five minutes so I could kick this bitch's ass! But then again, there was the whole gun factor in this.

"Give us the combination and we will let you go." The obviously slightly more intrigued rogue said and I swallowed hard, letting a tear slip down my cheek.

"And...and Lucius too, you...you will let us both go?" I said stuttering my words. Layla laughed and said,

"Are you sure you want that, just look how mad at you he is?" Lucius heard this and growled at her before looking to me, asking me with his eyes not to give them what they asked for.

"Yes, we will let you both go. My Master's fight is with Lucius, not with your family. But he is forcing our hand in this. So, give us what we want, and you are free to leave," he replied.

And after taking a deep breath I told Lucius,

"I am sorry, I have no choice..." The look of disappointment on his face was nearly soul destroying. But it was like I had said, I had no choice, as more than one life depended on it.

And in Lucius' eyes,

Depended on me becoming…

A traitor.

CHAPTER TWENTY-ONE

TRIPLE CROSS

The very first time I saw him.

Sixteen years old. I remembered it as if it was yesterday. It was the first time I ever felt the threat my father warned me about. Little did he realise that the danger he spoke of would last a lifetime and come at the hands of a Vampire King.

Once his greatest ally.

Once his greatest enemy.

Now my biggest threat.

It was the day we met.

"The combination is 1306."

I told them, ignoring the look of frustration and regret from Lucius, giving them what they wanted. The date we met. The date he first saved my life and then stole it for himself.

I would have shaken myself free of these thoughts, that is if I didn't currently have a gun to the back of my head.

The rogue released a sigh and told his men down the phone who quickly confirmed that the box was in there. After this, the creepy rogue nodded to Layla to let me go but this was obviously not something she wanted to do just yet.

She did at least lower the gun. But then she grabbed my hair, lowered her face to my neck and said to Lucius,

"Maybe after a little taste, this bitch smells too…" But she never got chance to finish, because for once it was *my* actions that were too quick for her. Because just when her head was bent low enough to my neck I made my move. And I did this by reaching up with my left hand, grabbing a handful of her hair and at the same time yanking her head down into my right fist that connected hard into her face as I twisted into it. The second she let me go, staggering back, I was up on my feet planting a heeled foot in her stomach, making her double over with a scream of pain. *Thank you very much hooker heels.*

The next thing I knew I was being grabbed from behind and hauled up over a shoulder.

"Let me at that fucking bitch!" I started screaming as my own rage hit new heights, thrashing against whoever held me now, trying to get back to her.

"Amelia, stop!" Lucius growled at me letting me know who had me and at the same time Layla, who had recovered, now swung up the gun and started firing in our direction. Only nothing hit us as this time it was Mr boring vamp himself that was at her, now pushing the end of the weapon up so the bullets sprayed out at the ceiling above.

"STOP!" The rogue roared before yanking the weapon off her. Then he turned to us and said,

"You are free to go, leave now!" Well, Lucius didn't need telling twice as, still with me over his shoulder, he stormed towards the double doors, kicking them open with an impressive amount of strength. Then he paused, looked back and threatened,

"Make no mistake, Samson, I will have my blood," he said

giving me Mr boring's name. Then he walked down the hallway and I looked up to see the doors close behind us.

After this, I thought it wise not to speak until we were back outside because I wasn't sure how Lucius was going to react with what I had done. Besides, I didn't think him capable of calming down enough to actually speak to until we were off the grounds of this damn house. I swear I could feel the rage coming off him like steam from a screaming kettle. I also didn't think it wise to remind him that all and sundry could currently see my ass and panties, seeing that I was still only wearing his t-shirt and being over his shoulder wasn't helping with that.

We walked out the same side exit I had entered with bitch face and the moment we walked to the front of the house, we passed a couple of groggy looking girls dressed like they belonged anywhere but here. This was when Lucius spoke through gritted teeth,

"Your handy work I take it?" I swallowed hard, ignoring their stares and trying to hide my face just in case one of them managed to get a good look at me. Although this wasn't hard seeing as I just let myself stare at Lucius' muscle clad back, holding the belt at his jeans so I wasn't just smushing my nose against his skin with the motion of his angry strides.

"Erm...maybe," I confessed making him growl. Then he walked straight up to what must have been where all the cars were being parked but seeing as my line of sight was near nonexistent right now, it was anyone's guess.

"Lamborghini," Lucius snarled, and I heard a muttering in return before we started walking again. I pressed my hands to his back and pushed myself up so I could see, now witnessing a man stood next to a box full of keys looking as though he had just had his mind taken over by pod people. Poor bastard was going to find himself fired by morning. Especially from what I

could make out the guy had just handed over the keys to someone's shiny pride and joy.

I heard the beep.

"Good, at least someone has some fucking taste!" he snapped opening the door and then bending so my feet touched the floor. I was about to say something when one look at his face and I wisely swallowed down the urge to talk. It was a good job too as he just barked,

"Get in the car!" I quickly sat down, lowering myself into what I could now see was a sleek matt black Lamborghini. I hadn't been in one before as my dad was a Ferrari man. But I also knew enough about them ever since I found out that Lucius was into their rivals, Lamborghinis.

So, I shamefully learned my stuff, wondering if there was ever a day I would get the chance to impress him with my knowledge. Well, that plan wasn't exactly working out like I had hoped it would.(You know, like foolishly making intelligent conversation on the way back from, say, our first date) But the second he slammed my door down, I watched him take angry strides to the other side before getting in and I knew you couldn't have got any further from that naïve, childish hope.

Then he pressed the start button and just as I tested that theory, I asked,

"Is this the Aventador...whoa?!" I was cut off the second he did a wheel spin out of there and shot off with nail biting speed.

"Shit!" I said as the car skidded around the turning circle, kicking up gravel as it did before he straightened it out to speed down the driveway. Then he pulled out onto the main road without so much as a look, his muscles tense and hard as he turned the wheel with an open palm so it slid through his hand with ease. Gods, but what was he, a race car driver in his spare time!

"Why aren't you buckled up!?" he snapped making me jump.

"Erm, because you just raced out of there like a bat out of…"

"Don't fucking say it!" he said cutting me off, so I was left to roll my lips in my mouth to prevent anything sarcastic coming out. After all, this was another one of those classic 'stressful moments' that usually prompted some smart mouth comment. But right then, well I didn't think Lucius would fully appreciate this as a reason.

So, I grabbed the belt and only just managed to click it in place, especially with Lucius not intending to slow down any time soon. In fact, from the moment Lucius had gotten in the car and demanded I buckle up, I knew he was seething mad. I didn't know if it was directed at me or just about what had happened in there. Either way he was driving the car like the road was on fire and we were trying to outrun an erupted volcano. Although the only volcano I could see was the lava burning in his deadly gaze.

"Lucius please, you're kind of scaring me here," I said still needing to hang on for what felt like dear life, but he was near beyond reasoning, as he wasn't yet slowing down what was obviously an insanely fast car. He was overtaking cars, zooming in and out of traffic, like he was on a bloody racetrack and didn't have a terrified woman with one hand on the dash and the other on her side window, looking petrified.

But then, he simply tapped the paddle on his steering wheel which made him change gear and the car shot forward even faster the second a section of the road was clear. And this was when I hit my limit, shouting,

"Lucius, stop the car!" but he gave me a look that said there wasn't a chance in Hell. He quickly confirmed this,

"No!" was his stern, pissed off reply. So naturally I tried again.

"Lucius, stop the car!" I said, this time as he went around a bend way too fast.

"I said n…" I quickly interrupted him, bringing that chance in Hell to him, in the form of a screaming, pissed off female,

"STOP THE FUCKING CAR!" I screamed this time the second I thought we were going to crash, which thankfully we didn't but it was enough to get him to do as I asked. As the next thing I knew I was being forced forward into my seatbelt and then back into my bucket seat as the car stopped at the side of the road. I was breathing heavy, panting and the second I felt him reach over to me, I batted his hand away, too annoyed that he thought it was okay for him to scare the shit out of me! Even when A, I asked him not to and B, (and it was a big fucking B), I'd just had to experience everything I had in the last few hours!

Which was why I unbuckled my seatbelt, looked to check it was clear and then started to get out the car.

"Amelia, what are you…?"

"What does it look like I am doing!?" I snapped and the door was up in the air like all Lambos, looking like the damn thing had wings. I was out the car and stomping off to the side of the road to get some much needed air. I knew he too had gotten out and felt his angry presence as if the air was turning static and charging around him.

"Get back in the car, Amelia!"

"No, not until you learn how to fucking drive!" I snapped back making him jerk back.

"I assure you that I can…"

"Yeah, well not without scaring the shit out of a woman you claim to care about, then no *you fucking can't!*" I snapped back making him flinch as finally I was cutting through his anger, forcing him to take control of his rage. I knew this the second his features softened. Then after releasing a sigh, his shoulders relaxed and he told me,

"You're right, I am sorry, I shouldn't be driving like that with you in the car." I had been ready to throw more of my argument at him but hearing the way he apologized right away, and with such sincerity too, well in all honestly, I was near flabbergasted.

"It's just knowing that they now have the box! Fuck Amelia, do you know what this could mean? The power it could give them against me...Gods, but I need to get you out of here, I need to get you somewhere safe, because now...fuck, I can barely think, let alone imagine what they could..."

"Lucius stop, it will be okay," I said cutting through his dire thoughts.

"No Amelia, it won't be okay, this is about as far from fucking okay as we could get, sweetheart!" he snapped back dragging a hand through his hair as his frustration was on a knife's edge of turning into full on rage.

"Lucius, I..."

"I don't blame you," he said quickly.

"What?" I asked frowning in question.

"I don't blame you. Gods, but you had a fucking gun to your head, of course I don't blame you for being scared," he ground out as the memory hit him once more. So, I took a deep breath as it was time to come clean,

"I wasn't scared, Lucius." His gaze softened as he took my words for trying to save face and act brave.

"I saw you, Amelia, of course you were..."

"No, I wasn't. I was just *acting* scared," I said, making him frown and lose his softness.

"But you gave them the box, you told them the fucking combination!" This time it was said to blame me, as his accusing tone couldn't be taken as anything else. So, I released a sigh of my own and said,

"Lucius, they don't have the box." He gave me a look of disbelief before shaking his head slightly as if trying to make sense of my words before saying,

"Come again?" And yes, it was confirmed as being definitely our thing. So, I took another moment before walking over to him, then I placed both my hands on his cheeks, framing his face so I could bring him closer to me.

Then I whispered up at him exactly what I had done...

"I switched your switch."

CHAPTER TWENTY-TWO

EVERYTHING OWNED AND NOTHING GAINED

"Say that again." I could tell with Lucius' tone that he was having a hard time with what I'd just told him. Meaning now it was my turn to run a hand through my hair, trying not to hiss at the pain there seeing as I had been hit with the butt of a gun recently.

"They have the fake box, the real one is hopefully still at the club," I told him wanting to snigger at the idea, knowing that they would probably kick themselves the second they realised their mistake, because if that had been me, I would have just taken both. Lucius then took out the phone he had kept belonging to the human name DeMars and rang his people.

"Sire we..."

"Shut the fuck up and just tell me, is the box they took from the vault still there?" he asked quickly.

"Yeah, well I mean it's on the fucking floor where they..."

"Thank fuck for that! Put it back in the vault and change the code to the day I sired you. We will be back in five..." He paused, looked at me and then back at the car before correcting himself,

"Make that ten minutes." I would have smiled, as it was obvious he no longer intended to drive at killing speeds.

"It will be done."

"Oh, and Clay…don't say a word." He replied but I didn't catch the reply this time. Lucius hung up, and I yelped the second he snagged my waist and yanked me to him.

"Fuck me, but you are one cunning little beauty," he told me making me hopelessly try to hide my grin. But then he was lowering his head to mine and capturing my lips, kissing me as if I was, well, as if I had just saved the fucking day!

Two minutes later we were back in the car speeding back towards his club, still breaking the law but no longer doing so as if I was hanging on like I was some forced co-pilot in a fighter jet. But then his next question came and I had to say, I wasn't sure I wouldn't have preferred to have been 50,000 ft in the air.

"How did they kidnap you?" Lucius asked making me tense as I knew it was coming, but had at least hoped we could have made it back to the club first. But then again, I was pretty sure Clay would have ratted me out the second I got through the door, seeing as I doubted he wanted to get blamed for it.

"I think that maybe we should get back to…"

"You weren't kidnapped, were you?" Lucius asked cutting me off and figuring it out for himself and I had to say, pretty damn quickly. I was either really predictable or he was just that good at cutting through someone's bullshit.

"Erm, no…not really," I said in a tone that said I was bracing myself for another bout of angry Lucius.

"For fuck sake, Amelia!" he shouted hitting the steering wheel in anger and I jumped.

"Look, I am sorry okay, I didn't know she was your crazy

ex-girlfriend, I mean she helped me the first time and saved me from getting kidnapped by who I thought were the bad guys, I didn't know she was..." He interrupted me again.

"Wait, back the fuck up...what do you mean, she saved you? What aren't you fucking telling me now!?" he shouted, swearing even more than usual and shooting me an incredulous look, finding my 'oh shit' one back in return. Because I hadn't actually told him anything about how I'd managed to break into his club. But then, in my defense, he hadn't exactly pressed for it either.

"Erm, maybe we should just..."

"Amelia, I swear if you don't start talking, as in right now, then so help me I will pull this fucking car over and..."

"And what!? Huh, what are you going to do, Lucius? Put me over your knee like a damn kid and spank me on the side of the fucking ro...wait, what are you doing?!" I shouted the second he pulled the car once more to a screeching halt the second it was clear. Then he turned in his seat and said,

"You have five seconds to decide, or you will find out!" he shouted and I swallowed hard before testing him,

"You wouldn't!"

"One."

"Lucius, come on, be reasonable."

"Two."

"Just stop and think about this."

"Three."

"You wouldn't fucking dare!"

"Four."

"Stop counting!" I shouted shaking my head and throwing my arms up in my anger, but he just looked at me in that stern and unmoving way of his, before saying,

"Five."

"Alright, alright! Gods alive, just fucking drive, okay!" I

shouted, giving in the second I saw him reaching for the door handle knowing he would make good on his threat. So, he put the car into drive and after less than twenty seconds, he said,

"This is the part where you start talking, sweetheart." Well, at least I was sweetheart again, which was exactly what I told him,

"Oh, so I am sweetheart again, am I?"

"Amelia." He said my name in warning and I snapped,

"What?!"

"Quit stalling." I released a sigh knowing there was no way around it, I was screwed.

"Fine! I got to the airport and there were men there waiting for me. Then bam, your psycho ex turned up out of nowhere, claiming she was there to save me and seeing as I was being chased by bad guys, then I didn't think I had many options but to jump in her car." I could see his grip on the steering wheel tightening as he listened to this obviously finding it difficult. But it was when the thing started to give way under the pressure, about to be crushed completely in his grip that I thought it best to speak up.

"Erm, I think you will need that," I reminded him and when he shot me a questioning look, I nodded to the steering wheel he was close to destroying. He followed my gaze and replied with a stern,

"Perhaps you're right, waiting until we are back at the club is wise," he said in a harsh tone that didn't scream fun things for me once we got there. I released a sigh and said,

"Yeah, that's what I thought."

Minutes after this and a not so leisurely drive back to the club, I knew that with one look ahead of me, that Lucius' night was only going to get worse.

"What the fuck!?" he snarled the second he saw the mess of the front of his club where the police had cordoned off the site of the car wreckage as it was being removed from the side of his building.

"Ah yeah...*that,*" I said letting him know that I already knew what happened. So naturally he shot me an 'explain it and explain it now!' look, so I told him,

"You have psycho bitch face to thank for that," I commented dryly making him mutter even more F words under his breath as he quickly took a different direction. I soon found out why, as it was the way to the back of the club. He then pulled up to a heavy security gate and after punching a code into the control panel and placing his thumb on the reader, the gate opened. Then he stopped right outside the back door I had used and cut the engine. He was out of the car before I even had chance to get my seatbelt unbuckled. In fact, I was still fumbling with it when my door opened and without a word, he reached down and across me, doing this so he could release it with the ease I lacked.

"Erm...thanks," I muttered taking his hand so he could pull me from the car. Then, without saying a single thing more, he led me over to the door and in less than a minute after that, I found myself in an elevator. Then I was out of it and in a lobby being pulled towards his apartment. So, I pulled back and looked towards my own, but he shook his head and said,

"Not this time, princess." I frowned back at him, but it was a pissed off look he ignored because well, his won hands down at being scary intimidating. And really, I couldn't say in that moment after all that had happened tonight, that I could really blame him. Oh, but I just knew it was about to get so much worse.

Clay suddenly appeared, coming from the VIP as he had obviously been waiting for him.

"Sire, I saw you arrive on the…"

"Do you want to explain to me how you let my girl escape, or how there is now a fucking car embedded in the side of my club, or why there are still police crawling all around it when I just stole a fucking car?" He snapped making Clay raise both his hands in surrender and say,

"Not really, no."

"I didn't fucking think so…now piss off and deal with it!" he said throwing Clay the keys to the car he'd stolen, making me wonder what 'dealing with it' entailed with that one. Then, without waiting for a response, because really what does a person say to that, Lucius tightened his hold on my hand and pulled me inside his apartment. The second the doors slammed shut behind me I jumped, and then shivered as I heard them lock, knowing Lucius intended to keep me here.

"Sit!" he snapped the second he let me go by his sofa and I was just about to tell him that I wasn't a damn dog, when he spun to face me, held up a finger and warned me,

"Not wise to push me right now, sweetness, so just do as you're fucking told…yeah?" I swallowed hard, backing away from the crazy scary vibe he had going on and sitting my ass down, deciding pushing him right now was definitely not on my 'wisest shit to do' list.

Well, at least he looked sort of grateful at the sight of me doing as I was told. After this he walked straight to his kitchen area, got himself a bottle of some sort of white spirit and came back with a bottle of water for me. I had to say, I think at this point I would have preferred what he was swigging back, but still, the gesture was sweet for him to care enough to think of me. Even when he was clearly blind furious. So, I took the bottle and the second I started drinking, I hadn't realised how thirsty I was, nearly finishing off the damn bottle.

"It's the blood loss and adrenaline kick," he told me as if I had asked the question. Then I watched as he sat down in one of the single chairs so he could face me.

"Now, you were saying something about being chased?" he said after first taking another long drink and a deep breath he obviously needed. I kind of wanted to ask him if he wanted me to get him a shirt or something, as all that muscle on show had been distracting me since he took it off, something I noted I was still wearing when looking down at myself.

"Amelia, you're gonna have to grant me some strength here, because if you don't start talking…" I decided to cut him off, as for the first time since knowing him, he looked beyond tired. So, I decided to just get on with it and give him what he wanted.

"She told me that she was the next oracle," I blurted out.

"So, you would trust her," he assumed as it wasn't a question.

"Well yeah, plus she gave me a key card to get inside here and explained how to do it. I just thought she knew I needed to get to the box, like she had seen it or something and had been prepared as she had been with the car, but now…well, I guess she was just hoping to use me as a way to get to the box," I said shrugging my shoulders and feeling foolish. Lucius released a sigh and looked as though he wanted to say something but at the last minute decided against it.

"And tonight?"

"She tricked me again. After you left, I went back to my apartment to find flowers waiting. The note said they were from you." He looked surprised by this and frowned before saying,

"And you believed they were too?" I gave him a small smile and said,

"I know you're not exactly the sending a girl flowers kind of guy, Lucius." At this he gave me a look I couldn't explain before it slipped from his face and he shrugged his shoulders once before taking another swig of his bottle. So, I carried on.

"Anyway, Liessa obviously thought you were, as she accepted them and put them where I would find them."

"Then?"

"Well, they were light pink, and the note spoke something about innocence, so I knew it was wrong. And I was right, as it turned out there was a hidden message on the bottom, telling me to meet her at the side door. She caused the distraction so when the alarms went off, no one would be suspicious that I had left, being too busy with…"

"Yeah, I get it. Then what?" Lucius said with a wave of his hand, clearly annoyed at his people *and me.*

"Well, then the rest you know really… we ambushed some poor girls, stole their clothes and snuck inside. Then she hit me with a damn gun and the rest is…"

"She hit you?! Where?" he snarled and was out of his seat before I could answer him. He slammed the bottle down on the coffee table and knelt before me like he had done in the cell.

"Well, just here, on the back of my head… but… but it's okay," I said stuttering the second his hands tenderly took hold of my head and started examining the back with his fingers, stilling when he found the lump I knew would be there.

"Gods be damned bitch! I am going to kill that…" I placed my hands on his, pulling them down from my head so they were between us and said,

"I know you will…besides, at least I got one good punch in," I added with a wink making him at least smile this time.

"That you did, sweetheart," he said softly bringing his

forehead to mine and holding himself there. It was such a loving gesture that I found myself unable to breathe the whole time just in case I ruined it in some way. But then he took a deep breath himself and asked a question he seemed to dread finding out the answer to, and I had to confess, it was one I dreaded telling him,

"How did you know I'd had a fake made?" Of course, he was talking about the box and the second I tensed, he felt it. He pulled back so he could look me in the eyes as I told him what he wouldn't want to hear.

"I went to the vault." I said starting with what was the most obvious. He knew it too as he raised a brow at me before saying,

"And?"

"And I...well I...I..."

"You?" he said and this time it was more than a prompt for me to continue, it was a silent demand.

"I was going to kind of, well... *try stealing it again,"* I confessed wincing as I expected him to erupt back into the rage part of the evening. At this he leant back, putting space between us but now sitting on the coffee table dead opposite me with less than a foot between us.

"But of course," he said putting his head back and looking up at the ceiling, or asking the Gods for strength, I was unsure which one.

"Why?" The question was out before I'd prepared an answer, or at least the lie I would have tried for first, which was why I did that age old tactic at trying to stall for time,

"Why?" I repeated the question, playing dumb and being shit at it.

"It's not a trick question, princess," he said gently and I could see that despite using this nickname, one I knew was usually reserved for a pissed off Vamp, he was trying to hold back his temper. Well, that wouldn't last long, that was for damn sure.

"I was going to try and hide it, until I…"

"Until you tried to leave me," he finished off for me and Gods but when he said it, I felt as if I had cut out his heart and handed it back to him on a platter with a knife sticking out of the centre. But what else could I do, there was no need to try and deny it.

"You know I can't stay," I told him quietly, scared of what his reaction would be.

"I know you can't leave!" he told me in return and his voice was definitely less gentle this time…*it was absolute.*

I closed my eyes, asking for strength to do what I needed to.

"Lucius, I am not your prisoner."

"Then are you willing to stay of your own free will?" he asked and Gods but just the way his muscles tensed like that, every single one on show…it had me licking my dry lips before I could answer,

"You know I can't do that."

"Then you're my fucking prisoner!" he snapped back, getting to his feet and walking away a little and making me release a sigh.

"You don't mean that."

"The fuck I don't!" he threw back at me, quickly turning at the waist to look back at me.

"You can't keep me here, Lucius." I said, once again trying for calm and deciding now was an excellent time to take the painful shoes off my feet, despite talking about leaving. Because, thanks to the blisters I could feel, then there was no way it would be in these bloody shoes!

"And why not?! Because you think you managed to escape once before that I would allow it to happen again!" I frowned, now getting to my own feet after kicking the shoes under the sofa and putting some more space between us, wishing I was back in my own apartment. Which was precisely what I decided to do.

"Where the fuck do you think you're going?!" he snapped the second I walked past him, now considerably lower than his towering frame. Maybe taking them off had been a mistake after all.

"I am going back to my apartment until you have calmed down and can talk about this rationally!" I snapped back.

"Rationally? There is not one Gods be damned rational reason for you to leave and you fucking know it!" he argued back, making me stop so as to face him again.

"Are you serious? Lucius, up until that damn box appeared I was nothing to you! I was a fucking nobody! Non. Fucking. Existent!" At this and the way I took a step forward to him with each word I threw at him he finally looked to be taking my words seriously. But hey, he pushed me into this, so it was time to give it to him straight, despite the angry vibes I could feel coming off him in waves.

"And now what, now I am here you think you can just amuse yourself with me but for how long, huh? How long this time, Lucius!? Seven fucking years I waited for you! Jesus fucking Christ…"

"Don't." he warned the second I said 'His' name, which was usually a big no, no for his people, for obvious reasons but I didn't give a shit. I was too far gone in that moment. I didn't know if it was after everything that had just happened that night, or the fact that reality just hit me. I'd had a fucking gun to my head and he still wouldn't give them the combination. What the Hell did that say?

"Fuck you! I can say whatever the Hell I want, human remember! Or did you forget?!"

"How could I ever fucking forget!" he snarled back making me itch to slap him again for that one, the bastard!

"Exactly, then you won't want me around, will you?" I threw back at him, making him rake a hand through his sandy coloured hair that looked close to being ripped out at the roots.

"That is not what I meant!" he told me and I took a deep breath before telling him what I knew was a heartbreaking confession on my side,

"Lucius, I have been dreaming of you near every Gods be damned night for the last ten years and you think that by you now deciding all of a sudden you want me, that I am just going to fucking jump into your arms without protecting my heart… you know, the one you destroyed the second I found out you loved my mother! So, I ask you Lucius, does that not sound fucking rational enough to you?!" At this he just snarled, but I could see the emotion it was hiding beneath. My words had got to him and burrowed their way underneath his skin, as if only for a second he looked guilty.

"You don't understand," he said after taking a deep breath.

"The fuck I don't! I understand more than enough. They had a gun to my head tonight, Lucius, a room full of guns and I know that you would have done everything you could have to protect me, but when it came down to it you still wouldn't give them that code…" I paused long enough to look to where his closet was, where his vault was and where the box now safely remained.

"You care more about that damn box than you do me, Lucius, and tonight, you… well… *you proved that.*" I said in a sad, lost kind of way, which was only half of what I was feeling. Because it was true, and I was only now just realising it. Or maybe I had always realised it, and at the time just didn't want to face facts. Because at the time I needed his strength. But now…well, now was the time I needed my own.

Strength to walk away.

"That's not true and you know it," he said, now looking as if I had all but tried to tear him apart with my words.

"Then explain it to me, Lucius, I had a gun to the back of my head, on my fucking knees and all you had to do was give them four little numbers. *Four numbers, Lucius!"*

"You don't understand, I knew they wouldn't have shot you… they were calling my bluff."

"You don't know that!" I snapped.

"Yes. I. Fucking. Do. They don't want a war with your family, they want a war with me, with the entirety of my own kind and if I had given them the box…then…"

"You would have killed my mother," I finished off for him, knowing that in that moment there had in fact been a gun to both our heads, even if my mother hadn't been in the room on her knees like I had been.

"Yes… No… fuck! You make it sound like I chose her over you, when if you understood one fucking thing about the past, then you would know that it couldn't be further from the truth!" he snapped back at me making me frown because he was making no sense.

"Excuses…it's all just an excuse," I told him turning my back on him and walking back towards the door.

"No, it's not and you know it! You're just running scared, it's what you do! You run when shit gets real instead of being the girl I know you could be…where is that fire now, Amelia, where is that defiant spark inside of you, or am I just not worth the fight to you?!" Lucius threw at me and that was exactly what his words felt like, a fucking hit to the chest. Which is why I hit back,

"You can't fight for something you don't have!"

"That's bullshit and you know it! I have been fighting for you every Gods be damned day since you were sixteen years old, so don't give me that shit!" At this I was stunned enough that I actually felt my hand reaching out to something to keep me from falling. Did he just say what I think he did?

"What...what did you say?"

"You heard me! You think the reason I didn't give them the combination was to protect your mother, well fuck your mother, Amelia! It was only to save you!" he shouted, his features beyond furious, where mine were beyond confused and most certainly in denial.

"No! It's not true... I'm not... not..."

"Why? Because you are scared to know the truth? Well, I will be fucking damned if I let you walk away without it!"

"Lucius, please don't..." I started, holding that hand out now towards him, near begging him to stop...*my heart couldn't take it.*

But he didn't stop.

He just continued to give it to me, and it felt *beautifully brutal.*

"I didn't give them the combination because for them to have that box would have guaranteed that bullet in your head!"

"Wh...what are you saying?" I asked, feeling now as though something bigger was being kept from me.

And it was.

"Gods girl! What I am trying to tell you is that you are linked to me! You're already fucking bound and you don't even realise it! If they had that box, then it's not just my life on the line, along with all my people but yours as well!" he confessed, every muscle in his body tensed as if ready to pounce on me any second.

Did he really expect me to run? I needed in that moment to push it, to test it. I needed to know just how far he would go. Which was why I said,

"No, you are just saying this to make me...to make me..."

"To make you what?! Not want to leave...I already know you don't want to leave, Amelia, not when you have every fucking reason to stay staring you in the face right now!" At this my mouth dropped before I snapped back,

"Why you arrogant...!"

"It's not arrogance when it's the truth! You say that you have been waiting seven years, dreaming of me for ten, well here I am, sweetheart...I am right fucking here! And all you have to do is find the guts, the heart, *the fucking bravery*, to take one fucking step towards me!" he said, holding his arms out as though he was some sort of Gods' greatest catch! But even if I knew deep down his words were true, even if I wanted to hate him for it, I couldn't. But that didn't mean I had to admit any of it. Which was why there was only one step I was taking and that was to the door!

"And why would I do that, I don't even like you!" I snapped back making him release a bark of laughter, before telling me,

"You may not like me, Amelia, but I know you fucking love me!" On hearing this I sucked in a quick and painful breath feeling it nearly getting caught there in my chest.

"No...no I don't," I said shaking my head, but he was still grinning in that cocky, I know everything about you, kind of way. The way that was infuriating.

"Yes... Yes. You. Fucking. Do," he said first mocking me and making me glare back at him as he said the words slow and distinct.

"I'm leaving!" I shouted back.

"But of course."

"And what is that supposed to mean." He took another step towards me and said,

"You know exactly what it means, princess...you are being predictable." If I could have growled like one of them in that moment I would have, but then I'd probably have bared my fangs at him too, because I had to say, just giving someone the middle finger wasn't half as effective or as badass as doing what he did.

"In fact, the only thing you have left to do is slap me," he said with a grin, taking the last steps needed to put him only an arm's swing away. Meaning that the urge to do so became too much and I felt it coming before I could stop it, but then again, so did he,

"And there it is...*there's my fucking fire,*" he said and it came out as a rumbling in his chest as he quickly caught my hand before it could make contact. Then, before I could snatch it back, he lifted it above my head and pinned it to the locked door.

"Let me go!" I snapped feeling my chest panting in both my rage and something else I could feel building...*undeniable, undiluted, unstoppable lust.*

"*Never!*" he snarled back low and menacing.

"I want to leave!" I snapped back, feeling with each lash I gave him in return, my strength was lacking.

"*Not... Fucking... Happening,*" he said again, the threat was there if I even tried, as though he was almost begging me to do it, just to prove to me what would happen when I did.

"*You don't own me, Lucius,*" I said, this time losing some of the fight in my voice and he knew it. Because his eyes got intense and he took that last step into me. Then he put two fingers under my chin and forced me to raise my face to his.

Then and only then, with our gazes locked, did he turn my whole world upside down.

"Yes Amelia, I do...*I own you*...every last piece of you will be mine...for I own your soul. I own your heart and I own your mind, for I already know these parts of you are consumed by me in return..." I shook my head or at least tried to, but his hold on my chin became firm as he snapped my head back to his.

"Don't try and deny it, Amelia...*not like I did for so long,*" he confessed and I sucked in a sharp breath.

But he hadn't finished.

"You have always been mine and the only part of you left for me to take, *to own*... is your body..." he paused so he could look down at me. His eyes ablaze telling a story of what was to come. Then he found my fearful gaze in return and told me exactly what that story was...

"...and finally, my Amelia, the time for that..."

"Is now."

CHAPTER TWENTY-THREE

PROMISED PROTECTION

The second after he said this, he kissed me and this time it only spoke of the promise of his words. Words that now, combined with the tender need his kiss spoke of, well then, I knew that I was lost. I was lost to everything that was Lucius and had no hope of walking away now. But it was much more than that. I had no hope of protecting my heart, because he was right.

He did already own it.

He owned every part of me he spoke of and the only thing left was what I had kept for him all these years. Because I had known right from the first time I ever saw him that he was the only man I would ever love and he was right, I was lying to myself if I thought any differently. Oh, I could try and convince myself until my last breath and had in fact spent years trying to do so. But nothing could stop this. Not now, not ever, and his kiss said that he knew it too.

"Gods, how I have waited," he whispered after pulling his

lips from mine just long enough to say it before continuing his kiss.

"Yes." The admission came out breathy and was swallowed by his lips as his tongue begun dueling with mine, tasting me, an age old dance we all knew set our blood alight. The kind of kiss that sparked that deeper part of you that felt strong enough to connect to your very soul. Well, it made me feel more than owned...

I felt consumed.

"Enough...enough waiting," he growled and suddenly I was in his arms, being carried to what I could assume was his bed.

That bed.

The bed that held the worst memory of my life so far. Which was why I couldn't help the small plea that escaped.

"Please I..." I didn't need to say anything more as he knew. He knew and yet, he didn't stop.

"It is time to let the past go and time to erase the lies with the only truth that matters," he told me the second he lowered me down to the sheets and I knew he was right. I needed to get over this irrational fear I had of his bed, and the only way to do that was to become his in it. But Gods, I was nervous and the second he smirked down at me I knew that he knew it too. Then he started to lower himself down over me and I shifted further up the bed.

"This is...erm, very Gothic," I said looking around his most personal space just for something to say to take my mind off what was about to happen. Only from the looks of Lucius, he wasn't about to let me off that easily.

"Indeed." He hummed the word with held back amusement and I knew then that he was enjoying watching me struggle with my nerves.

"I didn't think you were one for convention?" I added.

"Vampire remember, it was this or a frilly shirt and cape,"

he said, making me burst out laughing and right then I needed it to ease my fears. Which was precisely why I think he said it. But then he crawled up over me and one quick tug was all it took for me to slip underneath him.

"It's a nice bed," I said referring to the black, carved sleigh bed that had an equally high headboard as it did by our feet.

"It's nicer with you in it," he said making a show of looking down the length of me and in his torn large t shirt and not much else, I didn't exactly feel sexy, but his look said the complete opposite.

"And you have nice sheets, they're very soft," I said, again trying to focus on my surroundings to break through my nervousness. But his grin said he knew this too.

"Mmm, very soft," he said, this time running a hand up the inside of my thigh and igniting a breathy sound from my lips.

"And your pillows are very...*comfortable,*" I said ending this on a whisper as I saw the way he now fisted one hand in them by my head before he leant down to my lips and said,

"Amelia, my sweet girl..." he started kissing my jawline, pausing every time he went lower to speak against my skin,

"My sweet little princess..." Then he got to my neck, nipping at it before he was directly at my ear,

"Shut the fuck up about my bed." Then before I could argue, his lips were back on mine and this time his kiss was rough, hard and passionate enough to speak for him of what was to come. His hand was in my hair, fisting the black strands so he could pull my head back. My neck now held taut in his unyielding hold. It was nothing short of a brutal assault on my senses and soon all my fear evaporated, being replaced by nothing but my desperate need for him to take me.

My body arched up to his and the second he felt my breasts peaked and pressed against his bare chest, he had hit a limit of some kind.

"Not enough!" he snarled and I would have been hurt if his next actions hadn't explained to me exactly what he meant. Because he lifted himself up to his knees that now straddled either side of my thighs, so he could take hold of his shirt with both hands before he tore it straight down the middle. The action jerked my body with his rough treatment and the sound of material tearing echoed and merged with the song of my gasping and heavy breathing.

Then, with a touch the complete opposite to impatience, he brushed back each side of the now torn shirt with both hands as if he were about to open up a book, one solely to learn how to claim my heart. Or maybe one on knowing what to do with it, as it was as he already said, it was a piece of me he already knew he owned.

But opening me up now and it looked as though he had already ripped out that heart, because all that faced him was the remains of crimson stained skin and a blood soaked bra. I looked down to see what had him so fixated and was horrified to see what I looked like. So, I quickly tried to sit up, ready to try and slip from beneath him but his leather hand quickly shot out and collared my throat. An action I took seriously enough to allow him to push me back to the bed.

"You're fucking perfect," he growled down at me as if he knew where my thoughts were. I took a shuddering breath that in turn made my chest reach up before recoiling down again, but the sight was enough to have him fixated.

However, I wasn't completely convinced.

"I should go shower…"

"You are going nowhere…not this time, my little crimson doll," he said running his bare hand up over my belly and over my covered breast. His voice was like velvet laid over the danger of a blade. It was soothing, gentle and spoke of a deadly promise should you get on the wrong side of it. But being here, very much on the best side, well that voice had the power to make me do whatever he asked, had the power to make me bare my soul and beg him to take it...

Just like my virginity.

"Do you have any idea how addictive you are...?" he asked letting go of my throat and shifting down, lowering himself so his face was now just where his hand had started at my belly. Then he began to run his nose up and over my breast, stopping to nip at the blood soaked lace with his teeth.

"...The scent of your blood, mixing with the scent of your lust..." He continued up and back over me but reared back enough that I sucked in a fearful little breath. This was because when he looked to one finger he let a wicked looking demonic talon grow up over his fingernail. It looked far too deadly to come near me without causing damage, so naturally I flinched when I saw him bring it closer. But he ignored me and I felt its cool, smooth back when he hooked it under the middle of my bra, taking care not to let that deadly tip touch my skin. But I also knew he was getting off taunting me with the danger of it. Because this was who he was. I knew that when he told me,

"The scent of your fear...fuck me, my little Šemšā, it's intoxicating!" Then with a quick flick of his talon he sliced right through the middle of my bra, making it snap open. Then he lowered his head and licked right up the centre, coating his tongue with the blood stained there. Then he threw his head back, his pale corded neck straining, as he sucked air through his teeth as if the taste of me was sending him hurtling over the edge. And I was both afraid and captivated by the sight. Locked to the sight of him, the raw intensity in which he wanted me. I even saw his lips moving, whispering something I couldn't hear or understand as the language was one I didn't know. But then it suddenly came to me what it was he was doing...

He was praying.

The second a startled gasp left my lips his head snapped back to mine and now the eyes looking down at me belonged solely to his demon. I had never seen them like this before, like looking into the centre of a volcano circled by a raging storm of darkness. I even flinched back in reaction, but it was one he simply grinned at, and then his fangs emerged and he licked at one before telling me,

"Don't worry sweetheart, when I make you bleed for me...*you will like it.*"

"Ahhh, oh Gods!" My cry of pleasure came the second he suddenly shackled my wrists, held them above my head in a blur of motion and his teeth latched onto my nipple so fast it made me dizzy. But then what he did with his mouth and how it connected straight to my core, made my back arch. Which in turn pressed more of myself inside his mouth, making him growl around the hard tip. But then he rolled it in between his teeth, and I cried out ready to beg him to stop as it was too much. However, the breathy sounds wouldn't form into words the second his tongue circled the pain to soothe the sting. Gods, but the feeling was near maddening and I was in half a mind to ask if he was trying to kill me with sensation alone!

But I knew I needed more...more of something! Which was why I fought against his hold, trying to get at him, to touch him, to claw at his back, anything that it would take for him to give me more. So, he tore his lips from my breast, one still staining his lips red as my breasts were stained with my blood.

"When I am ready Amelia, only when I am fucking ready, do you understand?" he shouted down at me and my body reacted on its own accord as I hooked my legs around his waist and ground myself up against his erection pushing down on my shoulders to gain strength below. He hissed through his teeth the second he felt my soaked panties seep through the denim over his straining cock.

"You feel ready to me," I told him brazenly making him grin down at me and I swear the sight of his fangs on show caused my heart to beat faster and my pussy spasm.

"Oh, my sweet little virgin, I have been ready for you for a fucking age, the thought of you teasing me all this time, watching you from afar, well now it's time you made up for it... *now it's time I make you beg for me, my Šemšā,*" he said suddenly claiming my lips and at the same time, pushing my ass back to the bed by grinding himself to me. My shocked gasp died in his mouth where he claimed it as a victory, and the rocking motion of him grinding himself against me was keeping me on the cusp of coming.

"Yes!" I moaned as he left my abused, bitten lips in favour of my neck and I felt his hand skim down my side, making me squirm beneath his hand as though I was some kind of damn puppet of his. Only instead of pulling at my strings, he was fucking wrapping me up in them, like a spider to the fly, snarled in his web, he had me trapped without ever wanting to escape.

Now, I just had to hope he wouldn't accidentally suck me dry.

A sharp tug was my only warning that my panties were about to disappear as he tore them from me like the rest of my clothes. I had to say, when I ever thought about this moment, I had foolishly romanticised the moment. I would have been wearing some sexy dress hiding even sexier silk and lace beneath. But then again, this was my Vampire King featured in this fantasy. So, my bloody body quivering on top of ripped pieces of material he had torn off me was more fitting for a being like Lucius.

The moment his hand snaked in between our bodies, and he made contact with my soaked clit, I cried out, knowing I was far too close to last long with him touching me like that. But Lucius wanted something in return.

"Beg for me," he whispered against my cheek.

"Ahhh... oh Gods," I moaned arching against him, and I felt his knowing grin against my skin. Then he growled and nipped at me again, making me cry out at the little sting his bite created,

"I told you to beg."

It had been a warning to give in to his demands and to prove his point his fingers left my clit and I cried out at their loss. This was before sucking in a startled breath when instead they penetrated my unused channel. He swallowed that cry as well with his mouth. Then his fingers started to work me, and it built inside me once more. But just before it erupted, he cruelly pulled his fingers from me, making me cry again with yet another loss.

"No, please!" I said before I could stop it.

"Ah there she is...*now again,"* he demanded and I shook my head, telling him that I wouldn't. Because I wanted to be more to him. I wanted something more in return. Which was why I told him,

"I am not your plaything!" My breathy tone indicating differently. He seemed amused by this and his amber eyes glowed even brighter at my defiance. Then his fingers pinched my clit and I cried out again, my body trying to bolt upright, only his weight on me wouldn't allow me to move far.

"No? *Your body disagrees with you, princess."* Then to prove his point yet again, he released his hold on my clit and dragged more of my cream from in between my folds before working it faster this time. Again, my body arched and pressed into him, one hand breaking free of his hold so I could claw it at his back.

"Do you want me to have you...to take you and coat my cock with your crimson cream...to make you mine completely...?" he said speaking against my skin, licking at me before scraping his fangs up the length of my neck, making me shiver.

"I will if you only ask me to," he told me just as my orgasm was nearly there, it was so close...*I was so close*. Gods, but I was almost afraid of it, knowing just how powerful it would be.

Just that little bit more.

Just a few more seconds.

One.

Two.

Three.

And here it...

"NO!" I screamed the second he stopped, making the cruel bastard chuckle. I even found myself pounding my fist on his back and tears pricked my eyes.

"You want it, you know how to get it...so tell me, my little Šemšā, *do you want me to take your virginity?*" he asked with a growl to his words and I was so close, the only thing in my way was what he was yet to give me...*a promise*.

Which was why I started shaking my head, telling him a panicked little no, and instead of getting angry with me, he started to soothe me. He stretched out over me, and in that moment, I felt the denim of his jeans start to dissolve as if now nothing but a cloud of dust.

After that there was nothing left between us. I could finally feel the head of his solid length just there, a single thrust away. I could feel myself soaking the head, as I rubbed myself against him without being able to stop. It was as if my body was doing so of its own accord, screaming at me for being a fool and denying us.

"Ssshh now, why do you fight me, my Šemšā...*why do you fight your destiny?*" he asked me gently, as he stroked back my hair. A single tear escaped and ran down the side towards my hairline. Only Lucius saw it and like everything else, he claimed it, getting there first as he licked it, humming as he tasted my tears.

It was all just too much.

I couldn't hold out any longer.

"Will you…" this time I stopped myself by actually biting my lip, one he pulled free with his thumb.

"Will I what?" I decided to be brave and say it, knowing that in the next four words out of my mouth there was an abyss of meaning there.

"Will you protect it?" Once it was finally past my lips his eyes blazed and finally, he gave me everything I ever wanted,

Everything I ever dreamed of.

And he did this as he kissed his way down from my damp cheek all the way down to my neck,

"Body. Mind. Soul and your *tender little heart…"* I released a held breath of relief the second that last word was uttered against my skin. And I quickly took his face in my hands and brought his lips back to mine in a desperate need to kiss him.

"Yes," I told him the second he allowed me to take breath and I rubbed myself along his length to prove it. A rumbling sound vibrated in his chest. Then he collared my neck, pushed my chin up and was at my neck in a blink. He growled low against my taut skin and I knew the time was now. Especially when this time he gave me even more…

"Now it's time to say you're mine, my Khuba…*beg me to claim you, my love."* The second he called me his love I fell completely, knowing in that moment I would have given him everything I was and ever could be.

"Please Lucius…make me yours…*claim me, my…"* I never got to finish as this was enough for him, for in that single second it was as though the entire world stopped. Paused for the lovers. A single heartbeat for the both of us.

Because it wasn't all about what Lucius was going to take from me, seconds away from owning it all.

It was also about what he gave me back in return.

And in true Lucius fashion, it was a brutal and raw return of his heart, as he finally admitted who I was to him.

Admitting it in a way that only Lucius could, when he said, "This is going to hurt so sweetly...

"...My Electus."

CHAPTER TWENTY-FOUR

HARD LIMITS, SOFT LIMITS AND ALL THE LIMITS IN BETWEEN

Lucius made good on his promise.

He made it hurt so sweetly.

Because the moment after he called me his Electus, claiming me to be his Chosen One, was the same moment he claimed me in every other way. As he didn't just claim my virginity, he claimed my blood. He broke through the barrier of my sex, making me cry out the second I felt the length of him entering me. But then at the same time his fangs pierced through my skin, and my cries of pain ended up as long, ragged cries of pleasure.

I came instantly, being too overwhelmed by the intensity of it all. I felt myself screaming but couldn't hear anything over the pounding of my own heart. I didn't even know if there was any sound coming through my lips, but my mouth was open and every muscle in my body tensed as it continued to brace itself for the wave of rapture that assaulted me over and over again. The intensity of it all continued to build even as its release was erupting, as it just didn't seem to want to ever stop. And somewhere in the blissful fog that clouded my mind I asked myself was it because his movement inside of me continued to draw it out of me?

Every erogenous zone, every cluster of nerves was being discovered for what felt like the first time and I could do nothing but grip onto his shoulders, as he both fed from my neck like a wild beast as he took even more of me from below. But it was only when he must have felt my fingers gripping him go lax that he pulled his fangs from my neck, knowing he had tapped his limit, unless he wanted to lose me to unconsciousness. But then he had other ideas, because he first licked the length of the puncture holes he had made. Then he purposely looked down at me, letting my blood drip down his fangs and onto the skin by my lips, before he lowered his crimson lips to mine.

"I want you to see how good you taste...*how fucking addictive you are!*" he growled down over my mouth before his fangs disappeared so he could crush his lips to mine in a bruising, blood soaked kiss. The feeling, the sinful and wicked act, combined with the way his hips continued to pump his length into me. Gods, but it was no wonder I was coming again, a cry he consumed with his bloodstained kiss.

"Fucking Heaven!" he snarled down at me, and every drag of his large cock against my insides felt as though it was burning me up from the inside out. A pain merging into a pleasure of the likes I had never known. His hands at my hips, holding me locked to him, as he slammed into me, but he wanted more still. His hands found the back of my knees and he pulled up my legs so he could get deeper still. I cried out yet again, and he watched me with an intense gaze that told me he was drinking in every sound I made, every single expression of pleasure and pain. He was getting high off them, drowning in the sight of me taking everything he gave me and lastly, his own orgasm building in sight of every single fucking thing he took from me, knowing that after this moment our claiming was unbreakable.

He would own me completely.

"Now it's time for my own," he said cryptically before a talon grew and he sliced open an inch line at his neck. Blood pooled before dripping down the length and that was when I knew what it was he wanted.

It was time for me to claim him in return.

He lifted my head to his neck, guiding my lips to the blood he offered, and I hesitated for a second, long enough for him to fist my hair and tell me,

"My life is yours, as is my blood from this day forward... *now fucking take it!*" he snarled this demand and I opened my mouth the second he pushed my head to his neck and I latched onto him, knowing there wasn't a single thing between us.

Not. A. Single. Fucking. Thing.

I bit into him, sucking his blood like it was my very own elixir of life and in a way, it was. The taste of him burst across my tongue and instead of the metallic taste I was expecting it to taste like it was unlike anything I had ever had before in my life. But as my reaction had been to him drinking from me, his reaction was the same. Because he unexpectedly held me tighter in his hold, a desperate kind of need overtaking him as he suddenly roared his release into me. Now bellowing at the Gods in another language, swearing words I didn't understand as his pleasure erupted inside me.

I could feel his cock shuddering inside my core, thumping against the walls of my channel as my own orgasm milked his length, as it coated the walls of my sex with his seed. I felt it dripping out of me, coating my thighs as he continued to thrust inside me with speed, as if his own release wasn't yet over. I knew this when he tore his neck from my lips, threw his head back and this time when he roared his second release, it was powerful enough to crack the walls.

A hand shot out to hold himself from crushing me and instead it crushed the wood of the frame behind my head. This was when he finally started to come down from the rapture of his high, and we were both left panting, blood coating the upper parts of our bodies, the mix of our release soaking the lower, and beads of sweat in between.

And I felt utterly spent and knew my limbs would be useless as nothing felt as if it worked anymore. Nothing but the pounding of my heart that I could feel still thundering in my chest. I watched as Lucius lowered his head, letting it hang forward for a few moments as he took the time needed to regain control of his functions. The way his hair hung forward, his face looking strangely serene in a way I had never seen it before. As if the weight of the world had just been lifted and the damaged parts of his soul now fixed.

As if he had just felt his own heart beating for the first time.

But then he opened his eyes and the beautiful blue grey colour was back, staring down at me as though I was some holy being bestowing upon him a gift, and in a sense I guess I just had. He didn't say anything, but his eyes told me enough. He then started to move, and I was about to pull away from him when another thing I had never heard from him before slipped through the cracks of his hard exterior. It was a vulnerable sound, one said at the same time he quickly grabbed my hip, preventing me from moving and breaking our connection.

"No...not yet, I am not ready for you to let go of your hold on me," he told me gently and then he shifted our bodies both to the side after first hooking my leg over his hip, keeping us locked together, something I was more than grateful for as I too wasn't ready to let him go.

Then we lay facing each other, just like when I had woken up last time finding him looking at me with a tenderness and it nearly took my breath away. In that moment, when he brushed my hair back off my face, I didn't know what side of Lucius I loved more. The rough, demanding, dominant and 'says fuck a lot' King who had just fucked me raw or the tender, gentle, soft side of Lucius that looked at me now as if I was some precious rare gift he vowed never to return to my old life.

His little sun bird caught in the cage of his world.

"Are you alright?" he asked me softly and I blushed, only able to nod as I felt strangely vulnerable in that moment. It made me question if I always would? Was this what sex was like, was this the aftermath? The feeling as if you had just been cracked wide open and bared your soul to someone, praying that they would know what to do with it afterwards?

"Words, sweetheart," he demanded calmly.

"I am." He smirked at this and my obvious shyness. But then I decided to ask him the same… as well, I really wanted to know.

"Are *you* alright?" Now this question shocked him. I knew this as he placed his forehead to my shoulder and chuckled, muttering to himself,

"She asks me if I am I alright." Then he shook his head as if he couldn't get his mind around it, before lifting his gaze to mine, so he could tell me,

"Amelia, I just claimed my Chosen One, I am more than alright, I am…Gods, *but I finally feel blessed by Heaven."* The second the words were out I sucked in a breath holding it there, too afraid to let it go again, in case it had the power to take away this perfect moment along with it.

"Lucius I…" I started to say as I placed my hand to his cheek and he closed his eyes and simply said,

"I know." Meaning that I never got chance to finish before

he was kissing me and this time it was soft and gentle and spoke of those three words neither of us had said yet.

But it was eight letters we didn't need to put into words.

Not in that moment.

Not when it was there in our kiss. In our tender touch.

In our eyes.

"Are you sore?" Lucius asked shortly after our kiss ended and he was now gently running his fingertip over my lips.

"A little," I confessed making him grin wickedly.

"And we can't have that now can we. Not when I am far from done with you and your delectable little body." Then he winked at me and ended up laughing when I uttered in shock,

"Again?"

"No pet... *again and again and again.*" Then he kissed my nose as my mouth dropped in shock again making him chuckle.

"Hold still as I leave you."

"Oh, but I thought erm ...okay then..." I said in a small voice that he read easily because he whispered down at me,

"I meant leave your body, Amelia, as trust me, I am not going anywhere." I rolled my lips to stop myself from saying more, already feeling the heat in my cheeks from shame at appearing needy. Then he nodded down at me silently asking me if I was ready for him to move and I motioned that I was.

"Mmm, ah." I moaned as he pulled from my tender core hearing that I wasn't the only one that mourned the loss. But then I felt him pulling me up, and I was shy once more,

"Wait, what are you...whoa!" I ended that question when I was picked up out of bed and found myself being carried into what I assumed was Lucius' bathroom.

"I am taking care of what is mine to care for," he told me brazenly as we entered this new space, his sweet words staying with me.

The room wasn't what I expected in a bathroom but was

what I expected of Lucius, for the whole room except for the ceiling was different shades of black and dark grey. The floor was a dark grey slate and the walls were made of black painted panelled wood. In the centre of the room was a stone oval bathtub that looked to be carved from a single piece of granite. The edges were as smooth as they were on the inside and the only part of the bath that had been left to its natural rough state was the thick edge. But there were no taps and I would have questioned where the water came from if he wasn't now carrying me behind a granite stone wall, that held a shower behind it.

A large round shower head hung from above that was the size of a dinner plate yet when he turned on the water, it didn't just rain from this point. It actually rained down against the stone walls, creating a waterfall effect that looked kick ass cool. He placed me down on my feet and pulled what I only now realised was the rest of his T shirt from my arms and my bra that hung limp either side of my breasts. Then he threw them out from behind the wall so we were both naked in the shower.

Something by now I should have been used to, having done this once before. But after what just happened in his bed, well, it was like I was relying on him for guidance on what to do next. And what I was to do next was obviously let Lucius care for me and this seemed to be his time to wash me, something I was too stunned to stop. Besides it felt way too nice to stop, well that was until he started to travel lower and I shackled his wrist to stop him.

"It's okay I can do…" His growl silenced me and then he told me sternly,

"Nothing will ever stop me from touching you." So, my fingers uncurled releasing him and he continued on down, until his next command was issued.

"Open your legs for me." I swallowed hard and I swear I

nearly choked on what could only be described as pure fuckable desire. But I obviously wasn't obeying him quick enough as he tapped on my thigh and said,

"You heard me, sweetheart." So, I did his bidding as honestly, I couldn't find myself doing anything else. It was as if since having me, claiming me as he put it, I was locked into his command. As if I was actually his now and had unknowingly placed my body under his control, for I didn't seem to be questioning his authority over me.

"Ahhh," I moaned sharply the second his soapy hand came into contact with my sensitive folds and I reached out to grab hold of him, burying my face in his bicep. His gloved hand went to the back of my head and stroked down my hair,

"The tenderness will ease, especially once my blood has started to do its work." I raised my head at that and looked up at him over his impressive muscle.

"Its work?" I questioned.

"It will help heal you," he told me, affectionately running the back of his leather covered fingers down my cheek, making me wonder if he ever took the glove off. I had wanted to ask him about it so many times before, but I already knew, thanks to Pip, that even talking about it was a big no, no. And even though I had not long ago just been declared as his Chosen One, I didn't think it right to ruin the moment. However, I still wanted to test how far I could push it, so I covered his fingers with my own hand, touching his fingers lightly, bracing myself for his reaction.

And as I thought, his hand slipped quickly from beneath them and fell away from touching me all together. That was when I looked up at him and braved his gaze to see it looking for only a few seconds...*pained.*

This was when I knew that for Lucius,

This was a hard limit.

So, I let it go for now, hoping that he would trust me in time. But then again, I had a feeling that this was all as new for Lucius as it was for me and in fact, we were two people that were just learning what falling in love really meant. And right now, for Lucius it meant caring for me after what I had just given him. Which was why I let him wash my body in the gentle, tender way he did, and soak in not just the moisture but every single touch. The way he turned my body around so I was facing the wall with my back to his chest. Then he raised up my arms, linking my hands behind his neck that put my body not only on display, but naturally made my breasts lift as if begging for his attention next.

Then with his arms around me, his hands in front me, he added more soap and I became fascinated with watching his large strong hands rub together creating a foam coating them white. The manly scent was one I recognised as being all Lucius, meaning that he now purposely wanted me to smell of him and I asked myself was this his possessive nature making this decision? Surrounding me with everything that was him. His scent on my skin, my body in his bed, his seed still trickling down from inside me. He was everywhere even if his hands weren't.

Was this what it felt like to be owned by him?

If it was, then it was like he said...*it was fucking intoxicating.*

But then his hands, one bare, one leather, both wet and slick with soap started moving all over my body, cupping my breasts and with every breath I took, it pushed them further into his open palms. I couldn't help it when my head fell back against his chest at the same time a moan escaped open lips. I felt then the rumbling against my back as his own growls of pleasure vibrated from his chest.

"Gods, you're beautiful," he told me, making me take a

deep shuddering breath before I told him quietly,

"Thank you." But then I heard him chuckle softly, before he leant his head down closer so he could whisper,

"Ah, so this is what I must do to be granted your thanks." His voice was full of gentle humor and I couldn't help but grin, knowing that he had mentioned this a few times and I wasn't sure if he was right...was this the first time I had thanked him for anything? Even after everything he had done for me. Saving my life, giving me back my apartment after it was trashed, the clothes, the private space whilst here...and not once had I thanked him. Well, surely now was as good a time as any...

Even given my inexperience, it couldn't be that hard could it?

Well, it seemed to be my night for firsts.

Meaning that I turned in his arms, thankful that he let me, then with my arms wrapped around his neck I rose up on my toes and started kissing his jawline, making his grip on me tighten when I whispered,

"Then maybe it's time I thanked you properly." Then I started to lower myself before him and I heard his sharp intake of breath, and I had to say the sound of his surprise could quite easily become my new addiction.

"Amelia, you don't...ahh." He was cut off when I scraped my nails down his thighs as I lowered myself all the way to my knees stopping him from saying anything more, and I did this by looking up at him through the veil of my lashes and used his words against him,

"I claimed you back remember... therefore nothing will stop me from touching you," I told him before taking his thick length in my hand touching his steely length for the first time. The second I did, wrapping my fingers around his sizable girth, he sucked air through his teeth and at first, I wondered if I was holding him too hard.

The moment I loosened my hold on him his hand quickly covered mine stopping me. Then without words, he tapped me under the chin and nodded down to himself, telling me I was doing nothing wrong and asking me to continue. Because he knew of my innocence. He knew I had never done this before, and he was guiding me onwards. And well there was only one way to thank him and that was…

To keep thanking him.

So, I took a firmer hold and began using my tongue, starting at the base as I licked up to the tip, moving my hand as I went. Then the second I heard yet another guttural moan from him, this time I didn't stop, but I did smile to myself. Gods, but just knowing the power I finally held over this man was like a rush of adrenaline and lust merging into one. The knowledge combined with the act was turning me on enough that the second I took his cock into my mouth I ended up moaning around him, making him echo my sound with one of his own.

"Fuck!" I heard him hiss the second I sucked hard down on him before lifting my lips over his satin soft skin, one surrounding such a hard length. Then as I went down again, I twisted my mouth around him, letting myself gag a little and using the extra saliva to coat his cock.

He must have liked this as I felt him slap a hand to the wall, and I flinched a little when I heard stone cracking. But then he must have been worried about losing my mouth as a reassuring hand came to my shoulder. But when I felt it actually shaking, I couldn't help my grin form around him once more. Then I repeated the action, each time relaxing my throat a little more and pushing myself further down, gaining more each time. And in return, I gained more pleasure from the sounds of his.

However, I knew I would never manage it all, he was simply too big and the soreness between my legs was testament to that. But feeling the ache in my jaw I decided to get braver, licking at the head, paying it some attention, swiping at the small slit there and marvelling the second I tasted the salty precum. Gods, but he tasted divine and I started lapping at him, trying to tease more, now working my wet hand up and down his length.

"Lucifer's blood, woman!" he shouted as if I was killing him with pleasure and again, the knowledge that I could do this to him, accomplish such a thing, Lucifer's blood was right, having this power on someone like Lucius was addictive!

I heard more stone cracking, but this time ignored it as I continued to drive him closer, wanting to punish him with rapture just as he had done to me. Because I didn't just want to thank him, I wanted to brand this moment to his soul for the rest of his eternity, so he would never want another. I wanted to be the best he'd ever had. I wanted to be his everything!

So, I worked his length, this time too lost in my own pleasure gained to feel any ache or strain. I just wanted everything I knew he could give me and I when I glanced up, still with him in my mouth, I saw his hands locked to the back of the wall, bracing himself and keeping them there as if he feared any movement from him would end his pleasure too soon.

"Amelia, Gods woman but I am going to…I am fucking close so unless you…ahhh, fuck!" He hissed when I didn't stop and the second he knew I was fully intent on swallowing him down, I felt a possessive hand fist in my hair as he held my head to his cock the second he roared his release, giving me every piece of him. I am not going to lie, it took some getting used to, as I felt him shooting his seed into my mouth, I gagged around it as I tried my best to swallow him down, feeling it dripping down my chin.

But the roar of his release as he threw his head back and as the thundering sound erupted, I had never felt a thrill quite like it. Soon the fist in my hair went slack and once I was sure I had lapped up every last drop, I released him, making sure to kiss the sensitive head making him shudder one last time before I got to my feet.

Then I dipped myself under the spray one last time, grinning when I saw him still trying to catch his breath. Also taking note of the cracks in the wall around where his hands had been purposely locked to. Gods, but I felt good. Like some powerful siren that had the hidden power to bring this King to his knees.

Which was why I decided to end the moment on a 'aren't I a badass, giving my first successful blow job' kind of way. And I did this by walking up to him, kissing his jawline just as I had done when I first started and said to him,

"Thanks, handsome." Then I grinned against him before turning on a heel to leave him in the shower. Now this would have been a very cool way to make my exit after my power play…that was if Lucius had let me.

"Where the fuck do you think you're going!" he snapped at the same time snatching my hand and yanking me back to him. I fell spinning into him just as he took my head in his hands and kissed me with enough passion it made me dizzy and lightheaded. Especially when I felt myself being pushed up against the wall, feeling the spray of the waterfall cascading down my back.

"I am not finished with you yet, princess!" Then he suddenly grabbed my ass with both hands and lifted me so my legs fell open naturally, a space he quickly filled. Then as he lowered me back down, he did so this time impaling me on his length. I screamed in both pain at the intrusion but also at the pleasure it quickly bloomed into. My head fell back against the stone, feeling the water splashing over me, and I swear we could have been making love under some exotic waterfall in some jungle paradise for all I knew.

Because the pleasure was too intense to think of much else but the living fantasy his body was currently playing out. The way he held me, as if ready to fight the world if they dared take me away from him. The way he hammered into me, making me moan and cry out as wave after wave of my orgasm ripped through me, this time quick and fast without the slow build. No, this time it was raw and intense as this wasn't making love to me, this was wild desperately fucking me against the wall. As if his lust had taken hold and there was nothing he could do about it but sate his needs.

And me, *well I loved every fucking minute of it!*

"Yes, yes, yes…YES!" I screamed as I came again, this time letting it take me as I went limp in his hold, barely having the strength left to hold on. But then minutes later and he was following me in that release, this time swearing it,

"FUCK, YES!"

I remained clinging onto him as he lowered his head, panting through his euphoric state, with one hand holding my ass and the other holding us both up with a hand overhead to the wall.

After this and there was little else I could do but let myself be carried from the shower like last time. I felt as though my limbs had been replaced with soggy wet noodles as I clung onto him, with him still seated inside of me. Again, I moaned my loss the second he withdrew before sitting me down on the counter by the sinks. I felt a towel being wrapped around me and I let my head fall forward, placing my forehead to his chest as I muttered one last thing to him before I felt myself close to passing out.

Of course, I did, but doing so this time to the sound of his laughter…

"Was it good for you?"

CHAPTER TWENTY-FIVE

AND ALL AFTER BREAKFAST

This time when I woke up, I was awarded with a new sight and two things happened. The first was I silently gasped and the second was to replace the first with a secret grin. Because now I faced Lucius who was asleep. I don't know why I found the sight such a captivating and intriguing one, but maybe because like this, he looked so...*human*.

I was always so used to his presence being one that dominated the space around him, the whole room becoming aware of his entire being, it was sometimes stifling. The strength he portrayed as if oozing out of every pore and he didn't even realise it, certainly not something done for effect or some kind of act. It was simply him.

But like this, he looked so peaceful, he almost didn't look real enough to touch. As if when I tried, then my hand would simply pass right through him. The way those sandy coloured strands were tousled and giving real meaning to the term 'bed head'. It made me itch to run my fingers through it, to push back the strays that had managed to fall across his forehead. To run my fingertips gently along that strong jawline, now dusted with stubble a few shades darker than his hair. Gods, but he even looked younger in his serene state, with those long lashes casting faint fan shaped shadows under his eyes. It made me wonder if he was ticklish, and if I ran my nail gently across his lips now would they twitch or form that knowing, easy grin of his.

Gods, but just looking at him and my heart ached, he was so beautiful. And it made me think about all that he had endured in his long life on this Earth. My eyes continued to scan every inch of him that was on show, taking my time now that I was finally free to do so. The contoured lines, dips and hollows in between all that muscle, made me wonder if he worked out like I knew many of my father's kind did.

At one time, it was often I would be down in my father's training room, practicing all the moves he and Takeshi had taught me. Now thinking back to a time when I fooled myself enough to believe that if I became good enough that my father would trust me more. That I could be allowed to be more independent and do the simple things, like go to a party with my friends or fated Gods forbid, *a real date.*

I had trained to an obsessive point where each move had simply become as natural as breathing. I could use most weapons, with my arrows hitting dead centre and my throwing knives always on target. I had mastered the staff and spear and could sword fight as if I was a bloody samurai! But the simple fact always remained...

I was mortal.

And in the eyes of my father, these skills meant little in the face of an immortal enemy. I had once asked him what the point of it all had been? What was the point of me training so hard if nothing was ever to come of it? His answer had been a cryptic,

'Because even danger can come in the form of a weak wolf.' At the time I hadn't understood what he meant, and I still didn't. Was I the weak wolf, or did he think I could only ever hope to defeat the weak? I remember just throwing down the blade I had been training with, it landing at his feet, and telling him,

'Then I am done.'

And since that day I had never once picked up a blade again, not even engaging in a single fight until that day in the museum. I would be lying if I had said it didn't feel good and even had me wondering if Lucius had his own training room. His muscle and obvious fighting skills would suggest so.

But I remembered after that day, the first time my dad came into my room and asked if I wanted to train with him. I had told him no without explanation and we continued this for weeks later until eventually he stopped asking. I knew it hurt his feelings, but he wasn't the only one. He was the one always telling me,

'If you allow your opponent to make you feel weak, then you will be weak'. But what he didn't understand was that my father was a contradiction to that. As the only one who ever made me feel weak, *was him.* Even last night, Lucius never once made me feel that way. He was worried because he cared for me, but even with a gun to my head, he kept his shit together and in turn, I did the same. Later on, I had warped this into him caring more about the box, but then he explained it to me, and I found myself questioning my own doubts.

"That looks like some heavy thoughts for someone who had her carnal thirst quenched last night and... *so thoroughly.*" The sound of Lucius' lighthearted teasing brought me back from my thoughts.

"My carnal thirst? You're the vampire remember, I was just plain old horny," I teased back flicking him on the shoulder and making him laugh before grabbing my hand and bringing my captured fingers to his lips before he started to bite them. I opened my mouth, moaning but this time it was an over-exaggerated,

"Ooowww."

"Baby," he whispered in a soft voice that melted my insides. Especially when I watched him grin around the digits still with his teeth holding onto them, before he eased the pressure, now sucking them in his mouth to soothe the slight sting. After this he released them and ran a finger around my lips and told me,

"Mmm, now remind me again how talented this mouth of yours is," he said snagging me at the back of my neck and pulling me to him for a kiss, one that wasn't what I would have thought a morning kiss would be like. As this one ended up with me being slid underneath his body and moaning in his mouth.

"I must say, waking to this delectable little body and talented mouth of yours is going to be a most welcome addition to my day," he told me making me blush ridiculously.

"That's a little presumptuous of you, Vampy." I said as his lips were at my neck, well, they were until I said that, as he pulled back to look down at me.

"Vampy?"

"I have decided that's what I am going to call you, so remember that whenever the inclination to call me 'princess' takes you." At this he scoffed, lowered himself back to kissing my neck and muttered,

"We will see about that." I had to say, it felt amazing with his full naked length lay against my side, and his lips sucking and nipping at my neck and across my chest. So good in fact, that I nearly missed the next thing he said,

"It is not presumption, but an absolute."

The second his words finally sank in I tensed in his hold and this time when he felt it, he muttered,

"And here we go."

"I think we need to talk." At this he chuckled obviously not taking my tone seriously.

"I would rather hear you moan," he said and he did the second his lips took hold of a nipple as I arched my back to push myself further into him. I swear but my body was a traitorous bitch sometimes.

"You were saying something about talking, sweetheart?" he said after letting go of my breast long enough and I growled in annoyance, something he must have found adorable because he just grinned up at me.

"Yes, I did, and we do need...Oooh Gods." This again ended in a moan of pleasure as he shifted further down the bed and this time started biting my nipple in earnest. But then his chuckle around my flesh made me find clarity and I told him,

"We need to talk, Lucius." But he wouldn't listen, just continued, which was when I grabbed a fist full of his hair and pulled, knowing it wouldn't hurt the big guy. He let my nipple go with a pop and looked up at me from my breasts, baring his fangs at me. But it was a sight I didn't take seriously, as why would I...*I was his Electus.* Gods, but even replaying that name over in my head made me nearly give up on my task.

Nearly.

"We need to talk." I said more forcefully this time. And his response to this was to quickly retract his fangs and lower his head with a groan, resting it between my breasts, muttering,

"But of course."

"Hey, what's that supposed to mean?!" I complained the second he rolled away from me and got out of bed, and I had to say that shamefully I started to forget what we needed to talk about the second I saw his ass. Holy Gods in heaven! Talk about perfection, jeez, that sight should come with a warning attached to it. Like don't view and operate heavy machinery.

"See anything you like back there?" Lucius said looking over his shoulder and seeing me about ten seconds away from drooling, damn him! My eyes snapped to one side and still blushing I bristled a quick and mumbled,

"No, no." His bark of laughter told me he didn't believe me. I then watched him prowl into his closet and once out of sight I rolled over, taking the sheet with me and now on my front I buried my head in the pillow and groaned,

"Why me?" Then I shrieked as I felt the covers whipped off me and then Lucius was there.

And what he gave me was so much more than his ridiculously gorgeous body,

He gave me his thoughts…

"Why you…? You want to know why you, sweetheart, then I will tell you, because you're a lousy thief, fucking adorable most of the time, cute when you're not, hotter than the entirety of Hell, fucking funny and can throw a mean punch when you're not slapping the shit out of me like a girl…" He paused to lower himself to my shoulder and bite it a little before he carried on with his list and I had to say, I was stunned to silence,

"You also have the most incredible mouth, a fucking goddess in bed, have an ass I want to bite, and a pair of breasts I get to bite whenever the fuck I want…and you're also my Chosen One. So that Amelia, *is why*…now I'm hungry and unless you want to be on the menu, then I would get your fuckable ass up out of bed, sweet cheeks… before I make good on my words…*all of them,"* he said, now shifting off me and slapping my ass. He then walked away from me to the sounds of my whimper, both from the sting of his slap,

But most of all,

From the soothing words of his confession.

A little time later and I was dressed in a comfortable pair of stonewash jeans, and a casual off the shoulder sweater in navy blue, that I thought brought out the colour of my eyes. Eyes that this time were framed by my thick black rimmed glasses, as my eyes were sore from sleeping in my contact lenses. I pulled my hair up into a high ponytail letting a few of the short bits hang loose around my face. I wore thick socks forgoing the need for shoes right now, especially since I had enough blisters to last me the rest of the year, thanks to the stripper heels from last night. Meaning I was back to being just shy of a foot shorter than Lucius once again.

I was just glad that I had been allowed to slip on a robe and sneak back into my apartment to change while Lucius was on the phone. I made hand signals to let him know this was what I was doing, so as not to disturb him, when he lowered the phone and asked,

"Unless this is your idea of some task force style roleplay, then yes Amelia, you can go change in your apartment." I had frowned at him first before shaking my head deciding to bite my tongue. Of course, it still didn't stop him from halting me at the door, when he said,

"Amelia…you have ten minutes." And then he carried back on with his German speaking phone call.

And as for me, *I was eleven minutes.*

Which brought me back to his apartment, now staring at his door for over thirty seconds asking myself if I should knock first? This of course ended with the door being yanked open, just as my hand was up in the air ready to knock. Lucius took one look at me and frowned, then snapped in true Lucius fashion,

"Why the fuck are you about to knock!?" Then he hooked a hand in the waistband of my jeans and tugged me hard enough that I went falling into his chest. Then he gripped on to my ponytail so my head tilted back when he pulled and he snarled,

"That was eleven minutes you made me wait for your lips." Then he kissed me, not wasting another second. Meanwhile I was trying not to give in to the urge to grin in some sap happy ridiculous way because my big bad Vamp erm...*maybe boyfriend*...had actually counted the minutes.

By the time the kiss finished I was pushed up against the door with my hands still in his hair, his hands on my 'fuckable ass' (something that totally panicked me) and we were both breathing heavy. Then with his forehead lowered to mine, he whispered,

"We don't need words, my little Šemšā."

I wished in that moment that it was true, just so we could have found our way back into his bed. But then a delicious smell hit me and my answer to this was,

"Oh my Gods, is that bacon!?" Then I slipped out of his hold and sneaked a look behind me to see his forehead fall to the door where I had been, a fist next to it, at the same time he started muttering something about asking Lucifer to give him strength. Meaning that by the time I was in his kitchenette, I was grinning. Of course, it wasn't all down to him as there was in fact, *bacon.* Oh, and what looked like a gift from the Gods,

"Donuts!" I shouted in excitement and the second I felt him coming up behind me, I jumped at him and said,

"Donuts!" this made him chuckle and say,

"If just seeing them gets you this excited, then I know a

game you can play with them later if you like." Then he winked at me and I swear in that moment I had never been more shocked in all my life, even when I found out he actually liked me. Because I threw my head back and burst out laughing, and I don't mean cute girly giggles here, I mean full on belly shaking laughing with tears and everything.

"Oh my Gods, Lucius, you just told a joke and it was funny!" I shouted making him roll his eyes at me, but he couldn't hide the soft look he was trying to hide or even the way his eyes brightened at making me laugh.

"This might be a shocker, sweetheart, but when I am not dealing with fucking cults, crazy ex bitches, mercenaries with a death wish and ancient fucking boxes that want to kill me, then I do try and enjoy life and that includes a joke or two." I smirked at this, placed a piece of bacon on top of my chocolate sprinkled donut (because yes, I was a freak) and waved it towards him whilst I said,

"Good to know." Then I took a huge bite and groaned, ignoring his horrified look at my combination made and a show of saying with a mouthful,

"Thsooo Gooood" and he muttered asking for help as he turned around to grab himself some food.

"Gods give me strength."

I grabbed my cup of tea I had poured and sat myself down in a chair, with one foot up next to my ass and a sticky bacon topped goodness in my other hand. Then, because I had my hands full, used the knuckle on my thumb to push my glasses back up my nose, as I looked down at a German newspaper on the table. Die Welt was the name on the front and had a small picture of the Earth in between the two words that I knew translated meant, 'the world'.

"What other languages do you speak?" he asked coming to join me with a cup of coffee in his hands, but of course he took it black. He also had a plate with some bread and a few slices of meat and cheeses. I looked up at him over my glasses and smirked, especially when I saw his eyes glow slightly at the sight,

"Uh uh, I am not telling you that."

"And why the fuck not?" he snapped making me grin even wider now.

"Because that way you will never know whether I will understand you or not... you know for all those pesky little times when you are trying to keep stuff from me," I said winking at him this time and going back to reading the paper and forcing my brain to work harder at translating it in my head. He scoffed at this but didn't say anything. So, after a while and once my sweet breakfast was consumed, I decided to start it.

"So how exactly is this going to work?" I asked sucking the chocolate icing off my fingers, something he decided to do for me as he snatched out and had my hand in his just as he had this morning.

"That is what happens when you tease me with sweetness," he warned me once he had finished with me.

"Now be more specific," Lucius added now I had my hand back.

"You know, us dating and stuff." I said sounding very lame and nearly wincing at myself because of it. But then he frowned and crushed me a little when he stated firmly,

"We're not dating," he said then took the last bite of his bread before throwing a napkin to the plate and discarding it off to one side.

"Oh...well then, if this is just sleeping together then I..."

"And it fucking well isn't just sleeping together!" he snapped quickly interrupting me and with it confusing the Hell out of me.

"Then what is it?" I asked frowning.

"You're mine," he replied as if in these two words it explained everything. When, *It. Did. Not.* As in not at all!

"And what does that mean exactly?" I asked, thinking it was a bloody good job we were having this 'talk'. It was at this point that he placed his coffee down and slid it off to one side, before he steepled his fingers a moment as if doing so now to aid himself in gaining the patience needed to explain something to me.

"Alright sweetheart, I see you're struggling with this, so I will explain it in the best way I can. You. Are. Mine. That means I will soon be arranging for someone to pack up your stuff in that little flat of yours and have it shipped here." At this I balked before saying in a voice that was considerably higher that what it usually was,

"Why would you do that?!"

"That is what usually happens when someone moves to a different country, princess." I whistled and raised my hands at the sound of all of his crazy and said,

"Hold on there, Vampy, I am not moving here!" He growled at the name I gave him but well, I did warn him, and my look said this.

"You were ready to move here once before," he stated like seven years was bloody yesterday and yes, well to someone who still remembers what it was like to brush his fangs with a Miswak twig, then yeah, this would seem like yesterday. But still, I thought it best to make my point,

"Erm yeah, that was a while ago and was when I was going to study here. But I have a home, I have a job, friends…Lucius, I have a life in London."

"Yes, and if I remember correctly it was one you were ready to walk away from not long ago…you know, *a week ago when you tried to steal from me.*" he said making me cringe because really, that was a bloody good argument.

"That is beside the point," I said and he didn't have to say what a lame response it was, as his eyes said it for him.

"I think you will find it *is the point*," he pressed.

"I can't move in with you!" I said sounding strangely outraged by this.

"Why the fuck not!?" he snapped.

"Well, for starters, this is our first breakfast together and we are already arguing!" I said throwing my hands up, being slightly dramatic. At least at this his gaze softened.

"Alright sweetheart, I know maybe this is going too fast for you..."

"Uh yeah, like Nascar fast." He ignored this comment and continued on,

"But it is what it is and the sooner you accept your fate the easier it will be, *on both of us.*" I swear my jaw went slack, cartoon style!

"Tell me you are joking and did not just say that!" At this he leant back in his chair and folded his arms, telling me silently that he did. He did just say that!

"I cannot believe this is coming from you, of all people!"

"And what is that supposed to mean exactly?" he asked in a short tone.

"Oh, I don't know Lucius, do you want to remind me again just how many years you haven't been *accepting that fate!*" His face said it all, now it was my time to make my own bloody good point. Especially when he argued,

"It is not that same."

"This isn't a 'Potato, potahto, tomato, tomahto, Let's call the whole thing off' type of thing here Lucius, it is the bloody same!" I said making him smirk as he was obviously amused by my use of the song to try to make my point.

"Look, all I am asking is for you in my bed every night and you're there till we wake, your ass sat by my side every night in my club and not in London...*you are with me.* Now if doing so means that you want your own space, then fine, you keep the apartment next door until you feel comfortable enough to live with me fully, but just so you know, that is the only leeway I am giving you here, as no other scenario is acceptable. It's happening, so in the words of your precious Jean-Luc Picard, make it so!"

"Holy shit! You googled him!?" I screeched deciding this was far more important in that moment than him trying to bully me into moving in with him!

"Yeah, well that's what happens when a girl with a Gods be damned mouth like yours and a body I want to fucking ravish night and day, starts mentioning some other guy's name in her sleep, it makes you crazy enough to google shit!" he snapped and I couldn't help but bite my lip just to stop myself from bursting out laughing.

"I swear you start laughing, princess, and you will be over my knee this time, not my shoulder and don't forget, I still owe your ass my palm as it is," he threatened and this time I rolled my lips inwards as a grin was pushing to break out.

"Okay, so leaving Picard out of this, you have to understand where I am coming from here, Lucius, I mean, we haven't even been out on a single date yet," I said thinking this would help in making my point, but it totally ended up backfiring. Because he was striding to the door and before walking through it stopped at my words. Then he turned and said the very last thing I expected him to before walking out the door,

"Alright, princess, if a date is what it takes...

"Be ready at eight."

CHAPTER TWENTY-SIX

IN CASE YOU DIDN'T KNOW

7.57pm

I looked at the clock again and I swear that my heart was beating in time with the bloody thing! Gods, but why was I so nervous? Because you are stood here in a dress he had picked out for you, waiting for your first date with the guy you just lost your virginity to less than twenty four hours ago… and oh yeah, you have been in love with him since you were sixteen years old…that's why you idiot!

"Oh Gods, what am I doing?" I muttered to myself as I saw the clock tick down another minute.

It started from the moment he left me, with a head full of everything he had said to me, starting that morning when I first opened my eyes. Of course, one of the main things my brain was still clinging on to was the fact that now we had done the deed, 'the claiming' whatever that truly meant. Well, now he thought that meant the green light for a fresh new German start…as in, starting right now!

I mean how was it even going to work? Hell, how was I

even going to work?! I thought about all the logistics of it all day and nothing about a possible move was easy...well, other than the actual moving part that was easy considering I was already here and he would have his 'men' pack up my things and ship them here. Oh Gods, but what about the 'second drawer!?' I couldn't have just random people in my flat packing up my stuff! Okay, so yes, technically I had already had my flat trashed and then random people going in to redecorate and stuff, but surely, they didn't see...oh Gods, what if they did?

Needless to say, that for a solid hour after this thought I had then panicked about the 'second drawer'. Totally irrational thoughts like it being stopped at customs for vibrating its way through security and being surrounded by an entire swat team style bomb squad. All of them pointing guns at it from afar and a creepy featureless robot moving on in there and peeling back the sides of the box, one with my damn name written all over it!

I could see it now, YouTube videos from bystanders, Facebook statuses of laughing emojis, endless pictures on Instagram and my name making the six o'clock news as a box full of vibrators and dog eared erotic paperbacks was a suspected bomb!

Gods have mercy on my horny soul!

This was why these fears lasted an hour. Which was also why I made a mental note to ring Wendy and make her pinkie swear to burn its contents and promise on the death of a Wookie never to speak of it again. But then again, I did still have her jacket so at least I had a bargaining chip. Yeah, I could see it now, burn it or the jacket gets it!

Gods, but I needed a life...actually scrap that, I needed to get back to my actual life and quit leading this crazy ass one where people wanted to kill me, use me, throw me in a cell or just plain old shoot me...although that last one kind of goes hand in hand with the first.

But I wasn't wrong. My life before had been safe, quiet, cozy even. I had my work, and Star Trek pizza nights. I had my favorite cereal and my lame bird watching. I had my funny T shirts, cheap re-covered furniture and rug that I kept spilling stuff on...or at least I did.

I had my wall of collectables and my Lego sets. And as sad as it all sounded, for me, I had been living the independent dream. The life I always wanted the second I truly knew I didn't belong in any other.

But now being with Lucius threatened all of that in a big way. Things like, would he be okay with me just getting up and going to work every day? The 'see you later' and the 'honey, I'm home' becoming a regular thing. Because I just didn't see it. I didn't see the sitting down to dinner and Lucius being the, 'so how was your day, dear' kind of guy.

But then I hadn't put Lucius down as someone to sit and watch TV with me either, so he had shocked me there. It then stood to reason he could continue to shock me. And really, I loved him and had for over a decade, could I really just walk away now that I finally had my chance with him?

Of course, at some point I had actually started to get ready for the 'date part' of my self-interrogation, but even makeup, dresses and hair didn't stop me. No, in fact, the only time I stopped doubting my future was the second I found a box waiting for me on the table in the living room. I was back in my own space and had a towel wrapped around me after spending a good amount of time in the bath and shaving...well, everything apart from my head. After all, he had said he had been pleased to see me bare, so big plus for me with that one.

I found Liessa there looking down at the large white box tied with a blue ribbon. She nodded down at it and said,

"Okay, so he may not have been a sending flowers type of guy, but he is definitely buying you a spectacular dress type of

---

guy…which if you ask me is way better!" I smiled at her, knowing even without her saying it, she felt bad for allowing those flowers in the club. Of course, what she didn't know was even without them I would have still tried to sneak out and follow Lucius, because I had been worried about him. Then again, I doubted without the crazy ex bitch face, that I would have gotten far.

I turned my attention back to the box and beamed down at it the second I opened it. Because it was like Liessa had said, inside the box turned out to be a stunning navy blue dress with a note that said,

'To match my girl's pretty eyes.'

There was also a pair of shoes to match that were just as beautiful but with my blisters, I wasn't holding out much hope to be any taller tonight.

The dress, however, was perfect in size and shape and even elegant in style. It was also long enough that the shoes to match wouldn't be seen anyway, but I would still have to hope I wouldn't end up just tripping over the long skirt.

It was a striking navy blue silk in a maxi style, with a pleated skirt that floated around me in a wave, swishing every time I moved as though I was underwater. It also had a hint of a metallic sheen to it that caught in the light. The top half of the dress was also slightly pleated in design and one that cut across the breasts and gathered at one shoulder leaving the other bare. The back had a large section cut out of it in a diagonal shape that made it easy to get on as it was a simple zip up at my side and one thick piece of material that tied at my shoulder, its pieces of the bow hanging down my arm.

The only problem with the dress was what underwear to wear underneath, as a bra wasn't going to work and neither would a strapless one thanks to the cut out section at the back. Thankfully, Liessa came to the rescue and brought me a sweet and sexy looking body suit that had straps which could be changed to cut across my back and over one shoulder. It was simple, being black satin with rounded, layered lace at the cups.

After this I slipped on some simple but cute ballet flats that tied around the ankle with a thick ribbon. So, they were white but seeing as you wouldn't see them anyway, I rolled with it. As for my hair and makeup, I went with just a hint of smoky dark and shimmery blue on my eyes to match the dress. A subtle light plum colour for my lips and a swipe of eyeliner above and below made my eyes look even bigger.

Then, I styled my hair in a bun that had a few curls cascading around it and off to one side to mimic the shape of the neckline. I didn't have any jewellery and hardly ever wore it anyway so everything else on me was bare. Of course, due to my nerves I had also been ready a little over an hour ago. At the very least I had managed to find an inbuilt stereo system, meaning I was listening to the radio whilst waiting.

Which brought me back to now and one minute to eight. I didn't know if he would be coming here or if I was to meet him in the club or even go knocking on his apartment, although he didn't seem to like that much when I had gone to do it earlier.

"Ah!" I jumped the second I heard the door being knocked and guess I got my answer. It was dead on eight. Wow, who knew that Lucius was so punctual. I walked to the door and opened it, half expecting it to be one of Lucius' men come to escort me to him or something.

But the second my breath caught in my throat, anyone would have guessed who was standing behind the door.

"Lucius." His name escaped my lips as if I was surprised, which I wasn't, as I had been expecting him but what did take me off guard was the mere sight of him! Gods, but he was

utterly breathtaking and my eyes drank in the length of him, just as his did the same. But for once I did this not caring that he was going to catch me openly gaping at him. It was the first time I had seen him wearing a full suit, without anything missing, rolled up or unbuttoned. It was a dark grey colour that brought out the intensity in his eyes, eyes that in the moment I was sure the moon would have been jealous of.

The jacket was buttoned up and underneath I could see the tailored waistcoat and tie in the same colour but his shirt was black. He looked strikingly handsome, from his dress shoes all the way up to his messy hair that had been styled back from his face and fell slightly off to one side. I say styled but I could imagine that after a shower all he had done was run a hand through it a few times before it dried that way. Gods, but he looked good enough say to Hell with the date and drag him inside by his tie. However, I wasn't brave enough to do that.

But Lucius on the other hand…

"Fuck the Gods, you're exquisite!" he said snagging me around the waist and hauling me into his arms, a hand slipping to the knot of hair at the side, using it also to bring me to his lips in one smooth motion. And I opened up to him like I knew I always would, because this right here, *was my addiction*. The way he wanted me, Gods, but it was a passion that matched my own, the way every moment with him felt as though we were quickly burning out of control. As though we were both falling down some rabbit hole together, about to become buried under a mountain of mistrust, lies and fears that neither of us ever cared about when we were like this. Locked together in an already unbreakable bond that happened long ago and a decade before I was offered his blood and before he demanded my soul in return.

Like this, then every single word of his was true.

He owned every last inch of me.

I didn't know how long it was we were kissing for but the moment he pulled away I felt the loss of his lips like someone had just snatched that addiction out of my hands without warning.

"As much as I want nothing more than to tear this dress from you and claim this beautiful body on a floor of navy silk, I have something planned for you," he told me, running the back of his fingers down my cheek in a way that had me slightly leaning into the touch.

"Come," he said after taking my hand in his and leading me from the apartment and I had thought we were going to be walking straight inside his club, but this didn't happen. No, instead we turned left and walked toward the elevator.

"Are we leaving?"

"Not yet, no, but soon," he told me and then instead of getting in the elevator like I thought we would, he led me to the staircase and up towards the rooftop garden. The moment we walked through the metal doors I gasped at the sight as it came into view. It was as beautiful as it was before but now with the addition of thousands of fairy lights that had been wrapped around anything that could be lit up. Spirals of lights twisted up the small trees and entwined with the ivy crawling up over the wooden pergola making the green in the leaves glow. The steel sculptures at the corners were no longer just bare twisted lengths of corrugated iron as they had been transformed into something magical. Glowing a soft white, the lights became the leaves in what had been just dead metal branches.

Even the water feature in the centre was lit up and this, combined with the city that surrounded us all aglow, it was utterly breathtaking.

"It's...Gods, Lucius, it's so beautiful," I said taking it all in and he granted me a warm smile.

"Care for a drink?" he asked me and I couldn't help but tease him,

"That depends what's on the menu." The grin he gave me was nothing short of sinful.

"Oh, don't you worry, later I will get my fill of you, but it won't be here." I frowned at this, but he didn't give me anything more but instead popped open a bottle of champagne and I watched as he poured me a glass. The long stems of the black glasses were overly so, giving them an elegant gothic touch.

"So, are you going to explain that to me?" I asked him after taking a sip and giving him enough time to do so of his own free will, which only came when I pushed for it.

"I've decided we leave for Königssee tonight." I looked down at my glass just so as not to show him my disappointment as it felt for the moment as if it had stolen my breath.

"When will you be back?" I asked quietly, trying not to sound too needy but then he scoffed, and the sound startled me enough to look back up at him.

"You really think I would go without you, or anywhere for that matter…No, I said *we* for a reason, sweetheart."

"Oh, I thought you meant *we* as in you and your people." At this his eyes turned hard and he took a step into me, his leather hand coming to the bare point on my back, making me shiver against him.

"You are much more than my people, *you are mine.* You think I make such a claim that lightly that I would leave the very next day?" he asked his tone telling me he wasn't pleased. So, I decided to give him a little insight into my mind and I thought the best way to do this was to raise a hand to his neck, where I couldn't stop myself from creating little circles with my thumb at the place I had tasted him.

"This is all new to me too, remember." The moment he

heard this little admission his gaze softened, and he pulled me close enough to kiss my forehead before telling me,

"I know it is, sweetheart, and that knowledge brings me great pleasure." After this he took a step back and then took my glass from me and his own, placing them on the wall before coming back to me.

"Dance with me," he said utterly shocking me.

"You dance?!" He smirked down at me and said,

"Is it really so hard to believe, after all, I was once a gentleman of society and well, to not know how to dance...*was shocking?*" he said this last part getting closer to my face and whispering it in jest. Then he finished it with a wink, and I laughed. In all honesty it was too hard to imagine. Oh, not the elegant suits, top hats and the manor homes, or the sight of him sat upon a midnight black horse. But just seeing him out in society, the balls, the dinners, the dancing and such, it was just hard to picture.

But then he took my hand in his and placed that firm leather hand on the small of my back, pulling me into him. Gods, but what was it about that subtle move that had me gasping. It felt intense and so profound.

"There's no music," I said, first needing to swallow heavily or I was in danger of stuttering.

"Just you wait for it," he said making me unable to resist teasing him,

"Why, you gonna pull a string quartet out of your hat?" He growled playfully and snapped his teeth at me telling me,

"Behave, little bird." Then suddenly he closed his eyes and music started to play through what must have been hidden speakers.

"Oh...is this...Lucius I...I know this song," I said too shocked to form words at first and most definitely too busy asking myself if it meant what I hoped it did. Had he picked this one for a reason or had it just been pure fluke. I didn't have to wait long for my answer,

"Then you also know its words and by the end of this dance, you will know why I picked it," he told me, moving our bodies around in a slow dance that was more about holding me than the steps. But I was lost to the thought of those words, feeling the tears start to form the second the first line was sung,

I can't count the times, I almost said what's on my mind...

"In case you didn't know." I whispered the song's title as a tear slipped free this time rolling down my cheek, now knowing that he had picked it for its words.

Words like…

In case you didn't know,
Baby I'm crazy 'bout you,
And I would be lying if I said,
That I could live this life without you,
Even though, I don't tell you all the time,
You had my heart a long, long time ago,
In case you didn't know.

"Lucius." I whispered his name, just because I needed to, as if reminding myself that he was actually here, and this was actually happening. Asking myself if he was even real anymore?

"Amelia… my little Šemšā… *my Khuba.*" He whispered this last name, the one I still didn't know, down at me as he now framed my face with his hands and was closing the distance between our lips when I had to know. I had to know if it meant what I hoped it did.

What it felt like it could be.

"What does it mean?" I whispered making him kiss my jaw

instead, working his way to my neck and closer to my ear. Then just as my favorite words of the song started to play, he told me,

"Listen, to the words for this is what it means..." So, I did as he said for me to do.

I listened and what I heard nearly destroyed me in the most beautiful way...

You've got all of me
I belong to you
Yeah, you're my everything.

Then he pulled me to him and just as the song erupted into its meaningful words, he kissed my lips, softly, oh so softly before he whispered exactly what *my Khuba* meant. And the very moment I heard it spoken, I took hold of his face and pulled his lips to mine, kissing him and feeling that last word swallowed by my need,

"My Love,"

After this we kissed the rest of the song away, and this time it was one that didn't speak of our desire, our heat or our raw, sexual connection, but spoke only of one thing,

A declaration of love.

CHAPTER TWENTY-SEVEN

A BLOODY DATE TO REMEMBER

After this, along with many firsts Lucius had given me, I had to say that this was my most favorite. With our first kiss and making love barely missing top spot, because this was what I had been waiting for. Lucius already had my heart and he knew it. Hell, he had known it was his years ago. But as for his, well I had been left to heartbreakingly believe it belonged to another. But now, well it was like the song had said,

Now I knew.

After this moment I ended up minutes later wrapped in his arms with my back to his chest, looking out over the city as sweet music played softly in the background, just listening to him talk. He told me about his favorite places in the city, the Neue Rathaus, being one of them. It was the new town hall and a place he seemed to gravitate towards whenever he wanted to be alone, one of the highest points of the city.

He told me it was something about being surrounded by life and yet being completely untouched by it. Beyond its reach, beyond the reach of the world, he said. And it was in these moments that I realised there was a lot of hidden depth to Lucius that I didn't think anyone knew. And just knowing that I was the one who had the chance to reach for it, the one to discover it all one day, well it made my heart soar as if I was the one with wings at my back. Because I was the one all these years who had tried to reach it and finally, being here now in his arms,

I knew I was finally at my destination.

"And Königssee, is that where…?"

"My hidden winter castle is," he replied in a teasing tone and I shivered, something he took for the cool night air, especially from up here where we were exposed from all sides.

"Here," he said after shrugging off his suit jacket and placing it around my shoulders. I couldn't help but snuggle closer, letting both its scent and warmth seep into me as if it had the power to penetrate much deeper than just my chilled skin.

"We will leave shortly."

"Why?" I asked, after he told me this was where we were headed.

"Don't you want to see it?" he asked instead of giving me his reasons and I had to say that I was torn. From all accounts it was an intimidating place that wasn't easy to get to let alone escape from. I knew there I would be completely at his mercy and the thought both excited me and scared me at the same time.

"I do," I said making him chuckle behind me before whispering down in my ear,

"I call bullshit, sweetheart." I didn't even try denying it this time but just released a sigh, making him tell me why,

"We go because the threat is still in this city and as soon as they discover they don't have the real box, then I don't know what they will try next. Königssee is a fortress that no one is permitted to enter without first being loyal to me...*or leave without the same permission,"* he added on a knowing purr of words making me release a shuddered breath before saying,

"Ah, so that's why."

"I confess it is one of the reasons, yes," he admitted shamelessly.

"I had thought my title as prisoner long gone after last night," I asked him, this time turning around to face him.

"You are mine," he stated again and I frowned telling him,

"That isn't an answer."

"Yes, it is. It is more than enough, because until I am satisfied that you stay by my side of your own free will, then I am not beyond the means to force it upon you, and if that makes me a controlling bastard, than I accept that title gladly," was his stern reply as he gripped me a little tighter as if to prove his point.

"Oh good, 'cause I was thinking of getting a T shirt made." I said sarcastically.

"Amelia...ask yourself about your choices so far, each one didn't end the way you intended and whether each was born from good intentions or not, the outcome was the same. Meaning I long ago declared your rash actions not acceptable for me to allow to continue. It is simply not safe for you to be allowed to make those decisions anymore and I will not permit it." I frowned up at him, crossing my arms over my chest as I told him,

"Permit it? Lucius, I think we need to get you a dictionary because that isn't a relationship, that's a dictatorship." At this he closed his eyes as if asking the Gods for strength again but then he opened his eyes and said,

"Amelia, I think it is time you knew the truth about this life of yours, the one you think you..." he paused suddenly and looked above me to the sky,

"The one I think I what…Lucius?" I said but he was fixated on something in the sky and the second he growled, I knew it was nothing good. Especially when the next thing from his mouth was a vicious sounding,

"Fuck!" Then he grabbed my hand and pulled me quickly towards the steps down into the private room inside his VIP.

"Lucius, what is it?!" I shouted and then I heard it…*the distinct sound of the rotating blades of a helicopter.*

"GET DOWN!" he shouted the second the sound of gun fire started to explode all around us. Then he lunged for me, taking what I knew were some hits to his back, just like last time he had to protect me against gunfire.

"AHHH!" I screamed and covered my ears as he continued to move us with speed down the metal staircase until we reached the bottom but just at the moment we made it through the door, someone must have thrown a grenade or something. I was abruptly thrown forward to the floor, his sudden weight landing on me winding me enough that I had to try to drag in large gulps of air even though it burned, making me clutch at my stomach.

'Amelia!' Lucius looked as if he was shouting my name, but I couldn't hear anything but ringing in my ears. He grabbed onto the tops of my arms and shook me, his lips moving but I couldn't hear, which is when I first shook my head and said,

"I can't hear you!" or at least I felt my lips move because I couldn't hear myself. So, he pointed to the door at the end and mouthed only one word, and let's just say, it was one I wouldn't ever misunderstand,

'RUN!' I nodded and did as he said, but then just as I thought I was within reach of it, some sort of gas bomb went off in a flash of light, blinding me and filling the room full of smoke. I looked behind me and it was as if life had suddenly slowed down for everyone but Lucius. Because just through the

fog I could see his large form seeping into the cloud, disappearing from sight as if he were a viper lying in wait.

Then I watched as black clad figures descended down the stairs, each one wearing helmets and every inch of them packed with weaponry. And somewhere in the shadows was Lucius, in nothing but a suit, and left alone to fight these guys. That's when I knew that I needed to get help, his people, they needed to help him. So, I did as I was told and ran, now that I could see the door and just as I opened it hearing the first of the sounds of a dead man's screams behind me as Lucius claimed his first victim.

I burst into the VIP seeing for myself that we weren't the only ones who had problems as the entire room was now like one giant brawl. Only unlike Lucius, in here it seemed to be a mixture of the mercenaries and rogue vampires. There were also those running for their life, and the backdrop to this scene was the sound of all the mortals down below in the club trying to escape with their lives.

They were screaming, and the thundering of everyone trying to move as one, spoke only of everyone's panic. But then with hundreds of people all trying to pile out of one exit at the front, and a small door at the side, I knew it wasn't enough as I could already see people getting hurt. One guy fell over one of the lower balconies and a girl got knocked down before being trampled on.

"Fuck!" I cursed. I needed to help them. So, I looked around trying to find a way to do just that. That was when I saw Hakan lashing out his deadly wire as though it was an extra limb, or somehow alive being a part of him. It snaked out, slicing through anyone in its way, reminding me of a scorpion's tail spiked for slicing through body parts. And boy was it effective as at least about ten people went down in one go.

I then looked to Ruto, who was an incredible sight to

behold. A massive pair of glistening metal wings that looked as deadly as they did beautiful. Blades were being shot from behind his frame, as deadly feathers rained across the club, along with the ones from his capable hands.

Okay, so he also looked busy as he was aiming his fire at a group of rogues that were playing a deadly dodgeball. Even Liessa was there, now totally naked and completely covered in a slick black ink, her hair down and snaking wildly as tentacles slapped around, as if they were looking for water. She shot out her poison, laughing hysterically as it burned its victims, Vampires and soldiers going down in equal numbers. Then I heard the roaring of a beast and knew it would have been Caspian, also getting in on the action.

But it was when I saw Clay that I knew he was my best chance, as for one, he was closer and two, he had just finished twisting the head off one mortal…*eww.*

"CLAY!" I screamed his name and in that same moment I felt myself being grabbed from behind. A quick look down at the man's boots told me two things, mortal and military. So, my mind clicked into defense mode, blocking everything else out. I did a mental check list in my mind, assessing the situation in seconds. Feet were a no go, his boots were steel toe capped, and he would have a tactical vest on. I had to go for the known soft spots here, meaning I only had a few options left. Neck, sides, possibly kidneys, and definitely testicles… oh, why the Hell not. Suddenly I threw all my weight back, taking him off guard the second I started gaining momentum and running him back into the wall hard enough for him to let me go, then I quickly spun, dropping to a knee and as I went I grabbed his balls, yanking down as hard as I could before twisting the fuckers!

A sickening feeling I swear, as I felt something give that shouldn't have, but either way it worked as the man screamed in pure agony and went down like a sack of wet panties. Then, as he was going down landing on his knees hard, I was spinning out of his reach, gaining my feet just as quickly. Then before he could raise his gun and shoot me, I kicked out straight on, connected hard enough with his face that his nose exploded and his head snapped back, so he landed unconscious backwards.

"Holy shit, human." I heard Clay's shocked voice next to me and looked to see him actually cupping his balls with one hand before looking down at me with a wince on his face. So, I patted his massive bicep and said,

"Don't worry, your balls are safe...*for now.*" Then I winked before I plucked his knife from his vest and threw it up in the air to catch it the right way for what was to come next. Then just as I saw my target getting closer, a rogue baring his fangs at Clay's back, I threw the blade. It zipped passed Clay's head an inch away from taking his ear with it and he turned his head just in time to see where it had been intended. The handle stuck out of the eye of the rogue before he went falling backwards. Oh, it wouldn't kill him, but it was enough to put him down. Clay looked back to me, the utter shock plain to see before he asked,

"You're not just a human," he said and I smirked at him and replied,

"No, I'm also a Draven." Then I nodded down at the writhing Vamp and said,

"Do you wanna do something with that?" He followed my gaze and quickly stamped on his head with enough strength and power his head literally exploded. Yep, *now that was enough to kill him.*

I walked back over to the balcony and looked down as the chaos ensued.

"We need to help those people!" I shouted through the madness and he frowned down at me before he said,

"I need to get you out of here before Luc..."

"I am not fucking leaving until we do something, now either

you help me save them or I will do something stupid trying…
it's your choice!" I told him, folding my arms.

"They are not my people," he snarled down at me and I put
my hands on my hips, going toe to toe with the massive guy and
told him,

"No, but they are mine! Now what is it to be?" He looked to
the two I had taken down and realised that I wasn't lying, as I
wasn't exactly the type to shy away from a fight.

"Fine! What do you have in mind?"

"We need to create more exits, is there anything that can be
done about the windows on the ground level, they look big
enough for people to reach and climb out of, at least that may
thin out the herd," I told him and he nodded as he knew exactly
what he would do.

"Wait, what if they see?" I asked placing a hand on his arm.

"They will think it's an explosion," he told me with a grin
and my eyes widened, wondering what on Earth this guy was
going to do or what type of demon he was.

"Shit, okay, just try not to get glass in this side of the
building or they could get hurt."

"Who said anything about glass?" Clay remarked, with his
eyes already started to change like a fucking storm was
coming. A darkness overtook them before a bright glowing
dot of blood could be seen. Then he threw his arms back
behind him and roared like a wild beast of Hell. I felt the
rumbling and then he threw his arms towards the only wall
that people weren't stood near, being that it was on the
opposite end to the exit everyone was trying desperately to get
out of.

The second the energy hit the stone wall it exploded
outwards and it was like he said, it was as if a bomb had gone
off. Then a wind tunnelled through it, as if clearing the path,
one no one saw because the second they heard the boom,

everyone dropped to cover their heads. Which was when I screamed as loud as I could,

"THE COPS ARE HERE, THEY MADE AN EXIT, RUN, RUN, RUN!" but it wasn't enough, and besides, it was screamed in English, not having the time for my rusty German right now, so I turned to him and said,

"We only need a few and the rest will follow!" I said knowing he would understand what I was asking him to do. He snarled down at me but then turned that menacing demonic sigh to the hundreds below. Then he started whispering in an ancient sounding language, gaining access to enough minds to get them to start running through the large exit he'd made. Erm, wonder what a certain someone was going to think when knowing I had pretty much forced one of his men to blowing up a wall in his club. And speaking of Lucius, once I saw that people had started moving out of both exits now, it quickly created more room for others behind, I knew it was time to get back to my original mission.

"Lucius is in there, he needs help!" I shouted grabbing his meaty arm and pulling him, but he scoffed and said,

"I fucking doubt that," but he came with me anyway and the second he opened the door and barged his way in, I glanced around his shoulder and quickly understood for myself what he meant by that.

"Oh shit."

Lucius most definitely didn't need help. No, in fact all Lucius needed now was a shit load of body bags and a bath. The entire room had been turned in a bloodbath, and with one man at it centre. Lucius was standing with his back to us in the middle of the room, the fog of the grenades still lingering around him, making him look like some demonic God surrounded by his kill. The sight of his waistcoat tight to his large frame, one that tapered down to his slim waist and was now bloody, was getting tighter whenever he inhaled with his heavy breathing.

Because there was blood everywhere. On the walls one side, on the mirrored glass of the other, pieces of bodies, all still clad in black, but now torn in sections where their limbs had been ripped off with only jagged bloody flesh and bone seen at the ends.

But as Lucius sniffed the air, he turned on a growl, blood coating the majority of him, including the entire lower part of his face where he looked to have gorged himself. His eyes were like two hot coals in Hell, burning brighter the second they saw what I saw. Black veins branched out around his face, eyes and up his neck, like an infection had taken hold. He was beyond terrifying, but he was also my man and I was far from naïve when it came to Lucius' kind or that of my father's Demons.

They were Demons, for fuck sake. Of course, there would be blood.

But Lucius didn't know this and once again, he underestimated his Chosen One. I knew this when he snarled at us, and his demon issued the threat,

"Get her the fuck out of here!" but I purposely stepped out of reach of Clay, going further into the room, stepping around body parts and picking up my dress like a damn lady in waiting, holding down the urge to retch. Then I folded my arms across my chest, stood my ground and said,

"Oh please, like this shit scares me! I am not going anywhere without you, so let's go!" I snapped making him actually shake his head in confusion, or should I say the more demonic part of him did. Then when he didn't move or say anything more, I thought to add for good measure,

"Well, they're all dead, aren't they?" He actually looked around him and then down at the severed arm in his hand as if he'd only just now realised this was what he held.

"I think so," he said in a tone that spoke of his astonishment and it wasn't at what he had done, it had been at what I had witnessed and didn't seem to care.

"Yeah, well even if they aren't, then they won't be playing in a band any time soon, so that's good enough for me. Now come on, we need to get out of here!" I said making Clay suddenly throw his head back and howl with laughter. Lucius then snapped out of his bloodlust, dropped what had looked like his favorite human bat, and was at my side in a seconds.

Then he looked as if he wanted to reach out for me, coming close to tipping my chin up but the sight of his blood soaked hand stopped him.

"Are you okay?" he asked me, scanning the length of me and Clay scoffed,

"Oh yeah, she's fine but the poor bastard who had his testicles ripped out for touching her won't be." Lucius shot him a look and said,

"Good, I am glad you made him suffer." I growled at him, actually stomped my foot and said,

"Yeah, *I did make him suffer.*" Lucius snapped his head back to me and yep that same look of shock I received that day at the museum was back.

"You?"

"Yeah, you know, your new kick ass girlfriend, now you wanna start giving her some credit, so you can get laid again sometime this century!" Again, Clay burst out laughing, the deep rumbling sound almost infectious.

"Fuck boss, but I like her." Lucius snarled at that, but didn't take it seriously and neither did Clay.

"Let's go!" Lucius said, this time as punishment, wiping a bloody hand down Clay's chest to clean it of blood before taking my hand in his, and Clay grumbled,

"I fucking liked this jacket man." Which both of us ignored, or at least Lucius did, I, on the other hand, looked over my shoulder at him and winked. But Lucius caught me doing it and snarled at me,

"On the fucking edge here, princess, so try to behave, yeah."

"And how would you like me to do that, my handsome Vampy?" I teased making him spin me, pull me to him, coating my once pretty dress in blood, then look down at me with fire burning so close to the surface, part of me wanted to push and then see if I could tame the beast, as I had done with Lucius.

"By not winking at another male unless you want to catch the encore of what just happened in there," he warned making me wink at him this time after I said,

"Gotchya, boss man." He then shook his head as if he didn't in that moment have one fucking clue what to do with me. Other than maybe throw me over his shoulder and spank me.

"Tell me they are all dead!" Lucius snapped out after walking further into the VIP and taking in the carnage. Ruto appeared out of nowhere and nodded gracefully, his wings now folded back tucked against his back. Blood splatters dotted his pale face crimson.

"Yes Sire. The Rogues have been dispatched, leaving two to interrogate. We have cars waiting to take us directly to the helicopter and the chopper is fueled and waiting." It was strange because like this he was all business and it was a total contrast to how he usually was...a sulky teenager. It was times like this that it was obvious why he was deemed Lucius' second in command.

"Good, then get our people out and lock it the fuck down!" Lucius demanded, before turning back to Clay and issuing more orders. Then it was Liessa's turn, who like Ruto seemed to appear out of nowhere.

"Take Amelia back to her apartment, five minutes," he ordered before turning to me and saying,

"Get dressed and grab just what you need, I want you back here by my side in five minutes, Amelia and not one minute after, don't test me on this," he growled and I smiled up at him, saying,

"Five minutes, I promise." His gaze gentled somewhat, and he nodded once before gesturing to Liessa to take me. So, I quickly ran for the doors that led out into the lobby, when Lucius' voice stopped me and what he said shocked me more than the evidence of his bloody rage moments before,

"Don't forget your glasses, or your eyes will get sore again." And at this I wasn't the only one whose jaw went slack, as whoever was left standing was now doing the same in utter shock.

"Get fucking going! And does someone want to explain to me why there is now a great fucking big hole in the side of my fucking club!" Lucius roared in anger making everyone stop gawking and now find the floor with their eyes. And for me, well his first order was most definitely the best course of action right now, so I ran out the doors with Liessa in tow. Once inside my apartment, I told her to wait whilst I just ran into the bathroom to grab a couple of things.

I also wanted to ask her if she needed to borrow any clothes of mine because right now, she was just wearing what I assumed was her husband's Motley Crew T-shirt and leather biker jacket. But then I would ask once I had grabbed the stuff I needed, after all I wasn't sure it was a good idea having all those little secreting suckers on show.

I realised I might be quicker than what Lucius had said, thinking he could probably do with the small kindness right now. Especially considering my bag was kind of already still packed from when I had been determined to leave a few days ago.

So, I quickly grabbed that, then ran back into the bathroom, unzipped it and started swiping an arm across the top of the vanity so the contents all fell in. Then I grabbed my glasses and stuffed those in the inside pocket along with spare contact lenses, solution and the container I kept them in.

I was still processing his concern, reminding me to pick up my glasses. Amazed that even in the middle of the destruction of half his club, he still had me and my care in his mind. It was mind boggling to me and from the looks of things, his people too.

In fact, I was still grinning about it when I finally looked up, saw my grin and then quickly watched it die the second I saw another reflection looking back at me in the mirror,

As I was no longer alone and once more,

I had a gun to my head.

CHAPTER TWENTY-EIGHT

FOOTLOOSE AND EXCITED

"Ah shit!" I said the second I saw the mercenary with the gun, thinking at the very least it wasn't his ex, Bitch Face. Gods be damned, but when were people going to start taking me seriously here and stop underestimating me!

"If you scream, bitch, I swear the last thing I do will be pulling this fucking trigger!" The guy said with nothing but a handgun in his hand. Well, joy for small mercies I thought wryly.

"Now turn around and do it slowly." I took a deep breath, looked down and slowly wrapped my hand around the closest thing I could get. I then read the label and rolled my eyes thinking what was I saying about small mercies. Then I did what was needed and started to cry,

"No, no, please…oh Gods, please don't hurt me…I will do anything you want, please."

"Of course, you will!" He sniggered and the second he reached for me to force me into action because I was a useless woman shaking uncontrollably and crying, I made my move. I suddenly whipped my body around, hitting out at his hand as I went, and knocking the gun to the side, whilst bringing my other hand up and spraying him in the face with shaving foam.

The white foam covered the bastard's face, making him shout out in both shock and pain as I bet that shit stung. Then, before he had time to recover or see what was coming, I grabbed his wrist, and turned, ducking under his arm so I was now at his back taking his arm with me and forcing the limb where it didn't want to go. Then with a sickening twist I broke it with an echoing crack, making him scream out in pain and drop the gun. With my hold on him still in place I grabbed the back of his head and smacked it down into the counter, making the foam splat outwards around him. Then, just as another asshole came bursting through the door, he watched utterly dumbfounded as I let his buddy slip unconscious to the floor, covered in blood and foam.

"He said he needed a shave," I said in true aunty Pip badass fashion, before I dropped to the floor and picked up the gun from the floor and started shooting because really, how hard could it be? Guns weren't my bag, as for a supernatural they took the art and skill out of the fight. But then again, when up against an immortal being, they had to use what they had. And me, well I was using what I had because I was out of options here and I didn't think my little leg razor still with my short hairs clinging to it was going to cut it...like, literally.

But as the guy, who thankfully hadn't been armed and ready until that point, ducked from the bullets flying (because my aim was shockingly shit) he then fumbled for his gun. So, I gave up on the shooting part of the weapon and I threw it at the guy's head instead, this time getting my aim spot on. Oh, won't daddy be proud I thought before running head on at the guy whilst he was still clutching his head in his hands, blood pouring from the gash I'd caused. Which meant he didn't see me coming until it was too late. I rammed into him, taking him off his feet as we crashed into my bedroom.

We both landed on the floor causing me to jar my elbow, but I ignored the pain, using it instead to fuel my anger, putting it to good use. Then, just as I was reaching for a lamp to use as a weapon, he grabbed my ankle and yanked me back down. I fell but not before I grabbed the cord, pulling it hard enough that it fell into my hand. Then as I twisted my body to face him, I swung it round just in time as he brought a knife up, intent on stabbing me. Thankfully I was quicker, and the lamp ended up smashing against his face. But I had wished it had been a bit sturdier and made of steel but no such luck. So, with it only being ceramic, it pretty much exploded on impact without doing the damage I intended.

But what it did do was daze him enough for me to take his weapon. So, I grabbed his wrist, yanked his arm straight and rolled onto my belly, trapping it beneath me and in between my legs. Not where I really intended it to be, but at least I was now in control of his hand. And to prove this, I pulled it upwards making him scream in pain. Because bones weren't bendy and his was most definitely not supposed to move that way.

"Didn't your mother ever teach you it isn't nice to stab girls," I said before I then rammed a knee against his bent arm and yanked it up breaking yet another limb before kicking back into the guy's face, making him howl. The knife flew out of his hand just out of reach, which was unfortunate as the guy wasn't done fighting yet.

Because during me breaking his bones, he was using his less useless hand to grab his gun, and just as he raised it up to shoot me, my head jerked to the side, only just missing the bullet. So, I kicked out again, rolled once more to my back, and I grabbed the only thing I could.

I yanked the lamp cord out of the wall, just as he was recovering enough from two kicks to the face. But I was quicker, as before he could shoot again I had it wrapped twice around his neck and then I leant all my body weight back, placed my foot at his shoulder and used that to push against, as my back arched with the cord cutting into my skin where it was was wrapped around my fists.

But I ignored the pain, knowing that a bullet was going to hurt a lot more. I soon heard the gurgling strangled noises coming from him but I didn't look. No, instead I had my whole body straining with my shoulders to the floor, my spine and backside off it as I choked the life out of him.

"Come on you fucker, just die already!" I complained feeling the strain in my shoulder blades knowing that was going to hurt like a bitch in the morning. But the second I no longer felt any resistance, I finally looked down, my chin to my chest seeing that yep...he looked pretty dead to me. I breathed a sigh of relief thinking where the Hell was the cavalry by now, there was no way I had taken out two guys in under five minutes. Which then made me panic and I scrambled to my feet snatching the knife as I went, after muttering one name,

"Liessa!" I then ran from the bedroom, and just as I made it through the door, I swear it was like a bomb had just gone off as the whole building shook. I even found myself quickly gripping on to the wall, half expecting the building to start crumbling at the seams. But after a few loud crashing sounds echoing beyond the door, the shaking at my feet finished. It felt as if there had been a damn earthquake!

I then pushed away from the wall and felt my long skirt catch on something as it tore a long strip off it from the skirt. Well, that would at least make it easier to fight in, I thought as I skidded into the living space. But I skidded to a stop the second I found Liessa unconscious on the floor.

"Oh shit!" I muttered the second I made it to her, making sure not to touch the ink puddle she lay in, noting now about ten tranquilizer darts sticking out of her in different places. Her tentacles flapping around her head wildly as if trying to wake up their host.

"What the fuck!?" The sound of disbelief made me jerk my head towards the door and I spun away from Liessa. It was in that moment that I was seriously at that point of saying aloud, 'Aww come on, give me a freakin break'. However, they got in there first with,

"There she is! Get her!" One of the two guys who had just walked into the apartment, shouted as though I had been fucking hiding and not in plain sight just stood here...idiot!

Obviously, they had been expecting the two they sent in here to deal with us and have us already to go, 'cause I gathered this was a plain old kidnapping they had planned. Or that guy in the bathroom would have just shot me the first chance he got.

But at the least these guys didn't have their guns ready. But they also hadn't yet seen the damage to the other two that I had done. So, they each got out a knife and grinned, telling me,

"Now be a good girl and you won't get hurt." Then they both started to split up, coming at me from both sides. One was bigger than the other but that didn't automatically mean he would be harder to put down. Both looked like meatheads with shaved heads, thick necks and one was half a foot shorter than the other.

"Yeah, so put down the knife, bitch," Shorty said, so I made a show of looking down at the knife in my hand and then said,

"Oh, you mean this one...oh okay then." Then I threw it at him, wondering if Ruto would have been impressed when seeing it land directly in his heart, because this time I was aiming to kill. I had made that mistake once before back at the museum. So yeah, not doing that again.

"What the fuck! You just killed Kenny!" the bigger guy said shouting furiously,

"Kenny, seriously... you gotta be shitting me!" I said with a laugh because what were the fucking odds. My aunty Pip would be laughing her ass off right now. But this was when this guy went bat shit crazy at me, doing my trick by running right at me like some knife wielding maniac from a slasher movie. So, just as he was in range, I sidestepped and blocked his knife with my forearm. Then I brought my knee up and got him in the gut, but it wasn't as affective with his bulletproof vest on.

But then he grabbed my waist and picked me up, before throwing me against the wall. Then suddenly music filled the room as I'd banged into the stereo, cracking the side of my head on it. I staggered a little but shook the feeling from my head, now asking myself if I was hearing things, because seriously, the Pointer Sisters singing 'I'm so excited' coming over the speakers wasn't exactly what I would have called fighting music.

"Well, I hope you're a fan," I said making him sneer at me before swiping out with his blade and then making a show of passing it between his hands, as if this would put the fear of God in me or something.

"Seriously, just pick a fucking hand would you!" Then I braced myself for his attack, sidestepping him again and blocking each time he tried to slice me with the knife. I managed to get a good kick to the back of his knee, but the heavy bastard wouldn't go down like I intended, nor did he when I hammered down my elbow on his back when his legs buckled slightly. In fact, I only just managed to dodge his blade when he swiped out behind him, catching my blood stained skirt minus skin.

It was time to get rid of that knife. But he managed to catch me with a kick to the gut and I fell backwards into the piano of all things and I swear but what were the bloody odds of it being at the same time as the piano solo on the song!

"Fuck it!" I snarled and quickly picked up the stool by its legs, I swung out at him the second he got close enough. This knocked him into the wall, but still he kept hold of that bloody knife. So, I screamed in anger, spun the stool in my hands, so I now gripped the seat part and with him still at the wall, I ran at him with the legs pointing at his chest.

"AH!" he roared in pain and I grunted as the impact hit me in the chest, but the thin leg managed to get him good in the shoulder, pinning him there with the end of one leg now sticking in his flesh. He pushed back grimacing in pain as he did, making the wood travel another inch in his shoulder, bringing him closer to me. But I took the seat with me the second he thrust his blade closer. So, in turn, I twisted the seat, trapping his hand and forcing the blade from his hand, making it go flying from his grasp. It then landed against the wall with a thud and down the side of the sofa with a clatter. Then as he watched it go off to the side with the piano stool, I took this opportunity to uppercut him, knocking him back a few steps. The hit made his teeth slice into his top lip making him touch a hand there before looking down at it.

"Yep, it's called blood, asshole, get used to seeing it on yourself!" I taunted making him spit to the side before telling me,

"Bitch, I am going to fucking kill you!" I scoffed and snarled back,

"Yeah 'cause you're doing a bang up job so far, dickhead!" Then the song finished and the second Footloose by Kenny Loggins came on the radio, I couldn't help but say,

"Well, what are the fucking odds of that...I guess Kenny's not dead after all" He bellowed at me in anger and swung a punch, one I managed to block but Gods, this fucker was strong. Meaning that just as I blocked one, there was another and another, and then there was the one he managed to get me with. My head cracked to the side and I went flying on top of the coffee table that smashed with my weight before I ended up rolling off with a groan next to the sofa. Then I felt my head being yanked up with a fist to my hair just before he slammed it down on the floor, making me see stars… or should I say blurry spots because unfortunately this wasn't a damn cartoon and there wasn't an Acme anvil about to fall on this asshole and save my ass.

"Ah, but now you're nice and compliant, I wonder if we don't have time for a bit of fun, whilst your blood sucking boyfriend deals with the shit storm we had planned for him!" Then I felt him lifting my skirt and knew that my night was about to get a whole lot worse. But I also knew that if I panicked I wouldn't get anywhere. So, I needed to think, and to do that I needed him to think I was almost unconscious.

The element of surprise could be a person's greatest weapon, I remember being told enough times. Thanks Takeshi.

So, as the big skinhead was fumbling with what I assumed was getting his tiny little cock out, I reached out a hand, seeing something shiny…*the knife!*

It was under the sofa where it had fallen but damn it, I couldn't reach it! I just needed to stretch a little whilst he was busy, but then as I started doing this, my hand came across something else and only one thought came to mind…*Thank you, Lucius.*

So, the second I felt him coming back over me, no longer holding the back of my hair and thinking I was out for the count, he came to my ear and his stale breath wafted down over my cheek.

"I am going to fuck you 'til you bleed!" he snarled and nothing in the world could have stopped me from saying,

"Not with that tiny prick you're not!" Then with my weapon in hand, I reached across my neck and I hit up over my shoulder towards his head until the pencil I had in my hand embedded in his face! The very same pencil Lucius had plucked out of my hair only a few days earlier.

"AHHH!" he shrieked in pain, and when I felt the weight of him disappear it was only when I turned around, did I see why.

"Now that's what I call a pencil dick," I commented, now getting to my feet and wiping my bleeding nose with the back of my arm.

"AAAHHH MY EYE!" he screamed again with the pencil still embedded in the socket and his arms flapping around it as if he didn't know what to do. So, seeing that he was busy doing whatever that was, I walked right up to him and said,

"Here, let me help you with that." Then I grabbed the pencil without him even seeing me and yanked it out. This made blood spurt from the hole and he staggered back, now with a roar of agony. Then just as Bonnie Tyler's 'Holding Out for a Hero' came over the speakers, I kicked out his knees, knowing this time he was going down and he did...*hard*. Then I grabbed his hair like he had done to me, and with the bloody pencil still in my hand, I said,

"This is for ruining Flashback Friday!" Then I stabbed him in the jugular, knowing he wasn't coming back from that one. I then closed my eyes waiting for the gurgling sound of death to finish and with an exhausted sigh, I pulled the pencil free as blood still poured from his neck, being pumped out all across the floor. Then I let go of his hair and he face planted forward with a loud resounding thud. But it unfortunately wasn't loud enough to drown out the sound of clapping.

I looked up just in time to see the bitch it came from and I swear I nearly looked up at the Heavens and asked them why.

"Well, for a human, you're pretty resilient I will give you

that," Layla said and I looked down at the dripping bloody pencil still in my hand and then back up at the gun she had pointed at me. And somehow, I didn't fancy my chances. So instead, I dropped my pencil and said in a weakened voice,

"You should see what I can do with a sharpener." She laughed and said,

"Oh, I can't wait to see what my Master does to that smart mouth of yours, but until then..."

"AHHH!" I screamed the second pain hit me and seconds later I was falling backwards, landing hard enough to crack my head.

Then just as blackness overtook me,

Bitchface finally got her chance for revenge, as she stepped over my fallen body and with the end of her gun pointing down at my chest, this time without Lucius to stop her...

She shot me.

CHAPTER TWENTY-NINE

LUCIUS

SMOKE AND MIRRORS

The second I looked down at the floor below I saw that, apart from the few still limping towards the exit after picking themselves off the floor, obviously being the unfortunates who got trampled on, the club was mostly empty.

"I take it this is your handy work?" I said referring to the great big hole now in the side of my fucking club!

"Your human can be quite convincing," Clay replied making me scoff, because didn't I fucking know it!

"She can also handle herself, fuck but a word of warning Luc, don't piss her off too much," he said making me chuckle this time when I looked to the guy who, let's just say, I doubted would be fathering children any time soon. Yes, eye watering indeed.

"And this one?" I nodded to the rogue who used to have

something that resembled a head but the blade in his chest, now that wasn't Clay's style.

"Saved me from getting bitten, or at least she thinks she did," he replied with a scoff. But despite his words, it was clear to hear in his tone that he was certainly impressed. I had to admit, I was more than impressed, I was fucking astounded. She would have made a formidable vampire, that's for damn sure. In fact, it was hard to put the two sides of her personality together, being that they were a total contrast. Two polar opposites that couldn't get further apart.

I thought about her this morning, being unknowingly adorable whilst eating that monstrosity she called food, because who the fuck eats bacon and chocolate donuts together?! The way that even with her hands full, as her glasses slid further and further down her nose from reading the paper, she tried to push them up again using the back of her thumb. Gods, she was cute and impressive all at the same time. I found myself utterly fascinated just watching her and questioned if I would ever get bored of doing so, as I very much doubted it.

She was shy and yet she was fiery and confident. Fucking contrast wasn't even a word strong enough to describe her. The way she argued with me, challenged me on every fucking thing, but then was also submissive one moment and then playful the next, teasing me where others wouldn't have dared. She was witty, with her one liners and smart mouth...and Gods, what a fucking mouth! Hell's blood, but what that mouth had the power to do!

Fucking raw talent that was for damn sure, because for her first time, she had been incredible. But then that was Amelia, shocking me at every turn, like arguing with me about moving into my home. I knew that girl had been near obsessed with me since we first met, but now when she finally had me she resisted the change. It was fucking with my head and as frustrating as Hell!

So, I had forced the issue, but then she had made a point of reminding me she was human and the notion of dating her was a ridiculous one. She was mine and that was that. But then her vulnerable blue eyes had captured me and rendered me unable to just walk away without wanting to give her what she wanted.

So, I had done something I never had before. I had given her romance. And what's more shocking yet was that I had actually enjoyed it. Enjoyed experiencing the joy on her face, the surprise and appreciation in her gaze. The way when the song played it made her eyes water and glisten with unshed tears, held captive in those incredible blue depths. Those eyes alone told me so much and all I needed to know that spoke of her love for me.

Well, it quickly had me thinking of what else I could do for her. Because I wanted those expressions back and as often as possible. I wanted her to look at me that way, to see me as that person and to make her fucking proud and happy to be with me. Gods, but what was she doing to me and what's more,

Did I even fucking care?!

She was beyond perfect and I didn't just mean in the bedroom, or the shower…or anywhere else I could take that heavenly little body. But even the way she had stormed inside the room of death, surrounded by the evidence of nothing short of a monster. My beast had taken over and I had slaughtered the lot of them one by one. And the second she found me I had only felt one thing…*shame*. It was why I had ordered Clay to take her from the room, being ashamed at what she would see in me.

But then seconds later and there she was, astonishing me yet again! Because what did she see in me but me in my rawest form. A true son born of Hell and what did she do…? She didn't even fucking flinch, that's what! There had been no fear in her gaze but just acceptance and a comical expectant tone when she told me to come with her, demanding she would not leave without me. Gods, but if I hadn't been coated with the blood of my victims, I would have fucking ravished her. It was hard enough not touching her as it was.

Speaking of which, where the fuck was she?

"Heeer Masther…" Percy said handing me the wet towel I had requested, so I could at least clean the blood off my face and hands. I scrubbed it down my face and looked up in time to see one of the rogues. He had been one purposely left alive for questioning and now he had just broken free of Ruto's hold, if only for a moment before Ruto subdued him again, dragging him past us.

My hands itched to go and just snap his neck for being a traitor and coming here trying to destroy everything that meant something to me. I had once been their Sire, making them what they were today. He deserved my idea of a painful death and he would soon enough, but only once I had my answers. Because there had been a small army of rogues fighting here tonight and it was a feat I didn't think possible. Which meant a much bigger player was now sat at the table of Kings, and I needed answers as to who?

"Thank you, Percy…could you go and…FUCK, GET DOWN!" I roared the second I caught sight of what the rogue now had strapped to his chest and had broken free so he could activate it…

A bomb.

I grabbed Percy and spun with him in my arms, protecting him from the blast as much as I could as we were both thrown forward from the impact. I had just enough time to throw up a basic shield around us, to stop too much damage to my vessel, as I didn't have the fucking time to heal from internal injuries, even if it was only five minutes to spare.

But my shield hadn't been enough to stop us both from crashing through the glass barriers and hurtling over the edge of the balcony towards the ground floor of the club. I released my wings with just enough time to spin so as not to land on Percy, thus protecting him. Thankfully, he was unhurt and managed to get up in time to see the overhanging part of the balcony split from the rest of the floor and come crashing down on us both. So, I managed to grab Percy in time and throw him to safety before the whole thing came down on me.

And my last thought...

Oh yes, people were going to die for this.

Then darkness surrounded me.

"Lucius, are you coming?" I frowned as a voice I knew started to seep inside my mind, telling me something I couldn't see. But then it didn't say what I first thought it did.

"Lucius are you going..."

"I...who..." I tried to ask the question as a blurred figure approached me, stepping from the darkness. A white figure that looked like some kind of Angel of Death without wings. Now why would I think that?

"Lucius, why aren't you going to..." I tried to move but felt an immeasurable weight holding me down as the voice continued to echo around me, now gaining strength in volume.

"Who are...*Keira?*" I uttered her name the second she finally came into view and I frowned again, asking myself why she was here but then her face contorted, twisting in pain and panic was all her features screamed, then her voice did the very same thing as she suddenly cried out,

"Lucius, why aren't you saving my daughter!" The second I

heard this something in me snapped and my eyes opened with a roar the second I felt it. My Chosen One, she was hurt!

The feeling was faint, and it angered me that I hadn't yet had more time to build the connection between us. She needed more of my blood and I hers in return. And in that moment, I vowed that this would be the first fucking thing I did, when I had her once more safely in my arms.

But first I had to get to that.

So, I concentrated all my energy onto the weight on top of me and the next time I roared in anger, the rubble I had been buried under exploded outwards. I didn't know how long I had been trapped under half of my VIP, but I just hoped it wasn't long enough for the worst to happen.

I looked up and released my wings the second I was free, my body quickly making it to the top floor and landing with a furious crack to the already dangerous floor. Then, I took in the destruction around me and stormed over to Clay who was dragging Ruto's unconscious body from a piece of the ceiling that had collapsed on him. I tensed, hating the sight of my own people affected by this attack, but I also knew that they were the strongest of their kind and would heal.

My Chosen One, however, *would not.*

"Caspian and Hakan went to save her," Clay told me, and I soon saw why he hadn't gone with them, seeing as there was a jagged piece of metal embedded in his side. I nodded and raced to the lobby, fucking near praying to the Gods, just for her to be safe. But then the second I made it to her door, I caught the scent of her blood. Gods, but it was so strong I knew then that she was hurt and badly! So, I ran towards it, hunting it, and getting lost in my rage to claim it back, for I was nearly fucking blinded by it. I even staggered slightly, gripping on to the wall for support as my beast tried to take over me in its anger, tipping my sanity for blind rage! But I needed to keep a level head, at least enough to track her.

Focus on her blood...the blood will lead us to her!

So, I did just that, knowing that she had been put in the elevator. Instead I burst into the stairwell and threw my body down the centre, landing hard and cracking the floor under my knee and foot. Then I burst out into the back parking lot to see the gates wide open and Amelia screaming for me to save her as she was pulled into a car.

The smell of her blood in the air lingered and triggered something within me I couldn't have controlled if I had tried. It took me back to seeing Layla slitting her throat. The fucking agony that tore through me at the sight. Gods, it was all I could think about, so I destroyed the gates with my mind, crashing them together and crushing them so no car could pass, feeling somewhat assured that they had nowhere to go and I would soon have my girl back.

So, I started running to the fucking car she was in, ready to tear anyone to pieces that I found there keeping her against her will. What would I find when I opened that door, I didn't know and it fucking terrified me! Would she be alright, or in need of healing? Too much fucking blood! But there was something about it that I couldn't yet place. But then the closer I got, the more it started to infiltrate my senses and by the time I got to the door, I had a dreaded feeling in my gut.

Something about her blood hadn't been right.

Blind panic once more took over to the point that I ended up ripping the door from its frame and throwing it behind me. The second I did,

I roared in rage!

I had been fucking tricked! A mortal girl was terrified in the back of the car, but it wasn't *my girl*. She looked similar to

Amelia, as she had black hair and was a similar build, but that was when I noticed how I had been tricked so easily.

"It was a nice touch I think."

"Lahash!" I snarled her name and turned, seeing her with a rifle aimed at my head as she walked from the shadows.

"Now I know your first instinct is to kill me, but I must warn you, if you do then your little bitch is dead," she said and I looked to the screaming girl who was wearing the blood stained white dress I had taken off Amelia in the cell. That was how they tricked me. And now they had her. I silenced the girl with a single thought of will, before snarling back at my enemy.

"Where is she!?" my Demon demanded with deadly intent that was clearly a dangerous enough threat for her to take seriously as at least she had the good sense to flinch. But then she shook off her show of weakness and said,

"Oh, what a shame, you just missed her." Layla then looked up and I saw the helicopter flying over the roof of my club. I was just about to release my wings and then heard a radio crackle,

"If you see him follow, kill the girl." I snarled back at her to see Layla issuing this order.

"So, this was your plan all along, it was just a distraction to get the girl!"

"Oh no Luc, this wasn't my plan, my plan included putting a bullet in the bitch's head." I couldn't help what I did next as I grabbed her neck in my hand and started crushing her windpipe slowly. Even the sight of her eyes hemorrhaging didn't stop me. But then the sound of Liessa's voice broke through my blind fury, as she was running towards me with Caspian by her side.

"Luc, don't as she is the only one who knows where they are taking her. They told me to tell you that if you kill her, then you kill your chances of getting her back!" I let these words penetrate my mind, screaming at my other self to back the fuck down. Finally, I released my prey and she dropped to the floor, her neck severely damaged to the point where she would need to heal before she had the use of her voice again. She could barely even cough. Good, but not good enough, which was why I couldn't help but pick up the gun and snap it in two. Then I kicked her in the gut, before hammering down one half of the gun on her face, knocking her unconscious. Something I doubted was part of her fucking plan!

"Someone get this fucking bitch out of my sight! And someone track that fucking chopper!" I barked out the order, knowing that now was the time to go hunting. Because despite what Liessa had said, I knew that they wouldn't kill Amelia, they wouldn't fucking dare. Not when it was the only way for them to get me to give up the box, something this time I knew I might have no choice but to do.

Because I wouldn't let them hurt her, not like they already had. And if there was one small mercy from all of this, it was that at least I had her biggest threat in my grasp. For Layla couldn't hurt her now, the plan to control me and my actions had backfired. For this time she would pay. And she would continue to pay, until I had Amelia back in my arms, where she fucking belonged.

Because they didn't know who it was they were fucking with. Nobody took what was mine. I wanted my girl back!

And I would kill anyone who got in my way...

Even a fucking God.

CHAPTER THIRTY

A BIRD WITHOUT WINGS

The moment I heard the loud whirring sound, one that almost deafened me, I knew that combined with the jarring motion, I was most likely lay on the floor of a helicopter. I also knew that my fate at that moment looked pretty bleak unless I could escape these assholes. Of course, the only way to accomplish that would have been to hold the pilot at gun point, as I don't think a pencil was going to cut it with this one.

But I also knew I couldn't act rashly now, because I needed to know how many people were in here with me and mainly, if one of those people was bitch face. I didn't remember it being a particularly large helicopter but then again, I had been running from it at the time, so what did I know. Now, if it had been Lucius, he would have known all the specs and details by now, with just a mere glance when we were on the rooftop.

But thinking about Lucius and I felt pain in more than just my head from being hit repeatedly. I just hoped he was okay, as I knew they obviously had something planned to keep him busy. And it must have been pretty bad if he hadn't been able to get to me, as I knew that would have been his first thought. But if he had managed to get free or was unharmed, then the thought kept me hopeful that he would know what to do. I imagined that he was also going out of his ever loving mind right now with worry, rage and possibly even panic. Well, I bet he was regretting that date now, I thought with a painful slice of humour, one that this time didn't do anything to ease the painful ache in my chest.

The only thing I could guarantee was that they wouldn't have been able to get that box but then if they had me, then it was no question as what would happen next. Because I was just a pawn in all of this, just a simple mortal to use and all because of Lucius' obsession for me. Well, I was sick to death of these assholes underestimating me! Because I was not just some weak little mortal to be used as a fucking bargaining chip!

And it was time to show people exactly what a Chosen One was made of. Starting with getting away from these guys. Of course, the second something landed not far from me I tried not to flinch to give away the fact that I was no longer unconscious.

"I swear that bitch, Layla, fuck me I wouldn't mind a piece of that, that is if she wasn't a blood sucker...good job we are getting good money for this, that's all I'll say!"

"Yeah, well it's even more now seeing as over half our fucking squad is dead!" Another guy said, shouting over the sound of the engine and propeller. Then after a pause the same guy continued,

"Speaking of the hot Vamp, shouldn't we have heard back from her by now?"

"I don't give a fuck, man, we get paid as soon as we deliver this bitch!" One of them said and from the sounds of it, these were going to be like the same idiots that underestimated me back in my apartment. Well, it was a good job they didn't seem to know it was me who had put down four men, killing three. Because it meant that I wasn't bound in any way. Which meant they were either stupid, shit at their jobs or something else entirely. Maybe they thought that whatever I had been shot with shouldn't have burned out of my system yet, making me wonder if Lucius' blood had anything to do with that?

I decided to crack open an eye just slightly and I swear when I found out what the sound had been, I nearly laughed. A bloody gun had slipped to the floor and was literally now lying next to me and barely a stretch away.

"Did the other birds get back to the compound?"

"Yeah, well it's not like they were fucking needed, was it? Not with every single member from the four teams before us not fucking surviving!" One complained and so far, all I had heard were the two voices making me wonder if that was all I had left to contend with? Well, they had just said about their team mates not surviving as there must have been a few choppers in the air when they attacked us.

Okay, so I could deal with Tweedle Dee and Tweedle Dum, it was just the pilot I needed to be careful with. Because if shit went wrong then there was only one way this would end and that was down before the boom. And well, I'd only had sex twice so far and really, even though I wouldn't technically be dying a virgin, it would be even crueler now I knew what it felt like!

I heard something that sounded like a radio before a voice came over it,

"Delta two, come in, over."

"Delta two receiving, over," the guy said in reply and I held my breath to listen.

"Do you have the package, only people are getting testy here, need an ETA. Over."

"We are just coming up to the Isar River now, the bird will land at twenty one fifteen. Repeat two, one, one, five. Over." After this the radio call ended and I quickly realised that the raid on Transfusion must have been over a lot quicker than it felt, along with my kidnapping. But then again, I bet it felt longer for the guys I was beating up at the time. All of them had been trained in the forces at some point, that much was clear. But then they all had something else in common, as none of them believed they would get beaten by little me or that I would have posed any kind of threat. Each one had been taken by surprise, all but the last guy who knew that I had been capable to take them on after witnessing my skills with a knife.

That was why he had been the hardest to put down.

Well, daddy would most certainly be proud, now if I could just get out of this helicopter without crashing the thing, then that would be ideal and go a long step towards that proud daddy/daughter moment.

Okay, so it was time to make my move because without knowing what time it was now, then I didn't know how long until we arrived. So, it was basically now or never.

Now!

I quickly grabbed for the gun, rolled away from the voices and was up on my knees in seconds with the gun pointed at the two men now looking at me as if I had five heads and was asking them to choose the one they liked best.

"Nobody fucking move!" I shouted, thinking this was as good an order as any and it usually worked in the movies. But then the situation started to sink in as the men didn't look at me with any real worry and I soon discovered why.

"Bitch that is a tranq gun, so shooting us wouldn't get you shit!"

"Yeah, now be a good little girl and put down the gun before you get hurt by my fist as I knock the shit out of you!" said the other guy so I did the only thing left. I took a chance and pointed it at the pilot who looked over his shoulder quickly looking panicked and for good reason seeing as the first guy to speak said,

"You dumb bitch! He's the only one who can fly this thing, so if you shoot him, what you gonna do then, sprout wings and fly?"

"I'm dead anyway, so at least this way I have a chance, now land this thing or I fucking shoot him and we are all dead!" I said hoping they didn't call my bluff. They both looked at each other and I knew the moment something silently passed between them that they were going to make their move.

"Fine, then fucking shoot him!" one said and the second I fell for looking at him, the other lunged for me. He then grabbed the gun and as we fought for it, it accidently went off, shooting a dart into the pilot anyway.

"Fuck!" the other guy said rushing forward towards the pilot who was already being affected thanks to the dart now sticking out of his neck. Meanwhile, I was still being wrestled by the other one and the second I felt my head crack on the door, and a forearm pressed to my neck I held my breath. The gun was then wrenched out of my hands and his face was spitting mad in my face,

"You dumb fucking bitch!"

"What the fuck do we do now?" The other guy asked totally panicking and now trying to move the pilot. But then the second he did we started to do a nosedive forward, which meant the guy with his hold on me was forced to move back a bit.

"Pull it up before we hit the fucking water!" he shouted gripping on to a hold above my head to anchor him to the spot as the helicopter now jerked all over the place. As for me, I turned my head to look out of the window and saw that he was right, we were heading closer to the water, meaning that I had one shot here. So, I looked around for anything I could find when I finally saw it, a red handle that said emergency release. So, as he was still watching his teammate trying to pilot the thing, I reached down, bending my knees now his arm was no longer choking me. Then I grabbed a hold of it the second I felt the smooth rounded surface and yanked it up as hard as I could. The last thing I heard before falling backwards was my own scream and the door releasing with a loud bang, as the whole thing popped off.

But then I didn't get as far as the door, which was soon landing in the river below. Not as the bastard reached out and caught me just in time, meaning I was now dangling midair with his hold on the back part of my dress, gripping on and struggling to pull me back inside because his grip wasn't quite enough. His fist was by my shoulder blade and I could feel him twisting the material trying to get a better hold, before he started lifting.

I looked down and saw the river coming closer directly below us, and I had to admit that in that moment I had never been so scared in all my life. Because right now, there was no one here to save me. No daddy dearest or Lucius to come to my rescue. There was only me and the strength to survive. So, I looked up at the eyes of someone who now knew that he was most likely going to die and his very last wish in this world was to take the bitch that caused it, with him.

His features were twisted with both hate and the strain of hanging on with a hand to the frame trying to push me back inside, that would ensure the same death as these guys. But there was no way I was going down like that!

Death wasn't taking me today.

So, I reached up and the second I felt that length of material flapping around in the wind, I grasped it and pulled on it as hard as I could meaning that the bow unraveled, and his eyes widened with the knowledge. But it was too late as I started to simply slip down through my dress, one he still had hold of and as I fell backwards, the last thing I saw was the guy's face drop as he realised he had failed.

In every way.

So, with nothing else to do I closed my eyes and let myself fall, my mouth open as the descent captured my cry of panic as I realised now I had been falling for too long.

I was too high. I knew that the moment when I finally hit the water, crashing into it with such force it stole my breath and hammered every inch of my near naked body, that he hadn't been the only one that had failed. For it seemed that death might have been paying me a visit after all.

Because darkness started to consume me.

Water filled my scream.

Weightless, I started to slowly float to the bottom.

And then I knew that Afterlife was no longer my home…

It was to become my destiny.

To be continued…

ABOUT THE AUTHOR

Stephanie Hudson has dreamed of being a writer ever since her obsession with reading books at an early age. What first became a quest to overcome the boundaries set against her in the form of dyslexia has turned into a life's dream. She first started writing in the form of poetry and soon found a taste for horror and romance. Afterlife is her first book in the series of twelve, with the story of Keira and Draven becoming ever more complicated in a world that sets them miles apart.

When not writing, Stephanie enjoys spending time with her loving family and friends, chatting for hours with her biggest fan, her sister Cathy who is utterly obsessed with one gorgeous Dominic Draven. And of course, spending as much time with her supportive partner and personal muse, Blake who is there for her no matter what.

Author's words.

My love and devotion is to all my wonderful fans that keep me going into the wee hours of the night but foremost to my wonderful daughter Ava...who yes, is named after a cool, kick-ass, Demonic bird and my sons, Jack, who is a little hero and Baby Halen, who yes, keeps me up at night but it's okay because he is named after a Guitar legend!

Keep updated with all new release news & more on my website
www.afterlifesaga.com
Never miss out, sign up to the
mailing list at the website.

Also, please feel free to join myself and other Dravenites on my Facebook group
Afterlife Saga Official Fan
Interact with me and other fans. Can't wait to see you there!

facebook.com/AfterlifeSaga
twitter.com/afterlifesaga
instagram.com/theafterlifesaga

ACKNOWLEDGEMENTS

Well first and foremost my love goes out to all the people who deserve the most thanks and are the wonderful people that keep me going day to day. But most importantly they are the ones that allow me to continue living out my dreams and keep writing my stories for the world to hopefully enjoy... These people are of course YOU! Words will never be able to express the full amount of love I have for you guys. Your support is never ending. Your trust in me and the story is never failing. But more than that, your love for me and all who you consider your 'Afterlife family' is to be commended, treasured and admired. Thank you just doesn't seem enough, so one day I hope to meet you all and buy you all a drink! ;)

To my family... To my amazing mother, who has believed in me from the very beginning and doesn't believe that something great should be hidden from the world. I would like to thank you for all the hard work you put into my books and the endless hours spent caring about my words and making sure it is the best it can be for everyone to enjoy. You make Afterlife shine. To my wonderful crazy father who is and always has been my hero in life. Your strength astonishes me, even to this day and the love and care you hold for your family is a gift you give to the Hudson name. And last but not least, to the man that I consider my soul mate. The man who taught me about real love and makes me not only want to be a better person but makes me feel I am too. The amount of support you have given me since we met has been incredible and the greatest feeling was finding out you wanted to spend the rest of your life with me when you asked me to marry you.

All my love to my dear husband and my own personal Draven... Mr Blake Hudson.

Another personal thank you goes to my dear friend Caroline Fairbairn and her wonderful family that have embraced my brand of crazy into their lives and given it a hug when most needed.

For their friendship I will forever be eternally grateful.

I would also like to mention Claire Boyle my wonderful PA, who without a doubt, keeps me sane and constantly smiling through all the chaos which is my life ;) And a loving mention goes to Lisa Jane for always giving me a giggle and scaring me to death with all her count down pictures lol ;)

Thank you for all your hard work and devotion to the saga and myself. And always going that extra mile, pushing Afterlife into the spotlight you think it deserves. Basically helping me achieve my secret goal of world domination one day...evil laugh time... Mwahaha! Joking of course ;)

As before, a big shout has to go to all my wonderful fans who make it their mission to spread the Afterlife word and always go the extra mile. I love you all x

ALSO BY STEPHANIE HUDSON

Afterlife Saga

A Brooding King, A Girl running from her past. What happens when the two collide?

Transfusion Saga

What happens when an ordinary human girl comes face to face with the cruel Vampire King who dismissed her seven years ago?

Afterlife Chronicles: (Young Adult Series)

Stephanie Hudson and Blake Hudson

OTHER WORKS
BY
HUDSON INDIE INK

Paranormal Romance/Urban Fantasy

Sloane Murphy

Xen Randell

C. L. Monaghan

Sci-fi/Fantasy

Brandon Ellis

Devin Hanson

Crime/Action

Blake Hudson

Mike Gomes

Contemporary Romance

Gemma Weir

Elodie Colt

Ann B. Harrison

CPSIA information can be obtained
at www.ICGtesting.com
Printed in the USA
BVHW081106230421
605721BV00001B/85